PROUD WOLF'S WOMAN

KAREN KAY

AVON BOOKS  NEW YORK

PROUD WOLF'S WOMAN is an original publication of Avon Books. This work has never before appeared in book form. This work is a novel. Any similarity to actual persons or events is purely coincidental.

AVON BOOKS
A division of
The Hearst Corporation
1350 Avenue of the Americas
New York, New York 10019

Copyright © 1996 by Karen Kay Elstner
Map by Trina C. Elstner
Inside cover author photo by After Five Graphics
Published by arrangement with the author
Library of Congress Catalog Card Number: 95-96101
ISBN: 0-380-77997-8

First Avon Books Printing: July 1996

AVON TRADEMARK REG. U.S. PAT. OFF. AND IN OTHER COUNTRIES, MARCA REGISTRADA, HECHO EN U.S.A.

Printed in the U.S.A.

RA   10 9 8 7 6 5 4 3 2 1

He cautioned himself to show nothing, to feel nothing . . .

But he hadn't counted on the full effect of her. He urged the pony forward, feeling Julia's breasts pressed against his back, her breath on his bare shoulders. He smelled the uniqueness of her feminine scent: sweet, fresh, desirable. And involuntarily, a shudder tore over him, bringing with it a longing that made his loins stir to life.

He was Cheyenne. Cheyenne! He could control these urges. He *must* control these urges.

Neeheeowee made a low sound in the back of his throat. He wanted her.

Yet he must show nothing. There could be nothing between them. And though he endeavored to believe it, in truth, Neeheeowee knew he lied.

He'd never felt more alive than at this moment.

PRAISE FOR KAREN KAY'S
LAKOTA SURRENDER

"Immensely gratifying."
Romantic Times

"It will touch your soul."
Affaire de Coeur

To Santee Baird,
whose friendship has always remained constant

And to my good friend, Jeanne Miller

Special acknowledgment to Ella Deloria and her novel *Water Lily*. Many of the Lakota customs I mention, especially the kinship appeal, is carefully documented in her book; a work which, though fictitious, has preserved many Lakota traditions.

And oft by day upon a distant rise
Some naked rider loomed against the glare
With hand at brow to shade a searching stare,
Then like a dream dissolved in empty sky.

JOHN G. NEIHARDT, *The Song of the Indian Wars*

To the Reader

The beginning half of this novel uses many Cheyenne words which might prove a little difficult to pronounce. In view of this, I have included a small guideline to help with the pronunciation of this language.

Please note the following rules:

1. Every letter is pronounced.
2. The (') that you see here in the pronunciation guide is used to denote a stop. Because of differences in computers, certain letters and whisper marks (a dot over certain letters) were omitted entirely.
3. When a vowel is used to end a word, it is whispered.

For ease in reading, all marks were omitted from the words in the text. I am including a guide here to help in the pronunciation of some of these names.

As a note: Neeheeowee's name is pronounced Nee-hee-o-wee. It is a shortened version of the name Nee-hee-o-ee-wo-tis, an actual Cheyenne chief who was painted in the 1830s by artist George Catlin.

Cheyenne Names	Lakota Names
Ma'hoohe	Wah-ta-pah
Voese'e	Ta-his-ka
Aamehe'e	Min-ne-con-jou
Se'eskema	Wo-was-te
He-see-he'e	Cik-a-la Pe-ta
	Ke-ya
	Ko-ko-mi-kee-is
	Ca-pa Tan-ka
	Shon-ka
	Ma-to Was-te
	Og-le Sa

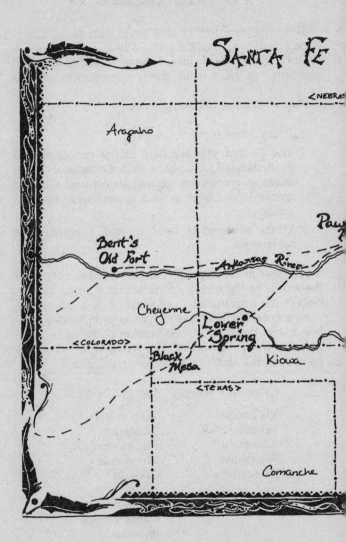

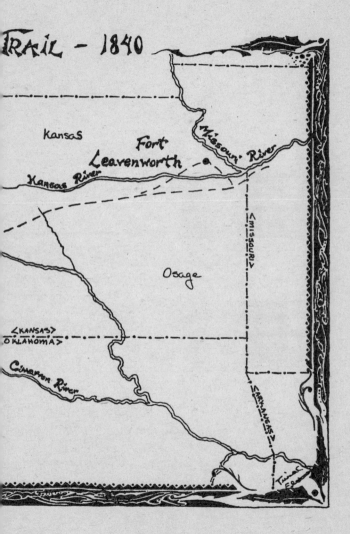

Prologue

Fort Leavenworth
Autumn 1833

"**Y**ou dropped a stitch there, Kristina."
Kristina Bogard grimaced. "I'm afraid it's not the first. I can't concentrate on our quilt. I can't help wondering what they're talking about. I feel it bodes ill for me."

Julia nodded, her long, dark brown hair falling around her shoulders as she glanced up at her friend.

The two young women were seated in the small parlor in Fort Leavenworth's largest home, while upstairs Kristina's Boston-bred mother spoke with a Mr. Carpenter, the owner of a wagon and team of horses recently arrived at the fort. Julia saw her friend's nervous glance toward the doorway, saw that Kristina worried.

"I wouldn't give it too much thought," Julia encouraged, smiling. "It's not as if your mother is planning to whisk you away today. I mean, you have plenty of time to try to find . . . Oh, Kristina," Julia broke off, seeing Kristina's reaction. "Forgive me. In attempting to ease your mind, it seems I have only reminded you . . ."

1

"No, no. It's all right. You've only stated the obvious. It's just . . ." Kristina choked on the words. "It's just that I don't know how much longer I can keep putting her off. My mother tells me every day that she plans to return to Boston and take me with her. You know how painful it would be for me to leave here, if I never were to see . . ." Kristina sighed. "I worry, Julia. I'm afraid someday I might give in to her from sheer exasperation. And then . . ."

Julia frowned, shaking her head. "Somehow I doubt that. You're too strong-willed. Besides . . ." Julia said, concentrating on a particularly stubborn stitch. When she chanced to look up at her friend, Julia gasped. Kristina was crying, tears streaming down her face.

At once Julia dropped her grip on the quilt, reaching out to take her friend's hand in her own. Julia closed her eyes for a moment.

What could she say? Julia had feared from the start that it might come to this. She'd known way back in the beginning of what could only be termed a clandestine affair, that what Kristina did could either bring tremendous happiness or estrangement . . . forever. Julia had warned Kristina of this, tried to discourage her from her unorthodox flirtation . . . at first. But Kristina had not listened, would not listen. And Julia had been lulled, herself, over several months into believing her opinion was wrong, hoping that she had incorrectly viewed Kristina's situation.

But it didn't help to remember this now. And it certainly wouldn't aid Kristina to mention such things. Which left Julia to do what?

Julia shook her head. She didn't know. These matters were simply beyond her experience. She raised her eyes to the ceiling as if she might find an answer there, and sighed deeply when nothing materialized.

It didn't matter anymore. The damage was done.

Her friend Kristina had committed a terrible faux pas, one that would ostracize her from the "best" social circles—one that, if the deed were known, could cause Kristina tremendous heartache.

Kristina had married—married an Indian. And the circumstances of it didn't matter anymore: that Kristina hadn't known the meaning of the ceremony; that Kristina wouldn't, on her own, have married the Indian. It didn't matter because Kristina was so much in love with the man now that, if he asked her, Kristina would gladly leave all behind her to follow him.

But when her Indian husband had left the fort this last time, he hadn't asked Kristina to follow him. In truth, the two lovers had parted on angry words. And it took no genius to know that what truly bothered Kristina was far removed from her problem with her mother and the newly arrived Mr. Carpenter.

Kristina worried. Had her husband, Tahiska, grown intolerant? Had he left Kristina without even a goodbye? Did he throw away all the good that had been between them?

Julia sighed. She had to do something, say something. Anything.

She squeezed her friend's hand. "Something has happened to delay Tahiska," she said at last. "I'm sure that's it, Kristina. You only need to keep heart. I saw the way Tahiska looked at you. I saw the tenderness in his eyes. It was as though he treasured you above life itself. And I swear I don't believe he would leave you. Besides, his two friends, Wahtapah and Neeheeowee." Julia paused, swallowing hard against the sudden lump in her throat. "They wouldn't just walk away without giving you word of him, would they?"

Julia held her breath, wondering if Kristina could read her own thoughts. But Kristina merely glanced around the room, her attention seemingly centered inward, and Julia breathed a momentary sigh of relief: Kristina hadn't guessed . . . didn't realize . . .

"Perhaps we credit them with too much." Kristina's words interrupted Julia's thoughts. "What do we know of their culture, really? As you once said, Julia, they're Indian. Lakota Indian, or as the people call them here, Sioux. Perhaps you were right from the beginning. Perhaps I should have listened to you and never become so involved, not fallen so much in love, not believed and wished so hard that it could work."

"No." It was all Julia said. But the force of the word, her conviction in it, carried over into her voice. She waited a moment, then, at length, she whispered, "I don't think so. I, too, grew to know them, gave them my trust, my heart . . . friendship. I . . ." She bit her lip and glanced quickly to Kristina. Had her friend heard that last?

Kristina, however, didn't appear to notice. She merely brushed a finger over the tears which had fallen onto her cheeks before turning to look toward Julia. And there she attempted a weak sort of smile. "You've changed," Kristina said at last. "You now see the Indians as people, not as you first thought, as savages. Tell me, Julia, do you agree that we've made some wonderful friendships?"

"Yes." Julia quickly looked down. She wasn't prepared to tell her friend that there could be more than simple friendship between herself and a particular Indian. Julia knew she must guard herself well. And so she kept her gaze hidden, her eyes focused on the floor. "Yes," Julia said again. "And I cringe to think I almost passed up the opportunity to get to know them. Without your influence, Kristina, I would have judged the Indians as savages without even giving them a chance. I'll never do that again."

"What does Kenneth think of your friendships with the Indians?"

Julia grimaced, bringing a picture to mind of her fiancé, Kenneth Wilson. That he compared badly when put up against the Indians, against one particular Indian, did not bear careful scrutiny. "He doesn't know," Julia said at length. "There's no reason to tell him. It's not as if we are married, yet. Besides, he has no right to dictate my feelings."

"Ah, I see and . . ."

"Sh!" Julia jumped at the chance to divert the conversation onto something else. "I hear something. Kristina, I think your mother is coming."

Julia saw Kristina sit up straighter, pinch her cheeks to draw color into her pale face, and rub away any trace of tears, while Julia became at once quiet and reserved.

"Hello, young ladies." Margaret Bogard, Kristina's mother, spoke from the parlor's entrance, with Mr. Carpenter, or so Julia assumed, standing at her elbow. "Kristina, I have some good news for you."

Kristina glanced up then, pretending indifference. "How nice," was all she said before she bent her head once again over her work.

"Mr. Carpenter and I have been discussing arrangements to return home," Margaret Bogard announced, seemingly not at all put out by Kristina's lack of enthusiasm. The older lady swept into the room, escorted by the gentleman. "I've rented Mr. Carpenter's carriage and horses to return us to St. Louis. From there we can book passage home. And this kind gentleman has agreed to start out within the week. Just think, dear, within only a few months we can be back in Boston, away from this horrible place and these terrible savages."

Julia's head jerked up. She glanced at her friend, but Kristina said nothing. Julia wondered at her thoughts. Was she, too, remembering the 'savages'? Their constant friendship which demanded nothing in return? Their devotion and honesty . . . ? Their love?

Slowly Kristina smiled and Julia drew a deep breath.

At last Kristina spoke, saying, "I know you've gone to much trouble, Mother, but I am already home. I don't wish to leave."

"Nonsense, you just don't know your . . ."

"No!" Kristina's voice was harsh at first, but then she smiled. "I love this land," she said softly. "I love these people. I belong here, not back East. You go ahead. You've always wanted to return to Boston, so you go on. We can write, you and I."

"Why I never . . . I mean I couldn't possibly . . ."

The sound of stampeding horses interrupted Mrs. Bogard's shocked reply. All glances swung to the window, and, at the sound of high-pitched war whoops, Kristina looked to Julia. Both women espied the look of surprise on the other's face. Both women grinned, quickly forgetting Mrs. Bogard, Mr. Carpenter, and the quilt as they jumped to their feet and raced toward the window.

"They've returned, Kristina!" Julia turned to her friend, catching hold of her arm at the same time Kristina reached out for her. The two friends hugged, smiling.

But Kristina looked back out the window. "I don't see him, Julia. I only see Wahtapah and Neeheeowee. What if he's not with them, what if he's . . ."

"He's here. I'm sure of it."

"Will you come outside with me?"

Julia smiled. "Of course."

Ignoring Kristina's mother and Mr. Carpenter, both Julia and Kristina stepped quickly to the door, pulling on the handle and swinging the large, wooden door open. Both women peered outside.

What a sight. Julia grinned. Three Indians, each one seated atop fine-looking mustangs, herding what must have been fifteen to twenty ponies, all brought to the front of Kristina's military home.

People and soldiers outside milled around the Indians and their horses, shouting out orders, everyone talking at once. There was laughter, wonderment, disbelief, and Kristina grabbed Julia's arm as though to steady herself.

He was there: Kristina's lover and husband, Tahiska. Julia saw him and smiled. She had been right. The Indian loved his woman, Kristina. He would never leave her. These things were easy to read, for someone who knew these Indians well. And Julia had certainly come to understand them over the past few months, learning to value their quiet strength, their soft-spoken advice, their friendship. Julia saw the way Tahiska gazed at Kristina and marveled at it.

Yes, the Indian loved his golden-haired bride; and within his look was a devotion to her that was as beautiful as it was fervent. And Julia, witnessing it, almost swooned.

Sitting astride a gray pony, the Indians presented a magnificent image of wild pride and splendor. Julia's gaze skipped over toward one particular Indian—toward Neeheeowee, before she turned quickly away. Proud, she thought, as she fixed her gaze upon a spot far away. It was a description that came easily to mind in connection with that warrior, whose namesake, Wolf, was so obviously befitting. Neeheeowee evoked the image of a fierce, proud wolf.

Julia shook her head as though to clear her thoughts just as Tahiska jumped down from his pony. His movement reclaimed her attention. Tahiska strode toward Kristina without a moment's hesitation, and Julia noted that he didn't smile at Kristina nor did he need to; his intention was clear.

"I have missed you," he said to Kristina, while Julia translated his words to herself, for Tahiska spoke to his wife in the language of the Lakota. Having spent the last few months accompanying Kristina in her clandestine meetings with this brave, Julia had come to understand the foreign language nearly as well as Kristina. Julia hadn't intended to learn the language— she hadn't intended to learn anything about the Indians. She had, however, discovered much. She had learned about nature, the earth, about honor and friendship; about a delicate, new love, fragile in its beginnings . . . "When I left you before, my wife, I left you with harsh words," Tahiska's voice broke into Julia's thoughts. "I forgot that without you, I would have no sunshine. I lied, Kristina. I could no more walk away from you than I could take my own life. I wish to spend the rest of my life with you. Now, here before all, will you be my wife?" He held out his hand to Kristina, palm up.

Julia shivered. It was beautiful. They were beautiful. They loved so well, it was as though they had loved all their lives. She shut her eyes. How she wished . . .

Julia flicked her eyes open. She couldn't dwell on these thoughts. She might admire Kristina, she might feel a burgeoning affection toward one of the Indians, herself, but she could never let herself harbor more than a fleeting thought of it. She could never live an Indian life. Never.

Still . . .

Julia stared at Tahiska's open hand, stretched out toward Kristina. And Julia knew the significance of this gesture, knew that if Kristina placed her hand in Tahiska's, the two of them, by Indian custom, were married. Julia sighed and, for a moment, just a flicker of time, she allowed herself the luxury of wondering what it would be like to have someone love her as this; to love beyond the restraint of culture, of worldly possessions, of censorship. She cast a surreptitious glance once again to the side, to one Indian, to Nee-heeowee. Quickly she looked away.

She could not allow herself to think of it ... to think of *him*. As though to cure herself, Julia tried to conjure up images of Kenneth, her fiancé, attempting to imagine the strength of Kenneth's embrace, Kenneth's love. But it was useless. With a show of sudden insight Julia knew that such a love could never exist between herself and the soldier. Where, then, would she find such a love?

Unbidden, again, the image of a tall Cheyenne warrior filled her thoughts. Her friend. Neeheeowee.

She groaned.

Shaking her head, Julia tried to sweep the thought from her mind. It could not be. She would not let it.

"I will love you all my life," she heard Kristina's words to Tahiska, spoken in English, and Julia glanced around, noting the disdainful glares, the looks of recrimination on the pale faces that had heard those words. And then her friend placed her hand in Tahiska's, saying, "I, too, wish to spend the rest of my life with you."

"Kristina!"

Julia heard Kristina's mother, realizing that Kristina, herself, had blocked out the sound, saw that Kristina heard only her husband's laughter.

"Kristina, no!"

Soldiers, youngsters, women swarmed around the group of horses and Indians, trying to see and to hear the goings-on, and Julia noted that Major Bogard, Kristina's father, joined his wife in the crowd, taking a hard stand beside the woman, effectively holding his wife back.

Julia turned her attention to Kristina and Tahiska once more and, seeing them, Julia swooned with the depth of their emotion.

Hand in hand the couple stared at one another as

if no one else in the world existed, and perhaps, for them, no one else did.

Then Tahiska picked Kristina up, swinging her around and around, the gesture at odds with Tahiska's normal stoic, Indian poise. And there, before everyone, white and Indian, he kissed her. Soundly, sweetly, a kiss of devotion.

"I will get my things," Kristina said at last.

"No, come! There is nothing here for you now. I will provide for you all that you need." Tahiska stared at his wife, the smile disappearing. "Come, it is time we went home."

Without releasing her hand, Tahiska led Kristina to his pony, and, jumping onto it, bent down toward his wife, sweeping Kristina up onto his horse. He placed the reins of two ponies he led behind him into Kristina's hand. "A wedding present," Julia heard him whisper to Kristina in Lakota.

Margaret Bogard screamed out a protest, but her husband, Major Bogard, supporting her weight against him, helped her to the side of the crowd.

"I love you with all my heart, Kristina," Tahiska murmured, ignoring the dramatics occurring all around them. "I have thought of you constantly since I left here. I would have been here sooner, but I needed these horses to win your father's approval and to show him my intentions. I will no longer have my intentions questioned. I wish no trouble, but it is time that I bring my wife home."

Kristina beamed, oblivious to the bystanders.

But Julia saw that Tahiska's gaze searched through the crowd, narrowing on Major Bogard, who strode toward the young couple. The major appeared neither shocked nor pleased by the proceedings. In the language of sign, the major asked of the Indian, "My friend, what is the meaning of all these horses?"

Tahiska released his hold on his wife, but only for

a moment. He smiled at the major. "I once asked for your daughter in marriage," he gestured back in his native language. "But you did not understand then. Let there no longer be any misunderstandings between us. I love your daughter with all my heart. These ponies—they are for you. I would live with your daughter, protect and care for her all my life."

Julia gazed at the two men who stared at one another, the Indian's glance proud, the major's . . .

Surely Kristina's father would give them permission to marry. And though this might seem strange to a bystander, that the major should condone such a union, Julia couldn't imagine it otherwise. Hadn't Tahiska saved the major's life? Hadn't the two men become friends? Hadn't the major shown that he considered the Indian honorable and brave without fault? Surely Major Bogard didn't harbor prejudice . . . surely . . .

Suddenly Kristina's father smiled, extending his hand to the young brave. "Welcome to the family, son."

A multitude of emotions flickered across Tahiska's face while Julia breathed a sigh of relief. She wanted happiness for her friend and Julia was certain that Kristina would not find happiness with anyone other than Tahiska.

The Indian took the major's hand, shaking it enthusiastically.

"Kristina"—Julia moved forward, touching Kristina's shoulder—"You'll be leaving now?"

Kristina grinned. "Yes."

Julia simply nodded, refusing to give way to the emotion she felt. "I will miss you," she said as an understatement. "But wait a moment, before you leave. I have something for you. Will you wait?" She asked the question in Lakota, looking toward Tahiska.

"Hau, yes." He nodded his head toward her, then said in English, "But hurry."

All this time, except for a few surreptitious glances, Julia hadn't really observed Neeheeowee. All this time she wondered if *he* would leave her without saying good-bye to *her*. Would she see *him* again, this man who had once saved her life, this man who, though as doubtful of her as she had been of him, had treated her with kindness and with honor, with affection . . . ?

She couldn't think of it. She couldn't consider such things. He was Indian. She was white. And these things mattered to *her*, to *him*.

Stifling a sob, Julia turned and fled to her room and, once there, she ran straight to her vanity and opened a drawer.

She could not have him. *He* could never take her with him, but Julia had determined that *he* would not forget her; she knew he would try, just as she knew that she, too, would attempt to erase his memory.

She grabbed the presents she had made, the gifts, and rushed back outside, fearing the Indians might not wait if she took a moment longer.

But they still waited, sitting before her proudly, fiercely; each one directing their attention upon *her*.

She didn't gaze back at them, she didn't dare. Approaching Kristina, she kept her eyes focused on the ground until she reached her friend. Once there she glanced up toward Kristina, handing her friend two intricately beaded necklaces, gifts inspired by the beauty and honor of Indian craft.

"The necklaces," Julia murmured toward Kristina, "are for my two friends, Wahtapah and Neeheeowee, the one beaded in blue, with the red heart, is for Neeheeowee," she whispered. "I'm afraid I lack the courage to give these gifts to the men myself. I am asking you to do this for me, Kristina. And these"—she handed Kristina two rings, each made of silver—

"these are for you and Tahiska. I noticed neither one of you have a ring to proclaim your marriage." And from somewhere Julia found the strength to smile up at Kristina. "I will miss you." Her voice caught in her throat.

Kristina took her friend's hand in her own. "Always," Kristina said, "we will be friends."

Julia was only able to flash Kristina a slight smile, and then, with a quick glance toward the other Indians, particularly toward the one Indian, Neeheeowee, Julia pivoted around, fleeing back to the sanctuary of her room.

And so caught up was she in her own emotions, Julia didn't see a sullen Neeheeowee watch her departure from him, every step of the way.

No, all Julia heard were the joyful whoops, the happy laughter, as her best friend, Kristina, with her Indian husband, Tahiska, and his two Indian friends, galloped out of the fort, out of her life.

And Julia, turning momentarily to her bedroom window to watch them go, wished that once, just once, she could ignore the restraints of her culture, of her upbringing to follow her heart. She shut her eyes, little knowing that at that same moment Neeheeowee, the young Cheyenne warrior who so disturbed her thoughts, wondered grudgingly if *he* might be able to ignore *his*.

Suddenly the young Cheyenne broke free of the others, racing back toward the fort. He stopped at the gates, turning his pony in circles, gazing back at *her* house, *her* room, *her* window. And Julia at that same moment opened her eyes.

Their gazes met across the distance—the Cheyenne warrior's fiery and proud; hers curious, yet uncertain.

What did he want?

Her heart cried out to him.

Did he want her? Should she run to him to see?

And though a part of her begged her to do just that, she couldn't.

She sobbed, instead; she cried, but she did not otherwise attempt to leave her room.

She held his gaze, heard his war whoops, saw him gesture toward her with his spear until, with one final look, he spurred his pony around, and, yelping and hollering, raced away to join his friends.

And Julia wondered, as she watched him go, if she cried for the loss of her friend, Kristina, or for the loss of another . . .

Well, it little mattered now.

Julia drew a deep, unsteady breath.

She had done the right thing, as had he. What was between them, she and Neeheeowee, could not be. Not for her. Not for him.

Not now and certainly not in the future.

And as she ran across the room to fling herself across her bed, Julia became aware that the thought was oddly depressing.

Chapter 1

Seven and one-half years later
The Arkansas River Area
Southern Kansas
May 1841

Spring had descended upon the land. The prairie was awash with the beauty of purple, blue, and yellow wildflowers while the scent of those same effusive blooms filled the air. The sun shone down, gentle and golden this day and its welcome warmth took away the slight chill in the morning air.

It was a perfect beginning to the day, a gorgeous day, whose beauty defied the somber mood of the few occupants who rested on this open stretch of prairie. Still, the young woman with dark brown hair and mysterious, hazel eyes smiled as she loosened her shawl and glanced around her.

Ah, the prairie in the spring. Was there any place on earth as beautiful?

Her gaze roved over the gently sloping hills straight to the horizon, where land met sky in splendid profusion of brilliant azure, spring green, and shades of golden brown. She reveled in the feel of the ever-present prairie wind which blew over her, ruffling her

hair and her bonnet, the air warm and fresh upon her
cheeks. Wisps of dark brown hair loosened from her
coiffure to blow back against the yellow of her bonnet,
but the young woman, with a delicate, pale complex-
ion and pink, rosy lips didn't notice. Instead she
raised her face to that breeze and inhaled deeply, enjoying, if only for a moment, the luscious beginnings
to the day.

She hadn't noticed these past few weeks that the
rains had brought such beauty to the prairie. But then,
why should she? She'd been too busy, too intent with
her work at the Colbys', with Mr. Colby's Indian wife,
who had delivered twins, to pay much attention to
her environment. But she did so now, and not even
the sounds of the disgruntled men who followed behind, nor the unsavory scents of horseflesh and sweat
could daunt her enthusiasm.

She glanced back at the company of soldiers, who
sat upon their mounts in two neat rows behind her.
Dragoons, they called them. Dragoons because during
the Middle Ages, mounted soldiers had worn a
dragon crest emblazoned on their helmets. Dragoons
now because these men here fought their wars on
horseback. There were about twenty men in this reg-
iment of soldiers, all of them under the command of
her husband, who, too, remained mounted, although
the entire company sat stationary.

The young woman glanced at the sun and, noting
its position, realized the company had been stalled
here, along this lonesome stretch of prairie, for almost
an hour, an hour during which they had all remained
in the saddle, herself as well as the dragoons, munch-
ing on a breakfast of dried jerky and water.

"Why do you think we're not traveling on?" she
asked, leaning down to whisper into her horse's ear.
"Do you wish that I were off your back?"

Her gelding whinnied as though in reply, and the

young woman reached down a hand to pat his neck. "Soon, boy, soon. I'm sure we'll be moving on soon. What I don't understand," she said, "is why we aren't making more progress toward the fort. Or if it is necessary that we stop, why aren't we dismounting?"

The horse shook his head, and the woman grinned, but only for a moment. She glanced over toward her husband and frowned. He sat gazing steadily about him, his look grim, daunting, while he listened to his second-in-command. She narrowed her eyes.

"Trouble." She hadn't known she'd spoken the word aloud until her gelding flickered his ears. "Yes," she said, her gaze still fixed on her husband. "There's bound to be some trouble before we reach the fort."

She pressed her lips together. No one had said anything to her. No one had to. She'd felt the agitation of the dragoons last night as though their distress were carried to her upon the wind. She'd heard the whispers, the rumors, even the muffled cursing of the men, and it had taken only a few inquires on her part to give her an idea of just why these men were moody, on guard, expectant.

"If they're attacked, it would only be what they deserved—if the rumors are true," she said her thoughts aloud, then shook her head. "When did I become so unsympathetic, boy?" she asked the horse as though the animal could give her an answer. "I used to understand these men. I used to understand their prejudice, I even used to agree with it. But that seems so long ago now. And fella"—she patted the horse's neck—"what am I to do? This is my husband's command; it's *his* men who may have committed these crimes. I'm supposed to support him . . . them, aren't I?"

The horse snorted while the young woman raised her chin, bringing her face full into the wind. "It's just that I don't know what to do in this situation," she

said, half to herself, half to her gelding. She bent
down over the animal. "All of my experiences out
here so far do not give me any sort of clear idea of
what I should do. The only thing I can do," she continued, "is to hope that my husband remains, himself,
innocent of the crimes that I suspect his men committed. Surely he would have tried to stop them,
wouldn't he?"

The young, dark-haired woman raised her head
and, in doing so, choked back a sigh, letting her gaze
fall onto this man who was her husband. Her look
was potent, as though by this simple action, she could
see into his soul as well as endow the man with a
strength of character he did not possess.

All at once, without her realizing it, a low moan
sounded in her throat, the utterance of it similar to
that of a wounded animal. She closed her eyes. She
released her pent-up breath as she came face-to-face
with a fact: If what she suspected were true, her husband could have restrained his men, and by doing so,
could have prevented their present misfortune. But he
hadn't. Why?

Was it because he, too, was guilty of the crimes?

She opened her eyes wide to gaze at the man who
was her husband. Was it true, what she suspected?
Had he participated in the crimes against the Indians?
Surely not, and yet . . . Even if personally innocent,
wasn't he guilty of the acts of his men by reason of
his command?

She grimaced, and the horse beneath her shifted.
She reached out a hand to pet the animal again while
she bent again over his head. She whispered, "What
am I to do? Do you know, boy? That man is my husband. Am I not sworn to love and understand him
despite the harsh bearings of life, despite his mistakes,
despite mine? But, dear Lord, if he really did what I
suspect . . . if the rumors are true, his men did more

than make a simple mistake. If true, they have committed terrible acts, acts I cannot condone, no matter my marital state."

She remembered again the mission of these dragoons: a peaceful visit to the Kiowa, one of goodwill and friendship. Where had it gone so wrong?

She had accompanied this troop at the start of their journey, staying with them until they had reached the Colbys', where she had left them to help with Mr. Colby's Indian wife. She had only rejoined the dragoons yesterday.

She thought back to what she had observed about this troop of men, and, unwillingly, mental images came to mind that she would have rather forgotten: certain of the men laughing at the misfortune of the "hang around the fort Indians," throwing those Indians bits of food as though they were no more than animals, antagonizing their leaders with cursing, with degradation of their women, their young girls. And she knew without doubt that these men were not only capable of the rumored crimes, that by the actions of her husband now, these crimes were most likely a reality.

She sat back up in her seat, pondering her predicament. There was danger here, and perhaps deserved danger.

And she knew that it was their plight now that bothered her husband, not remorse, and certainly not the actions of his men.

Unbidden, she heard his voice from out of the past, speaking to her as though that time were now: *The red man is a savage, an animal of prey,"* he'd said to her. *And like an animal, a bear or a cougar, we must kill him where we find him. If we don't, the godless creatures will soon murder us all. Remember this. The red man is a parasite and the sooner he is wiped off the earth, the better for us all.*

The young woman lifted her gaze to the heavens above her, staring at the light blue of the cloudless sky while she attempted to clear her thoughts. A pair of eagles chose that moment to fly overhead, causing the young woman to remember another time, another place, when someone from out of her past had told her a story of the eagle—a bold, adventurous tale. And for a moment, just a single instant of time, she experienced again the feelings she'd had then, the sense of being excited by the fullness of life around her, the affinity life holds for life, an appreciation for all living things, shown to her by someone she had respected . . . an Indian.

And she knew that despite what her husband said, despite the commonly held attitudes within the fort, she didn't believe. She did not agree.

She couldn't.

She shivered, though the sun encompassed and enshrouded her with glowing warmth. She had to stop thinking of these things, of the Indians she had known so long ago. If she didn't, the conflict in the cultures would confuse her.

She moved in the saddle, the action uncomfortable as her bladder responded to the motion, reminding her she had not yet seen to her body's needs since arising. She would have to do something about it; she would need a moment of privacy . . . quite soon.

She cast an uncertain glance at her husband, trying to determine what his response would be if she were to ask him to accompany her to a private spot. Although maybe she should not bother him. Perhaps she should just move out away from the line of men and relieve her natural callings discreetly, if that were possible in this land without a single tree for protection.

She grimaced. No, she would have to ask her husband to accompany her.

She closed her eyes for a moment, and swallowed hard. "What do you think I should say, boy?" she asked of her gelding again. "How can I ask my husband to help me when, by coming in close to him, I'll provide a target for his frustration? And though I know he may not be mad at me, I know he'll take his anger out on me."

Her gelding didn't answer and the young woman, shaking her head, gulped down a breath.

She lifted her head. Whatever her fears, it mattered little. Her needs, it would appear, could not wait. She gathered her courage, and, urging her gelding forward, she focused her gaze on his horse until at last, coming abreast of his mount, the young woman flicked her eyelashes up, a quick smile accompanying the motion; and she looked at Kenneth Wilson, her husband.

That his red, angry glance met her submissive one, should have cautioned her to silence. And, in truth, it did ... slightly. But her need was great.

And so she gave him her best grin, then, before courage deserted her completely, she asked him what she must, her voice quiet and gentle against the wind. She stared at him and awaited her husband's reply.

"Damnation, Julia!" Lieutenant Kenneth Wilson jerked his hat off his head and slapped it against his thigh. He glared at her. "Can't you wait even a moment? Why now and why must I be the one to accompany you? Why do you do these things to me? I wish I'd known what trouble you were going to be to me."

Julia stared into the harsh countenance of her husband's face, the man she had married almost five years ago, a man she barely knew today. That he looked more like a child at this moment, his face red and gaunt, did not bode well for her.

She knew it. She shouldn't have asked him to accompany her. She'd seen his frustration, had realized that if she approached him, he would vent his anger on her. She provided too easy a target for him.

The enemy was not here to fight; she was.

She cleared her throat, then in a steady voice, she said, "It's a simple request, Kenneth. It won't take me long."

He gave her a stormy look before answering, almost shouting, "I should have left you with the Colbys and let you find your own way back to the fort." When she visibly flinched, he moved forward in his seat, as though closing in for the kill. "Get out of here," he sneered, his voice raised. "Go on—get—if you have to go!"

Julia turned her head away while Lieutenant Kenneth Wilson's sunburned face turned even redder under the few censorious stares from his men.

"Damn!" he swore again, and Julia saw him smash his hat back on his head. He grabbed the reins of her mount then, and with a quick order to his next in command, he galloped away, Julia's gelding having no choice but to follow. He set a pace much too fast for a lady as he led them toward a small rise in the landscape, and Julia held back the retort she might have said had she not wanted to avoid further wrath.

She satisfied herself with a censorious glare instead.

"What?" he asked as they reached the crest of the hill. "Give me another look like that, and I'll make you wish you hadn't."

Julia's response was only a cool regard, though she felt like flashing back with an equally damaging remark. Stoically, she held her own counsel.

Kenneth had dismounted, she noted, though with his arms over his chest, she realized he had no intention of assisting her.

He sneered. "Well," he said, "Get down. And hurry. I have no time for you. *You*, who should not even be out here. I don't know what possessed you to visit the Colbys. My God, the Colby woman is Injun. Should have let her and the red-skinned kids die."

Julia gasped, though she said nothing. She supposed she should be used to Kenneth's viewpoint concerning the Indians, but she wasn't. Every time he insinuated that the Indians were somehow less than people, she cringed. But she no longer argued with him, learning long ago that arguments led too often to verbal and sometimes physical abuse.

And so she took a deep breath, the action somehow endowing her with a strength of will, a strength she would need in order to ride out Kenneth's verbal attack without feeling the need to retaliate.

She supposed she should dismount, but somehow her seating upon her mount, while Kenneth stood on the ground, gave her a slight advantage she would rather not lose, not when Kenneth was in one of these moods.

That he leered at her, voicing the word "Bitch," shouldn't have affected her. But it did.

She raised her head. "I wish you wouldn't call me that," she said, squaring her shoulders. And though she knew she shouldn't, she couldn't help continuing on, saying, "The Colbys needed me. And Kenneth, don't you remember that we had agreed on this before we left the fort a few weeks ago? You knew then what I was doing, and you had even agreed to bring your troops to the Colbys after your assignment was done at the Kiowa camp. It was *you* who offered to escort me back to the fort. You said even then . . ."

"Don't patronize me! Do you think I don't remember what I said? I have an excellent memory, I don't need to be told these things again and again and . . . don't raise your voice to me!"

"I am not—"

"You are, Julia. You are. And stop your constant prattle. You just talk and talk and talk. You smother me with talk. Well, I'm sick of it. I'm sick of your constant chatter, and I'm sick of you."

This last was said with so much venom that Julia was reminded for a moment just how much her husband's poisonous tongue could hurt, a fact she rarely forgot.

What had happened to the man she had married five years ago? She tried to conjure up images of that man: a man given to humor, to duty, a man who had appeared to desire her above all else. And she wondered with a deep sense of regret if this man she had known, this man she had married, had been all mirage, wooing her into believing he was something he was not.

Or was the fault partially hers? Should she have known he had another side to him? She had seen his prejudice, his cruelty on a few occasions before their marriage, but she had never dreamed he might turn that cruelty on her.

Julia debated for a moment as to whether she should raise another defense for herself, although, in truth, she knew it would do her no good. She sighed. This same scene was an all-too-common occurrence of late, and she wondered, not for the first time, if she would ever be able to live with Kenneth without a battle, both verbal and physical. Briefly she shut her eyes, wishing, if only for a moment, that it could be different.

She shivered, and, opening her eyes, she stared at Kenneth. That he turned on her, that he scoffed, that he cursed at her yet again, shouldn't bother her.

But Lord help her, it did.

Deciding no good would come from further argument, Julia dismounted without help and, taking the reins of her gelding from Kenneth, she began to lead the animal up and over the slight rise in the hill.

Once there, out of the eyes of the men, of her husband, and using the horse as a sort of shield, she attended to her "needs."

It took only a moment, but Julia hesitated before returning to where her husband waited for her. She sensed he was not yet finished with her and she wished to delay the moment of confrontation as long as possible.

Finally, several minutes having gone by, she knew she would have to return. Sighing, she gathered up the reins of her horse and, turning the gelding around, proceeded back up the rise the same way she had gone down.

He waited for her, her husband, his mood not at all improved, and for want of anything else to do, Julia gave him a quick smile. In truth, her grin was often her only means of defense against her husband's ill humor.

"Are you done at last? Now hurry," he ordered her. "I have no time for this, for you. There's trouble for my troops, and you are in my way. Now, mount up."

Julia nodded, although she hesitated. "Kenneth," she said, "I need a hand."

He groaned, but he came toward her all the same. "You know," he said, "this is all your fault. If we hadn't had to come back and pick you up at the Colbys', we would already be back at the fort. I hope you see what trouble you are."

Julia raised her brows. It was her only reaction to his accusation. And though she knew he might believe a part of his tirade, she also realized he baited her. Their predicament had little to do with her. She had heard the men talking, heard the rumors of what had happened in the Kiowa camp; she had asked questions. And it would appear that Kenneth's inability to control his men's baser appetites had borne so much ill will in the Indian camp that most feared the Kiowa might follow them now . . . seeking revenge for what could only be termed the rape of the Indian women. And it was this that most likely disturbed Kenneth's peace of mind—not Julia.

"What?" Kenneth folded his hands over his chest, as he halted, poised, ready for a fight. He pursed his lips, and when Julia further delayed speaking, he continued, "And what does my too sweet wife have to say? And don't tell me it's nothing. I know you too well."

Julia sighed, attempting to keep her gaze cool, assessing. Truly, she wished to say nothing. At this moment, anything she uttered would only serve to further enrage him.

Still . . .

Keeping her hands firmly wrapped around the reins of her horse, she took a deep breath and began, "Kenneth, I think the trouble does not lie with me, but with your own men and their violation of the Kiowa women. You were supposed to be on a peaceful mission in the Indian camp. You were supposed to do nothing but create goodwill toward the military, toward the pioneers who travel through their country. How could you have allowed your men to treat the Kiowa women in so degrading a fashion?"

She saw him flinch, saw his face redden even further. "What do you know of it?" he hissed at her. "You, with your great knowledge of military intelligence?"

Julia merely lifted an eyebrow, and though it mocked him, she could not help herself. "And what sort of intelligence does it take, Kenneth, to know that with the safety of Fort Leavenworth several days' ride away, one does not anger one's hosts in such a way?"

"You weren't there. How could you know how those women baited my men? The women begged for

it, I tell you. Why the savages even seemed glad we
had done it. Probably couldn't . . ."

His voice trailed off, but Julia barely heard any
more, her attention centered on one thing only. We,
he'd said. We?

Julia carefully schooled her features into revealing
nothing. Not her outrage at his logic, nor his justifi-
cation of what his men, and possibly what he himself,
had done.

We? Julia swallowed hard.

What could she say? Chastisement would accomplish nothing, would only serve to enrage him further. But deep inside, Julia died a little. We? She
licked her lips. It was her only reaction. Slowly, so as
not to draw attention to herself, she looked to the
ground.

"Well," he prodded, "have you nothing to say to
that?"

She hesitated. She kept her eyes focused on her
skirts, until at last she muttered, "I say there isn't a
woman alive who 'begs' for it."

He gritted his teeth in response to her; he glared at
her as though she had shouted at him and then, without so much as a further pause, he growled, "What
would you know about it?"

"More than you, it would seem," she murmured,
her head down.

Silence. Utter, deadening silence, until at last, with
a hiss, he snarled at her, "Stay away from me, Julia.
From here on forward you are nothing to me. Nothing
to anyone." And then, his lips twisted into a sneer,
he spit out, "I know you for what you are now, Julia.
And I don't like what I see. You're a bitch, Julia. A
goddamned bitch."

Julia didn't utter a word. Stunned, shocked at herself with her back talk, and at Kenneth with his ill-

chosen words, Julia, her dark hair blowing forward into her face, merely looked away.

It was some moments before she was able to regain her composure—enough to turn, to gather up her horse's reins, and begin her long, solitary trek back down the "rise."

She didn't look back. She didn't see her husband's red, angry face, and, in truth, it was better that way.

The gunshot came as a surprise.

Julia's head came up in an instant. Kenneth ran to her side. And together both man and woman stared out at the company of soldiers, the dragoons, who strove to assemble themselves while under the onslaught of attack. Dust clouded the field, making it impossible for either one to get a clear view of the action. The high-pitched war whoops, the whiz of arrows, the screams, the cursing, the orders to arms, to formation, told the tale.

More gunshots, more arrows, the squeals of the horses, the stench of raw flesh and sweat permeated the air. And still Julia and Kenneth stood transfixed, unable to move, to breathe.

The Indians clearly outnumbered the cavalry by two to one, and it was obvious that no white man would survive this attack. It was what the dragoons had feared, what they had expected, yet for all that, it came as a surprise to all of them.

It occurred to Julia that her husband, the superior officer, should be running back to his men to aid and assist them, but it was no more than a passing thought as Julia watched with horror the cloud of dust in the distance.

Their horses whinnied behind them, but Julia barely registered the sound until all at once, Kenneth pulled away from her, jumping onto his own mount. He might have helped her onto her horse. He didn't.

He might have encouraged her to do whatever it was he was going to do. He didn't.

He reined in his steed and Julia, reading his thoughts, knowing that he meant to flee in the opposite direction from the fight, felt her heart sink.

He means to leave me.

The knowledge hit her with the strength of an arrow. But he said nothing to her, he did nothing, not even inclining his head, until, with a click of his heel to his mount, he turned and shot over the rise.

"Kenneth?" She called, her voice no louder than a whisper, then, "Kenneth, come back here!"

She spurred herself into action and, trying to run, she stumbled after him. "Kenneth, where are you . . . ?"

War whoops interrupted her. Julia stopped. She froze.

More war whoops resounded around her. Julia spun around, screaming at the same time. A single warrior descended upon her.

She thought of running. She didn't. She couldn't move. Besides, it would do no good, and she knew it.

So she stood, fear gripping her, although the emotion became buried as she felt as if she were moving away from her body. It was an odd sensation, she was to think later, for she found herself contemplating the warrior as though from afar, as though none of this were happening to her.

It did occur to her once that she should feel something, yet as she stared at the Indian, nothing stirred within her, and she found herself studying the man, his body paint and his horsemanship, as an artist might, noting that white paint covered the warrior's face, neck, and chest, while black slashes jetted out under his eyes and along his cheekbones. Feathers dangled from his hair, above his crown, and also from his spear, which he held in his hand . . . pointed at her. He screamed as he raced toward her, his war cry carrying on the wind, and Julia, silently admiring the man's cleverness with his mount, watched, hypnotized, waiting for the death blow.

Closer and closer he sped, the sound of his approach deafening, until she thought she could see the color of his eyes, the yellow of his teeth. Knowing she could do nothing, she watched, she waited as though her body did not belong to her.

She noted the magnificent sight the warrior made, her own horse whinnying and stomping behind her, tugging on the reins she still clutched in her hands. Dust clogged her nostrils, stinging her eyes, stopping up the pores of her skin, finding its way into her system until she thought she might taste the dirt, and the warrior, ever closer, sprinted his pony right up to her, screaming. But at the last moment, he leaped on by her without more than a momentary pause, his spear coming a few scant inches from her face.

He hollered as he burst past her, and minutes later Julia heard the scream; a scream of horror, a masculine scream.

Kenneth's?

Lord, no!

She almost swooned, but something held her upright, some emotion that would not let her fall.

She heard the sounds of spear meeting flesh, of more crying, and then a horse blazed back toward her. She felt the jerk of motion as someone grabbed her around the waist, her hands twisting in the still-held reins of her own mount.

She felt hot, sweaty flesh next to her own.

The Indian's.

She felt the man's pony burst to full speed, saw the bloody scalp of brown hair he brandished in his hand: Kenneth's.

She closed her eyes, saying a silent prayer for a man she had never truly been able to love.

She began to cry, but the wind whipped the moisture off her skin, giving her the appearance of nonchalance; a look which, had she but known it, made her appear ethereal.

Her Indian captor gazed at her, his look expressing a sort of awe, but she turned away from him, feeling nausea building within her.

It didn't take long; within seconds, Julia convulsed over and over, losing her meager breakfast onto the ground until, at last, her stomach would heave no more.

She would never see Kenneth again. Not in this world.

She began to cry again, but the tears, she found, wouldn't come. Instead a sort of numbness filled her.

Perhaps it was that which gave her the appearance of strength; perhaps it was something else. Whatever the cause, Julia, raising her chin and, feeling her hair blowing back with the wind, little knew that her attitude lit a spark of admiration within her captor—an esteem that could win her guardianship or perhaps bring her terror.

But thankfully she was saved from this knowledge. For the moment, her insouciance became her saving grace, and she held on to it. It was, notwithstanding, all that she had.

Chapter 2

"Saaaa, my brother from the north has decided to join his southern Cheyenne relatives at last."

"It is good to see you." Neeheeoeewotis, or Neeheeowee for short, Wolf on the Hill, greeted his brother-in-law with these words and a brief shake of his head. He didn't smile, but then he never did.

"I see you have many ponies there." Mahoohe, Red Fox, maneuvered his steed around his friend in order to examine each of the eight mustangs which Neeheeowee led on a lariat. "I have never seen such fine-looking animals. It must have taken you much to accumulate such wealth. Where did you get them?"

"In our favorite spot," Neeheeowee responded, while he shifted his position on his mount. "I met with no trouble there."

"That is good," Mahoohe said. "Runners reported that you were approaching. I decided to come out and greet you before you came into camp."

Neeheeowee nodded, and, turning his head, he settled his gaze over each pony that he led before he gave his attention back to Mahoohe.

Mahoohe said, "It has been a long time."

Again Neeheeowee nodded.

"You will stay in my lodge?"

"I would be honored."

"Good, then," Mahoohe said, "that is settled. You intend to trade all of these at the Kiowa fair for . . . ?" Mahoohe raised an eyebrow.

Neeheeowee sat forward stiffly, hesitating to put his purpose into words. But Mahoohe was a friend as well as his brother-in-law and so, at last, Neeheeowee said, "I will trade all this wealth for the new fire-sticks of the white man. I have long been on the path of revenge. I would see the matter settled soon. This new weapon will enable me to do this."

Mahoohe nodded. "So. You are still on the same path. It is good, this revenge that you feel, and I understand that you must do this, but—"

Neeheeowee glanced up swiftly at his friend.

"But," Mahoohe continued, "do you not think it is time to settle down again?"

Neeheeowee shifted in his seating, unwilling to share his thoughts with his friend. What could he say?

"I came out here to welcome you because I wanted you to know that all here feel that you have done your duty toward my sister," Mahoohe continued. "All in our family have a glad heart to see what you have done. But it is time now to give it up. Do you not think so?"

Neeheeowee hesitated. His glance skimmed briefly over his brother-in-law, then over the land around them. "I will never rest," Neeheeowee said at last, speaking the words quietly, though firmly. "Never. Not until each and every one of my wife's murderers is brought to justice. I do not expect you to understand. I do not think anyone could understand. This is something I must do. It is something I will do."

Mahoohe shook his head. "It is over, my brother. It has been over for five years. You have done your duty

toward my sister. There is none who would question
your loyalty toward her."

"What others think has no meaning to me." Neeheeowee stared ahead of him. "This is something I
have to do. I do not care if anyone agrees with me.
What I do is what I must do."

Mahoohe sighed, and, looking back toward Neeheeowee, he said, "The Kiowa and Cheyenne trade
fair goes well this year. I believe you will find what
you want."

"This is good," Neeheeowee said, letting out his
breath. "I am glad the Kiowa and Cheyenne have
reached a peace at last. I have been waiting for this
trading fair a long time, ever since I realized it is the
Kiowa who live close enough to the Mexicans to bargain for the best weapons. But I have been unable to
trade with the Kiowa because we have been at war
with them. Now, however, I am ready. The Kiowa do
not have what the Cheyenne can obtain so easily:
these fine horses. And I am counting on the Kiowa
being willing to trade away those weapons of the
white man in exchange for . . ." He raised his chin.
". . . my ponies."

Mahoohe grinned. "Then it is a good thing we are
at peace with the Kiowa now."

Neeheeowee nodded. "Yes, it is a good thing."

"Come, then, my good brother-in-law. Let me take
you to my lodge. We have camped close to the trading fair."

Neeheeowee looked back upon his wealth of eight
ponies before, with a turn of his head, he nodded his
assent to his friend.

Both men clicked their own separate mounts forward, Neeheeowee's gray mustang surefooted over
the rough terrain.

It was only then, once under way, that Neeheeowee
surveyed the land around him as though he, himself,

were an eagle. He drew a deep breath. These were the lands of his southern, Cheyenne kin, the lands patrolled by the Cheyenne, the Kiowa, the Comanche. This land he loved; this land where dry, arid heat absorbed moisture and rain as though the earth itself were a hungry beast.

It was here where Grandmother Earth ravaged the landscape; here that Neeheeowee beheld the jutting cliffs set against the horizon in hues of brown, orange, and gray; here where the barren streams spouted red soil instead of water. He gazed around him at the brown-and-red earth with sprinkles of green, where hidden dangers lurked unknown in the dark recesses of the rocks.

These plains were his home; the sky his tepee, the ground his sleeping robe. And if the life he had made for himself out here was sometimes lonely, so be it. In truth, Neeheeowee preferred it this way, had lived this way since the death of his wife and unborn child.

"How long do you plan to stay with us?"

Neeheeowee shot a glance toward his friend. "I will stay long enough to trade and then, though I am grateful for your hospitality, I will be gone. Once I have the weapons I need, I will have other matters to attend to."

Mahoohe nodded his head. "That is as I had expected. I hope, though, that you will stay a while longer, perhaps relax with us."

Neeheeowee raised his chin, a movement calculated to cover up the feeling of vulnerability that had quickly come upon him. He said, "I cannot stay long."

"I know."

Neeheeowee nodded, needing to explain no more. His brother-in-law understood. At least, a little.

"You will go and seek out the Pawnee?"

"*Haahe*, yes," Neeheeowee said. "When I at last own the superior weapon, when I at last can make the enemy cower, I will finally put an end to the torture that my wife's spirit must endure. Only then can she walk the spirit path to the hereafter. And this, you must know, I will do. I will free her spirit. These eight ponies that you see here? They represent all my hard efforts this past year. I have known that if I could train these ponies, I would be in a better position to trade for the white man's fire-sticks. And now that we are at peace with the Kiowa, I can obtain all I desire. Plus I can trade also for supplies."

"We will give you all that you need in supplies."

Neeheeowee lifted his chin. He did not intend to take anything from his southern kin, except what good manners dictate that he accept. But he couldn't tell Mahoohe that. His friend would take it as an insult. And so, although Neeheeowee murmured a polite acceptance, he knew he would not infringe much on his friend's hospitality.

Hadn't he taken enough from them already? Wasn't their sister's life enough?

Their sister.

His responsibility.

His wife.

Neeheeowee frowned. Twenty seasons of the moon; five winters. All of it wasted; all of it spent in learning who had done it, who had killed those he'd loved. Which Pawnee? Who personally? Each and every one of them, for there had been several who had done it.

Though, in truth, only one had "turned the knife." Only one had raped his wife; only one had cut open her belly to slaughter the babe inside, while the mother had still lived.

Neeheeowee narrowed his eyes, his only show of emotion.

Only one would know a slow death.

Neeheeowee suppressed the shudder of reaction that always came with these thoughts and set his gaze, once more, to the fore, his lips set, his chin tilted forward.

As soon as he had these weapons . . .

A pony whinnied and Neeheeowee looked back with a quick reflex, but seeing nothing more than the horses nipping at one another, he turned his gaze again before him.

Such fine animals. At one time, he might have felt proud of the feat he had performed this past year in catching these ponies, but he would not allow himself to feel that emotion, not now. He did what he did in the service of another. Such things were expected of him. There was no glory in it.

He grimaced, thinking over these years—years of patience for him, years spent in search, years filled with the need to fulfill justice. Because as long as those few Pawnee lived, as long as those warriors still walked the earth, still remained free to rape and murder again, the spirits of his wife and unborn child would not rest, could not rest. Both were trapped in this world, forced to roam uselessly until the moment of full justice. A moment Neeheeowee must make happen, would make happen.

Nothing else mattered to him. Nothing.

He inhaled a sharp breath, and the tall Cheyenne warrior, who had only reached twenty-eight winters, sat up straighter in his seat as he drove his mount over the summit of the butte.

He stared out again at the land around him, at the valleys and the eroded, jutting cliffs. Mystic beauty abounded here, beauty which had become lost to Neeheeowee over these past five years.

All he saw instead was the endless space, all he felt was the waning warmth of the setting sun upon his naked back. And all he knew were the terrible nightmares of his own thoughts. They never abated. Not ever.

Neeheeowee urged his mount into a walk along the butte, the eight ponies trailing behind him, the reds and pinks of the sky giving in to those of lavender and deep gold.

Another might have at least noted its beauty. Another might have at least paused to look with appreciation. Another might also have left off his mission long ago.

Not Neeheeowee.

The Cimarron River Valley
Near Black Mesa, Oklahoma

Neeheeowee and Mahoohe joined the Cheyenne/ Kiowa trading fair long before the women had finished cooking their morning meals. Naked children stirred, scurrying about the camp while Neeheeowee breathed in the familiar smells of camp life, of horseflesh, of rawhide and smoke, of hundreds of different people. Even the wind carried the aroma of meat roasting or stewing and of something new: coffee, that white man's drink that Neeheeowee had never tasted.

The sun felt warm on the top of Neeheeowee's head, the ground hard, the short grass dry beneath his moccasins as he led his ponies through the camp. The sky overhead gleamed a light blue in the cloudless, morning sky, while the air cushioned the happy singing of the birds.

Mahoohe had gone on toward his lodge in the temporary camp while Neeheeowee lingered on the outskirts. He glanced up once, then away, impervious to the sounds, the smells, the happiness that burst all around him as people who had not seen one another throughout the winter months became reacquainted.

There was laughter, the happy sounds of gossip, the screaming of the children and the ever-present sound of drums as young men in the camp practiced their dance steps and songs.

Neeheeowee gazed around him at the gay evidence of life all around him. He started forward, across camp, his lips set into a grim frown.

He had no patience for this, any of this. He was here for one purpose, one reason only, and all else paled before it.

He looked away.

It was warm this day, the dry air promising an even hotter afternoon. But Neeheeowee didn't care. He would not conduct his trade in the heat of the afternoon. He would wait to finish his business in the cooler part of the day, in the evening. In truth, it would bode better for him that way. While others relaxed around the fire, listening to stories and relating their coups, Neeheeowee would negotiate, bargain. He would not relax; he never did, not anymore, not in these last five years.

His lifestyle demanded this vigilance anyway, it being necessary to remain on guard constantly when tracking, when traveling over the plains. But Neeheeowee carried it further; for him, this wariness was no momentary way of life. On the plains, in camp, in the company of others, he remained on the alert. Always.

"A-doguonko do-peya kuyo!"

Neeheeowee heard the harsh carping of a woman's voice and turned away, not interested. He had learned long ago to keep his own counsel when in camp, even when it appeared one should intervene. No one appreciated an interloper. Not even Neeheeowee.

"A-doguonko do-peya kuyo!"

He wasn't sure what made him turn toward the

sound. Something. He didn't really care what occurred there. In truth, he shouldn't have stopped; he should have gone on.

But he didn't. As though fate suddenly intervened, he turned.

"A-doguonko do-peya kuyo!"

He didn't know what he'd expected to see. Certainly all looked normal.

Nothing unusual there: Just a bad-tempered Kiowa wife harping at . . . what? Who? A sister? Not possible. Indian women treated their sisters with more respect.

Who, then?

A captive?

Haahe. Yes, it must be.

Neeheeowee shrugged, his long hair responding to the movement, the black strands of it falling back, over his shoulders. It was nothing to him how a Kiowa wife treated her captive. And though Neeheeowee rebelled at the idea of captivity or slavery, which went against the morality of his own tribe, he would do nothing here. The Kiowa tribes and the Cheyenne had only last year settled their differences. And with the peace between the tribes so new, Neeheeowee knew he would do nothing to break that truce, certainly not over something as insignificant as an inquiry about a captive.

Why didn't he turn away, then? He should have.

But he didn't.

He looked, trying to translate the Kiowa woman's words to himself: Idler? Coward? Something about an idler here at home?

He stared at the slave. Why did she appear familiar?

He glanced at her more closely. She was white, he could see that in her hair color, in the long, dark brown curls that could not be tamed, despite weather, wind, and uncleanliness. White? That should not make her familiar, and yet . . .

He knew few white people, keeping away from them instinctively. But there were a handful he had met once, long ago at a fort a little farther north and east from this place. A few men, a few women; one he had . . .

Neeheeowee narrowed his eyes and stared.

Hova'ahane. No. It could not be.

He studied the captive; her clothes were of white origin, though so dirty and tattered he could not make out their color. The woman sat on the ground next to the Kiowa lodge, her knees to the side, her head down. His glance roved over her, from the torn dress she wore to the very tips of her feet, the bottom flesh there red where the soles of her shoes had torn. Both the white man's *mo'keha,* shoes, and the woman, herself, were caked in dirt and mud.

Eaaa! Why did he look? Unable to help himself, his glance roamed back to the woman's face, hidden from him by the curtain of her hair, hair that gleamed dark, with reddish highlights only where a deterrent ray of sun struck it.

He had once known someone with that color of hair, someone . . .

He thrust his chin forward and turned his back. It was nothing to do with him.

"A-doguonko do-peya kuyo!"

He tried to translate the Kiowa words again; an idler here at home?

He stopped.

He didn't want to, he didn't intend it, but it happened anyway: He veered about.

The Kiowa woman grabbed a stick, hitting the captive, once, twice, again and again. But the slave did nothing; no flinch, no reaction, not even a look at her master.

Was the captive brave? Or was she simply degraded, her spirit broken?

The Kiowa woman raised her arm again and an anger coursed through Neeheeowee that he could little explain. He should do nothing—it had nothing to do with him. Again, Neeheeowee spun back around to go.

But not fast enough.

Suddenly the white slave girl screamed, jumping up and running as far as the noose around her neck would allow, behind the Kiowa lodge, and Neeheeowee, watching, stood still, his legs, his whole body suddenly wooden. A hundred thoughts might have gone through his mind—a similar number of mental images, as memory intruded upon his life.

He knew her. He stood, there in the middle of camp, eight horses patiently waiting behind him, little able to comprehend it.

Another man might have felt the warmth of remembrance. Another man might have, at least, felt inclined to smile.

But this was Neeheeowee; not his brothers, not his kin, nor his enemy. Neeheeowee.

He felt nothing.

And when he turned away from the path he had been taking, to march toward the Kiowa lodge, he told himself over and over that he felt nothing. But he lied, and he knew it.

Neeheeowee had never been angrier.

Julia didn't see the man stalking toward her until he was almost upon her, and then she cringed.

What did he want from her? Hadn't fate already dealt her too cruel a hand? What must she endure now?

Not even looking up, she sank to her knees on the ground, before the man, before anyone who would look, too distraught even to send a prayer to the God she felt certain had deserted her. She closed her eyes.

Perhaps when she opened them, he would be gone—he alone, not her circumstances. She didn't even dare to hope the latter: not anymore. She was beyond believing this all a nightmare, a mere dream to disappear upon awakening.

Hadn't she wished it so these past few weeks? Hadn't she prayed? To no avail?

She heard the muted sounds of the leather fringes of the man's leggings smacking against the ground as the man stopped in front of her. She smelled the clean smell of buckskin, felt a finger under her chin, lifting her face upward, curiously sending a shiver over her skin. But she would not, herself, look up; she kept her eyes firmly closed.

"*Eaaa!*"

She heard the man's voice.

Something stirred within her, some emotion, some . . .

"*A-doguoňko do-peya kuyo!*"

The harsh, feminine voice interrupted her thoughts.

Opening her eyes, Julia tried to turn her head, but the finger beneath her chin held her fast. She groaned, she tried to stir, but the man's grip tightened and after a few more struggles, she gave it up.

"*Nevaahe tse'tohe? Ne-toneseve-he?*"

Julia felt, more than observed, the man's intense look at her. She didn't know what he'd said, and for a moment she was glad, fearing whatever the words meant, fearing him.

Suddenly he let her go and she sank to the ground, praying the man would leave.

But he didn't. Instead she saw in her peripheral vision that he moved his hands, heard the slap of his shirt fringe as he spoke to her Kiowa mistress in the language of sign. But Julia was beyond caring what occurred between the two Indians. All she knew was that she had escaped the punishment her mistress had intended, at least for the moment, and she inched gradually backward, as far as the rawhide around her neck would allow.

The Kiowa woman responded to the man in rapid gestures and some moments went by where the two conversed in this way.

"*Saaaa!*" Had the man been speaking English, he might have cursed, and Julia glanced up to see a flurry of hand motions, none of which she understood.

Her Kiowa mistress spit on the ground, then into her palm, wiping the contents of it down the man's shirt and Julia at last peered into the man's face, if only to see his reaction.

She gasped. But it wasn't because of the Kiowa woman's action, nor was it due to the man's response, which was nothing save a stoic regard.

As though struck, Julia, barely able to breathe, could do no more than stare. Could it be? Too many years had intervened since they had last seen one another, but . . .

She recognized this man. Didn't she? He was . . .

"Neeheeowee," she said his name. Neeheeowee, a man she had once known, a man she had once . . .

For a moment, awe gave way to hope as it flared within her, and she almost reached out toward him. But at the last moment, she held back, returning her hand to her side.

She looked down at herself; at the tattered rags she wore, at the dirt and grime on her clothes, the marks on her body; she felt the scratches and bruises on her body, the filth that clung to her hair, the stench that exuded from her body. She closed her eyes, experiencing more: the degradation of her spirit, the sadness in her recent memory, the betrayal of her heart. She pulled back completely.

Why should Neeheeowee help her? He was Indian. Indian.

If her own husband hadn't thought enough of her to try to save her, along with himself, why should this man?

He was Indian.

She looked away, silently cursing the fates that had brought her to this. Why should destiny suddenly bring this Indian back into her life? Reminding her of all the good she'd once known, reminding her of friendship, of honor, of . . .

She didn't finish the thought. She inched backward, away from him, away from her mistress, trying to recall if she had done something terrible in this life to deserve these fates. Nothing came to her—not a terrible passion, nothing—not even the opposite. Neither the good she had done, nor the people she had influenced, brought her happiness.

At this moment, all Julia knew was despair.

And so it was with the despondency of one who has known defeat that Julia gazed up at Neeheeowee, blind to all about him, save only one point: He was an alien to her, an Indian.

She would beg no quarter; she would expect none.

Neeheeowee glared at the Kiowa woman, at Julia, back at the Kiowa.

"Where is your husband?" he asked of the Kiowa woman in sign language.

"Gone," the woman replied in kind.

"When will he return?"

The Kiowa gave him an assessing look. "Is my husband a woman that he needs to tell me his movements?" She smirked. "He is gone, I tell you. Do you want to purchase the captive? Is that why you ask? I will tell you now that if you want to purchase the woman, you will have to bargain with me."

"My business is no concern of yours."

"It is if you want the captive."

Neeheeowee didn't even hesitate. "I bargain with no woman."

The Kiowa smiled, though the gesture quickly turned to a sneer. "Then the captive still belongs to me, and I can do with her as I want."

Neeheeowee grunted while the woman scoffed.

"I will beat her if she does not obey me. She does little enough work, leaving it all to me." The Kiowa woman suddenly chuckled as though with great pleasure, although her glance at the man was shrewd, assessing. "I like to hear her scream."

Neeheeowee set his lips; it was his only reaction. "Is it supposed to mean something to me if you beat her? Am I supposed to care? The only thing I can tell you is that if you damage her, I will not want to buy her."

The Kiowa woman smiled, the gesture showing small, yellow teeth. "So. At last we get to the truth. You do want to buy her. Why?"

Neeheeowee glared at the woman's upright hand as she completed the sign motions. He had not meant to give away so much. Perhaps his time away from camp had caused him to forget how to deal with people. He gave the woman a blank look before beginning. "It is not the concern of a woman what a man wants," Neeheeowee said in hand motions. "If I intend to bargain, I will talk with your husband when he returns, not before. But know you this: If I find the captive damaged, I will tell your husband all you have said to me. I would ensure that he knows that I would have paid a higher price had the captive not been damaged."

The Kiowa woman snorted. "My husband cares not

what I do, especially as regards a slave. And as for your wealth, keep it. My husband is already rich in guns and horses. Why should he want yours?"

It was Neeheeowee's turn to mock; he did so, using all the ridicule at his command. Was the Kiowa woman so blind that she could not see the wealth in the ponies which stood at his back? Was she such a bad judge of horseflesh?

"I will return tomorrow when the sun is first up," Neeheeowee signed, "and if you are lucky, I will purchase the slave then—maybe." Here he leered at the woman. "But only if she is undamaged. Remember this, woman, for I will not hesitate to tell your husband all you have said if I find the captive with any more bruises."

"Naaaa!" The woman spit on the ground, into her hand, but catching the look in Neeheeowee's eye, she didn't dare rub her hands down his shirt again. She hissed at him instead.

Neeheeowee, in response, did nothing—no emotion at all to be witnessed as he signed, "Remember."

And with a quick look to Julia, to the woman he had once known, he spun around, the flap of his fringe, the restless whinnying of his ponies, noting his movement, and, leading a wealth of eight ponies behind him, he paced away, looking as though he weren't at this moment angrier than he could recall being in a long, long time.

Chapter 3

~~~~~~~~~~~~~~~~~~

"Neeheeowee . . ." Julia's voice trailed off.

She watched Neeheeowee's natural gait as he walked away, observing that not once did he glance her way, nor did he indicate he might still call her friend. She gulped, swallowing hard. No, this man she'd known—Neeheeowee—had plainly turned his back on her, shifting away from her as easily as her husband had done.

She glanced up toward the heavens, wondering what she had done to make those people closest to her hurt her the most. Even her parents . . .

Julia breathed out in a rush, trying to rein in her thoughts. It did no good to remember these things; it accomplished nothing.

She looked away, trying to think of other things, but the effort was wasted. The memories intruded upon her, the mental images bringing back old hurts, old wounds, she'd put to rest long ago. Suddenly, she recalled the day six years ago when she stood in Fort Leavenworth, watching her parents leave on a trip to St. Louis, never to return.

Some had said her parents were captured or killed by Indians, some had believed the two had lost their way, while others openly accused her father of desertion. But Julia believed none of it. In truth, she hadn't known what to think, though secretly she feared her parents had simply gone back East, deserting their daughter to her own fate. Hadn't Kenneth suggested this to her? Hadn't he plagued her with the possibility of it for months?

Julia slumped her shoulders. Kenneth. Gone now was the man who was supposed to have treasured her above all else, the man who should have loved her despite her faults, exalted her for her accomplishments, the man who, in truth, could find nothing right with her, nothing to admire.

Julia sighed convulsively.

She might have felt self-pity, but there was no time for it. Too soon the Kiowa woman stood before her, muttering words at her, making gestures that Julia couldn't understand and Julia, as though deaf and dumb, stared up at the woman in mute response.

That the woman flounced away, that she did not administer the usual punishment was lost on Julia. Submerged in a world of her own making, Julia barely registered anything else until, with a flutter of harsh words, her Kiowa mistress shoved three water bags into Julia's hands, and with clear-cut gestures, ordered Julia to fetch the family's water supply.

Julia didn't even blink. She knew the chore. In truth, this hauling of water had become a daily task, one she looked to with favor since it required the removal of the rawhide noose. And though it did no good to feel it, even to think it, for those few prized moments out of the collar, Julia felt free. And perhaps, by comparison, she was.

She waited now as her mistress removed the noose and Julia rubbed her neck where the tough rawhide had cut into her skin. That her fingers came away bloody seemed of little consequence. It made little difference to her anymore.

Since her capture, only a month ago, Julia had become resigned to the fact that her life offered little point. What had seemed barely tolerable to her before her capture, appeared by comparison a sort of haven now. She grimaced, grasping all at once the sadness of it, for Julia had found little happiness in her former life.

Tears formed in her eyes, but whether she cried for the injustice of her situation or whether perhaps for the final admission as to her unhappiness, Julia couldn't be certain. She only knew she hurt.

Kenneth had departed this world, and, despite all his faults, Julia mourned his passing. She had, at one time, loved him well. She began to feel tears well up in her eyes again when all at once her Kiowa mistress stood in front of her, interrupting her thoughts, shoving her toward the creek, and Julia, dodging out of the way, crossed camp to tread the well-worn path to the water.

"*Ehaeesenehe!*" Julia heard the voice of a child call out.

"*Enovo'e!*" another one answered

"*Epeheveene'e!*"

The children called out to one another, but Julia had no idea what was said and so she turned away, fixing her gaze on the ground as her feet, on their own, took the path through the weeds.

Why had Neeheeowee turned away from her? He had recognized her, she was certain of that. Why hadn't he rescued her, or at least attempted it?

Julia tried to imagine herself in his situation. If their places were reversed, if Neeheeowee had been caught by soldiers, would she have come to his aid? It would have been difficult; Kenneth would have objected, but Julia felt certain she would have at least tried.

Why hadn't Neeheeowee?

She shrugged, trying to recall what she knew of the

Indian man. It had been seven and a half years ago that they had met. She had been accompanying her friend, Kristina, out onto the prairie, to secret meetings with Kristina's Indian husband, who, along with his two friends, had journeyed to Fort Leavenworth on a mission of revenge.

But the two women hadn't known the Indian's purpose at the time, had only known that Kristina loved her husband as she loved no other. And Julia, Kristina's best friend, had aided the romance, albeit against her own best judgment; yet, when Julia had glimpsed Kristina, her friend had been so much in love, Julia could not resist meeting this man who set her friend to blushing, if only to witness the two lovers together.

That's when she'd met Neeheeowee.

She hadn't liked him at first. Moody to a point of rudeness, he would never speak to her, never acknowledge her presence. Still, after a while Julia had come to appreciate his quiet guardianship, for she was often left alone with him, he acting as her protector.

She remembered once she had been learning the Lakota language along with her friend, Kristina, and armed with this new ability to communicate, she had solicited conversation with Neeheeowee. It hadn't worked, he still hadn't talked with her and she had decided then that he did not know the Lakota language well; he, himself, being from the Cheyenne tribe.

Still, they had spoken, if only in quiet gestures, and it was this once that she had witnessed his smile . . .

"Why do you wear feathers?" she asked of Neeheeowee *in the language of the Lakota, her gaze centered on the buckskin pouch she was sewing. But he didn't answer at once, and Julia, looking up, gestured toward the feathers in*

his hair, raising her shoulders in a question.

He snorted as he usually did when he thought she had displayed stupidity, and Julia felt certain he wouldn't answer her. Still, she waited.

They were seated, she and Neeheeowee, along with another Lakota warrior, Wahtapah, out on the prairie beneath a few cottonwood trees. Beside them, a small stream of water ran through the land as though in a hurry to converge with some other large-body, while overhead the occasional song of a dove broke the usual silence of the prairie.

Neeheeowee took his time answering, and Julia wondered if he would ignore her, as he had done in the past. But at length he raised his hand. Pulling the two feathers from his head and pointing to them, he said, "Mee'e, epeheva'e."

Julia didn't understand since Neeheeowee spoke a language she did not know. But Wahtapah was there and Wahtapah intervened, saying, "My Cheyenne brother says that feathers are good medicine. We get them from the mighty eagle. It is not easy for us to obtain them, for the eagle is swift and clever. The feathers—they show a warrior's accomplishments on the battlefield. Here," Wahtapah said, pointing to one of the feathers that Neeheeowee held. "Do you see that feather there? Can you see how my brother has cut away a part of the top, with horsehair attached to it?"

Julia nodded, murmuring a "yes" at the same time.

"That feather there," Wahtapah explained for Neeheeowee, "represents his first coup."

Neeheeowee nodded his head at Julia, then at Wahtapah, then in broken Lakota, Neeheeowee asked of Julia, "Okicahniga coup?"

Julia could barely understand him, though at length Wahtapah translated, saying, "He asks if you can comprehend what a coup is?" to which Julia shook her head.

Neeheeowee frowned and raised his shoulders toward Wahtapah.

"A coup is an accomplishment," Wahtapah said. "It

means to strike the enemy. It is the mark of a courageous man. In our camps, these things are talked about and bring glory to a man."

Julia nodded her head, saying, "I see."

Wahtapah smiled and, getting to his feet, said, "I must go now to see what keeps my brother, Tahiska, and his wife. Stay here. My Cheyenne brother will protect you."

Julia nodded and glanced over to the Cheyenne warrior, who sat staring back at her. But Julia didn't flinch. She had come to realize that these warriors would do her no harm. In fact, she felt quite safe with them, protected. And so she smiled at Neeheeowee and he glared back at her for some time.

He didn't replace the feathers in his hair, however, and at length, he rose to his feet and came over to Julia, squatting down beside her.

Julia looked over toward him. His dark eyes stared back at her, and in them she saw a message, an emotion she could barely discern. And then all at once, it came to her. He liked her. Her heart seemed to stop beating at the thought, but soon her pulse began to beat again, not normally as it should, but rather racing as though she were running.

She stared back at him, unable to drop her gaze. The man was exotic, handsome, and alluring beyond description and he seemed to want her. She could barely breathe.

Neither of them spoke; there was no need for it. Instead, Neeheeowee extended one of the feathers toward her.

Julia reached out toward it, and, uncertain, she stopped, but Neeheeowee gestured her onward, and Julia placed her hand upon the feather, taking it from him. She wondered if Neeheeowee felt the touch of her fingers as they grazed over his own, and she glanced up to catch a slight shudder of reaction from him.

Was it her touch that had caused that reaction in him? She couldn't believe it was so. Still she looked up toward him, and, as she did so, she caught Neeheeowee's brief smile

*before, turning, he strode from the camp as quickly as if he
were chased by wolves.*

*She watched him for a moment, watched his graceful
walk, the way his breechcloth moved in and out, exposing
a bit too much of his backside for her view; then, sighing,
she glanced back down at the feather.*

*It was beautiful, and, as she gazed back at the man hur-
rying away, she was struck by an odd realization: Its giver
was just as beautiful.*

*It was a unique thought for Julia, who had been inclined
to believe the worst of the Indian.*

*And she wondered, as she watched him go, if all Indians
were as wonderful as he.*

Somehow she didn't think so.

It was sometime later that Julia had learned that the
giving of an eagle feather was something special to
the Indian. For a man to give a woman a feather
meant that he held her in high esteem and perhaps,
further, that he held her in affection. Julia had kept
the feather, tucked under her clothing in her room in
Fort Leavenworth. She had it still, not with her now,
but back at the fort. She'd never thrown it away, not
even when she had married Kenneth. She'd never
been able to bring herself to do that.

She sighed. That had been a long time ago. Too
many years had passed for her to know the Cheyenne
warrior anymore. Neeheeowee had changed. She had
changed. It was likely he was married and would not
be able to explain Julia to his wife. Perhaps that was
why he had not come to her rescue. Or perhaps, after
all these years, he no longer honored the special relationship they had once shared.

Julia shut her eyes, unwilling to admit to the hurt
that the thought caused. And suddenly she remembered other things: The possibility of love all those
years ago, her fear of it, her withdrawal from it.

She had been too prejudiced to see what was there. Besides, she had been so certain that she could create that same kind of love with Kenneth.

Julia sighed. What good did it do her to think of these things now? The past made little difference anymore. She grimaced. Could it be that Neeheeowee might bear her a grudge? He had, after all, given her the feather, he had as much as told her she was special to him . . . and she had . . . run away from it.

Was he now giving her back her due? She shut her eyes, frowning. What else could she expect from him?

"*Tsehetoo'otse!*"

A small, Indian girl suddenly appeared out of nowhere, jostling Julia. And Julia, losing her balance, fell forward, onto her knees.

"*Nestsehetoo'otse!*"

"*Tatsehetoo'otse!*"

Another child, then another and another ran on past Julia. Not one of them offered her assistance, not one even bothered to look at her, one kicking out at her, giggling, and Julia, looking up, felt hard-pressed at this moment to champion the Indians—any of them—including Neeheeowee.

What was she to do about her enslavement?

She couldn't run. She'd become forever lost. She wished now that she had paid closer attention when, seven years ago, the three young warriors had tried to teach both Kristina and her how to track and find their way on the prairie.

She looked up, wondering, if only for a moment, if perhaps it would have been better if she, too, had been killed along with that ill-fated company of soldiers. Again, she tried to make sense of it.

Why did the Indians let her live? What purpose did her life now serve? Wouldn't it have been better if they had just . . .

Enough! She swore at herself, her thoughts.

She was alive . . . alive, which meant she had a chance, if only she could run away. If only . . .

She bowed her head. What opportunity did she have? When not fetching water, she was constantly chained to the noose. And no one seemed to spare her a single thought, not even her male captor.

Julia raised her head, looking up toward the heavens, through the tops of the cottonwoods. She breathed in deeply. What was she to do?

Unbidden, an image of Neeheeowee came again to mind. Should she throw herself on his mercy? Should she beg him to set her free?

Never!

She remembered him, his backside today, his irritating, graceful gait as he had walked away from her—only minutes ago. Suddenly her situation seemed too much to bear, and Julia, unable to understand the why of it, any of it, silently denounced everything involved with it: her parents, her husband, white man and Indian alike.

She came slowly to her feet there on the path, and balancing the water bags on her hips, she continued her hike toward the stream, resigning herself to the fact that she no longer commanded her own life. And it was no small revelation that convinced Julia she could champion no one any longer—white or red. Betrayed by both cultures, her disenchantment toward life in general grew, spreading malaise within her as though she were on fire, encompassing all within its path: the good along with the bad. She closed her eyes, knowing that she could no longer consider herself a part of either world anymore, especially a culture which committed, even laughed at, the destruction of another human being, no matter what its civilized or savage aspect.

Without consciously willing it, she suddenly felt doomed, more so than at any other time—doomed to be neither white nor red, doomed to belong nowhere.

And it was this, perhaps more than anything else, which caused Julia to look within herself, searching for a spark of inner strength. And oddly, she found there, within herself, a shred of courage, a semblance of her spirit that would not allow her to quit. She found there an ability to cloak herself in insouciance.

And though another might not appreciate it, Julia knew she could at least pretend, if only for herself, that none of this mattered: not her captivity, not her heartache, not even Neeheeowee's disregard for her. She could assume, if only for a little while, a nonchalance. And if she might truly feel the apathy of her plight, she determined that no one would know it.

"I will not quit!" she murmured to herself, and squaring back her shoulders, Julia lifted her head.

Rags or no, grime or no, she would allow no one, especially not Neeheeowee, or any other Indian, to realize she had lost. Lost faith in herself, faith in her fellow man, in Neeheeowee, faith in the gods that be. And though outwardly she might assume the appearance of being unaffected by her captivity, deep within her soul, Julia knew she would never be the same.

Her world, she herself, had forever changed.

"What do you know of the white captive?"

Neeheeowee's question was met with silence. But at length Mahoohe, Red Fox, grinned, eyeing his brother-in-law with sly appreciation.

"*Eaaa*! She is pretty, despite her rags, is she not?"

Neeheeowee snorted. "Do you think I care whether a white slave is pretty or not?"

His brother-in-law merely raised an eyebrow. "And why would you not?"

Neeheeowee grunted, his only response.

The two men sat side by side within the lodge of

Mahoohe, a buffalo robe laid out comfortably beneath
them. Beside them, the men's war shields and bows
hung from the inner tepee lining, within their reach,
while their quivers full of arrows were strung from
the same, ready for use. The bottom flaps of the tepee
were rolled up to permit fresh air into the lodge while
the usual cooking stones and the buffalo-paunch
which served as cooking pot were relegated to the
outside, the cooking to be done in the open on this
hot, spring day. The scent of sage on the floor, of
sweet grass burning in the air, perfumed the atmosphere, already scented with the familiar tepee smells
of leather, rawhide, and smoke. Sounds of camp life,
of children playing outside, filtered into the lodge,
forming a sort of muted background to their conversation. Now and again, the aroma of buffalo and wild
turnip stew wafted into the lodge, enticing the taste
buds of those within, churning an empty stomach.

Neeheeowee glanced to the spot where Mahoohe's
wife had chosen to store the family's possessions. The
parfleches, which acted as a sort of chest of drawers,
now held Neeheeowee's things, too. They were neatly
set off to the side, these brightly beaded buffalo bags,
whose designs depicted the special dream sequences
belonging specifically to Mahoohe and his family.

The tepee flap suddenly opened, catching Neeheeowee's attention, and he looked up to see Voesee,
Happy Woman, Mahoohe's sister, leading her small
son into the lodge; both were followed by Aamehee,
Always A Woman, Mahoohe's wife.

It was an unusual sight, to see Mahoohe and his
sister, Voesee, together since custom dictated that after a certain maturity of age, Cheyenne siblings of different sexes could not be alone with one another, nor
could they speak to each other—at least not directly.
And though this might seem strange to an outsider,
to the Cheyenne, this conferred the greatest respect

upon one's brother or toward one's sister.

But Voesee was not known for keeping tradition, and Neeheeowee feared she had something to say to him, something which must be important since she dared to flaunt Cheyenne custom. And though the two women kept their gazes down to show respect as they entered the tepee, cloaked about the both of them was a sense of expectancy.

All at once Voesee looked up and smiled. "Tell these two, big warriors," Voesee spoke to Aamehee, as both women and the boy fully entered the tepee, Voesee and Aamehee moving off to the left to cross behind the men, while the boy sat down at once. "Tell my two brothers," Voesee continued as the two women made their way around the tepee to the women's quarters, sitting down across from the males, "that we heard them speaking of the white captive and that I believe the white woman should be bought. She would make a good wife, I think."

Mahoohe choked on the buffalo jerky he was eating, while Neeheeowee grunted. Mahoohe sent his wife an imploring look. "My wife," he said, being careful not to speak to his sister directly, "tell my sister that she does her brother great dishonor to speak of such things in front of him."

Aamehee looked down not bothering to say a word, though she brought a hand up to cover her mouth, as though she hid a grin. Voesee, however, smiled openly.

"Will you explain to your husband," Voesee quietly addressed Aamehee again, "that he need not worry overmuch. Tell him that I did not mean *he* should marry the white slave."

"My sister is surely not thinking of her own household!"

Voesee grinned while Aamehee laughed softly.

"*Hova'ahane*, no, no my husband," Aamehee said aloud. "Your sister was not thinking of bringing the white captive into her own home . . . something else . . someone . . ."

". . . from our northern relatives," Voesee spoke so softly, she could barely be heard. "Someone like . . ."

Neeheeowee heard. Neeheeowee groaned, but he said nothing . . . yet . . .

And Voesee, still addressing her brother's wife, said, ". . . like . . . Our northern brother-in-law has been too long without wife. It is time he came out of mourning and found himself—"

"I believe your sister would marry me to a white slave," Neeheeowee interrupted to say to Mahoohe.

And though Mahoohe chuckled, Voesee raised her head, looking down her nose at the two men, though she addressed only Aamehee. "Would you tell these two Cheyenne warriors that this is not something I say to make them laugh? I believe the white woman has great spirit."

Neeheeowee paused, giving Voesee an amused glance. At length he spoke, but still only to Mahoohe. "I believe the white woman has enchanted your sister, my friend."

And to Voesee's choked cry, Neeheeowee continued, saying, "It would appear your sister would like to see me united with someone who has no Cheyenne heritage. Do you think she forgets that the white woman is without family or kindred; without any moral or social standing in our community? I ask you, my brother, do you think your sister forgets that a Cheyenne husband would desire to know if his future wife is honorable?" Then, without even a smile, he leaned over toward Mahoohe, adding, "You had better watch your backside, brother, or next she will have you taking all the village widows as second, third, and fourth wives."

And while Mahoohe laughed, Neeheeowee silently congratulated himself. Voesee had a habit of ignoring tradition and poking into other people's affairs when she shouldn't, and he hoped that in this teasing way, his words would keep his sister-in-law from prying too carefully into concerns where she was not welcome, those matters being his own private life.

But when Neeheeowee glanced up to catch Voesee's gaze, he groaned. His sister-in-law was not to be put aside so easily.

Voesee had drawn herself up, her back straight, her head thrown back. She smiled, causing Neeheeowee to bring his brows together. "I must assume," Voesee said after a while, "that my brother-in-law from the north cannot see beyond this white woman's rags. I am greatly concerned about his eyesight." Here she leaned over toward Aamehee. "I will ask my son to tell him that I will solicit the village medicine woman to make strong brew to help him see."

Mahoohe grinned, while Neeheeowee scowled, sending a quick glance up toward the heavens. And looking over to Voesee, Neeheeowee found himself wishing that he could ignore the woman. However, he couldn't. For while custom clearly tabooed communication between brother and sister, the opposite remained true for brothers-and sisters-in-law. These relatives were expected to tease and to poke fun at one another directly, and the more people involved in the joke, so much the better.

He had just closed his eyes and sighed when a thought hit him. Ah, yes, here was a plan, here was a way to keep Voesee from prying too deeply into his personal affairs. And if it also had the effect of making Voesee think next time before she spoke, so much the better.

Neeheeowee didn't smile. He wouldn't. But that didn't keep him from leering at Voesee before he said,

"Sister-in-law, I have heard your words, and I have thought on them. I believe there is some wisdom in what you say and after thinking on it, I would be more than happy to purchase the white slave that you mention, but I will tell you now that I would not make this woman my wife. I believe that my sister-in-law forgets that I have other things to attend to that would not allow a wife into my life. I would ask my sister-in-law if she does not remember the Pawnee who . . ." Neeheeowee broke off. One did not speak of the dead, even if that dead be a beloved sister or wife. And so without so much as a shrug, Neeheeowee continued, "Sister-in-law, I will buy this slave. But I would buy her on condition, that condition being that my honorable sister-in-law should take the white woman as sister to her—"

"She is too old!" Voesee burst out, causing Neeheeowee to sit back, relaxing against the willow backrest as he watched Voesee struggle to subdue her urge to speak out. After a short while Voesee once again addressed Neeheeowee, saying, "My brother-in-law from our northern cousins has quick tongue, I think. But surely he knows that this white woman is too old for me to take her on as sister. It would be too hard to adopt her into our own customs. No, as I said. Not good sister . . . good wife."

Neeheeowee smirked and, leaning over toward Mahoohe, said, "*Eaaa*! Do your ears hear what mine do? Does my esteemed sister-in-law say that she will not have the slave, yet she would expect *me* to give up my life, to marry this white woman, and to tame this woman to our ways as well? Be careful, my brother, your sister has lost all sense, I think." Both men snickered.

"Tell my wise and great brother-in-law," Voesee broke into the two men's amusement and spoke to her young son as though Neeheeowee weren't pres-

ent, "tell him that I would desire to have the slave as
sister if she were fifteen winters younger. But tell him
also that it cannot happen now. The white woman is
too pretty, and I would worry that my husband might
find her so, also. No, not good sister would the white
woman make . . . good wife . . ."

Neeheeowee made a deep sound in the back of his
throat while Aamehee quietly spoke up from the sidelines, saying, "You must understand, my brother,"
she spoke to Neeheeowee. "Your sister-in-law, Voesee, is wise to protect herself. After all, what woman
would sanction the competition of another, beautiful
woman within her own household? Even if attractive
herself, a first wife would find the presence of such a
one as this white woman disturbing."

Neeheeowee nodded his head toward Aamehee,
not wishing to tease the shy, withdrawn wife of his
brother-in-law. "You speak wisely, wife of Mahoohe,"
he said, "though I would still query my sister-in-law,
Voesee, to ask if she has thought well on this. I wonder if she sees that here is a unique opportunity for
her—to have again an older sister; someone to share
the work, someone to help with chores, with the children. Besides, there would be no competition between
Voesee and the white woman unless her husband
were to solicit the white woman as second wife and
then—"

"It is that possibility that would torment me!" Voesee looked away, toward Aamehee, then back to Neeheeowee. At length, she addressed her son once again,
who sat at Neeheeowee's side. "Would you explain
to my northern brother-in-law," she said, "that my
husband may yet take another wife, but I would not
want it to be someone who is so . . . so . . ."

"Pretty?"

It was her son who spoke, and Voesee smiled, at
last agreeing, "Yes, pretty."

Neeheeowee didn't respond. Instead, glancing up and speaking as though to the air, he said, "It is too bad. I was hoping that either my brother-in-law, Mahoohe, or his sister, Voesee, would take the white captive into their home. Tell them, little nephew." Neeheeooe leaned forward, away from his backrest to try to gather the attention of the young boy. "Tell your elders here for me," Neeheeowee said, "that I am bound to purchase this slave, no matter the consequences of that purchase."

The small child of no more than ten years of age opened his mouth to speak, but instead of uttering a word, he gaped at his uncle. In truth, the whole atmosphere inside the tepee echoed the same response. Silence ensued.

At length, Mahoohe said into the quiet, "Tell us about this, my brother. Tell us about how a man who is too involved with revenge to even look at another woman, is now bound to purchase a pretty, white slave."

Neeheeowee said nothing, merely raising his shoulders, and Mahoohe continued, saying, "Come, come now. I am sure I am not alone in wondering, my brother-in-law, how a white slave could mean so much to you. All my life I have known you, and for these past seven winters I have beheld you as the man who married my younger sister; a man who even now would avenge my sister's death; a man without emotion, intent only upon revenge. And I cannot understand how a white slave girl could cause the sentiment I witness in you at this moment. For there is emotion in you today; emotion that I have not seen in you for . . . My brother, I see that this girl is pretty, but . . ."

"I know her."

It was a simple statement, yet it conveyed everything Neeheeowee wished to say on the matter; it also had Mahoohe straining up in silence for several moments, listening for more explanation while he gazed over to his brother-in-law, though, at length, Mahoohe merely asked, "You know her?"

"*Haahe*, yes." Neeheeowee nodded his head. "I met her some years ago when I accompanied one of my Lakota brothers on a mission of revenge which carried us into the soldier town the white men call Fort Leavenworth. She is the friend of my Lakota brother's wife, who is also a white woman. It was there that I came to know the woman they call Julia. It was there that I came to call her friend."

Voesee gasped. "You call a woman who is not a part of your kindred friend?"

Neeheeowee nodded.

"The white world allows this?"

Again, Neeheeowee nodded, saying, "*Haahe*, yes, it is so. They have many strange customs. But do you see now that I am duty-bound to purchase this white slave? I have pledged friendship to her, meaning that I must protect her. I cannot allow her to suffer the consequences of captivity. And I must see that she is safely settled, for I could not allow her to travel with me. It would put her honor at stake, plus it would distract me from my purpose. Would you not . . . ?"

"*Naaaa*!" Voesee came up onto her knees as she looked directly at Neeheeowee. "My brother-in-law, I have come to admire the white woman, but please, as I said before, it would be too hard for her to become sister. She would be feisty and she might attract the attention of my husband. No, I do not wish it." Voesee paused, then, after a moment, she sat back down and leaning over toward Aamehee, she said, "I have seen this white woman at the stream in the morning. I have seen her courage, have witnessed her stamina. I believe she has a good heart, I believe she is brave." This said, she glanced back toward Neeheeowee. "I can see that you have a problem, my brother-in-law, for if you do not make this woman your wife, as I think you should, and I cannot make a sister of the white woman, what will you do with her?"

"I do not know," Neeheeowee answered, then, turning toward his brother-in-law, he stated, "I had thought to make her a present to you, Mahoohe."

Mahoohe choked on the puff of smoke he had just inhaled. Amidst coughing and sputtering, he said, "As you have heard, my brother, one such as she would upset my household." Here he looked to his wife, who in her own turn, nodded.

Voesee shook her head, also in agreement. "Yes, she is too . . . pretty and already a woman. One such as she could not be brought into our households. Still . . ." Here Voesee smirked, a twinkle in her eye before she continued, "But wait, my brother-in-law, there is another in camp who would be only too happy to take the white slave into his household as wife: Se'eskema, Wart, is having trouble finding a woman. He would be easy to convince to take her." Voesee smiled. "I would only ask you, my northern in-law, not to judge the poor man on his looks. Wart would be kind to the woman."

"You would have me give her to Wart? I said that the woman, Julia, is my friend."

"He would make a good husband." It was his young nephew at his side who spoke, and Neeheeowee, rising up onto his knees, glanced down at the boy.

"Eaaa!" Neeheeowee spoke at last to everyone present. "Have you all lost your sense?"

No one said a word as all within the tepee, save one, grinned.

"Come, come, my brother." Mahoohe was the first to take pity on his northern relative. "If you must purchase the slave, then you must. But I hope you are ready to make a hard trade; for my brother, the Kiowa warrior who owns her, treasures his slave, I think."

Neeheeowee didn't respond—at first. Then, "What do you mean?"

Mahoohe smiled before he spoke. At last, he said, "My good brother-in-law, what would you trade for the slave?"

Neeheeowee shrugged, sitting back down into position. "I will have to part with one of my ponies since they are my wealth. But come now, you avoid my question."

Mahoohe paused, seemed to reflect for a moment, then said, "I am afraid, my brother, that it might take more than one pony to buy your friend away from her captor."

"Why do you say this?"

"Her Kiowa master refuses to part with her."

Neeheeowee took this message with a great deal more nonchalance than he felt, and he wondered why the matter affected him so. At last he spoke, again to his brother-in-law. "What do you mean," he asked, "refuses to part with her?"

Mahoohe raised an eyebrow, looking away, before saying, "Just as I said. We arrived here at the trading fair before the others. We saw the war party as it came in and settled into camp. We saw the white woman and we thought her Kiowa captor might have brought her here to trade. But we soon learned it was not to be. Her captor tells a story of killing the woman's husband in a fight with the blue-coated soldiers. He says because of her, he now has much medicine. He says she was braver than her husband."

Neeheeowee nodded, and, at length, he said, "That is a good story, but you evade my question, brother. How can a man refuse to part with a slave? It seems strange to me. Can you tell me what you know about these Kiowa people who own her?"

Mahoohe sat in silence as was Indian custom, the rule being, one should think before speech. At last, Mahoohe glanced up, saying to his brother-in-law, "I know little about them save that the Kiowa mistress is cruel, though it may be that the woman is only jealous. After all, would it not be appropriate for a woman to feel suspicion when her husband suddenly brings home a beautiful captive and refuses to sell her for offers worth a great deal more than her value?"

"Others have tried to purchase her? Is that what you have been trying to tell me?"

"So it is said."

"And who are these people?" Neeheeowee stared at his southern relative, drawing back within himself. He didn't like the sudden feeling of something gnawing in his gut. He didn't like it, he did not understand it, nor would he acknowledge it.

"Oh," Mahoohe said, a sly humor in his voice, "several of our young men have offered ponies for her. This is why I said it may take more than one of your ponies to purchase her."

"How many ponies have been offered?"

Mahoohe again took a long moment to reflect upon his answer, the action keeping Neeheeowee in suspense until at last he looked up. Then, still smiling, Mahoohe said, "I think I heard that one of our young men offered as many as two ponies for her, as well as two buffalo robes."

"And this Kiowa warrior who owns her turned down such an offer?"

Mahoohe nodded his head.

Something twisted inside Neeheeowee's stomach. A thought took hold, a terrible image Neeheeowee would rather not conjure up, his belly reacting adversely to the mere idea of it. This thing he saw, it wasn't something he wanted to think about, much less visualize. And though he didn't want to know it, didn't want to ask it, he still found himself forming the words, knowing he must ask. "Does her captor sell her out at night, then?"

Both Mahoohe and his wife, plus Voesee looked up to Neeheeowee; all teasing gone, all humor put aside, each one in the lodge appeared to feel their brother-in-law's hurt as though it was their own, although only Mahoohe answered, "No, my brother. He does not sell her out at night. Now do you understand why his wife acts as she does? I would not wish these things on my own wife. I know how she would feel."

Neeheeowee nodded, easing back against the willow backrest behind him. He drew a deep, unsteady breath, unaware that all within the tepee closely observed him. At last, he said, "This man, he will take my ponies as soon as he sees them, even though I may have to part with two or perhaps three of them. I have spent the last year accumulating this wealth. I have trained these ponies myself. There are none better. He will know it. Rest assured, I will easily buy the slave."

And with this note of assurance, all within the tepee relaxed.

Chapter 4

Neeheeowee did nothing to show his irritation, neither by word, nor manner. However, the sweat upon his brow must have indicated his mood to his opponent. The Kiowa warrior, seeing it, struck advantage.

"No trade," the Kiowa's hand motions said. "No trade. I keep woman."

Neeheeowee was dismayed. This couldn't be happening. He had just offered the Kiowa five—five of his best horses. There were no ponies better than these. Five ponies . . . for a woman. What did the Kiowa warrior want?

Neeheeowee gestured toward the pony herd at a distance, toward the woman, then in a flurry of sign motions, he asked, "Do you not see what you are turning down?"

The Kiowa hesitated. He seemed to think deeply before he replied in slower, more deliberate hand motions, "Yes, I do." He rubbed his chest before continuing. "And my fine Cheyenne warrior," he said, "do you not see what I own?" He smiled, looking back toward Julia. He licked his lips. "She is worth it, is she not?"

Neeheeowee almost spit; courtesy, however, for-

bade him such an action. And though he felt like
wrestling the Kiowa right there, right as they bargained, he could not. This was a trading fair—a
peaceful trading fair and Neeheeowee would do his
relatives no favor by breaking that peace either by
stealing the white captive or by fighting the Kiowa
warrior.

Neeheeowee looked over to his opponent, measur-
ing him, searching for strengths, for weaknesses. He
could find little, except one . . . Neeheeowee turned
briefly away, walking a few steps and gesturing to his
brother-in-law, who stood a small distance away.

"Summon your wife," Neeheeowee said as Mahoohe came within speaking distance. "I have need
of her to bring out the Kiowa woman who is wife to
this man. If this woman is truly jealous, it may be the
only weapon I will have to strike a bargain here today. And you know that if I do not do it today, it will
be all the harder tomorrow. Hurry, now. I will keep
bickering with this warrior until you return."

And Mahoohe, nodding, rushed away.

Neeheeowee retraced his steps, remembering the
week which had passed, a week while he and his
southern relatives had awaited the Kiowa warrior's
return to camp, a week during which both he and
others from Mahoohe's family had watched over Julia. And though none of them were obtrusive, always
watching Julia from a distance, the Kiowa mistress
had known of their presence, and had continued her
uneasy peace with the captive. At least, there had
been no more physical punishment, no more whip-
pings. And if the Kiowa woman's words were a little
strained because of this, if she were a little resentful,
it was to be understood.

And Julia? Neeheeowee frowned. He realized Julia's lot was not an easy one, still he could not understand her avoidance of him. He had once or twice

been within speaking distance of her, and she had ignored him as if she hadn't seen him. Why?

He wondered, as he had often done this past week, if she noticed the assistance he gave to her. If so, she did not show it, her head always held high, her gaze unseeing. And Neeheeowee began to wonder if she were one of those sorts of women who expected much and gave back little. Or to be fair, perhaps she did not recognize him.

Mentally he shrugged. It made little difference to him. He had once called her friend. He did so now, which meant he was honor-bound to rescue her, whether she remembered him or not.

The sun beat down an unbearable heat, and Neeheeowee strove to keep his composure, even though it meant letting sweat trickle down his face. He would not wipe the perspiration away, nor would he otherwise show his distress. To do so would be to display weakness. And Neeheeowee knew he needed every bit of strength he could muster.

It was not the right part of the day for bargaining. He knew it, but he'd had little choice. The Kiowa warrior had only returned to camp late last evening, giving Neeheeowee no chance to settle this matter in the evening, Neeheeowee's favorite hour to barter. Because the heat of the day did not always allow for clear thinking, he usually manipulated things so that he conducted business at night, such being the point in a long day when others reclined around the fire, relaxing. These were also the moments when Neeheeowee remained on guard the most, always alert. This he preferred; this gave him advantage. He did not have that favor now.

It had been his own fault. Anxious after a full week of waiting, Neeheeowee had approached the Kiowa captor in the early morning, intending only to set up the evening as a time for trade. But the two men had bickered, their argument continuing way past the sun's zenith, and now Neeheeowee stood in the heat of the afternoon, himself to blame, his final bargaining to begin.

He narrowed his eyes at his opponent. "Have you examined the ponies you decline?" he asked of the man in sign.

"No," the warrior answered back. "I have not, and I do not intend to. I have what I want. The captive has great medicine. I saw it during the fight with the blue-coat soldiers. Because of her, I have extra scalp in my lodge, extra pony. No, I keep her with me now."

Neeheeowee didn't change his expression; he didn't even move. He did, however, narrow his eyes. At length, he signed, "It is a foolish man who will not even view what he is offered, just as it is a foolish man who will not see. And I say that the man who will not look is no more than a coward."

The Kiowa warrior threw back his shoulders. He screwed up his face in the wake of the well-spoken challenge and glared at Neeheeowee. At last, he said, "I am no coward."

Neeheeowee nodded. "I am glad to see it." He glanced toward the pony herd. "Come, then, and have a look at these ponies I offer you, if you truly are no weakling."

"I will look," the man signed, his right finger snapping down to indicate his willingness. "I will see. It will do your cause no good."

Neeheeowee shrugged, his look saying, "We shall see . . ."

And as Neeheeowee led the Kiowa warrior away to the pony herd, he congratulated himself, knowing there would soon be a bargain. There were no finer horses on the plains than these.

*　　*　　*

"No?" Neeheeowee asked, his hand motions harsh. "How can you turn down six of the finest horses?"

The two men, having just examined the ponies in question, stood back at the Kiowa lodge.

The Kiowa warrior shook his head. "I do not wish to trade the white slave away for these. I already have enough ponies. Besides, the white slave keeps my wife company."

Neeheeowee took a moment before responding. He might have despaired, but upon looking up, he saw a gathering which gave him hope. It was probably the only weapon that could give Neeheeowee the power to win in this bargaining. The Kiowa's wife had appeared behind her husband, with Neeheeowee's two sisters-in-law, Aamehee and Voesee, in close attendance. And Neeheeowee, aware this might be his only opportunity to succeed in the negotiations, offered his best argument. "You say the white slave keeps your wife company. I say you speak only half-truths." His hand motions were slow so that all might easily understand them. "I say," he continued, "that you have other purpose. I say you keep the white captive here because you like to look at her beauty. I say you intend to take her for second wife."

The Kiowa man sneered. "And what business is it of yours if I do?"

Neeheeowee raised his chin. "I will give you six of my finest ponies."

"No."

"EEEEEEEE!"

The Kiowa warrior spun around to confront his wife. A moment passed, two. The wife screamed, her trilling voice causing others in the camp to run toward the sound. Frowning, the man turned back toward his opponent.

Neeheeowee, without so much as a flicker of emotion, pressed his only advantage as he motioned, "I will give you seven of my ponies. It is my final offer."

"You cheated. You knew my wife stood at my back."

Neeheeowee's expression didn't even change. "No, my fine opponent. I told the truth. It is too bad for you that she was here to witness it."

"EEEEEEEE!" The man's scream added to his wife's.

Neeheeowee waited.

Finally the warrior wailed at him, his hand motions quick, "I will have them all." The warrior paused. "Give me all your ponies, all your wealth, including your buffalo robes, all to me and then, only then, can you have the woman captive."

All? Neeheeowee, ready to accept, faltered. He looked to the heavens, he looked to the ground. All his wealth? All he had? For a woman?

"Well, my smart Cheyenne ally," the Kiowa sneered. "What do you say to me now?"

And Neeheeowee, barely daring to think of what he did, raised his right hand forward, in front of his breast. And extending his index finger upward, he moved his whole hand slightly to the left, the index finger closing over his thumb.

It was done.

He had agreed.

Where was he?

"*Pave-voona'o! E-peve-eseeva.*"

"*Ne-haeana-he?*"

Julia stared at the two women who stood before her, each one smiling and talking to her, both trying to shove multicolored, decorated, buffalo hide bags at her.

"No, no, I can't take them," Julia tried to explain, unable to return the women's friendly gestures and certainly unable to take what they offered. She held

her head high, hoping they would believe she felt no
emotion toward her situation, toward them.

She didn't know these two Indian women, she
didn't understand what they did, nor what they said,
and she did not want to trust them, despite the fact
that they had shown her only the best in courtesy.

It was early morning, the sun not yet arisen over
the darkened plains, yet the camp was alive with the
sounds of quiet voices, whining dogs, and the ever-
present echo of the wind. The scent of smoke and the
unmistakable smell of simmering breakfast permeated
the air.

She and the two other women stood in front of the
tepee where Julia had spent the night. Inside the
lodge, a fire remained lit from the night before, casting an air of comfort over all those inside, while outside, the entire tepee glowed from the light within,
illuminating the buffalo hide lodge in a multitude of
colors, as though the whole structure were translu-
cent.

Julia gazed around the camp, seeing other tepees
alight from inside as well. She could just make out
the figures of women and children moving about
within those lodges. The absence of warriors this time
of day was to be expected, most of the men having
arisen long ago, already out on the hunt.

The air felt dry, though slightly cool, the lack of
humidity in it making the atmosphere feel light to her
. . . light and fluffy.

Julia took a deep breath of the fragrant, desert air
and sighed. Why did they wait? For . . . what? She
couldn't be certain.

No one had spoken to her in words she could understand, making her unsure as to exactly what had
taken place. All she knew was that she had been removed from her enslavement yesterday to be rushed
into the tender ministrations of these two women,

who had fussed over her as though she were a new-born babe.

Julia recalled how these two had taken her to the women's section of the community stream last evening, there washing her clean with sand; the two women had then dressed Julia in a fine, elkskin gown, beaded with intricate designs and heavily fringed; they had brushed Julia's dark hair until the glossy waves had tamed, the whole mane of it falling down her back in a cascade of curls.

The pair had seemed to delight in Julia's hair, running their hands down the long locks much after the knots and snarls were gone. They had even left the mane of her hair free, openly defying the Indian fashion of tying the hair into two braids at the side of the head.

Julia felt pampered though she feared it no more than an illusion.

Where was he?

She understood that Neeheeowee had bargained for her, had bought her away from her Kiowa captor. And though she knew she should be grateful to Neeheeowee for her release, she couldn't help feeling resentful toward him: firstly because he *had* bought her and lastly because he'd had no choice but to buy her. It made her feel as though she were a commodity of exchange, not a woman of human flesh and feeling. It made her feel degraded.

He'd not said a word to her, either, not once. He'd not even seen her since the bargaining. And she wondered if he had given her over to these two women to use as their own, for they were all she had known since her "liberation" yesterday afternoon. Had Neeheeowee freed her from one form of enslavement only to rush her into another?

Where was he?

Suddenly, as if in answer to her unspoken question,

Neeheeowee appeared at her side, silently, his footsteps making no sound. He did not even glance at her.

"*Na-me'esta.*"

She quickly came to realize he did not speak to her, but rather to someone else, and it took her a moment to determine to whom he spoke. There appeared another man at Neeheeowee's side, who materialized as if by magic. And though Julia felt certain the two men were friends, it looked as though they were arguing.

"*Nesene, eesepeheva'e.*"

"*Saaaa!*" Neeheeowee expelled his breath with what seemed to Julia to be a curse.

More talk. More words, some angry, although Julia noted that the other Indian did not have as much to say—and that he often grinned, even laughed.

"*Saaaa!*" Neeheeowee said again, the word commanding such force that Julia almost jumped.

He directed his attention toward her, giving her a look full of such intensity, Julia would have run away, perhaps to cower somewhere else, had the man been anyone else but Neeheeowee. But this man *was* Neeheeowee; she *did* know him, and she felt her temper rise at what she felt were mounting injustices.

She glared at him. How dare he treat her in this manner? He avoided her, did not speak to her, threw her into the company of people she didn't know. He could have stayed close by to her. He could have given her comfort, let her know what he did, what was to happen to her in the future.

The more she thought about it, the more indignant she became. And Julia, staring angrily at Neeheeowee, resolved that, by the end of the day, the man would know her temper.

It was a pleasing thought but, oddly, the contemplation of it did not bring her the pleasure that it should. She would have to do better.

*　　*　　*

"Saaaa!"

Neeheeowee's brother-in-law grinned. "Why do you not stay here a while? You have what you want, my friend. You have the white captive."

"Haahe, yes." Neeheeowee felt like shouting, but cautioned himself instead to remain calm, to conduct himself with dignity. "Yes, it is true," he said, his voice low, even. "I have the white captive. But at what a price." He frowned. "Never have I heard of anyone carrying on such a trade. And I am afraid, my friend, that it will be talked about for a long time here in your camp. Do you not see that it would be better if I go? I do not wish to hear my name spoken with laughter. Besides, what is there now to make me stay? A chance to obtain superior weapons? The need to prepare for a fight? *Eaaa!* None of those. I have nothing; not a horse, not a robe, not even a scrap of food. Nothing! And why?"

Neeheeowee threw a scathing look toward Julia, while he tried to make sense again of how it had all happened. He had walked into camp a wealthy man; he would leave it now a pauper. His resources stripped; he stood to be perhaps the poorest man in camp. But it was not truly this that bothered him, since he believed, as most Indian males did, that material wealth signaled an inherent weakness; that the hoarding of goods was for the women, who, alone, could afford to remain tied down to them.

No, what bothered him most was that he had envisioned receiving something of value to show for his wealth, for all his hard work this past year: guns, ammunition, food. Perhaps a trinket or two. Something. Anything.

But what did he have? A woman. And not just any woman: A white woman!

"My friend," Mahoohe said, breaking into Neeheeowee's thoughts. "Do not think of this as a defeat.

Think of it as"—he looked at Julia—"a privilege. She is quite beautiful."

Neeheeowee narrowed his eyes. "Do you think I care about that?"

Mahoohe actually laughed. "I would."

Neeheeowee shook his head. "I do not believe that my ears hear correctly. How can you say this to me? I am stuck with a woman, my friend, a white woman; someone who could not find her way on the prairie if guided by *Maheoo*, God of all. And I am stuck with her for the next moon, maybe the next two moon cycles—until I can return her to her people."

Mahoohe only laughed louder. He said, "My poor brother-in-law certainly has much to concern him. This I witness as true. But my brother-in-law has also much to learn, I think. I am not sure I would do more than look at her if I were in your place. But very well, if you feel you must return the woman to the white men, then go. But take what I have to offer and pick out three of my finest ponies to see you safely on your journey."

Neeheeowee raised an eyebrow, the only indication that he struggled with an emotion. At length, he said, "I do not want to take more from you. Have I not already two of your buffalo robes in my possession? Do I not already need to take some *ame*, pemmican from you? I will accept no more. I do not want to feel more indebted to you."

Again Mahoohe shook his head and grinned. "You also rejected the present of the camping tepee that my wife and sister made for you, my offer of more clothing and food. It will not hurt you to take three of my ponies. After all, after you return the woman, Julia, to the soldier town, you will have to start over, new ponies, more capture. Take what I can give you now."

Neeheeowee snorted and, looking over toward Julia, sulked. None of this was in his plans. None of this was what he wanted. Yet, there remained no other path for him to take. He might not like it, he might not want to do it, but there was nothing else he could do—not if he wished to remain trustworthy to himself, to others.

Certainly he'd had no choice but to buy Julia away from her captor, just as he had no choice now but to take her back to the place where he had once met her; to Fort Leavenworth. He couldn't leave her here. He couldn't take her with him on a mission of revenge. He also could not dismiss her. She was friend—or at least, she had been . . . once.

He scoffed to himself. No, there remained no other path for him, nothing else honorable that he could do.

He had to return her to her people.

Mahoohe nudged his brother-in-law in the elbow. He said, "She is yours now. You do not have to take her back. Why not enjoy your purchase?"

"*Eaaa!*" The word, said almost like a curse, was Neeheeowee's only response at first. He gawked at his brother-in-law, then with quiet reserve, Neeheeowee asked, "Has my brother-in-law lost his mind? How can you ask me such a thing? Did I not tell you that she is a friend? What I do, I do for the sake of my honor—for hers. It isn't because of her beauty . . . it isn't because . . ."

Neeheeowee scowled. What was happening to him? Why did he suddenly feel light-headed just talking about Julia? Didn't he even know his own mind regarding her?

Mahoohe touched his shoulder, the amusement on his brother-in-law's face saying more than Neeheeowee cared to think about.

"Take my ponies," Mahoohe said. "I will worry if you do not."

Neeheeowee breathed out deeply, knowing the truth of his friend's words. He said, "I see the wisdom of what you say. I will take one pony, but it will be the worst one I can find."

"That will be fine," Mahoohe agreed, "since I own no weak ponies."

"*Saaaa!*" Neeheeowee shook his head, and, placing a hand upon his brother-in-law, he said, "Stay well and in peace while I am gone." And with a defiant look thrown toward Julia, Neeheeowee turned around, striding away as quickly as possible.

He stopped once, spinning around to signal Julia to follow him. That she might not understand his intentions, that she might perhaps even fear him, did not bother him. Besides, he was too angry at the moment to care.

He would leave it to his relatives to ensure that she followed him.

He paced on ahead, hardly able to contain his anger. He struggled with it, knowing that he must put an end to his hard feelings, and he hurried on in an effort to gain control over himself. But oh, how he wished to give in and vent his anger toward Julia. Just once.

And why not? Wasn't she the reason he was in this predicament?

Neeheeowee lifted his face toward the sun, momentarily oblivious to the world around him. What was wrong with demonstrating his anger? It wasn't as though he would actually hurt her.

Yes, he decided all at once, this is what he would do. He would show Julia his temper. And if he forgot for a moment the teachings of his elders, that one always made a guest feel as welcome and as comfortable as possible, he was to be forgiven.

After all, it wasn't as if he wouldn't do his duty toward her. He was bound to take Julia to the white man's fort, anyway, but it didn't mean he had to like it; it didn't mean he had to like her.

Yes, he decided, he would show the woman, Julia, no mercy.

None at all.

And strangely, though the thought should have brought him some measure of relief from his thoughts, it gave him nothing, not even the peace of mind which he sought.

Julia watched the early morning sun rise over the eastern horizon, shedding its glowing warmth across the endless prairie, where the buffalo grass and spring flowers waved in the strong, westerly wind. Behind her stood the Indian camp, now fully awake, the sounds of children and adults stirring in the breeze below. She gazed to the north, where Black Mesa rose to its majestic height, in defiance of the flat, sprawling prairie.

Neeheeowee stirred at her side. Encircled by the camp's pony herd, Neeheeowee inspected a few of the animals. Julia gazed all around her, doing her best to focus her attention away from Neeheeowee. She was angry with him for what she considered his mistreatment of her, and she refused to acknowledge him.

Still she could not help but notice how his breechcloth fell forward and back with his every movement. Nor could she keep her gaze away from his movements, which seemed to entice her to observe so much more than just a small portion of his firm backside.

She shouldn't look. She couldn't; she mustn't. Still . . .

She tried to tell herself it was only because she was female. Who wouldn't look at all that skin there, all that . . . ?

In truth, her preoccupation with the occasional view of his buttocks did much to incite her anger further. She had decided he would feel her displeasure.

She glanced back at him, determination in her gaze,

yet instead of a quick flare of irritation, she caught sight of his hands, firm and smooth, as he patted first one, and then another mount.

She looked away at once, a strange feeling washing through her. And breathless all at once, she inhaled deeply, smelling, as she did so, the clean scent of prairie air, the wind having chosen that moment to rush by her, its feel warm and smooth against her skin. She sniffed, and the aroma of prairie, mixing with the unmistakable scent of horseflesh, gave her a distinctive feeling of pleasure, not anger.

It was not something she wanted to feel.

"Darn!"

Neeheeowee glanced over at her as she spoke, but she pretended not to notice, turning her attention to scanning the plains stretching out before her, spotting not so much as a tree to mark where they stood.

"*Eaaa!*"

She glanced back over her shoulder to see that Neeheeowee had singled out a pony from the huge herd, and it took no genius to observe he chose the most inferior pony in the bunch. Shouldn't he be looking at another mount? Shouldn't he be . . .

Neeheeowee had reached out to run his hands down over the animal's haunches.

And a shiver tore over her skin, making Julia tremble. Quickly she averted her gaze.

Why was he concerning himself with that particular mount? Couldn't he see that the pony, a filly, had a curved backbone? That the animal's legs stood bowed out, and that a bluish film covered the filly's eyes. Didn't he notice these things?

The animal was truly inferior to the others, and Julia, as she stared at Neeheeowee, wondered at his knowledge of horseflesh.

"I always thought Indians were knowledgeable about matters pertaining to horses," she said aloud, wondering why she had even voiced the concern. He did not understand her, plus, in truth, his apparent inability to evaluate horseflesh gave her cause to think badly of him, something she greatly desired at this moment. For it kept her thoughts off of him and away from that flapping loincloth.

He didn't glance at her as she spoke, but he lifted his shoulders in a highly communicative gesture. At length, he finished his inspection of the mare, and, without once turning to face Julia, he motioned her forward, making several gestures toward her, as though she were half-blind, as well as dumb.

She knew other Indians understood this form of communication with hand gestures: she had even seen her friend Kristina communicate with the Indians in this way. But Julia had neither tried to learn it, nor had she ever desired to do so.

"I don't understand," she said, and stared at Nee-heeowee as though he were more alien to her than even this land on which they stood.

He looked over to her then, scoffing at her as he shook his head, clearly disenchanted with her; he grunted but didn't utter a word. Instead, he drew a rawhide lasso over the pony's head, making an effective bridle out of it. He then bent, picking up one of the buffalo robes which lay at his feet and, straightening, he threw it over the pony's back.

"*Ne-naestse!*"

He motioned to Julia to come forward and pick up the other robe, but when she pretended not to understand, he bent back down, lifted up the other robe, and advanced toward her.

Julia drew in her breath as he approached her. But it wasn't out of fear. No, not that.

Something else. Something much more disturbing. His breechcloth fell open with his stride, the motion enticing Julia with a view of the bulge that lay between the cloth.

She gasped, unexpected excitement racing through her.

This was not supposed to be. These things she was not supposed to feel. She was married . . . no she was not . . . not any longer. But she had only recently been widowed.

How could she even contemplate looking at this man, at this Indian, at his . . . ? How could she even . . . ?

She glanced to Neeheeowee, and this time her heartbeat raced until it seemed to challenge the wind.

She stood dumbstruck as Neeheeowee again motioned to her, telling her with his gestures that he wished her to walk around to the front of the animal. Yet this time, Julia came to her senses and did his bidding without even a whimper of protest. She didn't dwell on the fact that she walked ahead, while Neeheeowee sat astride the pony; she didn't even care. All she knew at this moment was that with Neeheeowee behind her, temptation no longer beckoned to her, luring her with images of just what lay beneath that simple loincloth.

Besides, it was a beautiful day. She wore a new elk-skin dress that grazed against her body as she moved, its softness feeling more like the finest silk than leather. Upon her feet, extending upward to her calves, she wore colorfully beaded moccasins, and around her neck she had fastened a bone-and-shell necklace.

These were all things given to her by the two Cheyenne women; they were all new and recently made. Giving in to the sensual pleasures, she gloried in the feel of new clothing and jewelry.

Without warning, life suddenly took on a promising new feeling. It was a welcome sensation for Julia.

And though her anger at Neeheeowee hadn't receded, she realized she could enjoy, at least for a short time, the beauty of the prairie and the safe feeling of being pampered. After all, no rope clung to her neck, and no noose bound her to the horse.

Julia held her head high, her spirits lifting up over the prairie, and she knew, if only for a moment, true freedom.

If nothing had truly changed for her, even if that freedom were to be taken away from her tomorrow, it did not detract from what she felt now. Let her worries take care of themselves. After all, there would be time enough to confront Neeheeowee. Why should she worry about it now, when right before her lay the vast expanses and beauty of the prairie?

She cast her gaze upward before shaking out her long mane of hair. And as she preceded her captor out of the pony herd, her feet seemed to find their own way out onto the prairie, as though she had walked this path a thousand times.

Truly, it was a good feeling.

And Julia, despite her resolve, silently thanked her captor.

"*Eaaa*!" Neeheeowee used the Cheyenne exclamation once, then again.

He stared at the woman before him. He didn't want to look at her, and many were the times he forced himself to focus on something else.

But it was useless. No matter how hard he tried, his gaze returned again and again to Julia as she walked straight and proud before him.

He, himself, sat atop the scrawny mare while he had forced Julia to march on ahead of him. Not that she had protested. No, she had given him a look of total disinterest and had walked on ahead without even a backward glance. It had come as a surprise,

this action of hers. He hadn't expected her acquies-
cence. He had anticipated a fight, had prepared himself to quietly bear her scoldings, only to have her
respond with nothing more than . . . boredom.

And oddly, her behavior grated on him. It was he
who was supposed to remain stoically reserved. It
was he who should have let her realize his total disinterest. It was he who had cause to display his anger.
And yet it was also he who found his glance returning
to her again and again, his gaze catching the errant
rays of sunlight that shimmered off her hair, her
dress, her skin.

He grimaced. He had forgotten the effect Julia had
on him, but he remembered now how his pulse had
always raced whenever she was near him, despite his
reluctance in the past to become acquainted with her.

He shrugged. He had made a small error today in
not remembering this, one he would not repeat.

But he hadn't realized the depth of her effect on
him. He had only known that he'd needed to show
Julia his anger. Wasn't it because of her that he had
lost all his wealth? Wasn't it also true that, because of
her, he could not follow his chosen destiny?

It had been a foolish thing for him to make her walk
on ahead of him. He could see that now. But he'd
needed to make her feel the weight of his annoyance,
and this had been the form of its expression.

Still it wasn't such a bad thing. Weren't there some
who would justify his action as correct? Wouldn't
they say he needed to ride instead of her, in case their
party were confronted with an enemy? Were there not
even some who would say it was his privilege as the
protector of their party to ride while she walked?

But Neeheeowee knew he'd done what he did for
none of those reasons. She had angered him. It was
that simple.

His plan, however, had backfired, and Neeheeowee

groaned as he watched the never-ending sway of Julia's hips as she paced on ahead of him. She moved with a grace that was as rhythmic as it was beautiful, the fringe and beads of her elkskin dress keeping rhythm to the movement of her feet. It was as though she danced instead of walked.

But it wasn't that which bothered him most.

No, it wasn't just the swing of her hips, which was, after all, barely discernible beneath her Indian garb. It was his reaction to her, the way his groin tightened as though he were seeing a female for the first time.

He was not supposed to feel these things . . . not for anyone . . . certainly not for Julia. She was white; she was foreign; she was a burden to him. Nothing more.

She also chose that moment to fling back the weight of her dark curls, causing the full cascade of her hair to fall almost to her waist, and Neeheeowee, all at once, could barely breathe. That the action only emphasized what he knew he shouldn't notice didn't help his cause.

And Neeheeowee, Cheyenne warrior, willing to risk his life for another, willing to face any pain, disciplined until he could confront and endure any torture, could not do one simple thing: He could not look away from the rhythmic sway of a woman's walk.

Suddenly she stumbled, falling down, and Neeheeowee sprang off of the horse, coming before her in a few, quick steps.

"*Henova'e he'tohe? Ne-toneto-mohta-he?*, What is it? How are you?" He knelt beside her.

"I don't know what you're saying." She looked up at him then and Neeheeowee's stomach fell. He almost groaned.

He had no idea what she said, but the way she said it, the way she looked at him . . .

He had to examine her, see to her foot, make sure she was all right. But how to do it without . . .

He drew a shallow breath and, keeping his glance as far away from her as possible, examined first the area around her, then the prairie hole where her foot remained trapped. He lifted his eyes upward, toward the heavens, feeling curiously glad—not that she had fallen, but rather that this hole was not part of a prairie dog town. This was good. Prairie dog holes held other dangers, mainly from snakes who liked to burrow in the abandoned nests.

Keeping the reins of the horse held tightly in one hand, he lowered his free hand to her foot, trying to ignore the feeling that shot through his arm when his touch briefly grazed over her skin.

He cradled her foot and gently twisted it this way and that as he eased it out of the hole. He listened for signs of pain from her, unwilling to look directly at her. But he heard no sound from her indicating that she was injured. And so at length, he raised his glance to her.

A shiver raced through him at once and Nee-heeowee almost dropped her foot, but he didn't, his practiced discipline enabling him to pretend he felt no reaction.

Again, he turned her foot, this time watching her face to catch any sign of pain. He saw none.

"*Ne-hoveoo'estse*, stand up."

He made to rise, but Julia couldn't arise on her own, and he frowned as he realized he would have to assist her. Drawing a deep breath, he picked her up, the feel of her in his arms more pleasurable than he would have cared to admit, and when a shot of pure longing ripped through his body, he nearly dropped her.

Gathering her more securely in his arms, he carryied her to the horse and, lifting her up and away from him, he set her down upon the mount.

He did it quickly so as to avoid further contact with her, but he noted, as he placed her on the pony, that she did not move to straddle the horse, placing both legs over its back. She sat, her legs drawn to the side, and though Neeheeowee motioned her to straddle the animal correctly, she did not budge from her position.

He almost did it for her, but he held back, more than aware of what touching her legs, her calves, her thighs, could do to him. He did not need to be told these things, nor did he need the movement of the front of his breechcloth to emphasize what resulted from such thoughts.

Realizing he could neither touch her, nor talk to her without severe reaction on his part, he did the only thing he could: He strode away. He took the parfleches from her, tying them onto the back of the horse. Then he rolled up the extra buffalo robe, settling it behind her and tying it onto the pony as well.

There. He was done with it.

She and the supplies were safely secured onto the horse. He no longer had to think about her. He no longer had to look at her. He was free now to walk out in front of her, leading the pony by the reins, this being what he should have done from the start, before his temper had gotten the better of him.

He lifted his shoulders and breathed deeply. This was better. No more would he have to watch the jiggle of those hips, nor would he have to witness her hair caught in the wind, blowing back in the breeze. He wouldn't have to see nor hear her movements. He wouldn't have to attend to the sound of the fringe and beads of her regalia keeping rhythm to the sway of her motion.

Yes, this he could handle. He silently congratulated himself on the wisdom of his actions and once more, his self-confidence reasserting itself, he looked down, only to observe it—not the tracks of an enemy nor even the path of an animal. No, it was his own breechcloth he observed, the evidence of her effect on him complete.

He groaned.

The westerly wind chose that moment to blow up behind them, bringing with it the sweet scent of her body. And Neeheeowee, his gut churning in ready response, despaired.

It was going to be a long journey.

Chapter 5

J ulia watched her moody captor from across the ashes of a dim campfire. Above her the sky burned with the brilliance of a million stars, all set to twinkling in the clean, dry air with a luminescence undreamed of by people who had not witnessed it. The half-moon this night shone down its radiance to the landscape below as though competing with the sun, while the ever-present wind whined across the deserted stretch of prairie, whispering its message of loneliness and fear.

But it was not fear Julia felt, nor loneliness. And as she continued to study her Indian companion from afar, she grew more and more confused.

She did not understand the man. First he'd made her walk while he'd ridden. Then, when she'd fallen, he had been beside her, ministering to her, pulling her into his arms, putting her onto the horse, letting her remain there while he had walked on ahead.

And tonight, after they had camped, he had taken the time gently to bathe her foot with a mixture of herbs, wrapping it up in a soft, elkskin bandage.

He hadn't, though, said a thing to her, hadn't even looked at her, and he'd acted in the strangest of ways. Having found a small stream, one which barely cov-

ered the ankle when standing in its center, Neeheeowee had spent more than an hour in it, bathing.
Or maybe he'd been doing something else? Praying?

Julia had once heard that the Indians said their
prayers in the early morning when they bathed. Was
that what Neeheeowee had done? In the evening?

Julia couldn't be certain of it, and she looked over
to him now where he lay across the campfire, his back
to her, his weapons within his easy reach.

She sighed. There was something else. He had
caught and roasted a small rabbit for their supper tonight. He hadn't expected her to do anything, he had
even started the fire, which she knew was a woman's
job in both his culture and hers.

Strange. She had thought Indian men lazy and Indian women no more than slaves to their men.

And perhaps they were. Perhaps. This was only
their first night together on whatever journey they
were making. Time would tell.

She could make no sense of it. Maybe tomorrow
would give her greater insight.

"I hope so," she whispered and, lying down, she
fell instantly asleep.

"Why did I not notice it before now?" Julia murmured to herself as she sat up from her bed of buffalo
robe and deerskin blanket. She should have seen it.
After all, the man wore only breechcloth and moccasins, his same outfit as yesterday. It was clearly there.
She should have seen it yesterday.

*Perhaps I didn't want to observe him too closely in case
I looked at his* . . . She broke off her thoughts.

What is wrong with me?

She shook her head, unable to believe she could not
get her attention off that one area of the man's body.

She had to get control of herself. Certainly there

was more to a man than one portion of his body. Certainly there was more to him than . . .

She looked up, catching sight of Neeheeowee as he returned from his lengthy morning bath in the stream.

She groaned. He looked more handsome than a man had any right to, and the way he was dressed, what he wore, the way he walked . . .

"Dear Lord above," she moaned, and jerked her gaze up toward his neck. And there she saw it again: Her necklace, the one she had beaded for him as a gift seven and a half years ago.

It was incredible. Neeheeowee wore her necklace. Did he even realize what he did?

She looked again, just to satisfy herself that she wasn't seeing things, but there it was. Sewn in blue pony beads, with a red-beaded heart in the center, it hung from his neck; the colors were a little faded, yet the strand was still intact.

She tried to observe him more closely, wondering if his wearing of it was recent, since his rescue of her, but when he bent down toward the fire, she saw a lighter skin beneath the necklace, indicating he had worn the ornament a long time.

How long? she wondered.

"*Nese'se'onotse*," he said, pointing toward her, then toward the stream, and it took no scholar to realize that he suggested she take a bath.

She sighed. "I take slight offense to that," she said softly, raising her chin. "Are you suggesting I am dirty?"

But he said nothing back to her, and she frowned, looking down at her gown of soft elkskin, the same one she had slept in last night.

She grimaced. She *did* need to bathe; she *did* need to rinse the gloom of the night from her mouth, but there was no way she would do it while Neeheeowee remained in camp.

She darted him a shy glance. "I cannot bathe while you are in camp here."

"*Na-ase-ohtse.*"

She knew he didn't understand her words, just as she didn't understand his, but something must have communicated between them because, as he spoke, he nodded, pointing first to himself and then to a point far distant from their camp. And Julia came to understand that he would give her the privacy she needed.

Julia met his gaze before he turned to walk from camp. She just as quickly looked away.

What was happening to her? Why did a simple glance from him make her stomach drop, her pulse beat a little quicker?

She tilted her head, finding herself studying the man's graceful walk as he trod away. And she didn't dare examine the reason behind why she also marked the movement of his breechcloth across his tight backside as he ascended a small rise in the landscape.

She waited a few moments, then, seeing he did not return, she got to her feet, treading leisurely to the water, her spirits oddly high for so early in the morning.

Curiously, she hummed, finding herself enjoying the quiet of the morning hours. She laid her dress on the nearby bank of the stream, and, slipping off her moccasins, left them behind her, near the bank. She trudged into the brook and, slipping to her knees, relished the refreshing coolness of the water.

She smiled, still humming as she bathed, gathering fistfuls of sand from the riverbed to scrub herself. She rinsed her mouth with the water, then wet and washed her hair as best she could in only a few inches of water.

Truly it was a welcome experience, and she lingered in the water until the last possible moment.

She could see Neeheeowee had returned to camp, and though his back was to her, his presence still presented her with a dilemma.

How do I get dressed?

If she walked out, she exposed her entire, nude body to his quick perusal if he so much as moved his head. If she grabbed her dress from the bank and pulled it on while she sat in the water, she might ruin the dress. The regalia of the gown was, after all, elkskin and most of the leather garments with which Julia was acquainted were ruined if ever they were wet.

It left her little choice.

Deciding her captor a sort of prairie gentleman, Julia rose from the water, pacing back to shore. She was almost there when the bottom of the stream suddenly fell out.

She screamed.

Neeheeowee jumped up and, spinning around, grabbed his weapons.

He stopped. He looked.

Julia, kneeling upright, gazed back.

A moment passed.

Another.

His gaze fell to the juncture of her legs—

She gasped and suddenly sat, covering her bottom with water, her bosom with her arms.

And Neeheeowee, snorting, turned his back.

But only a second elapsed before Neeheeowee suddenly burst into flight, running from the camp as though to a fire, while Julia, watching him, wondered what he did.

She glanced here and there, noting her surroundings, looking for smoke, any telltale sign indicating something was wrong. She saw nothing, nothing to have caused such a stir.

"That's odd," she commented aloud as she stepped fully out of the water. It wasn't until much later that

she saw Neeheeowee return to camp. And then she
saw it, the full effect of her on him, there under his
breechcloth.

She might have felt fear to have observed such a
thing. But she experienced nothing of the sort. No she
certainly did not feel afraid. And slowly, so very sub-
tly, Julia smiled.

Neeheeowee squatted on the ground, the reins of
the pony in his hands, Julia standing over him to the
side.

He looked up at the sun, back down at the tracks.
Sand still adhered to the blades of grass. It meant this
party had traveled by this spot in the morning, two
days ago, the only time there had been dew on the
ground.

Neeheeowee squinted, studying the imprints. No
travois poles indicating a family. Only ponies, at a
run. It was spring. A time for war parties, a time for
raiding.

His gaze moved upward, following the trail
through the grasses, the path easily discernible by the
different shades of the green grasses where the weeds
were still turned. There were four warriors in this
party, Osage, the tribe easily distinguished by the occasional moccasin print farther back on the trail and
by the manner in which these men rode their ponies.
They were also young warriors, the imprints told him
from their slight impressions, warriors out seeking
honor and glory, a coup, perhaps, to win favor of a
sweetheart.

Their trail intersected his own here, while up ahead
they had shifted course, turning east—traveling the
same direction as he and Julia, most likely going
home.

While they were four warriors, he was only one—
with baggage.

If the warriors circled back, they could easily pick up his own trail, he, then, becoming an easy coup. But he was fairly certain they would not do this. They were too far out of their own country. More than likely they were a raiding party, caught, fleeing for home.

Which meant someone followed them.

Neeheeowee sat for a moment, reflecting.

It was conceivable that this party had raided a Kiowa or Comanche camp, making it the Kiowa or Comanche who would follow, though perhaps not.

Neeheeowee gazed back, scanning his own trail. The terrain they had traversed so far did not make for an easy path to cover. All dirt and short grasses, there was no way to mask his own trail, unless he did it all by hand, a time-consuming endeavor. If the pursuers of this Osage party were Kiowa or Comanche, they were friend, and Neeheeowee had nothing to fear, except . . . the woman. They might try to bargain for her or even try to steal her, though they were allied tribes.

Or the following party could be Pawnee, a Cheyenne enemy. And if they saw his own trail, the singleness of his circumstances could present too easy a coup for an enemy to resist.

He'd not thought to be too careful these first few days on the trail since he was in his own and friendly country. Besides, he'd been distracted, paying too much attention to portions of his anatomy and to portions of Julia's to think clearly.

He looked up, scanning the barren horizon all around him; no trees, no bushes, no shrubs, only the short grasses blowing in the ever-present rasp of the westerly wind. He knew this country, the high prairie, knew it provided no wood for fire, little water for drinking. It also did not allow for any place to take cover, and with a war party within the vicinity, he

and Julia were more at risk here than he cared to
imagine.

He did not fear the Osage, nor their allied tribe, the
Kaw, or Kansa; no, in fact, he would relish the open
combat. For one thing the Osage were intruders into
this country. It would behoove him to seek them out
and fight them as his duty to his tribe. A battle would
sharpen his skills as a warrior, something he was always intent upon doing.

But more than all of this, though he did not like to
admit it, a fight would force his attention from Julia—
Julia, whose scent distracted him; whose grace intrigued him, whose feminine movements taunted
him.

He stood upright all at once and, glancing toward
the east, checked the hour by the position of the sun.
Then, lowering his gaze, he inspected the area for further signs.

He saw no indication of the Osage party circling
back, nor did he think they would.

However, it still meant someone followed them
from behind.

He scowled. He had been traveling north and east,
in a straight line toward the soldier town where he
had first met Julia. It was the quickest, most direct
way. And if he ever meant to return to his single-
minded purpose, he would have to conclude this journey with Julia as quickly as possible.

What choices did he have? He could follow the
Osage trail and hope that those in pursuit were Cheyenne allies. He could veer off the path and go in a
more northerly direction, chancing that the following
party would continue to pursue the Osage and not
him and Julia. Or he could take another path, one he
had considered taking from the start, but had disre-
garded since it was not a direct route.

It was, however, the safest course, and had he not

been in such a rush to return Julia and get back to his own business, he would have started off in this direction from the beginning. But he *was* in a hurry, plus he'd had his attention distracted, distracted by the sway of feminine hips and a delicate scent.

He grunted, disgusted with himself. He had to focus on the details of this journey.

He looked around him, searching for the best path to the nearly dry Cimarron River. This was his only choice now, to follow the river, if he wished to avoid confrontation. Their trail would be hard to pick up from the riverbed, especially since it was spring, and the recent rains had left some water there to cover his trail. It would allow him the advantage of leaving the water only when he encountered rocky terrain, thus rendering his tracks inconsistent.

It wasn't as direct a route, the dry river winding off course now and again. But it would be the safest course.

"*Eaaa!*" When had he become one to avoid danger? Had he been alone, he would have followed the Osage, had he been alone, he would have . . .

He stopped this line of thinking. He was not alone. He had a responsibility, another life to consider—Julia. And he had sworn his protection to her, not in so many words, but by action.

There was nothing for it. It meant adding more distance, more days to their travel. It meant being longer in Julia's presence.

He grunted, the sound deep in his throat. It also meant . . . frustration.

And worse, Neeheeowee could no longer afford to travel by foot. With an enemy in the vicinity, Neeheeowee would have to remain mounted, ready to fight should the need arise.

It meant he had to ride—with Julia.

He expelled a harsh breath.

As if things weren't already hard enough for him, he would now have to suffer the feel of her body against his.

He let out a low moan.

"We must go back to the river," he said, following his words with hand motions, indicating first himself, then her, then gesturing back in the direction from which they had come.

But she didn't comprehend him; or at least she didn't appear to understand. Instead of starting back, the way any good Indian woman would have without question, Julia stood, staring at him, her expression clearly puzzled, her stance stating she needed explanation.

"Go on back," he tried to explain to her again.

But when she just stood there, hands on her hips, he lost patience. He almost said something to her, but, catching himself at the last moment and holding back his quick retort, he stifled his impatience.

She was white. She didn't understand his ways. It was up to him to show her these things, thus bringing about her understanding.

He reminded himself of this, of the teachings of the elders concerning the care of women. So when he took hold of the pony's reins and turned the animal around, leading it back the way they had come, he merely motioned Julia forward.

But instead of moving, even a little bit, she crossed her arms, saying something to him in that white man's tongue he didn't understand. And Nee-heeowee, despite himself, almost smiled.

He was quite glad at this moment that he was unable to understand her. She had clearly not been complimentary.

And so Neeheeowee, letting go of the reins, approached her, oblivious to the fact that for the first time in five years, he had felt like smiling.

*   *   *

"No, I will not go back the way we've just come."
Julia couldn't believe the man was asking her to do
such a thing. "I will not return to that Indian village
... to that degradation and slavery. I will not, and
don't you dare smile at me!"

She planted her feet and crossed her arms, refusing
to acknowledge the half grin she saw on his face as
he stalked toward her.

She would not return. It was time he learned it.

"*Masaha-ve'ho'a'e,*" he said, stalking toward her, still
that hint of a smile on his face.

She saw that smirk, felt his resolve toward her, but
still was not prepared for his action when he picked
her up.

"Oh! Put me down!"

She beat against his back as he slung her over his
shoulder, as though she weighed no more than a parfleche full of belongings.

"Oh! Ah!" She struggled against him—a mistake,
for his arms only circled her more tightly, pressing
her into him more firmly, and Julia, giving up and
closing her eyes for a moment, breathed in his earthy
scent.

She flicked her eyes open at once to dispel the illusion of him, but upon looking down, she caught
sight of firm buttocks clearly outlined by his breechcloth.

"Oh, no," she moaned. "I think I need some guidance here," she said to herself, feeling safe in knowing
he could not understand.

The man was proving too much for her. The combination of the sight of all that skin, along with the
feel of him just underneath her garb, unnerved her,
and, with another deep breath, she squirmed.

At once shivers rippled over her skin, and it was
all she could do to hold herself back, to keep herself

from touching him, from exploring all that bronze skin with something more than a glance.

"*Ne-ve'-neheseve*! *He'kotoo'estse*!" he said, and Julia knew she had been scolded.

But worse, she felt his breathing quicken, and suddenly she imagined she could taste the warm saltiness of his skin.

"Oh, dear Lord, what am I to do?"

Again, she closed her eyes as if that action could keep his effect from her. But she needn't have tried. Everything about him encompassed her as though she were encased in a sweet cocoon, filled with his presence. And without her conscious knowledge of it, that part of her body most private began to ache.

She wore no undergarments, and it suddenly occurred to her that he could easily reach up and . . .

Sensations tore through her, shocking her not with the thought, but with the intensity of feeling.

"Oh!" She gasped out loud.

And then it was over. Just like that. She stood on her own.

He had deposited her on the ground, beside the pony.

And when she looked up at him, she thought she glimpsed—what? Passion? No, it couldn't be. Still . . .

I can't be having these thoughts. What has gotten into me?

She closed her eyes against the sight of him and turned her head away from him.

It didn't help.

She felt momentarily enraptured with him, and when he reached out to cup her chin gently in the palm of his hand, and when he said, "*Ne-mo'onaha*," and she knew that he complimented her, she thought she would surely burst.

But she didn't.

Instead she looked back at him and, catching noth-

ing more than his stoic regard of her, quickly brought
her own emotions under control, or at least she attempted it.

It was an odd thing to realize out here with the
wide expanse of prairie and endless sky: She wanted
him.

"Dear Lord," she whispered, "help me. I don't
know what to do."

How could this be?

After all these years of being apart from him, despite all that stood between them, their cultural differences, their language barrier, she wanted him:
Neeheeowee. An Indian.

It was that simple. She might fear his culture, she
might even despise Neeheeowee for what he stood
for, for what he might do to her, but it made no difference.

She yearned for him.

She looked him in the eye, and in his dark gaze,
she saw a reflection of her own passion.

She almost swooned.

It should have made her wary, or at least the
knowledge of it should have shocked her. But Julia
was far from being scandalized. In truth, she ached
with need. And she realized with a great deal of cha-
grin that if she had to be in the constant presence of
this man and she wanted to keep her honor intact,
she had to avoid further physical contact with him. It
was imperative.

And it was with no small fear that Julia realized
she was close to throwing herself at him.

"I must stay away from you," she said as though
making a vow to herself, and when he at last released
his hold upon her, Julia tilted her chin upward and
looked away.

In truth, it was all she could do. Had she done
more, she would have been in his arms.

It was an uneasy thing to realize.

*   *   *

Neeheeowee was far from immune. His whole body reacted to her.

Eaaa! He should have more control. He was Cheyenne, trained from birth to adulthood to control his body, his emotions. Why did these lessons desert him now?

And he realized with something akin to alarm that it was only going to get worse. He had to ride the pony with her now, and he knew the exact effect that would have on him.

But he wouldn't let her know it; he couldn't let her see it.

Still, as he looked down at her, he couldn't help reaching out to cup her chin, if only for a moment, bringing her face back around toward him so he could witness all of the beauty that was Julia.

He caught his breath, whispering, "*Ne-mo-onaha*, you are beautiful."

Was that passion he had espied in her eyes? No, it couldn't be, and yet . . .

His knees felt like buckling. He couldn't think of it. He couldn't even allow himself to ponder it.

And so he let her go, watching her chin go up in the air as she looked away, her gesture haughty, one of disdain.

He snorted, as though he reacted to her display of temper. But in truth, he didn't.

She intrigued him. She fascinated him. She . . . He stopped himself. She was beginning to rule his thoughts.

And this he could not have. They could not survive on the prairie unless he were wary at all times.

Hence without so much as another word or another gesture, he drew away from her, if only to put distance between them. He jumped up onto the pony, and there, fixing his position, he bent at the waist, offering a hand to Julia to help her mount.

And had she known that he bestowed upon her a compliment, that he normally would have expected her to mount the animal on her own, she might not have rebuffed his offer.

But she did reject it, retreating away from him.

"*Ne-naestse*! Come here," he said, making a movement of his head at the same time that he spoke, giving her to understand that she was to ride with him, not walk.

And she turned, gradually stepping toward him until at last she reached out, placing her hand within his own.

Excitement exploded between them.

A moment passed. Another.

Each stared at the other, at their hands clasped.

But too soon it was over, and Julia gained her seat on the pony, settling down in back of Neeheeowee.

The contact was immediate and Neeheeowee gritted his teeth against the silky feel of her elkskin gown against his own bare skin. He trembled like a newborn babe with the shock of it all. And as he felt her curves fit up against him, he thought he might likely lose all sense.

She squirmed behind him and he grunted, his only defense against her. He shut his eyes. And then it happened. She pressed her breasts against him, nestling her thighs into position on each side of his own, and as her arms reached around to grab him, he thought he would burst right there.

But he didn't.

He breathed deeply instead. And he cautioned himself to show nothing, to feel nothing, to . . .

Opening his eyes, he gritted his teeth and jutted out his chin while he pressed the pony forward at the same time, and as he did so, he determined he would put these feelings to rest, he must.

But he hadn't counted on the full effect of her; he felt her breath on his bare shoulders; he smelled the uniqueness of her feminine scent—sweet, fresh, desirable. And involuntarily, a shudder wracked him, bringing with it a desire that made his loins stir to life.

He didn't look down this time for the evidence of his arousal. He didn't need to. He could feel it.

"Eaaa!"

He was Cheyenne. Cheyenne. He could control these urges. He must control these urges. He could do it. He was certain of it.

But when Julia wiggled, bringing herself even closer to him, Neeheeowee made a low sound in the back of his throat: he, himself, uncertain all over again.

He tried to think of other things; he tried to remember other teachings; nevertheless, he kept coming back to one particular truth. He wanted her. He could not avoid it.

Yet, he must show nothing. There *was* nothing between them. There could be nothing between them. And though he endeavored to believe it, in truth, Neeheeowee knew he lied.

He'd never felt more alive than at this moment.

It was an odd awakening.

Chapter 6

The landscape lay about them, awash in red and gold. Clouds streaked the sky in a profusion of gold and yellow, pink and red. The sun, a globe of molten orange, illuminated the beauty of the hills and mesas, buttes and bluffs, creating a sort of fantasy world where nothing existed but them and the feel of the wind upon them. And everywhere there was silence, soul-stirring silence, the kind that allows the mind to expand, to think of goodness and beauty, of power, and of love.

They stood together, atop a small, golden mesa, having climbed there on foot, the pony tethered and waiting on a ridge below. Neither a word nor a gesture passed between them; neither felt the need. They stood as though paying tribute to the sun, lost in the companionship of silence and the knowledge that they both felt the overwhelming draw of the land.

"*Ne-naestse,*" Neeheeowee whispered, pulling away and motioning to Julia without touching her, to return to their pony.

She nodded but remained behind for a while until, with one last heartfelt look at the spectacle before her, she turned, following in the path her Indian guide had made, taking her back down the flat-topped mesa.

Guide. Yes, that was how she thought of Nee-heeowee now. She could no longer consider him her captor, not when he so obviously deferred to her needs.

She thought back over the last few days of their journey. On the move only a little under a week, she had learned to accept Neeheeowee's quiet companionship and to interpret his strange language of grunts and groans, although his attempts to communicate with hand signs became more and more successful.

She still had no knowledge as to where they traveled. And though she longed to ask her companion about it, she could think of no easy way to communicate it.

And so she remained silent on the subject, sitting behind him during the daylight hours, sleeping across from him at night, and though he behaved in some strange ways of late, she had come to realize that she held no fear of him. Something else, perhaps, but not fear.

She gazed down to where he squatted beside their mount, watched as he ran his hands over the haunches of the pony, listened as he spoke to it in quiet tones, and, without realizing it, she shuddered, imagining it was her skin those fingers explored, her ear into which he whispered.

"Stop it!" she admonished herself. She should not be thinking these thoughts. He was her friend, her guide. He was also Indian. Handsome though he might be, and, though desirable, she could not let her emotions rule the logic of her mind.

They had nothing in common save a past friendship and the current companionship of a long journey. That was all. Nothing more.

Yes, she was sure of it.

Why then, did her gaze seek out and watch his every movement, her ears listen for his softest whisper? Why then, was she even thinking these thoughts?

Julia tilted her head to the side, her attention inward on herself and outward on him, instead of where it should have been—on her footing.

She missed a step, and suddenly her feet went out from under her.

She fell backwards, hitting her elbows on the rocks, her fanny landing on something sharp, stony.

She screamed.

Her forward motion, its velocity picking up, carried her on down the incline, sliding on her bottom past rocks and scrub bushes and sand stickers. She screamed again, grabbing ahold of something.

Her hand came away bloody.

And then it was over. She lay flat, her dress hiked up around her thighs, her arms outstretched, while smaller rocks and dirt careened on by her.

"Ne-toneto-mohta-he?" Neeheeowee asked softly, appearing there beside her all at once. Squatting, he lifted her hands, her elbows, his touch pushing here and there, running over her stomach, her legs.

"Ne-haama'ta?" he asked. When she didn't respond, he reverted to signs, pointing to his arms and asking something, then to his legs, his chest, his head.

And at last she understood.

"Hurt?" she asked aloud. "You want to know where I hurt?"

He nodded his head. *"Haahe,"* he said. *"Ne-haama'ta?"* He touched his leg. *"Ma-htse'ko? Ne-haama'tovoho? Ma-nestane?"* And he indicated his knee.

She shook her head, holding up her bloodied hands for his inspection, then her elbows.

"Haahe," he said, gesturing yes with the movement

of his head. *"Tosa'a?"* He then indicated other parts of his body, then pointed to her.

She grimaced, saying only, "In my back."

He frowned, shaking his head and shrugging his shoulders.

She sighed and rolled her eyes to the side, too embarrassed to point to her backside.

He felt the sides of her body.

"No, no," she said, and he understood.

Again he questioned her, *"Tosa'a?"*

"Where?" she asked. "My backside. My posterior, my . . ." She pointed.

He narrowed his eyes and, lifting her gently, ran his fingers over her back.

Julia could barely contain herself. She sighed, she moaned, and Neeheeowee looked at once concerned.

She smiled up at him. "No, no," she said. "I do not hurt there. It's only that it feels good when you do that. No, I fell on something sharp and something prickly. I think I hurt my buttocks, but I don't think I'll tell you that."

Again he shrugged, and holding her gaze, he asked, *"Nehoveoo'estse-he?"* He stood up, making a motion of it, raising his shoulders at the same time, questioning.

"I think so. I think I can stand," she replied, getting up to her forearms, though when she sat up fully, she winced, falling back to her elbows.

Neeheeowee came down beside her at once, indicating to her that she should roll over.

Julia shook her head.

He just looked at her, waiting. After a few moments, he made the gesture again.

Once more she shook her head, and this time Neeheeowee took her into his arms, raising her up and running his fingers over her back as though he caressed her, and Julia relaxed against him. A mistake, for next she knew he had positioned her on her stomach, his hands making a search of her back.

She heard his indrawn breath. She knew what he'd
found and embarrassment swept over her. She'd
fallen hard onto a rock or something, whatever it was
slicing through her dress to cut her bottom. Most
likely the wound bled.

She bit down on her lower lip. It was bad enough
that she had fallen on her fanny, it was worse now
that he knew it, worse still that he had seen it.

But when he turned her back around so that she
faced him, taking her weight into his own and picking
her up, Julia found it hard to dredge up any sort of
annoyance at him. And so when she gazed up at him
and saw his open concern for her, she relaxed.

He looked down at her, catching her glance, and all
at once they both smiled, but whether in humor over
her situation or just for the pleasure of sharing a
smile, Julia could not be sure.

But of one thing she was certain: It was the first
time she'd seen Neeheeowee smile since they had re-
united . . . really smile.

And strangely, the knowledge gave her comfort.

They set up camp beneath a canopy of willow trees,
the soft grass beneath them cushioning their sleeping
robes while the nearly dry Cimarron River skirted
close to their chosen spot, coming right up to them,
then going on away, following its long-founded
course.

Julia looked up through the long, spiny branches of
the trees to gaze at the multitude of stars above her.
She breathed deeply. She never ceased to marvel at
the extent of the heavens one could see out here on
the plains. Before she had come here, she hadn't
known such grandiose beauty existed. Now she wondered how she had ever lived without it.

The wind whistled through the willow branches at

that moment, catching her attention, and Julia puzzled at how the thick stand of trees could survive the temperatures of this hot, desolate land. She had thought to question Neeheeowee on the subject, but not being able to work out how to ask him such a complicated question, let alone how to understand his answer, she had chosen to keep her silence, sitting quietly instead, enjoying the shelter of the trees after so long a stretch of barren prairie.

Unable to lie entirely prone, she reclined half on her side, half on her back. Neeheeowee sat across from her, his expression reserved, until all at once, he rose, coming over to sit beside her.

"*Ne-toneto-mohta-he*?" he asked.

"I don't know what you ask me," she said, his presence overwhelming her, and as he squatted down beside her, Julia gulped, her heartbeat picking up double time. She wondered idly if he could see the beat there, at the base of her neck.

But he paid it little heed, his attention elsewhere.

"*Ne-onesehe'onaohtse*?"

His gaze met hers. "*Na-nese'se'ona*," he said, producing a buckskin type of cloth. He wet it with water from a buffalo pouch bag and Julia knew that he meant to wash her.

"I don't think that you should—"

He had picked up her hand, Julia almost pulling back as a warmth swept up her arm.

He began to wash her hand, her fingers, moving up to her elbow. Then the other hand, all his actions repeated. And Julia tried hard to remember a time when someone had cared for her so well, so patiently.

She couldn't.

"*Ne-oneseohtse*?" he asked, and Julia opened her eyes to look at him. He grinned at her slightly, and Julia almost gasped.

But he didn't notice. He turned his attention to his

parfleche, searching through it quickly before he pulled out some ointment. He then proceeded to apply the mixture to her cuts, his touch as gentle as a babe's, as tender as a lover's, as . . .

She exhaled swiftly, gazing up at him, noting that his features had softened under the dim light from the stars and moon overhead. And as the willow trees waved their branches in the wind, sending fleeting shadows over his face, over his body, Julia thought she had never seen anyone more handsome, anyone more . . .

"Who are you really?" she whispered, and Neeheeowee raised his head, his glance catching hers.

Something passed between them, some emotion she couldn't define.

She almost reached out toward him, but he looked back down to her hand, and, as he continued his ministrations, she took the time to study him.

Yes, he was a handsome man, Neeheeowee. And she recalled now that she had always thought so. Tall, well proportioned, his body appeared as sleek and muscular as a Greek statue she'd once seen back East. His face was more oval than round, his eyes smaller than those of his white contemporaries, his nose slightly aquiline, his lips full and sensuous. Except for a section of bangs cut square on his forehead and centering down upon his brow, his hair hung well below his shoulders, almost to his waist, and he wore it without the usual ornamentation so familiar to the Indian: no feathers to boast of his prowess, no rawhide to tie it back, no oil to tame it into the sleek braids that appealed to so many of the warriors.

But it was more than all these things that gave to Neeheeowee his masculine beauty, more than all of these things that drew her to him. There was a strength about him, a strength tempered with . . . what?

"Kindness."

She didn't realize she had said the word aloud until Neeheeowee looked up to her.

She merely smiled back at him. And he, after seeing that she had nothing more to say, returned to his ministrations.

Kindness? How was that possible?

She looked at him again. Was she being fanciful? She stared. No, there it was. Strength, with a certain benevolence in his attitude that manifested itself in his every feature, an underlying resolve so powerful, yet so gentle, it gave her a feeling of safety with him.

She couldn't have said exactly how she saw it, it being more personal presence than physical feature. But there was something she could feel about him, some quality within him that set her at ease, and she realized that here before her was a man who would never desert her, a man who would stand his ground for her, a man it was an honor to call friend.

Her eyes widened slightly and she stared . . . and she stared.

His gaze, in contrast to hers, centered downward, his eyelids hiding his expression from her, especially since he sat bent over her arm.

But she didn't mind. It gave her ample opportunity to study him more closely, her gaze hungry to learn more. High cheekbones dominated his face while large, coarse brows complemented eyes that slightly slanted. His chin, she noted, was completely bereft of hair.

Her glance fell downward to where her necklace still hung over his chest.

Why do you wear it? she wondered, wanting to ask him. *Is it possible that you held me close in memory all this time?*

"No." She actually whispered the word aloud.

It couldn't be; she didn't want it to be, and she

shied away from the thought, barely daring to believe he might have held her in high esteem. She looked up to him, then.

He wore no shirt, his skin bronzed to a copperish tan from years under the sun, and she noted that not only was his chest barren of hair, but so, too, were his arms.

And unwillingly she wondered about other parts of his body, envisioning what they might look like. She glanced downward, toward that area of interest, but realizing at once what she did, she shot her gaze back upward, her stare stopping midway between his shoulders and his waist.

She glanced over to his arms. His fingernails gleamed white, his nails clean, set off as they were against the tan of his skin. His fingers were long and his touch sure, gentle; Julia, watching him, felt quite mesmerized.

As though he suddenly became aware of her scrutiny, he glanced up toward her, the pale moon accentuating his foreign beauty.

Julia breathed deeply, returning his look. He held an allure for her, this man, and she wasn't sure just what to do about it.

He didn't smile at her at this moment—he didn't do anything. He just stared at her, and Julia's heart tripped over itself as though unable to beat quick enough for the extent of her emotion.

His gaze lowered to her neck, centered on that tell-tale pulse, and, slowly, so that she didn't even notice it, he raised his hand to the spot there, a single finger tracing the throbbing outline.

"*Ne-mo'ona'e*," he said softly and Julia knew he complimented her.

At once, sensation swept over her, the enticing sweetness of it seducing her.

But he wasn't finished. He smoothed out her skin

with those fingers, he gazed at the pulse, at her neck, then back up to her face.

Their eyes met, his survey of her searching, cool, controlled.

She held her breath.

What did he intend? Did he intend to make love to her?

She almost stopped breathing at the thought, her body responding with frightening intensity, yet she hesitated. Was it what she wanted? Truly?

She thought back over this past week. Except for a few shy looks and some unusual behavior after he'd been close to her, Neeheeowee gave her little indication as to his mood, keeping his distance from her whenever possible, even during those times, like now, when she wanted his attention. There had been moments this past week when Julia had even wondered if the man regarded her as female, so reserved was he. But the look he sent her now . . .

Did he want her?

The thought made her feel faint. And while a part of her reacted to the idea in quite a womanly way, a voice within her cautioned her to go slowly, to think this thing through.

She glanced away. Would he attempt to make love to her? Did she want him to?

Yes. No. Maybe. She didn't know.

Had they been the only two people alive, she would never have hesitated. If there were no one else to consider, no cultural barriers to surmount, she would have already fallen victim to his charms.

But there *were* cultural barriers, there *were* other people who would judge them, especially if a child were made from the union. And Julia couldn't help but think that a match between them held little future.

He was Indian. She was white. They had nothing in common, not even those things commonly held true within a culture: no alignment of goals, no similarly held ideals. If they ever did make love, where would they go from there?

Julia didn't know.

An image of her friend, Kristina, suddenly came to mind. Kristina, who, seven years ago, had married an Indian; Kristina, who had gone to live with that man in the Indian world. Was her friend happy in the foreign culture? Had her relationship with her Indian husband worked? Could Julia do the same?

She had no husband now, no family to censure her decisions. Could she leave all she'd ever known and learn to live within an entirely different culture? Would Neeheeowee even ask it of her? Or would he love her now only to discard her later?

Suddenly her heart lurched, her head hurt, and Julia knew she could not think of such things any longer. Whatever her future might be, she could not see it with Neeheeowee; she only knew she could not allow him to love her at this moment. And with sudden intuition Julia knew that Neeheeowee did not intend to keep her with him.

She gazed back at Neeheeowee, and as she did so, she knew, if he asked it of her, what her response would be, what it had to be.

But he just stared back, saying nothing, asking nothing, and Julia, though she tried, could not read a thing from his scrutiny.

She closed her eyes, steeling herself with all the reasons which kept her from him, and unbidden, another thought came to her.

Wasn't she now a widow . . . just? Wasn't she still in mourning? Were she back in her own society, wouldn't her actions be censured? In truth, how could she even entertain the idea of another man's touch? How could she even . . .

She shuddered. Neeheeowee had just run his fingers up and down her arm, albeit briefly, yet the contact, the sensation of his touch over her skin, the feeling it invoked proved almost more than she could bear.

She flung her head back, exposing her neck to his wandering touch. She wanted more. She wanted . . .

She inhaled, the sound of it more gasp than inspiration. And she realized, she could not allow this. She must make him realize it.

And so, as she lay prone, there on the windswept prairie ground, beneath a thousand stars, twinkling majestically above her, she lifted her gaze to his. They stared, the two of them, communication passing between them without a word being spoken, and slowly, so very, very gradually, she turned away; her cheek, her gaze, her whole body rejecting Neeheeowee, his tenderness, his kindness, his care.

And Neeheeowee, receiving the communication as though she had spoken to him, stood up and quietly slipped away, the sound of his going lost forever amidst the rustlings of a hundred willow branches overhead.

What did she think he wanted?

What did *he* think he wanted?

Neeheeowee stood beneath a large willow near the edge of the river and glanced back to their camp. She still lay on her side though he could see that she had bent over, her hands reaching around behind her, trying to pick out the sand burrs and stickers lodged there in her backside.

He had tried to ask her if she would mind if he did the task for her, but she had misinterpreted his intent.

His intent? He snorted. When had he resorted to lying to himself? He might have originally intended only to care for her cuts, but at first contact with her skin, his best intentions had evaporated as moisture did to dry air. And Neeheeowee, striving to remain honest with himself, knew he'd given her reason to mistrust him.

He'd not been able to resist the temptation of touching her more intimately than simple care and good manners dictated were necessary, and despite himself, he'd almost hoped she might respond to him. It was what his body demanded of him, of her.

Neeheeowee groaned, knowing he had a serious problem. While he remained duty-bound to protect Julia and to treat her as though she were a favored guest, his body demanded of him that he make more of their relationship than mere honored guest.

In truth, his groin had begun to ache in ways he would rather not think about. And though cold baths held good medicine under normal circumstances, Julia was ever in his vicinity, her presence never giving his body a chance to recover fully.

But that wasn't all.

Since embarking upon this journey, Neeheeowee seemed to have lost sight of his purpose: the hunt for the Pawnee murderers, his wife's and unborn child's atonement. These were not things he could put aside. These were not things to be taken lightly.

And yet, something had come over him recently, a welcome change that Neeheeowee knew had everything to do with Julia. He no longer had those terrible nightmares that for so long had haunted his every thought, his every action. With Julia beside him, he felt freer, more happy than he could remember being in a long time. And he wasn't quite certain he wanted to give it all up.

Still, he could not turn away from his duty, his pledge to the memory of his former wife. He had made vows to her, had given up the last five years of his life for her. These things remained vital to him.

Yet, hadn't he traded away all his wealth, all his

means to avenge these deaths with a need to buy Julia? Why?

Duty? Honor? Yes, all these things. But there was some reason beyond the fact that she brought him a glimpse of happiness, a peace of mind.

Was Julia some sort of trial that Maheoo, God of all the Cheyenne, had set for him? And if so, how was Neeheeowee supposed to respond to the challenge? By returning Julia to her family as quickly as possible? Despite his own frustrations and desires? Despite his own happiness?

Perhaps Julia had been set before him not to tempt him, but to give him the physical gratification he appeared to need. Maybe that was all there was to it, but Neeheeowee rejected the thought; his attraction to her was not entirely physical. There was a quickness of spirit to her and a kindness of heart that he recognized instinctively, such qualities endearing her to him.

And then there was her beauty, an inner loveliness as well as her womanly essence.

Was it any wonder, then, his body reacted to her every movement? His heart raced at her very nearness? It left no doubt as to why, when he thought of her, her image blotted out the pain of the last five years.

Neeheeowee scowled. If all these things were true, it would seem Julia meant more to him than he cared to imagine. And this he could not allow. At least, not now.

It meant that he would somehow have to bring his body under control, for he could not have Julia. He could not turn away from these last five years, his duty, his purpose in life.

Julia had been right to reject him just now, and Neeheeowee knew he respected her for it.

He glanced upward toward the stars, and with a

slight lifting of his shoulders, made a decision. It might kill him to do it, but what choice did he have? He must keep himself away from Julia.

She could not fit into his life. He had no place there for her. Perhaps if he weren't such a wanderer . . . perhaps if he were free to . . . he sighed. He had his own life, his own purposes to fulfill.

She had hers.

And so it was that Neeheeowee determined that, despite all, he would respect the boundaries that Julia herself had erected tonight. No matter the responses of his body, no matter the imaginings of his mind, nor this fleeting feeling of happiness, he could not have her; he would not have her.

He would avoid further contact with her as best he could.

And as Neeheeowee prepared to lie down for the night, he wondered why his spirits took a deep plunge.

He had, after all, made the right decision.

He knew it. Didn't he?

Eaaa. What was that sound?

Did she cry?

Neeheeowee shot straight up from his bed, listening.

He groaned. Yes, she cried. Why?

He glanced over to where Julia lay on her side, still huddled up next to the campfire. She looked like a small child, alone, scared.

He sighed. He didn't want to know it, he didn't want to do it. And most of all, he didn't want to go down there to her. He knew the consequences of what might happen if he went to her in the middle of the night; he knew where it all might lead.

Still . . .

He grimaced. Did he have a choice?

She cried.

He shook his head as he looked down, his eyes staring without really seeing the ground below him. If he went down there, he would take her in his arms and comfort her, trying to discover whatever it was that ailed her. And his body would react all the more toward her, making him ache with a desire he thought reserved for adolescents, not for grown men.

He breathed out heavily.

She sniffled just then, the sound muffled, as though she tried to hide it, but it made no difference. He'd heard her, no matter the volume of her voice.

He moaned; he cast his gaze upward, yet even as he did so, he threw off his coverlet of buffalo hide, easing his tall frame out of his sleeping robes. He came up onto his haunches, quickly positioning his breechcloth around him and shaking out his moccasins before he put them onto his feet. Next came his quiver full of arrows, over his head, onto his back, then he picked up his bow.

Quietly, so as not to alarm her, he slipped toward her, squatting beside her once he reached her.

He touched her shoulder first so she would know he was there, then gently, placing a finger beneath her chin, he brought her face around toward him.

"*Ne-oneseohtse*?" he asked. "You are in pain?"

And she shook her head as though she'd understood him, tears streaming down her face. Neeheeo-wee's gut wrenched in response.

He did not want her to cry. He did not want her to hurt. In truth, such a protective feeling toward her washed through him at that moment, he might have jerked away in response to it had he not been so concerned about her.

He didn't say a word. Instead, looking down into her eyes, he traced her tears with a single touch of his forefinger, raising his shoulders at the same time in the age-old gesture of inquiry.

"*Henova'e he'tohe*? What is it?" he asked.

She sniffed, she sobbed, she held up her hands, showing stickers so deeply embedded into her fingers, they bled more now than they had done when she fell.

"*Eaaa*!" Neeheeowee stared down at them, at her. What had she done?

And then he remembered—her backside, her bottom. He had not attended to it. She hadn't wanted him to and he had shunted away from it, knowing the inevitable result of such an action.

He raised his eyebrows and sighed. There was nothing for it. He would have to attend to her there. She had tried to do it herself, all to disastrous result. He would have to do it.

And though his body jerked in reaction to the mere thought of it, Neeheeowee strove to bring his responses under control.

He would do it, he could do it, and perhaps if he pretended she were a child instead of an adult, he might come away from the experience with his senses still intact.

It was all he could hope for.

And as he raised Julia's hand toward him, feeling the inevitable quickening of his pulse, he moaned.

It was going to be a long night.

His touch felt like the warm caress of a lover.

He had looked into his bags, dragging out a bone object looking much like the pluckers women in white society used to pull out unwanted facial hair. And though Julia had buckled at the sight of them, they had proved a useful tool.

Neeheeowee hovered over her now, her hand in his

as he pulled first one sticker from her hand, then another and another.

She couldn't understand it. She'd been so sure she could handle this all herself, yet the stickers had adhered to her hands as she had reached around behind her to pull them from her derriere. It had gotten worse and worse, the burrs embedding themselves deeper and deeper into her hands.

She'd not had the courage to call out to Neeheeowee, yet he'd come to her anyway.

Julia gazed at him, the flickering firelight illuminating first one, then another of his features. And all at once she became aware of other things: the feel of his hands holding her own, the aroma of the fire mixing with his own spicy scent, the soft resonance of the wind as it drifted on past her.

Neeheeowee looked up to her.

She gazed back, unaware of the breeze blowing her hair back from her face.

And then it happened. Her heart felt like it had burst.

She caught her breath, groaning, the sudden realization of what was happening to her rocking her with the emotional impact.

She knew. She had feelings for this man, deep, heartfelt feelings, and the power of her sentiments gave her pause.

Did she love him? Was that what she felt? Or was the sensation more one of . . . well, she didn't know. But of one thing she was certain: She cared for him greatly.

"Maybe it's just the sort of adoration I might feel toward a brother," she whispered to herself. "Or maybe I only feel devoted to you because you are my rescuer. Is that all it is, my friend?"

Neeheeowee looked up at her, then back down to her hand.

She frowned. Whatever it was, it didn't matter. She held him in affection. It was all she needed to know.

"Maybe I feel this way because you have never lost your temper with me, though I am aware that you have been angry with me on numerous occasions. You have never raised your voice to me, nor have I heard a harsh word from you. Instead, though I can often feel your frustration with me, you continue to treat me with kindness and . . . with respect. I believe, sir," she said in an undertone, "that you are a rare sort of gentleman in any society."

Julia, watching his handsome features in the flickering light from the fire, came to another conclusion: Nothing mattered between them—not where admiration was concerned—not race, not culture, nor even prejudice. What she felt transcended such things.

She gasped, whispering, "It is beautiful, what I feel for you." And it was in that moment that she knew that nothing, not even the censure of her own people, could make it less.

It was a sobering, startling awareness for Julia, who had striven all her life to fit her needs neatly within the boundaries of her own society. And with intuitive realization, she knew these feelings would not go away. And so she breathed out a deep sigh, settling back to enjoy the quiet ministrations of Neeheeowee, her proud, proud wolf.

"Who are you truly?" she asked, her voice soft in the wind. "Are you Neeheeowee? Indian? Brave warrior? Are you my hero?"

She gazed up at him. "Yes," she said at last, answering her own question. "I think that you are my hero, truly."

And as he looked back at her, she very slowly smiled.

* * *

Neeheeowee had heard her soft words, had glanced up, only to catch that smile.

His heart did a flip-flop, then burst on with a rate of speed equal in intensity to that of a long-distance run. He stared away. What was that he had seen there, heard in her voice?

Admiration? Perhaps love? No, it could not be. He did not want it to be; he could not handle such things from her.

He was supposed to keep his distance from her, he was supposed to protect her, cherish her; yet that smile of hers did things to him, made him think thoughts he shouldn't, made him wish for things he could not have. It gave him ideas, it set his blood to racing, it made it hard for him to breathe.

What was he to do? The worst of his ministrations was yet to come, and, with calm resolve, Neeheeowee cautioned himself to move slowly, to think first and to think clearly.

He pulled out another sticker from her finger, then another and another, washing her hands after each one. But soon there remained no more stickers left in her hands, and Neeheeowee, sending a shy gaze up at her, motioned her to stay here while he got to his feet.

The medicines he needed to spread over her fingers remained in his parfleche, and he was glad for the opportunity to leave her, if only for a moment. He had to collect himself before he continued to attend to her. If he did not, well . . .

He took several deep breaths, his body already responding to the mere idea of what he had to do. He dallied, he paused, fussing over his bags and then, looking over to her, realizing the delay did not lessen his agony, he threw back his shoulders and, thrusting out his chin, set about to do the deed.

*   *   *

Julia stirred under his touch, his fingers gentle as he turned her onto her stomach.

Her buckskin dress remained slit where she had fallen, exposing a portion of her anatomy she would rather he not see, and she hoped the slit there would be enough for him to help her without the necessity of pulling the dress entirely up and over her hips.

She felt his fingers there now, felt his exploring touch, winced as he ran his fingers over something sharp.

"Julia?"

She heard his deep baritone voice. It was the first time he had called her by name, the first time he'd voiced anything she could understand. She marveled at the warmth of it, the way her name sounded on his lips.

"Julia, *Na-heese-tsehestoestotse.*"

Julia shrugged her shoulders, moving her head from side to side.

He sighed and pulled on her dress, repeating, "*Na-heese-tsehestoestotse.*"

And Julia, at last, understood. He needed to pull up her dress.

"No, I don't think that I want you to—"

"*Na-heese-tsehestoestotse.*"

He'd said the words softly and Julia, knowing what he had to do, nodded her assent.

He inched her dress up gradually, gently, as though he, too, were afraid of the result of such an action, though perhaps, he just took care not to hurt her.

Slowly, inch by inch, he pressed the dress upward until at last, he grabbed her hips, holding her slightly up and easing the dress over her hips, up to her waist. Cool night air immediately assaulted her buttocks and Julia shivered as his hands touched her, easing her back into place while his fingers explored her wound.

And then he bent forward, hovering over her. She

could feel it, she could sense it, and though she held her legs firmly together, she felt a response toward him building there where his touch came so close, yet hovered so distant.

She wanted him to touch her *there*. She wanted it. She . . . shame burst through her. How could she think these thoughts? How could she . . . she squirmed, just a little. And though she was sure color diffused through her face, she couldn't help herself. At least he couldn't see it. At least he couldn't know that she wanted . . . so much more.

He touched her other buttock cheek, the one uninjured; his touch fleeting, still . . . she moved in response to him . . . just a bit . . . she . . .

He removed his touch, making her feel immediately bereft.

"No," she murmured before she knew what she did. But he didn't hear her, or at least he didn't appear to.

No, it seemed he set about his task of cleansing her wound as one who had no interest in a woman's bare bottom, as one who had seen such things so many times, it had lost its effect on him long ago. Gently, using the tweezers he'd produced, he did nothing more than pull each sticker from her behind, carefully avoiding further contact with her.

One after the other, he worked at his task, washing her after he removed each sticker, carefully spreading ointment over each place. It took too long, yet not long enough.

At last he had finished, and still he hadn't felt her where she longed for the contact. She lay still, wishing, hoping, aching. And though she little knew it, a moan escaped her throat and, involuntarily, she moved her hips, not much, only a little.

But it was enough.

"*Ne-ve'-neheseve*," he groaned just before he caressed her, his stroke fleeting. But it came back again, his fingers, his hands brushing her up and over her buttocks, one hand finally centering over one soft mound of flesh, then squeezing.

Julia sighed, the sound more a high-pitched moan.

"*Eaaa,*" she heard his soft exclamation, sounding as though he were in pain, and she felt the touch of his fingers on her; then his lips were there, too, kissing the wound better, his lips, his touch roaming farther afield while his fingers dipped ever closer and closer to that spot that . . .

He touched her there, and Julia murmured a soft reply.

She shouldn't do it. She knew it. She had just decided she wouldn't do it, and yet . . . His touch felt like warm velvet against her, his fingers searching, and Julia could no longer hold back.

She fretted. She sighed, but with a slight wail of relief, she did it. She opened her legs . . . just a little, allowing him the access she had earlier denied him.

And when she groaned aloud, she no longer heard herself.

Neeheeowee, however, registered every soft whimper, its effect devastating to his tight control, and, with his own groan of frustration, he prepared to give to her all she could need.

Chapter 7

Neeheeowee was almost beyond control.

He'd had to bend down too closely to her in attending to her. And too many things about her filled his senses; the sweet, erotic scent of her, the smooth feel of her skin, the sounds of her quickened breathing, her moans. He could envision the taste of her, and he longed to run his tongue over the soft flesh there, if only to experience the flavor of her skin. Was it sweet, salty, spicy? How would she respond to him?

Just wondering about it set his head to spinning.

And then she moved—only a little, but it was enough.

She was aroused.

The knowledge sent him over the edge. She wanted his touch, and Neeheeowee was past the point where he would deny her.

He looked down at her. She lay before him, her feminine beauty fully exposed to him, and he would not have been a man had he not stroked her, giving to her all he felt she desired.

Up and over her buttocks, down lower and lower, his fingers trailed a path around and into the sweet recesses of her body. And then, she did the unfathomable. She opened her legs—just a little. And unable to help himself, Neeheeowee bent to her, kissing her skin there, the wound and then more—he had to know more. He traced his tongue over the path where his fingers led, up over her back, down lower and lower.

She moaned, the sound as erotic as if she had begged for his touch, and Neeheeowee could think of nothing at this moment save the ache in himself, the ache in her.

She spread her legs, again—only a bit, but it was more than enough for him.

Neeheeowee let his fingers trail down toward that area of her body demanding attention, touching her softness there, exploring her body, his touch as vibrant as if he had lived all his life for this one moment. And when she opened her legs even farther, he removed his breechcloth.

He would make it good for her. He would . . .

What was that he felt there? Curls of hair?

He ran his fingers up farther toward her stomach, his touch exploring her every crevice along the way. Yes, it was hair he felt in that region of her body. He knew the white race to be a hairier race of people than the Indian. He had seen it in their men's faces; but he would never have imagined discovering such a protective covering in this region of a woman's body, for Indian women had no such markings. He remembered seeing Julia naked in the stream that once, but he hadn't registered it all then.

How far did these tiny curls extend? He wanted to see them, he wanted to touch them, he wanted . . .

She whimpered and Neeheeowee looked down at himself, at her, and all at once sanity returned to him.

Saaaa! What was he doing? This was Julia—an honorable guest. Julia. And he was ready to use her as though he were some animal in heat.

He let out a cry of frustration and withdrew from her, taking with him his touch, his passion, his curiosity. He sat up, giving her backside one final squeeze before he came up onto his knees.

He groaned, aching for her, wanting her, still knowing that he could take no further action. For of one thing he was certain: He had no intention of keeping her with him, of making her a permanent part of his life. He couldn't.

Not now. Not in the future. Even if he made love to her. He would still return her to her people, which would do what for Julia? What if their union brought about another life? Mightn't it alienate Julia from her people?

He thought back to what the grandfathers had taught him so many years ago, their words running over and over in his mind. Wasn't it true, they had said, that a woman pushed too far into passion, could not return? That it was up to the man to call a halt to the lovemaking before it went too far? That it was up to the man to preserve her honor?

Neeheeowee shut his eyes, all at once disgusted with himself. Hadn't he been taught these lessons from the time he was a small child? Hadn't he been instructed that to take a woman without the sanctity of marriage meant only to disgrace that woman? That a man should do this only if he meant to bring shame upon the woman?

Neeheeowee despaired. He did not wish this for Julia. Never.

Yet, here he sat, naked; there she lay, naked, her body aching for his, and it was his action, his failure to control himself, that had caused her this. Without thought, he'd almost taken from her that which a woman holds most precious.

Neeheeowee stood up all at once, barely daring to look at Julia. He scooped up his breechcloth lying on the ground close by and moved around to face her.

"*Hena'haanehe,*" he said to her, motioning in gestures that he would go no further so that she would understand he would not bring dishonor to her. "*Nohoomanahtsestse,*" he said, then, "put on your blanket." He motioned with his hands, throwing a buffalo robe to her at the same time. And with one last look at her, at all the beauty of her, he turned and stalked away.

And if his walk were a little crooked, perhaps a little pained, he could only hope she didn't see it.

Julia had never felt so embarrassed.

Not only had she offered Neeheeowee the use of her body, he had turned her down! Never could she remember feeling more the fool—more used.

"What happened?" she voiced her thoughts. "Why did you turn away? Did you find me undesirable?"

No, that couldn't be. Julia had seen the outline of his body as he'd left, leaving her in no doubt as to his own state of arousal.

"So what happened?" she asked, receiving no reply except that of the lonesome whine of the wind.

She didn't know, she just didn't know, and as she eased up onto her knees, pulling her dress down in the process, she determined that he would not have another chance to dishonor her. She would pretend he meant nothing to her . . . even if it hurt her to do it. And with intuitive insight, Julia thought her withdrawal from him might do just that.

Grimacing at her thoughts, she lay down to rest, and if she didn't sleep well that night, she was at least comforted by the fact that Neeheeowee spent the night in the most restless fashion she could ever remember.

Served him right.

And with this unpleasant thought, she turned over,

pulling the blanket with her, seeking in sleep the solace she had hoped to find elsewhere.

It had been a wet spring so far that year, and for this Neeheeowee was glad. At least there was still water there at the lower end of the Cimarron River. And Neeheeowee, knowing what lay to the north and east of the spring, drank gladly of the milky white substance that oozed into the deep hole he had dug from the river's dry bed. He filled his water bag to overflowing with the unusual-looking white water and, gazing back at Julia, gestured her over toward the spring. But she didn't respond, nor did she come forward, and Neeheeowee, looking back at her, debated what to do.

All at once he frowned, twisting his gaze away from her with a jerk of his head. His breathing quickened, his pulse raced, and moisture beaded up over his forehead. He shrugged his shoulders.

What was he to do about Julia? About himself? The soldier town where she lived was still a moon, maybe more, away, and he realized that if he didn't do something soon to curtail his response to her, he would not be able to ensure that she would arrive there with her honor still intact.

What was he to do? His action, only a moment ago, had been innocent, yet his gaze, quick though it had been, had looked at her, at all the beauty of her, and his body had responded as though he could make love to her right now, in this spot.

And it was worse: The ache within him was spreading farther and farther afield, the hardening of his body demanding attention. Neeheeowee set his lips together. This craving for her was becoming too constant a companion these past few days, ever since that night he had attended to her, and Neeheeowee had begun wondering if his groin would ever return to its more normal size. As it was, he felt nearly crippled over of this sensual appetite he felt toward her, and he wondered if Julia knew of his discomfort.

He gazed over to her now, realizing his mistake at once, for his body responded with newfound excitement, that area of his body causing him such pain growing larger.

But he couldn't help it. She looked good, beautiful, and he stared and he stared at her, from the bottoms of her moccasins up farther, over her gown of elkskin and beads. And unable to deny himself, he found his glance lingering there where the beads on her gown, set in round circles, hovered over her breasts.

A force hit him in the gut, and he shot his gaze up to her face, outlined by her dark hair blowing back in the wind.

She looked wild, she looked potent, she looked . . . Indian.

But Neeheeowee knew she wasn't. He shook his head and turned his gaze away, attempting not to remember the exact differences in race that were hidden so well beneath that Indian garb.

He silently chastised himself. Why could he not put aside this lust for her?

He looked back to what he was doing, and taking one last drink of the chalky white substance called "water," he motioned Julia forward once again. But she didn't move, and he set his gaze back to her, studying her features more thoroughly.

She glanced at the awful-looking stuff in disgust, causing Neeheeowee to wonder about her. Didn't she understand that there weren't many places at this point along the river where water could be found, even if dug? Didn't she know the barren straits that lay ahead of them? The land his people called "land of no water"?

He supposed she might not, even though she had

lived close by to this country for at least seven years,
perhaps longer. But then, being a woman, maybe she
had never traveled this far south and west.

He frowned. It would be his duty to educate her, it
being no easy task since they neither one seemed able
to deny the passion that sprang up between them
whenever they were close.

So far it was a circumstance they mutually avoided.
Still . . .

He glanced over to her, carefully masking any
thought or emotion from his expression. Again, he
motioned her forward.

"*Mahpe*," he said, gesturing toward his water bags.
Then, shaking his head, he said, "*Hova'ahane mahpe
ese'he-tsexe-heseme'enese notama*," and motioning toward the north and east, he tried to make her
understand there would be no more water until they
hit the big river where all streams flow into it, the
river the white man called the Arkansas.

Still she did not come forward, nor did she drink
the water, and Neeheeowee struggled to determine
what to do. He would not force the water upon her;
he could also think of no way to make her understand, which left him little choice. He would have to
prepare another water bag, since she would soon
come to learn why Indian and white man, alike, drank
from this spring, despite the water's awful appearance.

Straightening, he stepped over to the pony, pulling
another bag from his parfleche, and taking it back to
the spring he'd just dug, he began to fill it with the
white-colored water. Hopefully it would be enough
to see both the pony and Julia through this next
stretch of land that the Mexicans called the *Jornada*, a
desert march.

He could only pray it would be so. At least, he
thought with slight self-disgust, the march up ahead

would keep his thoughts from Julia, a condition he would more than welcome.

Also, the hard journey might help to relieve this pressure in his groin, the ache there becoming worse and worse each day.

Yes, he would welcome the hard march, yet he would make the journey across the *Jornada* as quick as possible. He would have to, he thought as a scowl crossed his face. He would have to because until he reached the end of the *Jornada*, there would be no further opportunities to take a cold bath.

And with Julia's presence ever beside him, a cold bath was fast becoming more and more a necessity.

Chapter 8

"**P**awnee Rock," Julia said, looking out upon their campsite which ran from a tree-lined stream up to what was the highest point on this, the flat, boundless plains. Julia knew this place, recognizing Pawnee Rock by its sheer black walls rising a good fifty feet above the flat, endless prairie.

"Did you know," she asked of Neeheeowee even though she knew he couldn't understand, "that this place is named for a fight that took place between the Comanche and Pawnee, where the Comanche wiped out a small, but terribly defiant group of Pawnee."

There were hundreds of names inscribed on that black rock up there, homesteaders passing through the country, leaving their signatures behind to pass into history, but she said nothing of this to Neeheeowee, not sure how to describe the concept of writing.

She remembered hearing that Pawnee Rock was also a prime camping spot for the pioneers, despite the frequency of Indian raids and attacks. Nestled in the shade of the hill, it provided the pioneers' herds with ample grazing land and the people with water from the nearby Arkansas River.

Food was no problem either. Game abounded here,

antelope, wild turkey, deer, and the ever-present scattering of buffalo.

Seated in a safe spot, under a nearby cottonwood tree, Julia let her gaze turn to the south, to the sand hills of the Arkansas valley, as barren and forlorn as the African desert, but seeing nothing there, she looked westward, over the unmarred stretch of prairie, her gaze searching out the herds of buffalo and antelope dotting the landscape.

They had been traveling from that way for some time now, and always, after they had reached the Arkansas River, there had been buffalo. But before that, before they had reached the river, there had been nothing.

She remembered again the harshness of the last few weeks of traveling. It had been a cruel trek across what she now came to realize had been the *Jornada*, or Horn Alley, as the Americans called it: a desert march.

She remembered being glad to drink of the chalky white substance Neeheeowee had called *mahpe*, not even caring anymore if the water might be contaminated.

It was also during this time that she'd become aware that they traveled the Sante Fe Trail, and she remembered wondering if she might come across white travelers. So far, though, she had seen no one ... up until now.

She looked down again upon the scene below her, her gaze taking in the herd of buffalo that seemed to stretch out to the horizon. Sometimes she and Neeheeowee had been forced to move amongst those numerous herds these past few days, Neeheeowee seemingly at ease over it, Julia half-afraid of the huge beasts. Often they would follow a buffalo trail, seeking out the hollows where buffalo had lain down and rolled over and over, these spots dotting the flat, endless land as though they were shimmering aqua beads strung out on a necklace of brown and green grasses. It was in these hollows that she and Neeheeowee would water the pony and stock up on their own water supply, if low.

She smiled, watching the sun as it began to set in the western sky, the magnificence of color there, the golds and pinks, the reds and oranges, unlike anything she'd ever seen, and as Julia watched it, she experienced a sense of well-being that was as pleasurable as it was unusual. There was something about this limitless space that did something to her: the prairie that looked more silver than green under the hot, spring sun; the grasses that waved in the wind; the expanse of sky and high clouds. Even the air seemed magnified in purity, and she breathed it in now with a satisfied sigh.

She listened to the wind, the breeze blowing the faraway sounds of the trailblazers to her.

She supposed she might have gone down there to them, since they camped so close by, but she didn't and she wouldn't, content to continue her travels with her Indian companion, her proud wolf.

Yes, that was how she had come to think of Neeheeowee now: Proud Wolf. It was difficult not to picture him this way; not when he tilted his head a certain way, sometimes looking down his nose at her, although she knew it was all a facade.

She wondered again at how the white man had ever come to think of the Indian woman as a slave. Clearly there were divisions of labor as to the men's and women's work, but Neeheeowee did not balk at taking on her tasks when she didn't know them or couldn't do them.

And never did he scold her nor make her feel his inferior. Never.

In truth, she had never felt so cherished.

Still, there was something else: She had never asked, she had not thought to, but she had come to understand that Neeheeowee was taking her back to Fort Leavenworth. Another chivalrous move on his part.

She straightened up, away from the tree, looking out upon the camp that Neeheeowee had pitched. Stretched out beneath a canopy of cottonwood trees, their site disappeared into the landscape. And she knew it would take more than a little expertise for anyone, even an Indian, to find their camp.

She had noticed that Neeheeowee made no moves to light a fire this night, and Julia could only assume that was because of the close presence of the pioneers. And though she had come to realize that Neeheeowee did not much fear the white man, he did go out of his way to avoid them.

She glanced over to Neeheeowee now and watched him as he worked at camp chores, untying his bow, working over the wood, even chipping away at an arrowhead and shaft. These actions had become so commonplace to her of late, she barely even noticed him doing them.

As though aware of her scrutiny, Neeheeowee inclined his head just slightly before turning it quickly to his left, a gesture which had become familiar to Julia, and she couldn't help but believe it an Indian custom, with some meaning to it.

He looked over to her, his expression stoic, unreadable.

"Ta-naestse," he said, making a gesture toward her, indicating her voice. With a lift of his shoulders, he gave her to understand that he asked a question and Julia realized she had been humming, something she'd not been aware of until this moment. She stopped, but he motioned her to continue and then, possibly by way of a compliment, he smiled.

Julia was immediately captivated; so rarely did he honor her with such an expression.

She smiled back and continued to hum in tune along with the lazy fiddle, whose notes drifted up to them from the pioneer camp below. She knew the song being played down there and had she felt more at ease she might have sung along, but, being a little self-conscious, she contented herself with a mere hum.

At length, she rose, wandering to the edge of the ridge and there, looked over to the pioneer camp. Dusk had fallen all around her, bringing with it the scent of the pioneers' campfire, the soft feel of evening air, and the nightly squawk of prairie hawks. Also, too, were the sounds of laughter and of happy music which filtered up to her. All at once, a sense of melancholy overcame her, and Julia wondered at the cause. Perhaps it was only her desire to be near to the things she had once known, or perhaps it was simply the melancholy which she had heard so often attached itself to the prairie traveler.

Whatever the cause, Julia began to recall the dances, the jigs, the excitement of being young, unattached, and in love, the thrill of being asked to dance by the most handsome of beaus.

Caught up in her reminiscence, she swayed to the rhythm of a jig, her feet finding their way into the simple steps of the dance. And all at once, she twirled once, again, until at length she spread her arms, spinning round and round, the leather fringe of her gown flowing outward and swaying like so much prairie grass in the wind.

She smiled as a slower waltz took over the beat and melody, remembering when she'd danced to this very song not so long ago.

And without even thinking about it, she curtsied as though to a suitor.

"Oh, my, yes," she said to this most handsome of

imaginary partners. "I'd be more than happy to accept this dance."

Her arms came up to rest on her partner's strong, invisible shoulders as he began to twirl her around and around the carpet of prairie grass, the hard earth beneath her feet her dance floor, the darkened sky overhead her ballroom.

"Are you planning to ask me to walk with you in the garden after the dance?" Julia asked into her shadowy partner's ear, throwing her head back while the dark curls of her hair fell down around her waist.

She giggled as she pretended her fanciful partner's reply, deeming it to be a most naughty of answers, and she feigned a blush, saying softly, "Why sir, how dare you speak to me as such."

But when she smiled, it took the edge off her words, so that the dreamy figure holding her continued to whisper to her, the words so terribly naughty, it made Julia laugh.

She reached down, to sweep the train of her fictitious gown over her arm and then it happened.

Neeheeowee stood before her, stepping into her arms as though he were her fancied prince, his very real arms encircling her, his hand over hers.

His steps were smooth and slow, his look at her intense under the beginning shadows of a softened night.

She matched his steps, looking up to meet his gaze.

The moon appeared as an imperfect disk in the soft hush of evening, its radiance already beaming down, basking them in a glow of silvery light, and, as she looked up to him, Julia thought Neeheeowee more handsome than anyone of her acquaintance, and at this moment he bore more traits of what is considered the civilized man than anyone else, white or red.

Her one hand rested over his smooth shoulder, her other hand he clasped tightly within his own and he twirled her around their ballroom of softened prairie grass and hushed, moon-filled night. They danced as though to the tune of a hundred violins with thousands of spectators watching, yet they danced only for themselves.

The music from below had long ago ceased to play, but not so these two dancers. They swept around the circle there on the ridge, each twirl bringing her closer and closer into his arms, neither one aware that they danced to none other than the music of their own hearts.

His head came breathlessly close to hers, his lips hovering over her own and Julia, looking up, begged him silently for his kiss, her gaze pleading, her lips trembling.

She didn't have to wait. As he completed the one last twirl, his lips pressed sweetly over hers and Julia responded as though she had waited all her life for this moment, or more particularly, seven and one-half years.

"Julia," he murmured, his tongue sweeping into her mouth while his teeth bit gently down on her lip. His breath, tasting minty and sweet, mixed with her own.

Suddenly they stopped, her body thrust up close to his, the imprint of his masculine form forever pressed into her memory. He bent a little lower, his gaze seeking out hers until, at last, he kissed her . . . once, twice, again, this time raining kisses over her face, then, down to her neck, tracing the pulse at her neck with his tongue.

"Julia," he groaned again, and she felt the unmistakable evidence of his desire pressed up against her.

"Love me," she pleaded, and she might have surrendered to him right then. But she didn't.

A gun fired off in the distance, near to the pioneer camp.

The two lovers pulled apart, Julia barely able to move, her gaze still lingering over Neeheeowee, from the silvery outline of his dark hair down over his chest, still lower to his . . .

She gasped and he seemed to swell.

He grabbed her hand, bringing it closer and closer to him, until with a shudder, he seemed to realize what he was doing and let her hand go, let her go, and, stepping away from her, he took several deep breaths.

But he didn't leave. He did nothing, staring at her as though that action alone would fulfill his need.

But it didn't. He didn't, and as though he at last gained control over himself, he turned swiftly away, striding so quickly from her that Julia was reminded of the swift movements of an agitated stallion.

And as she watched him leave, she came up straight against a sudden realization, one she would rather not have known: Her heart went with him.

Neeheeowee, her Proud Wolf, her trusted guide. Neeheeowee, her love.

"I love him."

She sighed. Well, at last she had admitted it. And maybe, if she were truthful, she might confess that she had always loved him, ever since they had met over seven years ago.

But she wasn't quite so bold, nor so truthful. And so she shut her eyes instead, not quite willing to think of it.

Yet she couldn't stop herself, and the thoughts kept coming back to her. She was in love—in love with a man who, though kind, was as foreign to her as the prairie across which they had traveled.

Neeheeowee. Proud warrior, Indian . . . love.

And Julia, unwilling to envision more, murmured a quick, "Oh," and turned away, rushing toward her

remote spot beneath a cottonwood tree, where, at
least for this night, she could be alone.

And though the wind howled cool that evening,
making red man and white alike shiver beneath their
covers, neither Neeheeowee nor Julia sought out the
other, both knowing what lay between them, neither
one willing to acknowledge it, neither one willing to
see it to fruition.

It was clearly a standoff.

Neeheeowee was perpetually alert now. It was necessary, for he no longer strode over grounds belonging to the allied tribes of the Cheyenne. He now was
the intruder into the country of the Pawnee, the Kaw,
and the Osage. And though the latter two tribes were
weak, none would hesitate to count coup on a lone,
Cheyenne scalp.

They were camped in a beautiful spot this night,
where the water tasted as pure and clean as if it had
been driven here from icy mountain streams, a place
where trees abounded, where lush grapevines
tempted one's appetite.

It was an idyllic setting for what Neeheeowee knew
would be their last night in camp, their last night together. On the morrow, they would reach the outskirts of Fort Leavenworth, and there Neeheeowee
would set Julia free.

Free. It was what he had intended to do all along,
to bring Julia home, to set her free.

Why, then, did he feel a great sadness?

They could have arrived at the fort a few days earlier, but Neeheeowee had deliberately delayed along
the way, not quite willing to part ways . . . yet, leave
one another, they must. Julia had her life to live there
amongst her own people, and he . . . he had to consider his deceased wife and unborn child, his resolve
to avenge their deaths, to free their spirits.

There was nothing here for him with Julia. Nothing. Just the stirrings of his body and the tempting sensations of his spirit. Once she was gone, so, too, would his body return to his own control.

But would his heart?

Where had that thought come from?

He shut his eyes and had Neeheeowee been alone, he might have groaned, but Julia lay only a few feet away, and Neeheeowee knew that if he spoke, she might stir and then he might . . .

He wouldn't think of it.

With a power borne of long practice, Neeheeowee returned his attention to his guard. He would not think of her. He would also not sleep this night, not in enemy lands. Besides, he hadn't really slept well since he'd begun this journey with Julia, his body too rigid, his thoughts too erotic, his emotions too extreme.

He wished to keep her with him.

The thought came from nothing, yet the power of it struck him as though sent to him through the magic of thunder, its medicine streaming through him with every pulsebeat in his body. And he knew: He might seek revenge, he might even have purpose to free the spirits of his wife and child, yet nothing was more vital to him at this moment than keeping Julia with him.

How could this have happened? And to him, a man who needed no one, a man who especially wanted no female in his life?

Yet, he could not deny it. He wanted Julia, with her quiet strength, her soothing companionship, and unerring faith in him . . . and he wanted her to stay.

But would she come with him?

He snorted. He remembered several seasons ago, a little over seven to be more precise, he'd made an indirect bid for her, not with her parents, as he should have done, but rather with the intention of stealing her away.

She had acted wisely, however, not even acknowledging him, and, Neeheeowee, realizing her wisdom, had put her and her memory away from him.

Caught up in his thoughts, he fingered the beaded necklace he still wore around his neck, the necklace made and given to him by Julia. And though he'd told himself over these years that he wore it for its beauty, and not for its giver, he knew now he had only fooled himself. Even his wife had once asked him about the necklace, but Neeheeowee had been unable to tell her all of it, merely indicating it had been made by a friend he had not seen in many seasons. And at the time Neeheeowee had believed it true. Julia had been only a friend—or so he had thought.

But his heart had never faltered. Not once. His heart had always known.

What good were these thoughts now? Julia was still white, still connected to her own world, a world completely foreign to his.

And he?

He could no more afford a wife right now than he could possess the moon. It took wealth to keep a woman; wealth he did not have. It also took companionship, something he would be hard-pressed to give, his solitary lifestyle one he favored over camp life.

And didn't women need camp life? Didn't they value the presence of others to talk to, others to help with the many chores that fell to the Indian woman?

Besides, there was the matter of the Pawnee murderer that he sought, the danger involved with that, something no man should subject a woman to.

No, he could not have Julia.

He jerked his head swiftly to the left, as though to give emphasis to his thoughts, and breathed deeply. It was true. He could not have Julia.

And as Neeheeowee glanced out over the awe-inspiring landscape, the vast sky, and the stars that twinkled forever against the blackness of night, he despaired.

Chapter 9

J ulia recognized this land over which they traveled: the rolling hills and tall grasses that grew as
high as a man's hips; the wild plums and strawberry
patches; the stands of walnut and hickory, of oak and
pecan.

"Home," she murmured, the word leaving a bitter
taste in her mouth. Fort Leavenworth. The end of the
journey.

Julia gazed up toward Neeheeowee, who strode out
in front of their pony, the animal held firmly by its
reins. Sweet melancholy assailed her, and Julia closed
her eyes, sighing.

She didn't want to leave him. She didn't want to go
"home."

She opened her eyes to look before her. She didn't
see the fort, but she knew it was close. Hadn't she
been out this way a thousand times?

She didn't want to go there.

What was there for her now, anyway? No parents,
no husband; friends, maybe, though her best friend
no longer resided there.

Besides, Julia seemed to have grown attached to
this wandering lifestyle these past few weeks.

She wasn't sure just when it had happened, nor was

she certain when her attitude had changed. She only knew she didn't wish to leave it. There was something out here for her: the call of the open prairie and wide-open sky; the softness of spring over the land; the resonant songs of the meadowlark and sparrow; the multicolored flowers of poppies, of coreopsis; the opening squawk of the nighthawk in the twilight of day . . . Neeheeowee.

And she realized with a deep sense of longing that she felt whole out here, free and independent, a sense of well-being washing over her that she found hard to explain, let alone acknowledge.

She wanted to stay with Neeheeowee. She wanted . . .

She pulled up her thoughts.

She couldn't have it. She couldn't have him.

There was no bridge which existed between their cultures, at least none that she could cross.

And so when Neeheeowee turned around to face her, no expression on his face, Julia cautioned herself to think long, to think wisely, and to think with her head, not with her heart.

But most of all, she cautioned herself to show no emotion, lest Neeheeowee should suspect her feelings. For somehow that he might know of her longings, that he might even foster sympathy for her plight appeared so much worse to her than having those feelings in the first place.

She couldn't have his sympathy, she didn't want it. So she gazed at him, her glance carefully devoid of any emotion, despite the hasty beating of her heart.

He came around the pony toward her, the reins of the mustang still held in his hand. He gazed up at her as soon as he reached her, placing the reins in her hands.

"Ta-naestse," he said, motioning her on in the direction of the fort.

Looking down at him, she feared she would be lost in the depths of his eyes. She tried to smile at him, but her lips shook so badly, she only managed a slight opening of her mouth.

She looked away, whispering, "Thank you," but still her lips trembled, and Julia knew she was close to tears.

She was saying good-bye not only to the man who had rescued her, a man who treated her with kindness and care, but to a man whom she loved.

She would not cry. She resolved herself against it, yet the wetness clung to her lashes, threatening to spill over onto her cheeks if she so much as blinked.

"I will always appreciate your kindness to me," she said to him, although she kept her head turned away. "And I want you to know," she said in English, "that I will remember you till the moment I die because you see, Neeheeowee"—she shut her eyes—"I have fallen in love with you."

She didn't translate in gestures. She didn't know how to. And Neeheeowee, himself, said nothing.

Yet, she could see in her peripheral vision that he nodded his head as though he'd understood her every word and then, before he set the pony in motion, he looked up to her, his feelings clearly etched there in his glance.

And he might have set the pony to run right then, but he didn't.

Instead he said to her, *"Yagla'sni ye."*

And Julia, afraid to turn her head toward him, nodded back, as he had, just as though she'd understood his every utterance.

He waited. He hesitated. But at last, he switched the pony on the rump, setting it into a gallop across the prairie.

And if she'd only known that Neeheeoee, watching her go, died a little inside, she might have turned around. But she didn't know and so, holding her head high, she continued onward.

Julia cried . . . openly, no longer afraid to hold back the tears.

"Why couldn't he have asked me to stay?" she wept. "Why couldn't he have kept me with him? Doesn't he know of my feelings?"

But it seemed that he didn't. And Julia had to face the fact that she might never know him again.

Yagla'sni ye. Why did the words sound so familiar?

Yagla'sni ye.

Yagla'sni ye.

It struck her all at once.

Yagla'sni ye.

He did not speak in Cheyenne, a language she did not understand; he spoke in Lakota. Lakota, a language she had learned with Kristina over seven years ago. A language she could understand.

Yagla'sni ye. It meant . . . "Please do not go."

Please do not go?

Julia reined in the pony. Please do not go?

He wanted her to stay with him? He wanted to keep her with him?

Please do not go!

She turned the pony around, setting it to a run back toward the spot where she'd just left Neeheeowee.

She saw him in the distance.

She kept his gaze as she raced toward him. She drew up close to him, full speed, only reining in to stop the pony at the last moment.

The pony snorted, shaking its head. But Julia barely noticed.

She stared down at Neeheeowee, he back at her. She didn't speak, neither did he; nothing uttered, no words spoken, and a dozen or more thoughts rushed through her mind all at the same time.

Had he meant what he said? Had she mistranslated it? Mortification raced through her at the thought that she might have it wrong, and she wondered if she should offer some excuse for returning to him, perhaps to ask him to take her to Kristina. She could always . . .

Julia drew a strained breath and at length, summoning her courage, she questioned, "*Yagla'sni ye?*"

Still he said nothing, he took no action. until at last Neeheeowee stepped toward her, one step, another, then, in a flurry of motion, he swept Julia off the pony, saying over and over to her, "*Yagla'sni ye, yagla' sni ye.*"

Julia sighed in relief and there, on that open stretch of prairie, he began to kiss her once, twice, again, and still, not satisfied with that, he showered her with kisses, over her face, down her neck, over her shoulders. He held her so closely to him, she felt safer here now than she had ever felt within the tight confines of the fort.

"I love you," she whispered, then said it again, liking the sound of it.

"*Ne-mehotatse,*" he murmured back, and as Julia listened to his foreign tongue, she knew he told her the same thing.

And then he dropped to his knees, taking her with him, the tall grasses hiding them, though neither were aware of their surroundings.

But if someone could have seen them at this moment, they might have thought there knelt two Indians, so deeply in love, so enraptured with one another, their admiration outshone even the majestic surroundings of big sky and flower-laden prairie.

Neeheeowee and Julia had found one another . . .

again. And at this moment, nothing else in the world mattered.

All thought fled. In truth, they could have been raided by an enemy at any time, so deeply were they enveloped in their own world.

They knelt, facing one another, holding on to each other as if one of them might disappear.

He kissed her face, her neck, his arms circling her, his hands stroking her spine.

Suddenly it was too much. She couldn't wait. She wanted it all now.

She had been married. She was no innocent to the wonders of passion.

And she wanted Neeheeowee now.

She drew him in closer, her own hands running over his shoulders, his arms, his chest, down farther and farther, feeling all that lay there beneath his breechcloth.

He drew a shuddering breath and, his gaze meeting hers, he pulled up her skirt, thrusting aside his breechcloth and fitting himself within her.

No preamble, no whispered murmurings. Both knew what they wanted. Neither could wait.

She met his gaze as she fit her legs around him, her eyes rolling back as sweet sensation tore through her. She didn't moan, she didn't scream, unwilling to utter any sound that might give away their hidden location.

He kissed her neck, pulling her dress up farther to run his tongue over her breasts, all the while driving deeply within her.

He groaned and she lifted her head, seeking out his gaze. Passion, love, admiration were all illuminated there in his eyes, and Julia could not look away.

She watched him, reading the passion there as hips pushed against hips, movement drove against gyrating movement.

Still neither shifted their gaze; neither one spoke.

Motion met motion as she strained against him and she knew this, their first time, would be quick, if sweet. She had wanted him too long.

And he? She knew he barely held back, and with a shuddering sigh, Julia tripped over the edge, Neeheeowee following her at the same moment.

They strained, they groaned, they held on to one another, dark eyes meeting those of hazel, until with one final thrust of pleasure, it was over, panting breaths and racing hearts the only accompaniment to their joy.

They stared at one another, both breathing heavily until, with a tinge of mischief in his eyes, Neeheeowee grinned, pushing himself forward until Julia's back met the ground.

He laughed then, the sound more than a little musical to her ears as he rolled over on top of her.

But Julia pushed him over, coming up on top of him, meeting him grin for grin. And then it happened, he rolled her over, himself on top, then her, then him; both of them laughing, the sound of their joy carrying on the wind as sweetly as that of any melodic song of a lark.

And as Neeheeowee came up on top of her, his smile disappeared into a look of raw hunger as he once more took her lips with his own.

And passion flared between them again, although they were to be forgiven.

Truly they had endured much. The time to enjoy one another had at last come to fruition.

And Maheoo smiled kindly upon them this day, for no enemy met them, no enemy found them. No, the world this day was a very happy one.

The sound of their laughter echoed over the golden, sun-drenched hills of the plains.

They strode almost leisurely through the tall, spring green grasses of the valley, Neeheeowee in front, Julia behind, and the pony pulling up the rear. The clean scent of the grasses, the flowers, the stubborn pea vines permeated the air while the occasional serenade of crickets accompanied their passage. Dusk would soon be upon them, and Neeheeowee had been traveling toward a spot he remembered from seven years ago, a spot where stands of hickory and oak trees bunched together, a place which could have hidden the two lovers for the night, but now he hesitated, changing direction.

There was a storm brewing in the western sky, and he knew any tree-surrounded area would not be safe refuge during a prairie storm. They would fare better here on the open prairie, at least until the storm had passed. And so he searched for a place, not too low, nor too high, where they could sit out nature's fury.

Neeheeowee knew he should be more discreet as they made their way through the valley. He knew he strode through enemy land—knew also that he could attract an enemy eye here all too easily—but he couldn't help himself. He hadn't felt this good, nor been this happy for so long, he barely knew how to respond.

And he did nothing to stop it.

It felt too good.

He glanced again toward the western sky, at the storm gathering there. The clouds did not have a brackish green-gray color to them indicating a twister, but judging by the speed of the gusts, the winds were high, the probability of thunder and lightning was strong, and a drop in temperature to that of a winter's night, was likely. With all this threatening to happen so quickly, one barely had time to erect a shelter. But in truth, after his quick study of it, Neeheeowee barely gave the blower further heed. He knew this area, had prepared himself for such occurrences, and knew they could sit out the worst of it beneath the warmth of their buffalo robes.

No, at this moment, all he knew was Julia, all he cared for was Julia, and if he were a little less diligent in his observations, a little less cautious because of it . . . well, so be it.

Nothing could harm him. Not now. He knew it. All of nature knew it, and incredibly, nothing challenged him.

He had been leading them through the tall grasses, following a buffalo path a little south before turning off of it to travel once more to the west. Julia walked along behind him, holding the pony by its buckskin reins, the animal keeping a significant distance from them, as though it, too, was unwilling to break the intimate bond between its masters.

Neeheeowee narrowed his eyes. How he wished to impress Julia. He wondered if she knew just how good a tracker and a hunter he was, and if she did, would she be proud of him, knowing she would never have to want for meat or for clothing? He wanted her to feel safe with him, he wanted her to admire his skill, he wanted her to know he could provide for her. And, oh, how he wished to provide for her.

There wasn't much else he could give her, not even the stability of a home; yet he wanted to give her the best that he could, within his ability. He wanted her in his arms, in his life, in his home, he . . .

What was he thinking? Had he gone mad? He could not take her home. To do so would be to degrade her, for he could not marry her, not ever, not if he wished to keep good his promise to the memory of his wife. It was a startling thought for him.

He could not take her home, not if he wished to preserve Julia's honor. Why hadn't he remembered this earlier? He grunted, the sound deep in his throat.

He had not thought his actions through. All he'd known was that he couldn't let Julia go, the thought of her leaving more than he could bear. But in keeping her with him, wasn't he treating her falsely? He had asked her to accompany him and in doing so, hadn't he implied that he would marry her? Wouldn't she expect it of him?

"I need to stop," Julia said in Lakota, reaching out to touch his shoulder, interrupting his thoughts.

And though it took him a moment to translate the unfamiliar Lakota words, when he finally did, he nodded his head and turned his back to her, giving her the privacy she required.

Neeheeowee gazed out over the prairie, frowning while he waited for her.

It was true. She would expect marriage from him, and he couldn't give it to her.

He might live with her ... might even perform most of the duties of a married man with her, but he would not marry her ... nor would he take anyone else as wife ... ever. At least, not unless the path he had chosen for his life changed forever, which was a very unlikely prospect.

No, he couldn't marry her, and not just because she was white. Neeheeowee carried within him deep scars. Scars in the form of vows that could not be broken, paths that could not be changed, not ever, unless ...

An image swept before him, and Neeheeowee suddenly saw his grandfather's face appear before him, the old man's words clear, as though he were speaking to his grandson even now.

"There will come a point in your life, my son, when something new will enter your life. Do not fight it when it happens, for it will bring good things to you. But I must

*caution you to think with your heart at this time, for the
senses of your mind will only confuse you."*

Neeheeowee shook his head. The image dissipated,
the words faded, leaving Neeheeowee feeling wholly
disconcerted. He hadn't thought of that conversation
in years, had barely even remembered it. These had
been his grandfather's parting words to his young
grandson, the old man straining to speak even as he
lay dying all those years ago.

Neeheeowee drew his brows together. Why did he
remember it now? Had his grandfather's ghost returned to deliver the message?

Was this a message related to Julia? Without doubt
she was something new in his life. Yet what could
Julia, a foreigner, an alien to his culture, have to do
with him, with his life? Hadn't he already chosen his
own direction, a path he had vowed to take—a life
devoid of anything Julia could offer him?

Julia touched him on the shoulder and Neeheeowee
turned so quickly, she gasped.

He smiled. "I did not mean to frighten you," he
said in Lakota, his words broken and slow. He drew
her into his arms, hugging her to him as though she
might suddenly disappear. And as he stood there, his
arms wrapped around her, it all came back to him.

*It was the summer of his thirteenth year and Neeheeow-
ee's mother had just rushed up to hug him as he returned
to camp from his first vision quest. It had been a fruitless
quest, for Neeheeowee had not dreamed, had seen no visions. He had been gone into the hills four days and four
nights, with no food or water; clad only in his breechcloth,
bearing only his wits for protection. He had fasted as his
elders had instructed him; he had waited, sung his medicine
songs, opened his arms to the wind which blew on up to
him as though it would speak. But it said nothing. It blew*

on by him. He'd waited, but nothing else had visited him.

And there, up on that hilltop, it had started.

The young boy had despaired. Nothing had happened . . . no vision had visited him, no illusion had materialized in the wind.

He had left camp jubilant; he came home, downtrodden and miserable, trudging into camp as though he had been to war and lost. He'd been gone four days, and he had nothing more to show for his efforts than the tattered rags of his breechcloth and moccasins.

"There goes Neeheeowee after his vision quest," he heard people say as he passed. "Do you think he will take his place with his fathers as a great medicine man?"

"Look, there goes the son of Heseehee. What do you think his vision is?"

And so it went. He tried to tune out the voices of the others, but by the time he reached his mother's tepee, Neeheeowee felt worse than when he had climbed down from the butte that morning with his uncle who had been his sponsor. Neeheeowee then had to relay the bad news: He'd had no vision.

His mother followed Neeheeowee into their lodge and smiled at him, yet she said nothing, simply setting about doing her normal chores, putting out food and new clothing for her son.

After a while, his father entered the tepee and, moving around to the men's side of the lodge and sitting next to his son, his father said, "You are welcomed home, my son. There will be plenty of time to speak of your vision quest. Do not feel you have to talk now. Rest, relax. We are glad to have you home."

And Neeheeowee, not willing to admit to his failure all at once, gladly agreed.

"There is a storm brewing up ahead," Julia spoke to Neeheeowee, breaking into his reverie, and Neeheeowee nodded, coming back to the present. He thought of the softness of her words, and immediately he tried to think of something to make her speak again. He wasn't sure when he had ever heard such a pretty, lilting voice, and he wanted to listen to it some more.

They had begun to speak to one another in Lakota even though the going of it had been slow at first since neither of them had been given call to use the language much. However, it was better than nothing and at least they were able to converse and understand one another now.

Neeheeowee groaned as he let out his breath, wondering what would have happened if he hadn't remembered that Julia might still understand a little Lakota.

"Come," Neeheeowee said, setting Julia away from him. "I must find us somewhere where we can wait out the storm."

She nodded and, stepping from his embrace, picked up the buckskin reins of their pony. Neeheeowee waited until she was ready, and then, with a quick motion of his head, turned, striding back through the tall buffalo grass.

But Neeheeowee hadn't gone far before his past began to intrude upon the present, the weight of his memories reminding him of a gathering gloom, moving in and spreading a gray hue over all it touched. Neeheeowee felt his happiness begin to fade, if only for a little while, and although he still paced through the grass, leading his party, his attention stuck on the past, beginning to replay scene after scene of incidents he would rather not recall.

"You are the favored son of a great medicine man," Neeheeowee heard his father speaking as though the older man stood before him. "Do not worry overmuch that you have not yet had a vision. It will come, my son. It will come."

* * *

But it hadn't come. Neeheeowee had made several vision quests, some in his youth, some as he'd grown older. And always the result was the same; the wind would visit him, would rush on up to him, but just as quickly would blow past him with no dream there in it, no vision to carry back to the medicine man to interpret, no purpose to fulfill. And while it might seem strange to an outsider that a vision quest could either make a man or break him, to the Indian male, the vision quest was a necessary part of life, one he did not engage upon lightly. For to dream meant that Maheoo, maker of all, had shown one his chosen path, it then being up to the individual to ensure that the dream came to fruition.

But Neeheeowee had no dream; no path to follow, no purpose to fulfill. He stood a man alone.

"My son," Neeheeowee heard his father's words again. "You try too hard. Maheoo cannot speak to you when your heart is already full. Forget that you are the son of a powerful family of medicine men. Perhaps the ways of your fathers are not within your true path."

"Or perhaps I am not worthy," the young Neeheeowee despaired. "Maybe I do not have the power to heal and to see things as you do. This could be Maheoo's way of telling me."

Heseehee, or Ridgewalker, as Neeheeowee's father was called, smiled at his young son. "You speak with all the fervor of youth, my son," he said. "I see in you great power, but you do not know it, have not felt its influence in your life. But you will, and it may be that you will have to live, to experience life before you can dream. My son, I think Maheoo tests you."

"But why?" Neeheeowee asked. "Why not someone else? Why can I not have a vision as all my friends have?"

His father only smiled at him. "Only you can answer this, my son." Heseehee laid his hands on his son's back.

"I do not tell you this to comfort you. I tell you this because it is what I see. When Maheoo believes you are ready, you will dream. But you may have to prove yourself worthy first, for, my son, you have great power. And this is all I have to say to you."

Heseehee had taken on another youth as apprentice for the role of medicine man amongst their people and Neeheeowee had stood back, watching, wondering what was wrong with him that he couldn't dream. Finally Neeheeowee had approached another, one known to dream, and, as was custom, had solicited that one to seek the vision that Neeheeowee lacked. Effectively, Neeheeowee had bought himself a vision.

The vision brought back to him by another had been in the form of a hunter or a tracker, and Neeheeowee had done his best to fulfill that vision, becoming the best hunter, the best tracker within the entire Cheyenne nation. His skills as a hunter had been renowned, and he had earned himself great recognition within the bands of his tribe. He had even become a sought-after matrimonial "catch."

But Neeheeowee remained dissatisfied. He had married, he had even felt happiness with his new wife and yet, there had been something within him that would not let him be, something that made him ache for more. And he knew there lay some other purpose to his life—just ahead—but what, he could not grasp.

And then, he'd taken his wife on that fateful hunting trip, and Neeheeowee knew that had he been stronger, wiser, more able to dream, she would have never died. In truth, Neeheeowee blamed himself for his wife's death as much as he blamed the Pawnee, and he was uncertain he could ever free himself from that guilt.

It had been a wonderful, sunny day, that day. All had gone well for him on the hunt and Neeheeowee was feeling quite happy with himself. The wind blew at his back as he approached their makeshift camp, so he had no sense of what lay ahead of him.

The camp looked the same as when he'd left it only a day earlier except that no dogs barked, nor did any birds sing. Perhaps he should have taken note of the lack of activity ahead of him, but he didn't. He'd had too good a hunt to worry about things he didn't know, couldn't perceive. Besides, his spirit soared at his good luck on this and the previous day, and he was anxious to share the stories of his encounters as well as the meat of his hunt with the others.

It wasn't until he was well within the camp that the smell of death assailed him, horrible and exacting in its message. It hit him hard. His spirits, which had been sweeping the heavens, plummeted. He knew at once what had happened.

"Hova'ahane! No!"

He dropped his game, running to the camp tepee he and his wife shared. Perhaps she had been taken captive, perhaps she still lived. He could rescue her.

He threw back the rawhide at the entrance to their lodge and, looking inside, he screamed. "Hovaahane! Hovaahane!"

She lay on the ground, there inside, her head scalped, her stomach torn open, their unborn babe cut apart from her.

Neeheeowee screamed. He cried. He wailed, the sounds horrible upon the afternoon breeze. But his grief did not bring his wife or his child back, did not bring the others back. Nothing did.

He knew then, as he picked up the remains of their bodies, what he would do. He knew then the reason for his lack of a vision. His life became suddenly filled with purpose, and a truth took hold within him: The hunter's life had not been a true path for him. It had been a mistake. No wonder Neeheeowee had felt there was something more for him. No wonder he had lacked purpose, almost ached with it.

But no more. He knew with certainty where his future now lay. And for the first time since he had started his string of vision quests, he knew why he had become the best tracker, the best hunter within the Cheyenne nation. He *would use those skills to accomplish his true purpose in life: to kill the Pawnee murderers.*

He fell to his knees, right there in that small hunting lodge, his tears falling onto the dead bodies of his wife and child.

> *"Ehani nah-hiwatama.*
> *Napave vihnivo."*

He sang the song over and over.

> *"Ehani nah-hiwatama.*
> *Napave vihnivo.*
> *My Father,*
> *He hath shown His mercy unto me.*
> *In peace let them walk the straight road."*

And there, bent down, in that lodge, it hit him, a sudden "knowledge," the awareness that he had caused these deaths; indirectly, but caused them nonetheless. He had been following the wrong path. If he had been on the right course, none of this would have happened. For all knew the grandfathers' teachings: Following the wrong trail in life will bring a man nothing but disaster.

Neeheeowee wailed to the skies above, moaning his sorrow, his grief. But nothing brought his loved ones back. Nothing. And there, on the floor of that tepee, before Maheoo, before the ghosts of his wife and child, before all, he vowed complete devotion to their spirits, promising that this man to whom his wife and child had looked for protection, this man known to others as Neeheeoeewotis, this man would not rest, would not marry, would not even live again until the Pawnee murderers breathed no more.

* * *

Lightning streaked across the western sky, bringing Neeheeowee back to the present, reminding him that he had better keep his mind on finding some sort of shelter before the storm caught them unprepared. He paused, looking around him, finally seeing off in the distance a spot which was not too high, not too low. It was not the best he could do, but it would afford them at least a meager amount of safety.

He headed toward it now.

It was odd to think of it now. In all these years, nothing had tempted him away from his purpose; nothing, not family, not duty, nor even the seeking of honor in battle. Nothing, that is, until Julia.

Julia.

He wondered again why he had asked her to come with him without being more prepared to accommodate her. Had it been momentary aberration on his part? A sudden drop into insanity, thinking he could make her happy despite the type of life he led?

No, he decided, closing his eyes and sighing. It had been none of these things. He could not part with her. It was that simple a truth.

And though he knew he did her a great injustice since he could offer her none of those things a woman seemed to desire most, he could think of nothing else to do but to find a way to make it up to her. For of one thing he was certain: Julia had insinuated herself into his life, into his affections, and he would do all he could to keep her with him.

No longer did he have the terrible nightmares that had plagued him for so long. No longer did his face show a constant frown. No, he would not let her go, not unless she decided she could not stand the life he offered her. And even then . . .

It left him in an interesting dilemma.

He longed to protect Julia, to save her from any possible harm, yet he remained the one person most likely to bring her the greatest hurt of all: the inability to make her wife, in fact.

He would have to tell her. She had the right to know it all. But oh, how he shied away from the telling of it. She would not understand. And why should she? She was white, unused to his ways, his beliefs. How could he expect her to understand what even his own people found hard to comprehend?

He breathed out loud. There was nothing for it. He would have to tell Julia. He would also have to suffer the consequences of her demands on him to take her back to the fort, her possible hatred. For of one thing he became suddenly certain: he would not take her back. Somehow, some way, now that she was with him, he would keep her with him.

There, it was decided. Neeheeowee brought his head up and gazed overhead to where the sky remained blue, despite the ominous appearance of the blackened clouds to the west. He would speak with Julia, and soon.

But not now. For now, he would enjoy her, the love they shared a little while longer, still knowing that on the morrow, all could change.

Oddly enough, Neeheeowee's emotions settled back down after his decision to talk with Julia, and he continued to lead her out over the prairie. He looked to the west where the sun set farther and farther down, the orb finally taking refuge behind the darkened clouds. And though he tried not to think of it, he couldn't help wondering: Would Julia stay with him willingly when she knew the truth? Would she put behind her all those things a woman seemed to need most: a home, a husband, family? It seemed doubtful that she would, but Neeheeowee knew he wouldn't back away from telling her the truth. And he would face her decision as he had faced many others in his life, with stoic reserve, his hurt only acknowledged to himself in the darkness of night.

"Neeheeowee," she spoke to him, touching his shoulder and, pointing off toward the west, where the sun peaked out from behind the storm clouds, she said, "look there."

He nodded his head in answer to her and gazed behind him. But when he said, "yes," to her question, he wasn't at all surprised to find that he spoke not about the sky at sunset, but rather about *her*.

Ah, his Julia. When he looked at her, his troubles fled.

And if all else paled before his feelings for Julia, if Neeheeowee were temporarily blind to the complete and full extent of the emotion within his heart, he was saved from the realization of it . . . at least for the moment.

Beauty filled the prairie, which even the dark clouds in the west could not hide. Flowers bloomed within the tall, tall grasses, the pinks and blues of the flowering pea vines as pretty as if purposely planted there, while a type of purple wildflower Julia had no way of identifying grew abundantly. Winds had come up from the west, bringing with it the cooler scents of rain-drenched prairie. Birds soared through the sky as though hurrying home to their loved ones, and elk scattered, sensing the storm.

She and Neeheeowee trudged within the buffalo paths, which generally ran north and south, no more than eight inches wide, though Neeheeowee turned to the west more often than not. And though Julia wondered where he took her, what their plans were from here, she did not ask. In truth, it was only a minor thought, most of her attention centered on Neeheeowee.

He looks so handsome when he smiles.

Julia grinned at her thoughts. He was handsome no

matter what he did, but so very much so when he smiled, which was rarely.

Julia stared, dreamy-eyed, at the man before her. Stripped to only breechcloth, leggings, and moccasins, she caught brief glimpses of his tanned buttocks as he moved before her. And oh, how she longed to reach out and touch him there, how she desired to capture that buckskin cloth and pull it away, exposing all of him to her view.

Julia sighed, more than a little scandalized at her thoughts. But what was she to do? Neeheeowee possessed more potent sexuality than she had ever imagined a man could have, and she could barely believe she hadn't been aware of it seven and one-half years ago. Or perhaps she had noticed it then, unwilling to acknowledge it.

The sun dipped at that moment, falling behind the storm clouds gathering off to the west, the result of which threw the prairie into a darkness that rivaled the very skies at night. Julia shivered and reached out to touch Neeheeowee, her fingers brushing lightly over the skin at his shoulders.

It was a simple stroke, nothing more than a fleeting caress. Yet she witnessed his shudder.

He broke stride and Julia almost bumped into him. He turned.

She smiled, taking her time to look up at him as he stood before her.

He drew in his breath. He reached out a hand toward her. He touched her once, gently, then again, himself quivering in response.

"I love you," he said in Lakota and then he took a step toward her, taking her in his arms so quickly, Julia barely had time to register the fact that he'd moved. He kissed her, his tongue searching out the taste of her mouth, imbuing his own taste within her. Conscious thought fled her mind, leaving nothing behind for her to grasp onto except the feel of him, his muscles hard beneath the satiny tone of his skin. His scent filled her nostrils, the slight muskiness of it mixing with the fragrance of sweet, prairie grass.

They might have stood there a moment or perhaps an hour. Julia couldn't be certain. All she knew was him, his tongue, his body, his kiss still creating havoc with her stomach, her senses, her very being.

The ground felt warm and firm beneath her feet as the cooling winds of the storm blew in upon them. And still he kissed her, Julia responding with all the ardor within her, returning his passion one on one, her hands pressing against his chest, running over the smooth skin and sharp muscles there, up and down. She couldn't get close enough. She wanted more; she wanted . . .

He dropped to his knees, she too, his lips, his touch never leaving her. His kiss deepened, his mouth, his tongue demanding more from her while he pushed her dress up and over her hips, her breasts, then over her head until she knelt before him in nothing more than her moccasins. He ran his hands over her skin, from her breasts, to her buttocks, over her stomach to that secret place between her legs.

He groaned and, tearing away his breechcloth in one savage movement, broke off the kiss. But the moment of reprieve was quick. His gaze hungry, he looked at her, his hands following the movement of his glance. But it was too much.

"I want you," he said in words she could understand.

"I want you, too," she replied. And without another word being spoken, he drove into her, moaning as the tight recesses of her body fit around him.

"Julia," he cried.

And Julia, hearing him, drew in her own breath, her body shivering in response to his. She needed this.

She needed him. She moved up on him, her legs straddling him, her response to him wild, complete. And perhaps it was this that caused him to lose control. Julia could never be sure.

"I cannot wait," he cried out, straining against her.

"Don't," she said as her sighs, her moans got caught in the storm winds blowing up all around them.

Lost in enchantment, Julia looked up to him, his gaze locking with hers. His hair tangled in the wind as did hers, his pitch-black locks and her dark ones intertwining, blowing around them as their only covering.

They strained toward one another, each one seeking a pleasure that was as delirious as it was sweet. Sweat broke out on them both, despite the cooling winds. Passion raged, emotion flared, Julia unsure she could endure the intensity.

"Neeheeowee," she screamed.

"Julia."

They came together, the culmination of their pleasure flaring into splendor. And still neither one dropped their glance from the other. They stared, both gazing at the other as a desert traveler might at water.

He moved. She met him.

And it started all over again, the pleasure, the intensity, the love, neither one looking away from the other.

Storm winds blew up, bringing with them the clouds, the rain, the thunder, and still neither one of them paid the storm heed. They loved through the rain, through the winds, the occasional lightning only throwing their bodies into better view. And if her screams were lost to the thunder, no one noticed. Certainly not Neeheeowee.

Somewhere in the night he brought the buffalo robe

more fully around them. But it didn't stop them. Their passion could not be tamed, and if they made love again and again throughout the night, they were to be forgiven.

After all, they had just found one another...

Chapter 10

"Taku ote eciciyapi kta yustanpi,* I have much to tell you."

"Han, yes," Julia said, "I know." She smiled and looked over to Neeheeowee. The baritone timbre of his voice, its quality, caused her to quiver, and she wondered again, as she had done over these past few weeks, why neither one of them had remembered the language of the Lakota—a language they both understood. Although neither of them spoke it well, they could have at least understood one another sooner. Perhaps the intervening years had buried the memory in them both, awaiting only the jar of their situation to bring it back to them. What if Neeheeowee hadn't remembered? What if he hadn't . . . She shivered, unwilling to finish the thought.

"Are you cold?"

Julia shook her head and sighed, a tingle of satisfaction racing through her. It would seem that after a few weeks of traveling, of listening to Neeheeowee, she would have become used to the sound of him speaking to her, to his low, gravelly voice. Yet, she hadn't grown tired of it, and she found herself looking forward to each moment they talked.

They sat now in front of the evening fire, camped

out as they were at a place Julia had never seen, a place where thickets of cottonwoods and willows dominated the scene, where the trees scented the air, pouring pure oxygen into the evening atmosphere, where their branches hid the two amorous travelers. Giant roots dug into the sandy soil beneath them, the ground feeling soft and cool to a weary back, although Julia couldn't have known this firsthand. She reclined atop Neeheeowee in his lap, her backside toward the fire.

"Neeheeowee?" she asked, basking in his gentle ministrations. "What is the full meaning of your name? I remember that part of it means wolf, but I do not recall the rest of it."

Neeheeowee shrugged. "It means Wolf on the Hill. It is the name of my grandfather."

"Wolf on the Hill...," she repeated. "It fits you well." She smiled at him as his touch roamed over her back, her stomach, his hands and fingers soothing away her fatigue. She could never remember being so happy, and she reveled in the fact that he could not keep his hands from her; nor, if she were honest, she from him. She tilted her head, recollecting their recent journey over the prairie, remembering how neither one of them had been able to put the other out of mind, or rather, out of hand.

They had been traveling a westwardly course, Neeheeowee intersecting, though not quite following what the white man called the Sante Fe Trail. And though Julia might have wondered from time to time where they traveled, she never asked, her attention centered more on Neeheeowee's touch and the delirious sensations it sent running through her.

Neither of them had kept strict vigilance over the land as they had passed through it, and perhaps it was pure luck that they had traversed over enemy grounds without so much as a chance encounter with another tribe. Or perhaps her God or his had watched over them.

Whatever the cause, they had laughed and loved their way across the prairie, walking through it as though they were children out for a leisurely stroll, he teasing her, she, him. They had loved more often than they had traveled, and Julia had gradually discovered in Neeheeowee a gentle companion, one given to laughter as easily as passion. And she had discovered that she wished to share in his laughter as well as his lovemaking.

She shivered now as Neeheeowee trailed his touch over her back, his hands coming around toward her breasts, and she reached up quickly to help him, to untie the straps of her dress, letting the article fall down around her waist. Neeheeowee looked at her, smiling, before dropping his gaze to her chest, letting his hands caress everything he could see ... and more.

Julia moaned her pleasure, Neeheeowee echoing the sound with a groan of his own.

"We go toward Bent's Fort," he informed her after a while, speaking in Lakota, and Julia nodded her head, though she could barely focus her attention on what he said, her mind centering more on what he did. At length, he asked, "Do you know of it?"

She shook her head, it taking her a while to translate the words, and he smiled. "We will be welcome there. My brother, Little White Man . . ."

"William Bent?"

"*Haahe*, yes." Neeheeowee's hands smoothed over her breasts while he talked; kneading the softened mounds, making Julia's eyes roll back with the pleasure of it. "My brother," he continued, "Little White Man, will welcome us. But we must be careful, you and I, and you must keep your eyes always down while we are there. There are many white men there,

many traders, and they might not understand a Cheyenne warrior with a white woman. I do not wish to
cause you any trouble. If they know you are white,
they might try to take you from me. I have heard that
white men do this, that they do not always respect a
woman's choice."

Julia nodded, and though she wished to say
something back to him, she couldn't, her attention too
centered on what he was doing to her breasts with
his hands. She breathed in deeply just before Neeheeowee said, "Julia?"

She knew that note in his voice. She knew he, too,
was aroused, but still he persisted in speaking, saying,
"We need to talk, you and I. I need to tell you some
things." He stopped, scrutinizing her for a moment
before burying his face in her hair. He nuzzled his
face into her neck, inhaling deeply. "I must talk to
you and I hope that you will understand all that I
say," he said after a while, his voice muffled against
her hair. He lifted his head, looking back toward her,
seeming to hesitate before he took her more fully into
his arms. "Did I tell you," he said, "that Little White
Man, William Bent, married a distant cousin of mine,
Owl Woman? I would like you to meet her. It is my
desire that . . ."

He groaned suddenly when Julia reached up to run
her hands through his hair, though at length he continued to talk. "Did I tell you, too," he said, "that
Little White Man is considered Cheyenne because of
his marriage to my cousin?"

Julia, after a moment of translation, shook her head
and gazed up toward Neeheeowee before she asked
in Lakota, "As I am now, too?"

Neeheeowee frowned, a darkness coming over his
features that Julia found hard to explain. It was a
small change in him, minute at first. But when he
drew back, his hands stopped their handiwork over

her skin. He looked at her, his glance puzzling. He paused. A moment passed, another. At length he gazed away from her, the wind catching a lock of his hair and blowing it into and around his face. After some time, he spoke, saying, "You are not Cheyenne."

"Yes, I know. I am white but I . . . we—"

"You are not Cheyenne because I do not make you so."

Julia straightened herself and gazed at Nee-heeowee. Not one single emotion could be distinguished on his features, and Julia all at once felt bereft. What was wrong here?

Cool night air blew in upon her and Julia suddenly felt the need to protect herself. She brought her hands and arms up, covering her breasts from the night wind, from Neeheeowee.

What did he mean, she was not Cheyenne? And why did he look so solemn all of a sudden? She gazed up toward him, but he still peered away from her, into the darkness. She cleared her throat, an attempt to speak, but no words would come. What was happening here?

They had just been in one another's arms, wanting each other, barely able to restrain their passion for one another. How could something have changed so abruptly? She didn't know and yet . . .

She narrowed her eyes, gazing more intently at Neeheeowee. Perhaps she mistook his reaction. Perhaps he merely played with her. Or perhaps she had translated it incorrectly.

She stared at him, a frown forming over her brow. No, she had it right. She'd not heard incorrectly. Neeheeowee appeared more moody than she had ever seen him. Why?

She set her gaze away from him, staring out into space, looking for some distant spot, trying to get her thoughts in order. She shivered once, then again. At last she said, "I do not understand."

He hesitated, and though Julia looked back toward him, he still stared away. In due course, he lifted his shoulders, saying, "I have delayed speaking to you on a matter of great importance and by not saying anything to you before now, I have misled you and I never intended that." He frowned, then, "Know you that I can never make you Cheyenne as my cousin, Owl Woman, did for the white man, Bent. If you ever do become Cheyenne through marriage, it will not be because of me. I will not ask you to marry me—I cannot."

Julia sat still for a moment, shock keeping her silent. Marriage? The thought of marriage had not even entered her thoughts, her attention too focused on her physical relationship with Neeheeowee. But now that he mentioned it to her, she realized that the thought of it, the knowledge that she expected it from him, had been there in the back of her mind all the while. Why otherwise would she have come with him? Given up her world for his?

"I still do not understand, Neeheeowee," she said, speaking in Lakota. "Kristina once told me that in Indian culture when a man asked a woman to go away with him, he offered her marriage. Is this not so?"

Neeheeowee hesitated. "This is true in many tribes," he said, his voice steady for all that he appeared reluctant to talk. "It is true for the Lakota, but it is not the custom of the Cheyenne. For the Cheyenne, even if a couple steal away to be together, the marriage custom must follow or the two people are never considered married, the woman will be dishonored."

Julia sat still, unable to breathe. Suddenly she felt light-headed, as though her world were spinning for a moment out of control.

It was incredible, the effect his statement had on her. And she realized all at once the great amount of trust she'd granted Neeheeowee. Perhaps it had been misplaced, or perhaps she truly did not know the Lakota language that well.

She cleared her throat. "Did you not ask me to come away with you? I thought that—"

"I can never marry you."

There, he'd said it to her, correctly, plainly. There was no mistaking his intent, no misinterpretation of the language.

Julia shut her eyes, her throat muscles working convulsively. He meant to dishonor her. He meant to heap shame upon her. She could not credit it. How could she have been so wrong about him? Hadn't she witnessed his care of her, his attention to her needs? Hadn't she known his desire? She'd been so certain of him; he whom she regarded as her Proud Wolf. Hadn't he rescued her when there had been no one else to come to her aid? Treating her with kindness? Hadn't it been Neeheeowee who had asked her to stay?

She pulled the top of her dress up over her bosom, needing the material around her as a sort of defense. She retied the gown at her shoulders, slowly, so as to give her time to think. But at last she took a deep breath. And without another thought as to what she was about to ask, she queried, "Neeheeowee?"

He turned. He faced her, his gaze seeking out hers, and it was all Julia could do not to back down and falter. But she didn't. Instead, she thrust out her chin and looking at him directly, she said, "If you do not intend to marry me, I think you should tell me just what you do intend. I am away from all that I know and I am dependent upon you and your goodwill. I believe that you owe me at least this, and I think you should tell me why you cannot marry me . . . ever.

Did you know this when you asked me to stay with you?"

He nodded his head.

"And you have waited until now to tell me?"

Again, another nod of his head.

With a great deal more calm than she felt, she said, "Then perhaps you had better explain to me why you asked me to stay with you."

He said nothing. And she waited.

"Did you ask me to stay only so that you could have a warm body next to yours at night?"

"*Hova'ahane*, no."

She said nothing more, hoping that her silence would invite him to speak, but when several moments passed and still he said nothing, Julia leaned forward, asking only, "Why, Neeheeowee?"

He breathed out all at once, then lifted his shoulders; he sucked in his breath, throwing back his head, and Julia thought he might not answer. But at last he opened his mouth to speak, his voice barely audible as he said, "I need you."

Julia could barely move. Had she heard him right? She asked, "What?"

But Neeheeowee had already turned away. He raised his chin. "You bring life to me, *Nemene'hehe* . . . Julia. These last few weeks have been as though I were suddenly a younger man. When you are near me, I see things more clearly, I feel things more vividly. I no longer suffer the nightmares that have haunted me for so long. It is as though I feel life again. And I believe, *Nemene'hehe*, that this has something to do with you. If you were to leave me, I would only be half a man, I think."

His admission sucked her breath away and Julia found it hard to speak. "Neeheeowee, Wolf," she said at last, her voice barely above a whisper. "When you speak like this, I am greatly affected by it. It makes me feel certain things, but I do not understand. If you truly feel this way about me, why do you say you will not marry me and make me your wife?"

He hesitated. "There is much about me you do not know," he said after a while. "There is much I have to relate to you. But I will tell you now that I am a man haunted, a man without a vision, and understand, Julia, that to my people, a man without a vision is a man without purpose, a man left, not to live, but only to exist. I have lived my life in the service of others, in service to my wife and child who have been dead since five springs ago. Only through them, have I a purpose to my life. And I have a vow to keep to them, a promise I made to free their spirits so that they may walk the path to the afterworld. I failed my wife and child once; I will not fail them again."

Julia paused a moment, unable to take in all he said. Purpose? Visions? Vows? Ghosts that walked the earth? A wife and child?

"I did not know you had been married." It was the only thing out of all he'd said that her mind seemed to focus on.

Neeheeowee nodded his head.

"And they are dead now?"

"*Haahe*, yes," Neeheeowee said, again with a nod of his head.

"Would you tell it to me again, Neeheeowee, so that I can be certain I understand all you said to me? Did I hear you say that you are bound to free your wife's and your child's spirits?"

"*Haahe*."

"And where are they now, the souls of your wife and child?"

He pointed to the ground, then placing his hands in front of him, palm down, he advanced one, then the other. Finally, he said, "They wander the earth, their spirits restless. And so it will be until I set them free."

Julia gulped, swallowing hard. She'd never heard of such a thing. And she wondered what other strange ideas she would find here with Neeheeowee, with the Indians. Had she been mad to follow him?

After a long pause she asked, "How will you free their spirits?"

"I must fight the Pawnee," he said. "I must find those Pawnee warriors who killed my wife, and I must ensure none of them walk the road to the hereafter."

Julia took a moment before speaking. But at last, gazing up at Neeheeowee, she said, "Give me time to comprehend this, Neeheeowee, for I find this hard to understand. You see, I do not believe as you do. Now, tell me again, why must you do this?"

"My wife and child died horrible deaths," he said. "I had been away from our hunting camp while the Pawnee stole into it, killing all who were there, including my wife and child." He paused and Julia noted how distant he looked as he continued, "Sometimes the dead will not leave to go on their path to the afterlife if their dying is too terrible. And so it is with my wife and my child. When such a thing happens, it is up to the nearest relative to seek revenge upon their enemies. As I said before, I was a man without a vision, and when this happened, I knew why Maheoo, God over all the Cheyenne, had never allowed me to dream. My life's fulfillment will be to kill the Pawnee. It is why I live."

Julia didn't dare blink. She nodded instead, asking, "And when you kill these men, what will you do with your life, then?"

"I may die seeking their revenge."

"And if you do not die?"

"Then I will return to my people and live to be an old man."

Julia shook back her hair, looking away. And though all her ingrained beliefs begged her to shout out to him, "Pagan," she didn't. He believed what he told her; it was enough.

It took her several minutes to respond, but at last, she said, "I find what you tell me hard to comprehend because I do not believe as you do about the dead. It is my contention that it is not up to you to salvage these people, though I know you loved them. I believe that it is the life that they led here on earth that will either speak for them or not. And I do not believe in ghosts, Neeheeowee."

He looked taken aback. He hesitated, seeming to choose his words well before he said, "Many of my people have talked of the white man, have said that this man is unable to see beyond this world. But I had never believed it . . . until now. Is it true? Have you never talked to the dead?"

"I do not believe in such things, Neeheeowee—no ghosts, no spirits that walk upon the earth—only what you, yourself, keep alive."

"I see," he said, moving back away from her, if only a little bit. He peered at her. "How is it that you do not know this? Is the white man so disconnected from all things spiritual that he thinks nothing lives on after death?"

"Yes, but not in this world, not—"

"They live," he said, emphasizing his words by pointing to his chest, to his heart. "They live on, trapped here to the physical world, yet apart from it. I vowed to them I would free them, I vowed to them to bring the Pawnee murderers to justice and I promised them I would never marry again, that I would always hold their memory above all else, at least until they are freed to walk the path to the afterlife. These are things I am set to do. And do not mistake me. I will keep my promises."

Julia took a moment to gather her thoughts, and though there were many things in his speech she found disturbing, only one of his statements stood out from the rest: He could never marry . . . at least not while his wife's and child's spirits roamed the earth.

But Julia knew such things were ridiculous, that such things didn't exist. And he might as well have said to her that he could not marry her—ever, for that is how she understood it.

She felt stunned, and not just with the weight of their different beliefs. He would not marry her. He could not marry her.

Again she felt as though her world tilted, all out of control.

She'd never heard any viewpoint like this—ever. And she wondered, was Neeheeowee saying these things just to avoid marriage to her? Or did he truly believe them? Ghosts?

She looked at him, wondering for a moment as to his sanity and her own inability to observe such things in another, but upon gazing up into his eyes, viewing there his dark, steady gaze at her, she realized she saw not insanity, but rather difference in viewpoint. She sighed.

She didn't understand. His beliefs were too different from her own. And she wondered: Were there more to these Indian customs which bound him?

To her credit, Julia tried to put aside her own opinions on such things, trying to understand his. But she had been raised all her life to a white man's view of the world, and she found she could not grasp the idea of a dead person influencing another as though living, nor a ghost acting as though it were still a part of their world. And though she felt the urge to guide Neeheeowee toward what was for her a truer point of view, she didn't. She held back what she might have said, clearing her throat instead before she said, "Neeheeowee, if you are this indebted to your wife and child, perhaps," she said, "you do not truly need me. If I were you, I would see me as an obstacle in your purpose in life. I do not fit into this, Nee-heeowee. I am afraid I see no place in your life for me."

"No," he said, lifting his hand to run his fingers down her cheek, so very, very slowly, downward and back, brushing her hair, stroking her cheek, the edge of her ear.

She shut her eyes, taking a shaky breath, and still he touched her, his fingers caressing her face, her lips, his touch roaming downward, over the curve of her neck.

"I am a man with a past," he said, his voice husky, "but it does not mean that these things are more to me than you. I tell you only what I can and cannot do. But do not mistake me, *Nemene'hehe*, I will find a place for you within my life if you decide to stay with me. I must, for you see, you, *Nemene'hehe*, hold my heart and without you, I . . ."

Julia jerked her head away from him, away from his touch, his words. She didn't want to hear what he said. He played her unfairly. He spoke words of love, yet none of permanent attachment. And Julia knew she needed both. She felt a war beginning to wage within her. She loved this man. She wanted to stay with him. And oh, how she wished there were within her that spark of adventure that would allow her to follow him no matter their relationship. But she found she couldn't.

All her life, she had been raised with stories of morality, of goodness and faith. These were not things she could ignore simply because she loved a man.

Was Neeheeowee turning away from his beliefs or his vows?

No, nor would she expect him to. But within that same breath whispered the idea that neither should she. She squeezed her eyes shut, opening them only when she took a deep breath. At last she was able to speak, but even then, she only asked, "What does it mean, *Nemene'hehe*?"

He took his time answering, as though he, too, needed a moment to shift his attention away from that subject most prevalent. Finally, he said, "Singing Woman. It means Singing Woman."

"Ah," she said, turning her head back toward him. "That is right. I remember," she said softly, lifting her gaze slowly, her eyes at last meeting his. "I was humming along with the tune from the camps that evening not so long ago."

He nodded his head, bringing a hand up to play with a stray lock of her hair. "You brought me much happiness that day, the music of your voice remaining with me long after we had gone to sleep. I will always remember it, *Nemene'hehe*, as I have always remembered you."

Julia caught her breath, his words, his intent a heady mixture, for as he said it, one of his hands played with her hair, the other stroked his necklace. The necklace she had given him. She breathed out a heavy sigh, suddenly reminded that through her necklace, he had kept her in memory all these years.

She shut her eyes briefly, opening them almost at once. What could she say to him? That she loved him? Most assuredly. That she wished to stay with him? Without doubt.

But she couldn't, not if she wanted to maintain her self-respect.

Julia almost wept. Not from grief, not from anger, but rather from pure emotion. Never had she felt so much love for another person, yet never had she needed to turn away from someone more.

The firelight shimmered over them, casting shadows over the ground as she sat before him. A tear fell softly down her cheek, and Neeheeowee wiped it gently away.

She knew she should tell him to go. She knew she *should* go. But she didn't. She couldn't, the conflicting emotions within her almost crippling her. And so she did the only thing she could do right now: She wept.

"Neeheeowee, my proud, Proud Wolf," she whispered, unable to speak any louder, not with his touch still caressing her face, her cheeks, her tears. "Neeheeowee, please," she said. "I do not know if I can follow you."

"I know," he said. "You must make your choice— and soon, for I am destined to continue my search for the Pawnee. I only tell you about me so that you know what the life ahead of you would be. If I could, I would give you more. I cannot."

Julia nodded her head, her hair falling forward with the action.

"*Nemene'hehe?*" he asked, and when Julia looked up, he ran his hand lightly over the darkish-red highlights of her hair. "I wish to honor you. You have a troublesome decision before you and you take it well. I am proud of you. You have thought well on all this, despite the differences in the way we each one view the world. You have much courage, and I honor you."

Julia paused for a moment, Neeheeowee's touch still a warm caress upon her body, and then she couldn't keep it in any longer. She cried.

Chapter 11

"**C**ome, Julia, it's time to get ready for church."

"Yes, mother."

Her mother smiled, brushing her hands through Julia's dark locks. In the background the smell of smoke and of Sunday dinner cooking made Julia's mouth water. "You must hurry," her mother said. "We can't have you growing up to be a heathen, can we?"

Julia giggled. "There's very little chance of that."

Julia gazed down at herself in a dreamlike haze, at her buckskin gown, the moccasins upon her feet. She ran her hands through her hair; hair pulled into braids, with buckskin tying them back.

"No, Julia, bright beads like that are for women of ill repute or for savages, they are one and the same, you know. Here now." Her mother gathered up the necklaces Julia had been making. "Julia," her mother reminded her, "no more of this beadwork. You embarrass me. Do you want friends of your father's to wonder if you've gone Indian? Why don't I get you some silk or perhaps some taffeta material? You could make yourself a lovely gown instead of . . ."

* * *

191

Julia gazed down at the brilliant beadwork on the Indian regalia that she wore. Blue, yellow, and red trade beads lay in intricate designs all over her dress and moccasins. Bold patterns and bright beads mixed together in her vision, swimming before her eyes.

Outside, a church bell tolled.

"Come, now, Julia, it's time for us to go to church." Her mother took Julia's hand in her own, both ladies walking with the army lieutenant, Julia's father, along the wooden planks toward the chapel.

Her mother gasped all at once. "What are those heathens doing going into our church?"

Her father answered her mother while Julia watched the Indians with interest, unaware of what the two adults said. To Julia the Indians did not look heathen; they seemed to her to be dark and proud and certainly, to a youngster's eye, they looked magnificent. They dressed with more color than she had ever seen on anyone, and they lavished themselves with jewelry that caught a young girl's fancy. Frankly, she was impressed.

"Stay away from them, Julia," her mother admonished, reading correctly the admiration there within her daughter's gaze. "Those Indians would kill you if you get close to them. They have customs we will never understand, ceremonies that are pagan to us, and their women are nothing but slaves when they aren't outright . . . well, a proper woman doesn't mention such things. Be careful when you go near them, Julia, for no white woman has ever come away from their camp with her purity intact."

Julia gazed upward to find a mirror and gradually, so very gradiently, she looked over to it until she saw the image staring back at her. She screamed. It couldn't be. She looked into the eyes of an Indian. An Indian—herself.

*   *   *

Julia awoke with a start, Neeheeowee coming up on his elbows beside her.

"What has happened, *Nemene'hehe?*"

"Nothing, I . . . I just had a bad dream," she said in English, then remembering, translated it into Lakota.

He soothed back her hair, comforting her with the touch of his fingers. He smiled down at her, saying, "Do you wish to talk of it?"

"No. I . . . I cannot."

He nodded and at length, said, "Sometimes the things we like the least only visit us in dreams. They have no meaning and have no effect on us. They are not like the visions or dreams that my people seek for wisdom. Sleep now, and we will talk some more of this in the morning if you wish it. Do you think that you can?"

Julia nodded her head.

"Good, then," he said, and, bringing her in toward him, he cradled her up within the warmth of his body. "I will hold you through the night. Come, rest now."

Julia tried to sleep. She closed her eyes, she moved little, she tried to think of other things besides her own problems. She couldn't make herself fall asleep and finally she settled down, her eyes open, to think over her predicament.

Her heart longed to stay with Neeheeowee. Logic, the moral fiber with which she had been raised demanded she leave. These were not things she could put aside.

Besides, if she went with Neeheeowee now, she had only the security of the moment; no friends or relatives to care for her if something should happen. Nor would she be able to lift her head in either Indian or civilized society, always troubled that she lived not quite within her own moral standing.

But it wasn't any of these things that bothered her most. It was her dream that unsettled her—seeing herself as an Indian. Did she want to live and die amongst a people to whom she had not been born?

She had loved Neeheeowee, she loved him still, but was it enough to become, herself, Indian? Perhaps if he had offered her more than the life of a mistress, she might have considered it. But now? After having been brought up within the gentle ways of society, could she throw aside all she felt was right?

No, she didn't think so. Which meant what to her?

She had no family left at Fort Leavenworth since her mother and father disappeared on a trip to St. Louis several years ago. And with only a few scatterings of friends within the fort, the idea of returning there was less than appealing. But what else could she do?

As she pondered over her situation, dawn settled in over the prairie, washing the land with the pinkish glow of morning and bringing with it the scent of a clean, fresh day.

Perhaps this day, she thought, her future would become clear.

She'd known it all along. She'd just been unable to admit it. There was only one path for her, and that was to return to her own people.

The problem was how to do it. She couldn't find her way back to the fort on her own, she was quite un–prairie-wise. She'd get lost, or, even worse, she might starve.

But she couldn't continue to travel with Neeheeowee; otherwise, she could have simply asked him to take her back. But she couldn't do that; it wouldn't work. And not because he might not take her back. No, she simply foresaw the result of it. If he were to bring her back there, their parting would be too painful for her, for him, for them both, and she knew she would never leave him.

There was nothing else for it. She had to get away now, while she still had the strength to do it.

That's when the idea came to her. She knew that they followed closely to the Sante Fe Trail, but until last night, she'd had no indication of pioneers traveling that route. But this past night as she had lain awake, she'd listened to the faraway sounds of a country fiddle.

And she decided. She would travel down to those people on the trail below her and, once there, beg them for passage to Fort Leavenworth.

She might not see Neeheeowee again, but she knew this was for the best. It had to be.

Just as he had his vows to live up to, so too, did she.

She left at the first light of day, while Neeheeowee was away from the camp on his regular early morning hunt. She didn't take many supplies with her, certain that she'd find camaraderie down there amongst the people of her own race.

And so it was that on this day, Julia left Neeheeowee's guardianship. The travesty of her heart was mirrored in the few gray clouds overhead which grumbled out a protest, but Julia, seeing it, chose to ignore it.

Neeheeowee watched her go, knowing he would not stop her . . . at least not right now.

He saw her take some supplies from their pony, noticing that she packed only a meager amount of food. He shook his head.

He realized that she probably thought to go down to the white travelers along the road, but even still, she should have taken more. He could always hunt for food, whereas she would starve if her supplies ran out.

Despite her obvious intentions, he would not let her

go, and he considered his choices. He could appear before her right now and put a stop to her leaving, perhaps treating her as though she were a captive, forcing her to continue with him. It was an action he looked to with favor since it meant that he would keep her with him, something that he intended to do no matter the consequences.

However, such an action would override her own power of choice, something he was reluctant to do. Besides, he had no great wish to subdue the spirit in her that he so greatly admired. Somehow it would make her less alive, and this he didn't want.

There might be, however, another way to keep her with him, a more difficult way, but it could provide her with more opportunity to think and perhaps, if Neeheeowee were lucky, she might eventually change her mind without his having to say a thing. It was possible. The only problem was how to go about it.

He would keep her from reaching the white man's camp, perhaps by putting obstacles in her path, maybe by making it easy for her to lose her way. It would mean he would have to follow her, to plant wrong tracks for her to follow as well as to ensure she came to no harm.

It would be more difficult for him, but it would have the advantage of not overruling her ability to make decisions, nor would it take away her independence. After all, he wanted to strengthen Julia's belief in herself, not overwhelm it.

Neeheeowee narrowed his eyes as he watched Julia prepare to leave. Yes, this is what he would do. He would follow her. He would somehow prevent her from reaching the white man's camp and he would keep her on the road to Bent's Fort . . . somehow . . .

What does she do?
Neeheeowee had been following Julia from a dis-

creet distance, intending to plant obstacles in her path
to ensure she did not arrive at the white travelers'
camp. But so far, he'd had to do nothing.

He glanced up toward the overcast sky, then back
to Julia, and frowned.

If she meant to meet up with the white travelers,
she grossly miscalculated their direction from her.
They lay to the south and east of her. She traveled to
the north and west, the direction *he* wanted her to go.
Was she traveling elsewhere than he had originally
anticipated, or could she simply not tell direction?

He lifted his shoulders in pure bafflement. Never
had he seen anything like this. All Indians possessed
an innate sense of direction, even the women. Finding
one's way was something no Indian thought extraor-
dinary.

Yet, he saw before him what appeared to be a
woman who could not find a camp which lay no more
than the distance of several hills and valleys away.
He raised an eyebrow. She must be heading elsewhere. It was the only explanation he could fathom.

He scowled. Even if she traveled in the direction he
had hoped to coax her into, and especially if she had
some other destination in mind besides the white
man's camp, she went greatly undersupplied. He
made a mental note to teach Julia the basics of survival techniques on the prairie at the first opportunity.
Otherwise, he would never be able to trust her out of
his sight.

Julia suddenly stumbled into a hole, most likely a
rattlesnake hole.

Neeheeowee prepared to shoot out of his cover toward her, but when she picked herself up, no apparent harm coming to her, Neeheeowee held back.

Muttering a quick "*Eaaa*" to himself, and then a
grunt of disbelief, he set off after her, gazing into the
hole she'd fallen into as he passed by it.

That he had to act quickly to send an arrow into the snake that slithered out of the hole did not sit well with him, especially when that snake almost bit *him*. He shook his head, hoping against hope that this wasn't an indicator of things to come.

Somehow he didn't think so.

"None of this looks familiar," Julia said to herself, gazing around her. Perhaps that should have disturbed her, but it didn't. She dismissed the idea of familiar territory as ridiculous. Why should any of this look familiar? She was on the prairie, alone, after all.

It seemed to her, however, that she should have crossed the pioneer camp several hours ago. Mayhap it was simply a greater distance away than she had at first estimated. She would just have to keep going onward until she ran across them.

She felt optimistic. *It isn't that hard to find my way on the prairie*, she decided. *I can always tell direction from the sun.*

She looked upward, wishing the sun were out.

"Oh, well," she said to herself. "I'll find the pioneer camp eventually. I'm certain of it . . . I think."

Julia congratulated herself on escaping Neeheeowee without his being aware of it. By now he would have returned to their camp to find her gone. If he were to follow her, she could only hope that when he did eventually catch up to her she would be safely ensconced within the confines of the white camp.

And though she wasn't elated over her escape from Neeheeowee, life still had a pleasant feel to it, and she found herself humming a tune as she trod over the grounds of the prairie, certain she would find the pioneer camp any moment now.

* * *

Neeheeowee and the pony lagged behind Julia far enough so that he knew she couldn't spot him—if she even looked for him. He rolled his eyes at the naïveté she demonstrated on the prairie, and he admonished himself for not teaching her better.

She strolled over the ground with no concern for where she stepped, as though there were no danger of awakening a rattlesnake or a copperhead or even a bull snake. He shook his head.

How could he ensure her safety when she didn't know the dangers? He wondered if she would have the sense to check the ground each night before she made camp? Did she know how to find fuel for a fire out here on the barren prairie? Did she know when to start a fire and when not to? Did she even know how to build a fire in the first place?

In the distance, far away from him, a pack of wolves followed her, they, too, aware of her naïveté, waiting for her to make a mistake.

He lifted his shoulders and shook his head. He would have to scare off the wolves. He couldn't allow them to come too close to her.

He sighed, deciding that if Julia ever returned to him of her own free will, he would teach her the basics of survival on the prairie. But he couldn't think of that now, and, with one last glance at Julia, Neeheeowee picked up his bow and lance, slung his quiver of arrows over his back, jumped onto the pony, and set off in the direction of the wolves.

Julia heard the growls and whelps of some animals in the distance, wondering what could be causing such mournful sounds. She thought about investigating the disturbance, but seeing that it lay the opposite way from where she was headed, she decided against it.

"I hope it's not too important," she said as though to someone else. She sat down upon a rock, thinking to bask under a few rays of light, the sun having decided to poke its head through the clouds for a moment. She smiled to herself, at the wonderfulness of being able to survive alone on the prairie. Who said a woman couldn't do it by herself?

She stood up all of a sudden and stretched, ready to continue her journey, unaware that a snake coiled at her feet.

Just then thunder roared in the distant sky and Julia lifted a hand to look off in the direction of it, missing completely the swish of an arrow as it hit its mark deep in the body of the rattlesnake, that reptile just poised to strike.

In truth, she wasn't even aware of the snake or of any danger at all and so as she moved away from the rock, and, feeling her spirits high, she hummed softly to herself.

Neeheeowee watched Julia from the cover of several bushes and rocks. He looked down at himself, at the numerous scratches and wolf bites over his body, and grimaced, while Julia, unaware of his plight, happily sang a song.

He had sneaked into her camp, confiscating some of the ointment Julia carried in her parfleche bag, and he was even now thinking of applying the mixture to his cuts when, ever watchful, he noticed a bear moving in Julia's direction. He looked back at Julia and almost shouted his frustration. She sat in front of a black bear den and didn't even know it.

He let out a soft cry of exasperation before he looked back to see that a bear approached them.

And then he didn't think. Neeheeowee sprang from his cover as though shot out of it, sprinting toward Julia in his fastest run, but he needn't have bothered.

Julia had finished her meal long ago, was already strolling away as though unaware of anything at all, while Neeheeowee, having fled in the direction toward her, stood dead center where she had been. He heard a growl and snapped around to confront the bear.

And though Julia heard the growls and yelps in the distance, she didn't connect them with anything to do with her, and, unaware of any danger, she continued her hike over the prairie.

Julia tripped over something in her path. She looked down. Why, this was just what she'd been looking for, just what she needed, wood for a fire. It had been growing dark and she had begun to wonder how she'd ever be able to make a fire when she could find no buffalo dung and all she could see for miles was flat, treeless prairie.

How wonderful. It was almost as though someone had set the wood right here for her.

She smiled at her fanciful ideas, although she did look around her to see if someone watched her. It seemed a little too good to be true.

But she saw nothing, and so, shrugging, she set about making a fire, her last thought before she drifted off to sleep being how much she missed Neeheeowee. She wondered where he was, but most of all she wondered, why didn't he follow her?

In a camp not far away, Neeheeowee applied ointment to his many scrapes, gashes and wounds while he cut himself out a new breechcloth from some buckskin in his bags. He tried to lie down, but found his body wouldn't obey his command, still sore from the near miss with the bear.

He'd just barely escaped with his life, having abandoned his breechcloth to the bear's claws, the animal having gotten that close to him. He'd finally escaped, running downhill as fast as as possible, this being the only way to outrun a bear, since the animal needed to be more careful in its footing.

Neeheeowee had picked up Julia's trail later, just in time to drop the wood conveniently in her path.

He grimaced, knowing it would go better for him if he went to her now and just took her captive, giving her no choice but to come with him. But he wouldn't do it. He had decided on his course of action, he would see it through, even if it meant giving up his life in the process.

He smiled at his thoughts and shook his head. If things continued on as they had today, forfeiting his life might not be that unreal an outcome.

Chapter 12

❧ ❧

Neeheeowee shook a bush as though there were an animal in it, the noise discouraging Julia from turning south when he wanted her to go west. It hadn't been difficult to keep Julia on the path that he wanted, since he had cleared a course for her, making the trail look like a buffalo trail.

It wouldn't have fooled another Indian, most prairie travelers observing that buffalo paths generally trailed north and south, not east and west. And although he congratulated himself on his clever maneuvers, he frowned over Julia's lack of understanding of this land and of her terrible sense of direction.

Neeheeowee looked up. The skies were no longer overcast. She traveled along his path, north and west, as though she knew where she was going. Didn't she realize Fort Leavenworth lay in the other direction? Or was she simply following the trail, hoping that she might eventually meet up with the white travelers?

But then again, perhaps her path was deliberate. It could be. She might be considering meeting up with other travelers at Bent's Fort. If she kept moving at her current pace and in the same direction, she would reach Bent's Fort within a day, maybe two. In all likelihood Julia may have been smarter than he had originally thought. Perhaps, he thought, he should have given her more credit than he did.

Neeheeowee still followed her from a distance, taking care to ensure her welfare, even going so far as to throw berry bushes and wild turnips into her path when he thought she might be hungry. He had considered leaving a rabbit on the trail before her, placing it in such a way that she couldn't miss it, but had decided against it, there being no logical explanation for an arrow hole in its carcass except the obvious one—if she noticed.

They were closer to the mountains now than they had ever been, and the land, which had been gradually drifting upward, had begun to change its scenery, a few mountain peaks visible in the distance. Certainly they were still in the flat plains area, but here and there the land allowed for more timber, especially along the Arkansas. He glanced at the river now, realizing it, too, had changed, the waterway sprouting an outcropping of islands in places.

Up ahead, within only a short walk, they would run into a valley his brother, Little White Man, called Big Timbers. Long an area of prime campground for the Cheyenne and the Arapaho tribes, this precinct boasted big, mammoth cottonwoods, their trunks sometimes as large as the bottom half of a tepee.

He hoped Julia would stop there within the grove of cottonwood trees for the night. At least she would be safe there for the evening, and he wouldn't have to watch over her so strictly, this being his land, the land of the Cheyenne.

He would have to keep some sort of watch on her though, for there were other dangers there besides the human kind: cougars, wolves, coyotes, and bears. He sighed, realizing he would have to keep a watch over her no matter what she did. For of one thing he was certain: if there was danger out there in any form,

Julia would find it, or rather he would see it and fight with it in order to save Julia.

He frowned at his thoughts, but seeing that Julia moved on up ahead of him, he set his mind to her trail.

Julia stood aghast, looking out over the enormous "park" she had just discovered. Immense cottonwoods filled the valley of the Arkansas River, the width of these trees, she judged probably ranging anywhere from seven to ten feet in diameter. The area underneath the trees, too, had been cleared of the numerous bush and smaller trees which usually grew in great profusion in these areas, making this stretch of land look as though it were a well-groomed, though shaded park.

"How welcoming this looks on a hot day like today," she said, as though someone stood beside her.

Julia took a deep breath, sighing. "Lord, how I miss Neeheeowee."

She gazed out before her. "It would have been nice to camp here with him. It would be fortunate also if he were here to tell me exactly where I am."

Julia frowned. It was true. She was lost—hopelessly so. And she didn't know what to do about it except to keep going on in the same direction she had been traveling all along. Sooner or later she would run into something, or someone—or so she hoped.

She remembered Neeheeowee saying that Bent's Fort lay in this direction. He had also said it sat within walking distance of the Arkansas. If all that were true, it made sense, she kept reminding herself, that if she kept on her course and followed the river westward, she would eventually find the fort.

She didn't feel the mounting panic that some associated with being lost. In some ways she felt she knew where she was, and she did—somewhat—as long as she had the river beside her. Besides, somehow she always had enough to eat, firewood for her camp each night, and water for cooking. In truth, she'd had little to do each night but pick her campsite, build a fire, eat, and go to sleep.

It seemed awfully suspicious to her, and she wondered if Neeheeowee were somehow following her, providing her with her needs. She hoped so. But she could find no trace of him to confirm her speculations even though it seemed more than likely, and so she continued on her journey, pretending that Mother Nature truly wielded a helping hand.

She found a wonderful camping spot, in a shaded area under a huge cottonwood tree that looked as if it had been transplanted from a land of giants.

"This tree must be ten feet across," Julia said, voicing astonishment. "Why, I can hardly see to the top."

Suddenly Julia had the odd sensation of feeling as though she were in a park back East. She looked around her, half-expecting to see a dozen or more people using the "park" as a picnic area. But as she gazed around, she realized she was quite alone, and so she went about setting up camp.

"Indians have been here at some time," Julia murmured aloud. It was easy to see, she realized, from the circle of stones they had left behind—the stones used, she knew, to hold the tepee down against storms and high winds. She moved around her new campsite, matting down the grasses and collecting up all the branches and small trees for firewood.

She would start a fire early, she decided, and eat a meal, leaving the evening free to indulge in a leisurely bath. She almost sighed contentedly. A bath would be heavenly.

In truth, the "park" was so nice, she thought about resting here for a few days, but she ruled out the idea almost as soon as she'd thought it. Indians had been here. Indians would be back. And she had no idea what tribes she could expect to find here.

Something caught in her peripheral vision and Julia quickly turned her head. She looked back toward the fire, smiling.

Ah, she thought, *Just as I'd suspected. Neeheeowee trails me.*

She'd just caught sight of his dark hair, blowing in the breeze.

Elation filled her and she sat back in relief. She had feared she'd never see him again. It was nice to know she'd been wrong.

Neeheeowee surveyed Julia from the confines of his own campsite. He was quite pleased with himself. So far today, he'd had no scrapes with wolves, nor snakes, nor even bears, and the scratches on his body were beginning to heal.

He'd also been able to leave Julia a good amount of food, including the tree ears, or tree mushrooms, which grew in such abundance here on the cotton-woods. He'd also left a buffalo calf lying at the side of her campsite, making it appear as though the animal had died from a struggle with wolves. Although this would fool no Indian, Neeheeowee knew Julia would hardly question it.

And so Neeheeowee relaxed, content merely to watch Julia with only half an eye cocked to her whereabouts.

He'd almost been asleep when it happened. One moment she'd been sitting quietly in camp, the next she'd gotten to her feet, walking slowly toward the river, shedding first her shoes, then her leggings, then her dress; up, up and over her hips, over her breasts, her head, until she stood in nothing save the chain of beads around her neck.

She turned around, so that she was facing him, then

she stretched, leisurely, almost as if . . . Neeheeowee sat up at once. If he didn't know better, he would have sworn that she flirted with him. But she couldn't know that he was here . . . or did she?

He groaned. It didn't matter if she knew he was there or not. He would not stay hidden very long, not when she looked like that.

He crept down toward the river, hoping to observe her a little more "close to hand." She droned a song as she washed first her hair, scrubbing it with sand from the river bottom and then her face, her neck, her arms, her breasts, her . . .

Neeheeowee gazed all the harder, not needing his body's reminder to tell him he found her attractive. She had finished her washing, and Neeheeowee thought she might leave the water at once. But she didn't.

She flung a glance in his direction, then turned onto her back, floating in the water like some shimmering goddess, a patch of evening light following her as though it had nothing to do but watch over her. Neeheeowee groaned and shut his eyes, but he didn't turn away. He couldn't. And as he opened his eyes to catch her glimmering beauty, he knew he would not make it through the evening without going to her.

The game was up. He would have her tonight.

She stood now within the water, her hair flowing down her back in a cascade of wet curls, and Neeheeowee thought he would go insane with the wanting of her. His desire was worse now than it had been when they had first traveled together. He'd made love to her now. He knew the warmth of her response, the fleeting caress of her fingers. And he wanted her; oh, how he wanted her.

He would go to her now. He would tell her the truth, that he could not let her go, that if necessary he would take her captive, and he stood up out of his cover just as she gained her footing in the water.

That's when he saw it. There in the trees. A movement. Something watched them—or someone.

Neeheeowee crouched back down, looking out toward Julia, who hadn't yet become aware that danger lurked close by. What was it? Animal or man?

He caught a glimpse. A Comanche brave, he identified. He let his senses scour the surrounding area. How many were there and where were they? Neeheeowee waited, counting two, unmounted. Because of the Kiowa alliance, an uneasy truce existed between the Comanche and the Cheyenne, but Neeheeowee would not put it to the test. These men meant harm, and *he* would not allow it.

He waited. Let them make the first move. His would be a maneuver of surprise.

He didn't have to wait long. Yelping and hollering both men stood at once, brandishing their arms and running down to the river toward Julia. Julia screamed, and, plunging down into the water, struck out toward the other shore.

War paint streaked from the Comanche's faces and Neeheeowee read the symbolic slashes there in the black, snagged edges of the paint. He grimaced. These warriors were on a mission of revenge. Unless victorious, no one who met these men would live to tell of the encounter. It meant that if they caught her, Julia would die.

He watched them. He waited, until the men were at last within range of his bow and arrows, Neeheeowee stood up, screaming out his war cry and firing within seconds first one, another, another, and another arrow all in an arch calculated to hit the two Comanche. He'd sent up eight arrows into the sky before the first one even fell, hitting its mark without error.

One Comanche fell. One Comanche injured and running.

Neeheeowee charged, screaming, his lance held high. He paused just long enough to throw it, missing his opponent only because the Comanche, dumbfounded by Neeheeowee's ferocity, ran away in the opposite direction as fast as he could. Neeheeowee shot another round of arrows into the air, the scream in the distance testifying to the accuracy of his aim.

Neeheeowee ran down to the first man, taking the warrior's hair off as trophy before running off in the distance toward the other Comanche warrior, returning to Julia, two greasy, black scalps in his hand.

Julia still hugged the farther shore, her look at Neeheeowee more one of disbelief than pleasure.

"That's disgusting," she said in English, as though the crimes here in this camp were his, not the Comanche. Then she switched to Lakota. "How could you do this to me?"

Neeheeowee didn't say a thing, not knowing to which of the things he had done she referred. He didn't have to wait long to find out.

"You have followed me," she said. "At first I was elated to find that you were with me, but now, I do not know. You have been with me all along, have you not?"

What else could he do? He nodded his head.

"You have tricked me. You have led me to believe I could survive out here on the prairie all alone, and I have not, have I? It is you who has been putting food in my path. It is you who threw firewood along my way as though such things were natural. It was you who slaughtered the buffalo calf. What was your intention? Did you think to play me the fool?"

He didn't get a chance to defend himself, and, in truth, what could he say? He understood her reaction, her fear, her need to strike out at something after having experienced an attempt upon her life. But to Neeheeowee's utter amazement, as he stood there, bewildered, wondering what to say, how to speak to her to make it better, she cried.

"I owe my life to you," she whimpered between sobs. "What would I have done if you hadn't been here? And yet you don't want me as your wife and I do not know if I can . . ." He couldn't understand the rest, for she now spoke in a tongue he could not comprehend.

Neeheeowee raised his eyes to look at the tall trees above him. And suddenly he knew what he would do.

Throwing down his weapons, his trophies, he advanced out into the water, toward her; there to take her in his arms and comfort her until the tears went away.

And when she hiccuped, "What has happened to you?" seeing all his scratches and bites, Neeheeowee merely smiled, shaking his head and picking her up to trudge back through the water to the other shore.

Chapter 13

❦

"**B**y thuneder, did ye iver see such a sight?"
Neeheeowee saw that Julia almost raised
her head, but at the last moment, she stopped, focus-
ing her gaze back toward the ground as he had instructed her to do earlier. "What be it? Injuns?"

"I couldna rightly say. But if ye're askin' me, I'd
say it most likely looks like fire."

"In the spring?"

"Thar's what I said. Did ye iver hear the tale 'bout
the man jist beginnin the business of trade an' the fire
he lit? Why, the way I heard it . . ."

Their words were lost to Neeheeowee as the two
men passed by as though they didn't even see the two
young people. Neeheeowee let out his breath, knowing his ploy in making Julia look Indian had worked.

And why not? Hadn't he taken the time this morning to braid Julia's hair; two plaits, one on each side
of her head, meticulously fashioning them and tying
them?

He thought back on their morning, on their evening
just passed. After the attack by the Comanche, Neeheeowee had held Julia in his arms all night. He
hadn't said much, nor had she. He had wanted to tell
her many things; he said nothing. He wanted to tell

212

her he wouldn't let her go, but instead he had just held her and Julia, after a while, had relaxed, accepting his embrace.

They needed to talk, he knew it, yet he couldn't bring himself to speak of the things that he must; of captivity, of kidnapping, of sabotaging her attempt to find the white travelers. He still hoped Julia would decide on her own to stay with him. It would be best if she did. And though it seemed unlikely that she would settle in his favor, he patiently awaited her decision. He merely declined to tell her it wouldn't matter: He would not let her go.

He knew he took a chance in bringing her to Bent's Fort. He knew that white people might discover Julia and try to take her from him, but he had little choice in the decision. He could not leave Julia alone upon the prairie, there being too many other dangers to consider. He had business to attend to with Little White Man, business involving Julia's future, and he could not delay his visit. That left him only one solution to the problem of Julia, and that had been to make her look as Indian as possible. That way, when he approached the fort with her, perhaps no one would notice that he led a white woman in an Indian's place.

To this end, he had taken his time with her this morning, fixing her hair, dressing her in the style of the Plains Indian. And, in truth, he had enjoyed himself. He had adorned one of her braids with a patch of rawhide and had hung a shell from the other, finishing the job by smearing vermillion paint down her center part and over her cheeks and brow.

He frowned. He remembered it now, their morning together. He had paid her the highest compliment possible by combing and fashioning her hair.

But Julia, perhaps unknowledgeable of this Plains Indian custom, didn't understand what Neeheeowee did, didn't know that he performed a very husbandly duty for her, one known to the Plains Indian as that of bestowing great affection and honor.

And so she didn't acknowledge his actions, and though Neeheeowee tried not to, he knew his attitude conveyed his disillusionment.

"Neeheeowee," she asked sometime later. It had still been early morning when they had stopped by a stream on their way to Bent's Fort so that she might bathe and wash her clothes. "Have I done something to injure you?"

Neeheeowee hesitated to answer. He wasn't certain Julia had recovered from the attack by the Comanche. True, she hadn't been harmed, but she had been frightened, and he did not wish to burden her with criticism so soon after a shocking incident, not when she might still be weak from fear. Although perhaps he shouldn't worry overmuch. She appeared more angry with him for what she thought was his deception than upset with the Comanche for threatening her life.

And so he thought for a little while and then, gazing away, he answered her question with a shrug, returning his attention back to the task at hand, that of scraping and polishing his bow. He made no other comment.

"Neeheeowee, what have I done?"

He put down his equipment, looked over to her, and gave her a half smile. At last he said, "Please excuse my ill manners if I have made you feel that you have injured me. Our customs, yours and mine, are different. There is no reason for me to assume you know mine. And it is a man with no honor who constantly corrects another."

Julia snorted. "How am I to know your customs if you do not tell me?"

Neeheeowee rose up onto his haunches, and poked a stick at the fire, turning it round and round as

though it held interest for him. At length he said, "It
is true that you are new to the way in which I view
things. There are some things you do that I do not
understand and there are things that I do that I know
you find incredible. And so I will tell you this once
about a custom we have within our tribe." He
stopped, he rose to his full height, backing away from
their camp to lean next to a tree. He smiled slightly
before saying, "I performed a husbandly act with you
this morning by combing your hair, one that is reserved for married couples who love each other
deeply."

Julia gasped and threw down the clothes she'd been
washing. She swung around, coming up onto her
knees. "You did?"

He nodded.

"What does that mean, Neeheeowee?" she asked,
and Neeheeowee, staring at her, wondered at the look
he saw in her eyes. Was that love that he saw there?
It seemed incredible. She had walked away from him,
causing him to believe she did not feel deeply about
him, and yet . . .

He grinned all at once. "It means that I think of you
more and more as my woman," Neeheeowee said. "It
means that I honor you and that I . . . *Nemene'hehe*, tell
me, how a woman honors her man in your culture."

Julia paused, but after a moment, she got to her feet,
and, straightening her skirt, she tread slowly toward
the spot where Neeheeowee stood. "Well," she said,
her gaze never leaving his, "if she really loves him,
she will cook for him and wash his clothes."

Neeheeowee glanced to the fire where a stew
brewed over the open fire, then to the water where
Julia had been working over his leggings. He sent a
startled glance back to Julia, asking, "And what else
does she do for him?"

"Well," she said, pacing closer and closer to him,

and Neeheeowee prayed she would not see him shudder, a reaction to her nearness. "If she is wise," Julia continued, "she lets him take her into his arms from time to time." She stepped right up to him. She teased him with her closeness, she played with his necklace and Neeheeowee, a willing victim, at once encompassed her within his embrace. "And," she said, her lips no more than a hairbreadth away from his, "when a woman really loves a man, she'll let him kiss her."

Neeheeowee brushed her mouth with his, his teeth nibbling at her lips. It was the first kiss they had shared since their recent trouble with one another had started.

"Julia." He gasped for breath all at once, his hands running quickly up and down her spine. "Julia," he said again, then deepened the kiss, his tongue finding hers, tasting her over and over, deeper and deeper, until breaking off the kiss, he whispered, "Julia, I need you. I want you. I—"

Julia cut him off by the simple action of reaching up to untie the strings of her dress, letting the dress fall to the ground.

She stood before him then, in all her feminine allure, and Neeheeowee sucked in his breath, his response complete. He waited only a moment, looking at her, and then he felt her everywhere. He couldn't get enough of her, his hands roving over her back, her buttocks, her breasts.

"I cannot wait, Julia, I—"

"I want you, too, Neeheeowee, please."

He didn't need any further urging. He pulled her up to him, taking her full weight upon him and, pushing back his breechcloth, he drove into her. He gazed at her all the while, at all her beauty, as he reveled in the warmth of her body surrounding him, her inner spasms mixing with his, and Neeheeowee thought he might burst.

He tried to hold back, but as he watched her, she smiled at him before sighing and moving over him, meeting her own pleasure. "Julia," he cried, echoing her own response. "Julia," he wailed again, releasing himself into her. On and on it went, Neeheeowee wondering if he had ever felt anything more intense, more enthralling.

And as he drifted back to earth, he whispered to her, his shaft still aroused and warm within her. "I promise you that sometime I will take you with all the finesse and longing of couples well acquainted. Not always will I act the young brave, unable to hold back my passion."

And to this statement Julia said, "I hope not, my love. I hope not."

And with her legs still wrapped around him, her weight still on him, she began to move, and then he, too, and if Julia did anything at all this day, she proved to Neeheeowee that the moment of which he spoke still lay in the distant future.

Bent's Fort lay just ahead of them, the proof that they were close to it being the amount of foot traffic they encountered, from traders and Indians to pioneers and white covered wagons.

Julia and Neeheeowee were approaching Bent's Fort from the southeast this day, their route allowing Julia to get an excellent view of the trading post which stood situated in the heartland of the plains, almost in the center of what most called the Great American Desert. Here, dry winds blew incessantly, depriving the land of water and developing within the traveler an urgent sort of thirst. To the south, across the Arkansas, lay barren sand hills and to the north, bluffs of chalk and rock.

She and Neeheeowee had been lingering upon the
outskirts of the fort from its southern end, both of
them reclining on a rocky bench a hundred yards or
so up from the river. There they had been able to see
the long stretch of valley and rolling plains spread out
before them, the distant mountains of the Spanish
Peaks glittering off to the southwest and Pikes Peak
to the northwest.

By mutual consent, ever since the Comanche attack
at the river only a day or so ago, the two had traveled
together, Neeheeowee taking the lead of their party,
as was Indian custom, Julia following along behind
him. She also led their pony by its buckskin reins, the
animal having been brought by Neeheeowee as he'd
followed Julia over the prairie. The pony was laden
down with their supplies of parfleches and buffalo
robes, for which Julia was grateful. Not only did it
allow her to have more of her own things around her;
so, too, was she spared the burden of carrying the
heavy robes.

She kept her head bent, her eyes looking down as
they approached the fort, only venturing to look up
to catch an occasional view of the activity happening
all around her or to snatch a quick view of the fort.

Bent's Fort—she gasped at the magnificent sight of
it. The morning sun hit the gray-brown, adobe bricks,
making the high walls of the structure appear remi-
niscent of a hundred-year-old, stone castle, with tur-
rets and domes, rounded walls and belfry towers. The
only thing missing, she decided, was a moat. But its
lack was more than made up for by the scattering of
Indian villages, stationed all around the fort; and the
laughter in these camps; the incessant beat of the
drums were more welcoming than Julia would have
liked to admit.

Neeheeowee, however, avoided the camps, leading
Julia instead up to the fort. And Julia wondered why

he evaded his own people. Did he avoid them because of her, because he did not wish to introduce her, or was there some other reason?

Julia shook her head at her thoughts and tried to recall instead what she knew of the history of this fort, recollecting that Charles and William Bent had opened this post several years back, hoping to cash in on the abundant fur trade to be had in the area. Friendly toward most tribes, the Bents particularly catered to and allowed free rein within the fort to the Cheyenne and their allies, the Arapaho. Some said this was due to William Bent's marriage into the Cheyenne tribe to a pretty Indian girl, Owl Woman, but most knew the alliance between the Cheyenne and the Bents had begun from the very first incident of Cheyenne meeting Bent. It was rumored that William Bent saved the lives of two Cheyenne warriors when, unannounced, a warring tribe of Comanche had entered the fort. The Cheyenne had never forgotten the incident, and a strong alliance had been forged from then on.

Neeheeowee had told Julia he had business at Bent's Fort and that there would be many white people at the fort, some en route back to Leavenworth. He had asked her if she intended to find passage back to her home, to which Julia had shrugged, not knowing what to say. She didn't want to return to Fort Leavenworth, but she couldn't stay with Neeheeowee.

What do I do? she wondered. She just didn't know, and the conflicting emotions were almost more than she could bear.

Julia tilted her head, watching Neeheeowee now as he paced along in front of her, his path heading toward the main entryway. He stood tall and proud, his black hair fluttering back against the quiver of arrows upon his back, and Julia had an urge to reach out and touch a long lock of it where it fluttered out against the wind.

But she quelled the urge and quickly looked down. Truly, he was the handsomest man she had ever seen.

They came right up to the fort without incident, passing into it by way of a tunnellike entryway, the two of them blending in with the other Cheyenne and Arapaho Indians so much so that no one gave them pause, not even the other Indians. Julia still led the pony by its reins and quickly found herself dispatched away from Neeheeowee, ushered on toward the corral. She feared leaving him at this place, but she had little choice in the matter since Neeheeowee turned back toward her, nodding his approval of her leave-taking, though he signaled her to return to him swiftly.

An old Mexican woman led her to the south of the main building, where stood the most beautiful corral Julia had ever seen. She let her breath out in awe.

Here the adobe walls were shorter than those of the main building, perhaps six or seven feet tall to the sixteen-to twenty-foot-high walls of the central structure. But it wasn't that which made the enclosure so pretty. Along the tops of the walls, mayhap for safety, a heavy profusion of cactus had been planted, their spring flowers in tremendous bloom. There were startling reds, mixed with the stark white of other blossoms, growing in great profusion and sitting atop the most green of cacti she had ever seen. And the sun, beaming down on the flowers, seemed to make the walls come alive with color.

Julia smiled, feeling dazzled by the effect, but she had only a moment to appreciate its beauty, for the old Mexican woman, in a cascade of Spanish, shooed her young charge onward, indicating where Julia could corral her pony, and also where the young woman could store her belongings. Julia nodded her thanks to the old lady, uttering one of the few words she knew in Spanish, a simple *"gracias."*

She watched the Mexican woman for only a moment more as the lady departed before, with a flick of her wrist, Julia turned her attention onto Neeheeowee's mustang pony and to that animal's care. She and Neeheeowee had taken only a short walk this morning with the pony, and so the mustang needed no rubdown, and Julia merely tethered the animal, reaching up to grab their parfleches from its back.

The sun felt warm upon her back while she listened to the singing of the birds that had nested near the cactus. She almost smiled, remembering another time when she had felt this good, listened so intently to all that took place around her. The smell of food cooking, of meat set over campfires, of goodies baking in wood-burning stoves made her feel homesick, and Julia realized that this was the first time she'd been within white company for several months. And the irony of it was that she was now stationed within a white man's fort, surrounded by white men with white tradition and here she stood, Indian.

It got worse. She wasn't quite sure she wanted the white company. She liked Neeheeowee's just fine. If only he . . .

I can't think of it, she scolded herself. *When I do so, it only brings me more heartache and confusion.*

It was true that she would have to make a break from Neeheeowee—and soon, but she didn't have to do it right now. Tonight, tomorrow would be soon enough. She had a whole day before her, a beautiful day, and she expected to enjoy every minute of it.

The thought did intrude upon her that it might be the last day she would spend with Neeheeowee. But feeling the tremendous emotional upheaval such ideas brought her, she chose to ignore the possibility of that altogether.

* * *

Julia took her time seeing that their belongings were safely stored and the horse properly watered and fed before she returned to Neeheeowee. And though he feigned indifference to her appearance upon the scene, Julia knew that he had been watching for her. It was evident in the way he relaxed as soon as she entered into the main area, the way he seemed to concentrate so deeply on those around him.

Julia smiled to herself, her head down as she stepped toward him, taking her place in back of him, as was Indian custom. Neeheeowee ended his conversation right away, and moving through the crowd, headed toward the corral.

"*Wimunga.* Julia?" Neeheeowee spoke to her without turning around to see if she followed. "I had grown worried about you. Did you need some help?"

"No," she said, smiling. She bent her head at once so that no one else could catch her smile. "It was just such a pleasure to be here, to be out in the sun with no worry as to whether some warring tribe would find us, that I took my time over my tasks."

He grunted, before he muttered, "*Haahe,*" in acknowledgment, then said, "I have spoken with my cousin, Little White Man, who is the chief of this place, and I have made good with him for us to spend the night here. It is quite an honor my cousin extends to us since usually no Indians, even the Cheyenne, are allowed within the fort after sundown. I will honor him with the pony I have brought with me in payment for what he does for me."

"This is good," Julia said. Then, "Did you tell him about me?"

"What about you?"

"Did you tell him I am white?"

"No," Neeheeowee said. "Why would I do that and

bring attention to you? Are we not trying to make others believe you are Cheyenne?"

"But there are so many white traders here that I thought I might—"

"It will do you no good, *Nemene'hehe*."

"What do you mean?"

Neeheeowee sighed. "If you mean to beg passage from the white travelers, I may as well tell you now I have no intention of letting you go with them."

"Is that why you followed me when I tried to escape?"

He thrust out his chin. "I did more than just follow you," he said in answer to her. "I kept you from finding them. I cleared a path for you to follow each day, keeping it going west and north, so that you would not find those travelers."

"Well, that explains . . ." she began in English, then aware of what she'd said, the language she'd used, she raised her head and gazed around her, finally asking in Lakota, "Why?"

He tossed his head. "I do not intend to let you go."

Julia was taken aback by the incongruity of the statement. "But, Neeheeowee, I am surrounded by white people. I could approach anyone here and tell them all that has happened to me and obtain passage back East."

"Yes," Neeheeowee said. "I know this. But I think I should tell you that I would follow you and take you captive." He shrugged. "It makes no difference to me. Go ahead if you must. I will still come for you."

"How can you be so certain you could take me?" she asked. "I would tell them what you plan, and they would watch for you."

He smirked. "Do you think they would stop me? White men do not guard well, nor do they track well. Be assured, I would do it."

Julia hesitated in her footing for a moment while

she tried to make sense of what this Cheyenne warrior said. She lost pace with him and found herself having to run to catch him. But once again, falling into step behind him, she said, "I do not understand this, Neeheeowee. You have made it clear to me what you intend to do with your life, and I do not see any place for me within your plans. Why keep me with you? Wouldn't it be better just to send me back to Fort Leavenworth?"

"*Hova'ahane*, no."

"Why not?"

Neeheeowee stopped so quickly, Julia bumped into him. He spun around to face her. "I know that your husband was killed," he said, silencing her with a signal of his hand when she would have interrupted. "The Kiowas who captured you told us the story. I also know your best friend lives with the Lakota. Is there someone else at this soldier town that waits for you? Is there a child that needs you, a parent, perhaps?"

Julia shook her head.

"Then we do not go back there."

They had reached the corral, and Julia glanced up at the sky before she returned her gaze to Neeheeowee, once again eyeing this Indian brave who stood before her. "I do not understand this," she said. "Am I not a bother to you?"

He nodded. "Yes."

"Would it not be easier to travel without me?"

Again he nodded.

"Then, why—"

"Some 'bothers' are worth the trouble. I intend to keep you with me. I have from the first moment when I asked you not to leave me. Now that you are here, you stay. Leave if you must. Taking you captive would solve many problems for me since I would never be expected to marry a captive. At least then I would not feel guilty every time we share one another's sleeping robes."

"Oh!" It was all she could think of to say, and though she physically backed away from him, he followed her, his eyes staring into hers.

At last, though, he stopped and, straightening, said, "I am sorry. I should not have told you all of this. I have been trying to let you make your own decision. Leave if you must."

"But you would only follow."

Neeheeowee shrugged and, looking around him, he said, "Come, I wish to show you something."

He turned around without responding to her statement, beckoning Julia on with a wave of his hand. He led her in and around different corrals until he came to one set way off to the side. There he leaned up against one of the wooden posts.

"There," he said, pointing. "Do you see the black pony out there in the middle? The stallion?"

Julia nodded.

"That is a pony I left in Little White Man's care last time I was here in this fort. It was the best from my herd and I did not wish to take it to the Kiowa trade. I left it here to retrieve later."

"He is beautiful. What is his name?"

"He has none yet. I had just captured him before I brought him here. He is one of the best from the wild herds. It took me much effort to catch him."

Julia grinned. "I can see why that is."

Neeheeowee turned his head toward her. "I have just given him to my cousin, Little White Man."

Julia spun about. "You did?" she asked. "Why?

Neeheeowee didn't answer for a while, looking out over the corral toward the stallion instead. In due time, however, Neeheeowee spoke up, saying, "I did not know what kindred you had, if any, which were left at the soldier town. I only know that if something happened to me, I would see you safely settled. I have arranged with Little White Man to take you in as though you were cousin to Owl Woman, his wife, and her sister, Yellow Woman, if ever I were to perish. Remember this because from here, you could either return to the white soldier town or you could stay with my people, whichever you would choose." He cast her a fleeting look from the side before he grinned. "I worried."

Julia didn't say a thing. What could she say? She just looked at him, meeting his gaze.

He had traded away the best that he had—and for what? For her. How did one respond to such generosity?

"I thank you," she said in English before realizing he could not understand her, but he was already turning away from her.

"Come, now, *Nemene'hehe*," he said, striding away from her, back toward the main structure. "I will show you the lodge area where we will stay this night."

"Neeheeowee," she said, catching up to him and touching him on the arm. He stopped, turning toward her briefly. She gazed up at him, squinting her eyes, "I am overwhelmed by your generosity. I . . ."

"It was nothing," he said, and, turning aside, he led her to their room.

They climbed a ladder to the second floor, Neeheeowee opening the door to her room and entering first, as was Indian custom. He looked around the room, checking under the bed, in the corners, and behind bureaus, but, finding nothing, he motioned Julia forward.

She stepped into the room, feeling as though she had gone back in time, to another life, another place where she had been white. Almost at once, memories

assailed her, items she had quite forgotten were called
back to mind; a four-poster bed, a dresser, chairs, a
washbasin, and a table.

She looked around her. The room was a mixture of
dirt floors, adobe walls, and a large post set in the
middle of the room, its purpose to give the roof
greater support, she supposed. There were two windows set well into the thick walls; but tucked off into
a corner of the room was a vanity, and Julia walked
over to it now, her fingers gliding over the wooden
structure as though its drawers were made of marble,
not solid oak.

Julia glanced back at Neeheeowee where he still
stood at the door. "*Wapila*," she said in Lakota. "I
rejoice. Thank you for what you have done."

Neeheeowee nodded his head, and, coming farther
into the room, he closed the door behind him.

"Little White Man says we will eat our evening
meal in here. I will finish my business with him tonight, and we will leave in the morning.

Julia nodded, saying nothing. She looked away
from him, her gaze taking in the solidness of the
walls, their color, their size. She studied the sturdiness
of the floor, saying at last, "So soon? Do you fear that
I will leave you, Neeheeowee? If you do not want me
to, there is a simple remedy; marry me."

His chin shot in the air. "I do not make my plans
because of fear. If I could offer you marriage, I would.
I cannot."

Julia looked away, going to stand by one of the two
windows in the room. This one looked out onto a
patio. At length, she said, "I appreciate all you have
done for me, Neeheeowee. You have come to my rescue many times. You have even saved my life. Perhaps if I had not been raised so strictly, I might be
able to set aside these things that I feel, but I cannot.
And Neeheeowee"—she caught his glance from

across the room—"without marriage, I cannot go with you."

"I know."

"I do not seem to be able to leave you either."

He sighed. Then, at last, he said, "I know."

The noises of horses neighing down below, of children crying, of men fighting and scolding one another blurred into the background, second to the turbulence of her thoughts. She breathed in deeply, and Neeheeowee quietly left the room.

Chapter 14

As it turned out, they dined with the Bents that evening: William, Owl Woman, her two children, and Yellow Woman, sister to Owl Woman. Neeheeowee and Julia had been invited to the Bents' private chambers, the entire party feasting on buffalo meat and wild turnip stew.

Julia observed William Bent to be a short man with dark hair and midnight black eyes. His nose was long, giving him a hawklike appearance, and when his gaze fell upon her, Julia felt much as a small rodent might if under the watchful eyes of a soaring buzzard.

She kept her gaze down in an effort to hide the color of her eyes, but during a long meal, it wasn't possible to keep her gaze always locked to the floor, and from time to time she chanced a glance up, only to encounter that same, watchful regard from William Bent. She thought of many things she could say if he queried her on the hazel color of her eyes. She could easily claim to be a half-breed. Didn't William Bent have half-white children of his own?

But he didn't ask her, and she didn't volunteer the information. In truth, after a while she had set her mind onto thinking about other things, since everyone in the room, save her, spoke the Cheyenne dialect.

So when William Bent asked, "What part of the country are you from?" she jumped.

It wasn't his question, really, that startled her, it was the fact that he had just spoken in English and Julia had almost replied to him in that same language, catching herself and holding herself back at the last moment.

She said nothing, not even raising her eye level above the table. Still, she heard Mr. Bent sigh.

"I know you are white," he said after a while in distinct English. "I don't know what you are doing here with my Cheyenne cousin or why you are trying to pass yourself off as Indian, but it won't work with me. There are too many things about you that give the truth of your race away." Mr. Bent seemed to smile at this point, and Julia risked a quick glance upward. "For instance," he said, "you eat with utensils. My good woman, take a look around you. Do you see my wife or her sister, or even my cousin Neeheeowee eating with utensils? I would suggest that the next time you desire to masquerade as an Indian, learn to eat with your fingers."

Julia did lift her gaze to look around her then, noting that not only William Bent, but Neeheeowee gave her critical stares. She cleared her throat, and, ignoring Neeheeowee to address William Bent, she said, "Next time, I shall take your advice, Mr. Bent."

"Ah," the man replied, "now we're getting somewhere. I would like to ask you what you are doing here with my cousin. Are you running away from something?"

Julia shook her head, glancing quickly toward Neeheeowee and catching his scowl at her. "I am running from nothing," she said. "I was captured by the Kiowa tribe of Indians and Neeheeowee rescued me. That is all. He has been seeing to my welfare."

"Humm," was all William Bent said. Then, "It won't work."

Julia hazarded a startled gaze upward.

"Your disguise," William Bent said. "Others will see through it if you stay here any length of time."

"We are leaving on the morrow."

"Ah," William Bent said. "That is good." And if he meant to say more, he certainly gave her no further indication. As though all were settled with her last remark, he gave his attention back to the Indians, speaking in the Cheyenne dialect until, one last time he glanced up at her, saying to her in English. "There will be traders through here soon, heading back East. You could go with them if you would like. I could arrange it."

Julia lifted her gaze toward the man just briefly before she answered. "That is very kind of you, Mr. Bent," she said, "and I appreciate your offer. If I desire it, I will let you know soon. Thank you."

William Bent sent her a quick inclination of his head by way of acknowledgment before centering his attention back onto the others at the table.

The evening was young. There would be more than enough time for Mr. Bent to pry what information he could from the young Cheyenne warrior whom he called cousin. However, William Bent, owner and proprietor of the most influential trading post west of the Missouri, was to find himself the loser in this situation, coming away with no more data about the white woman than what he had already learned.

Clearly, the Cheyenne warrior held advantage, nor, it would seem, would he relinquish it.

An hour later, Julia sulked in her room.

Neeheeowee still remained downstairs, talking with his cousins and with William Bent. Julia had excused herself from their meal shortly after William Bent had spoken to her and, unknowing of anything else to do, had gone directly to her room, where she still remained.

She'd needed to think. And she did so now.

Why didn't she take advantage of Mr. Bent's offer? It wouldn't take much effort on her part. She could easily slip away without Neeheeowee being able to do anything about it. She would have the protection of Mr. Bent.

So why didn't she do it?

It was, after all, her decision to leave Neeheeowee, wasn't it? Hadn't she already decided that this was for the best? For him, for her? Why, then, did she delay acting?

Julia moped, unable to answer her own questions, and she began to pace back and forth in front of her window, wondering what she should do. Evening had begun to descend upon the land, but the darkness that had started to fill the air remained unobserved by her, involved in her predicament as she was.

A knock sounded at her door and she called out in English, "Come in," without thinking.

Yellow Woman, sister to William Bent's wife, opened the door in answer, standing at the entrance to the room and smiling at Julia. That the Indian woman held a blue gingham dress didn't register at first with Julia.

"Hal-lo." It was Yellow Woman who spoke.

"Hello," Julia returned, "Won't you come in?"

Yellow Woman nodded but she didn't advance farther into the room. "I bring you *hoestotse*," Yellow Woman said in Cheyenne, "dress," she finished in English as she stood in the doorway, her head down as though she were reluctant to enter. "Little White Man," she continued, "says you may want to wear this," she added.

"Thank you," Julia returned, smiling, and again she motioned Yellow Woman forward. "Won't you bring the dress over here, Yellow Woman?" Julia asked. "It has been a long time, many moons, since I have held the fabric of the white woman's dress." She glanced up toward Yellow Woman. "Have you worn this?"

Yellow woman giggled, shaking her head no, while at the same time, she stepped one foot into the room.

Julia thought a moment. "Would you like to? Wear it, that is?"

The young Indian woman lifted her gaze to Julia's. Dark eyes met Julia's before at last, the Indian woman cleared her throat. Then, speaking in English, she said, "I like very much the white woman's dress. I have tried on several of them in the past. They do not good ... look ... " She grinned. "They do not look good on me."

"That cannot be," Julia said, appraising the young woman up and down. "Why, you have a wonderful figure. Perhaps you just do not know how to make the dress fit you. Maybe I could help you to look 'good' in it. There are certain ways to wear the white man's style of clothing and certain ways not to. I could teach you some of it. I could even do it right now. Would you like to try?"

Yellow Woman brightened up all at once, saying, "Yes, very much. But first I have come to attend to you. Little White Man said that you might want to dress like a white woman, even to the combing of your hair. He has asked me to help you do this if you would like it."

Julia hesitated and Yellow Woman, as though sensing something amiss, said, "My cousin from the north does not know that Little White Man has asked me to do this. Somehow I do not believe he would ... approve? He appears taken with you, my cousin. Is that not strange?"

Julia gave the young girl a puzzling glance, repeating, "Strange?"

"Yes," Yellow Woman said, advancing still farther into the room. "My cousin from the north has long been without a woman and we had begun to think that he might never find one again. But all who have seen the way he looks at you would know that, at last, he has found someone."

"And you approve?"

Yellow Woman nodded, saying, "*Heehe'e*, yes, why would I not?"

Julia didn't answer all at once. She hesitated before she spoke, finally saying, "Because I am white. Because our cultures are so different. Because if other white men knew I was with him, they would try to take me away from him."

Yellow Woman tilted her head. "I think that I understand what you say but I do not understand what you mean," she said, and when Julia gave her a puzzling glance, Yellow Woman continued on, saying, "Those things you speak of mean little. Look around you. Little White Man is white and is married to my sister. No one tries to take him from her. Little White Man and my sister are able to blend our two cultures together."

"Yes," Julia said, "that is true. But somehow white men think differently when it comes to white women, I think."

"Little White Man does not," Yellow woman said. "He knows you are white. He knows you will leave with my cousin. He does not try to prevent it."

Julia sighed. "Maybe. But he has sent you here with a white woman's dress. I think he may be trying to tell me to go back to my own people."

Yellow Woman shrugged. "I do not think so. He only tries to make you feel comfortable."

"I see," Julia said. "Then maybe he is different. Maybe because he is married to your sister, he understands both sides. Most white men do not."

Yellow Woman nodded in agreement, saying, "I think you are right."

Julia shook her head as though clearing it before she turned and smiled at the Indian maiden. "Come in further, won't you, Yellow Woman? Let's see what we can do to make this dress look good on you."

Yellow Woman smiled back and, with a chuckle of delight, hurried into the room.

Julia stood back, admiring her creation. Yellow Woman did, indeed, look beautiful in the blue gingham dress. She had only needed to be shown how to wear it correctly, how to tuck it in here, push it out there, how to adjust the shoulders, pull it into place.

"Come," Julia said, standing in front of the mirror and motioning toward Yellow Woman. "Come and have a look at yourself."

Yellow Woman did as she was bade and soon stood in front of the mirror. She looked. She gasped. "Is that me?"

Julia smiled. "Yes," she said. "I'm afraid it is. You look quite beautiful."

"Do you truly think so?"

Julia nodded. "Yes, I think so. Yellow Woman," she said, hesitating, "I have certainly enjoyed myself with you tonight. I had forgotten, I think, what it was like to have a friendly chat."

"What is this 'chat'?"

"It means just to talk to somebody about something."

"*Naaaa*, you are right," Yellow Woman said. "It is always good to have someone to talk to." The other woman paused, then, as though she had thought for a while longer, she said, "Some say Yellow Woman is a good person to talk to. Many people tell their troubles to Yellow Woman." She paused again, then,

"Yellow Woman senses that you have this need in you. Do you?"

Julia sighed. She looked away. "Yellow Woman," she said, "it is true. I am deeply troubled."

"*Naaaa*," she said. "It is how I thought."

Julia gazed over to her before turning to sit on the bed. "Come," she said, patting a place next to her on the bed. "Will you come and sit here with me and let me talk for a while? So much has happened that I do not understand that perhaps, if I am just able to say it all, I can put my thoughts in order."

Yellow Woman nodded, and, coming forward, said, "What is troubling you?"

Julia couldn't help smiling at the girl. "Many things are worrying me," she said, "but I think what is bothering me more than anything else is that I do not understand some Cheyenne customs that Neeheeowee speaks about. And I was wondering, perhaps if I were to ask you, if you could help me to understand these customs better?"

"Yes," Yellow Woman said. "It would be my honor to do whatever I can for you. For you see"—here the Indian maiden smiled—"we think very highly of our cousin. And I can see that you are important to him. I think that if I can assist you, it will help him."

Julia nodded, saying thank you, then, "Tell me," she said, "the Cheyenne custom of marriage."

Yellow Woman lifted her shoulders before saying, "It is simple. A young man will often court a girl one year, maybe more. He asks for her agreement to marry through an elder of the tribe and offers many horses as a gift to her parents to show how highly he regards her. If she accepts, they are married."

Julia nodded. "Is there a ceremony?"

"Yes," Yellow Woman replied. "The young girl is put onto one of her father's finest horses and is led to the young man's lodge. There, she is sat on a beautiful blanket and friends of the groom then carry her into the lodge. After that, they are married."

"I see," Julia said. "And is a couple considered married without the ceremony?"

"Never."

Julia paused, but at length, she chanced a glance up at Yellow Woman. "Neeheeowee and I are not married by your customs and, Yellow Woman, Neeheeowee tells me he cannot marry me . . . ever . . ."

The Indian girl shrugged her shoulders. "He protests marriage overmuch, I think."

"Yellow Woman, please." Julia gazed over to the maiden. "Neeheeowee has asked me to stay with him."

"*Naaaa!*"

"Yes," Julia said, and she would have confided more, but Yellow Woman sat up suddenly, climbing onto a spot on the bed behind Julia. There she smoothed down Julia's hair, and, taking each of Julia's braids into her hands, she began to undo the braids, one strand at a time.

Finally she spoke, "My cousin from the north," Yellow Woman said, "long stands on tradition as is his right, I think. But he worries sometimes where there is no need to worry. He has so long been without a woman that we would give him most anything, if it would only make him happy. And when he is with you, I see happiness in his eyes. I would only listen to him with half an ear, for I do not think he knows his own mind."

"Hmmm," Julia said, then, "Do you really see that?"

"What?"

"Happiness in his eyes when he looks at me?"

"*Heehe'e,*" she replied. "Yes, have you never noticed it?"

Julia shook her head.

"*Naaaa*! You should look. He does not hide it well for all that he tries to be reserved."

"Yellow Woman," Julia said, "he tells me that without marriage, he would dishonor me if he were to take me to his village. Is that true?"

A long moment passed before the other woman spoke, but finally she said, "*Heehe'e*, yes, it is true." She hesitated again, but at last she ventured, "My grandmother once told me that the most precious gift one could give another was love. She did not speak of physical love, but rather of the love one can see between mother and child, a sister and brother, or a man and his wife. And where such a love exists, it is never wrong. My cousin from the north has not yet learned this. His heart is still too full of hatred from the past to see that the best of his life could be right before him." Yellow Woman hesitated, then she continued, "I have lived here with my sister for many seasons of the moon and I have seen many different ways of living and I wonder, why do you have to live with the Cheyenne? Why not find a place among our allies, the Arapaho, who do not have such strict rules of conduct?"

Julia shook her head. "No," she said. "I do not think Neeheeowee would do it. He longs to be again amongst his own people."

Yellow Woman shrugged. "It should not be his choice where he lives."

"What do you mean?"

"In our tribe, it is not the woman who follows her husband to his kinship and family. Usually the man goes to the woman's family. How else could she be taken care of if something happens to her husband? It is necessary that she remain within her own kinship circle for the sake of herself and her children." Here Yellow Woman paused in her grooming of Julia's hair. She looked around to catch Julia's gaze. "So you

see, it is not unusual that he would go to another
tribe, and that other tribe might not have such rigor-
ous rules on marriage."

"I see," Julia said. "Is that really possible?"

Yellow Woman grinned. "Yes, it is possible, and if
you truly love him and if he loves you, which I believe he does, there is a way that you two can marry."

Julia sighed. "That's what I thought at first, too."
She shook her head, causing her hair to fall from Yellow Woman's hands. "But Neeheeowee is haunted by
the ghosts of his former wife and child, who not only
will not let him go, but who solicited a vow from him
never to marry again. Yellow Woman, have you ever
heard of such things?"

"*Heehe'e*, yes," Yellow Woman said, "but it is not
always a wise man who courts communion with the
dead." Yellow Woman placed her hands on Julia's
shoulders. "There will be a way, my friend. You have
his love, his passion. All who look at him can see it.
It is up to you now to find a way to make that love
blossom."

"But I do not know your ways, your customs."

Yellow Woman merely tilted her head. "It is up to
you."

"I would like to think so," Julia said, "but I have
no wish to cause Neeheeowee to break a vow, even
though that vow hurts me."

Yellow Woman sat forward, bringing her face
around to look at Julia. "You are a good woman.
There will be a way. Besides, nothing is forever. Our
grandfathers understood this, and we have many ceremonies within our culture that can break such a
pledge. Do not despair. You already hold his heart,
and when you have that," she said, "anything is possible."

And Julia, listening to her, believed for a moment

that perhaps it was true. Maybe, after all, there was a way.

Julia paced in front of the window, looking up now and again anxiously to scrutinize the scene outside her window. There wasn't much movement that she could catch out there, it was too dark. The Indian camps stood off to her left. She could see those. Their campfires were bright, plus the singing and drumming from those areas drew the eye to look toward them, as well as the ear to listen to them. Julia grimaced, realizing that the incessant drumming was becoming a more and more commonplace noise to her.

She gazed outside once again. She could see figures dancing out there in the firelight, and she wondered if Neeheeowee were among them.

He hadn't yet returned from dinner, and Julia had begun to wonder what was wrong. She worried, although, she tried to tell herself she had no basis for it. What, after all, did she truly know about Neeheeowee? To her, it appeared that his long absence was out of character, but on what did she base this?

She had come to know him on their journey, a time set apart from any other. She had never experienced what he might be like, how he might treat her when others were present. Perhaps his staying out till very late at night was usual for him.

She had no way of knowing.

Still, a voice within her reasoned, she knew him well enough to know that this was unusual for him. Something was wrong. What?

It made it all the worse since she had made up her mind as to what she would do, and she was eager to make it known to him.

She stared outside again. Stars glistened in the heavens above while a light breeze filtered in through the gauzelike window covering, the softness of the light wind bringing with it the scent of evening and the late spring aroma of prairie.

Julia sighed. The prairie in the evening was just as alluring as the prairie during the day, maybe more so. The hooting of an owl, the squawk of a nighthawk accompanied the ever present whine of the wind as it blew in upon her.

She closed her eyes and felt the sweep of the brief, strong wind. She wasn't sure when it had happened, but somehow the lure of the plains had called to her. There was something out there, she felt. Something ... although maybe it was just the sensation of knowing that one was a part of something tremendous. Maybe it was that which had seeped its way into her soul. Or perhaps it was the utter freedom of the open space that cried out to her; or mayhap it was the feeling of a wholeness of being.

Whatever it was, Julia felt the vigor of it lift her spirits, carrying away the weight of her worries, as though her troubles were mere phantoms, easily carried away by the wind. Julia sighed, barely hearing the door open and close behind her, and so when Neeheeowee spoke to her, she jumped, not expecting him to arrive before her so quietly.

"You are ready to go?"

"No, I mean..." Julia stopped and looked more closely at Neeheeowee. He wore all of his clothes. And though this might sound a strange observation to make, Julia had become used to seeing him in various states of undress; usually in nothing more than breechcloth and moccasins. So to see him before her in leggings and breechcloth, long shirt and moccasins seemed odd. "No, I am not ready to leave. I thought we left in the morning. Are you planning to travel through the night, now?"

"*Haahe*, yes," he said. "This is not a safe place for us right now."

"What do you mean?"

"Little White Man tells me that many soldiers have been spotted on the road traveling toward this fort. Also, there is a party of Comanche just arrived into the camps outside. Although there is an uneasy truce between my people and the Comanche, I do not wish to expose you to that danger, for the Comanche can be a cunning enemy."

"That's all very well, Neeheeowee, but I would rather leave after a good night's sleep. What difference does it make if we leave now or before first light in the morning?"

He paused before he spoke, his features completely unreadable. "It makes a great deal of difference. Prepare your things," he said. "We leave at once."

"But I—"

"Unless you have decided you wish to remain here and go with the white travelers, you will have to come with me now."

Julia frowned, but she didn't argue. Instead she asked, "Where do you go to now?"

He shrugged.

"I have a request, then, if you have no particular place where you are headed."

"I am listening."

Julia shot a quick look at Neeheeowee and nodded before she shifted a lock of her long hair back behind her shoulder. She moved away from the window to walk over to the vanity. Once there, she looked in the mirror, seeing before her a woman who looked both Indian and white at the same time. Gone was the red paint Neeheeowee had spread over her face; gone were the braids. Instead Julia had freed her hair to hang loose, falling down almost to her waist.

She sat down at the vanity noting that she was still dressed in the Cheyenne dress given to her so long ago at the Kiowa camp. It had been washed and

cleaned, the tear in the back mended so that it barely
showed, and Julia realized there was a reason she still
wore the dress, why she had not donned the white
man's clothing offered to her. And it wasn't because
she had become Indian.

She was still very much herself, a white woman in
Indian clothing. But she had realized something very
vital to her. She loved Neeheeowee. She might never
find another one such as him again. Now that she had
him, she did not intend to let him go. But she would
not live with him, she could not. Not until he married
her.

And to do that meant she had to stay with him. The
problem now, as she could see it, became one of how
to remain close to him and still keep her resolve.

She wasn't sure she could do it.

She sent him a quick glance and then, standing up,
she said, "This has been a very hard decision for me
because, as you know, there is much feeling between
us. At first, I thought to leave you. But there is nothing at the fort for me anymore. You were right when
you said that my husband is dead. We had no children and my parents disappeared while making a trip
east over five years ago."

She glanced away. "My husband and I . . . we did
not have a good marriage. You might even remember
him because he is the one who used to torment you
and your friends all those years ago at the fort. I was
unhappy with him. I do not want to be unhappy
again. While I have feelings for you now, without
marriage, I am afraid those feelings would begin to
fade. How long could I stand to feel the inferior of
others? How long would it take before I would want
to feel at peace with myself again? To be able to walk
freely with my head held high?" She gazed back at
Neeheeowee. "I am afraid it would not take me very
long."

"Then you wish to leave now?"

"No," she said, glancing quickly toward Nee-heeowee. But there was nothing to be read there upon his features. Stoically, he kept hidden any emotion he might feel. "I . . . I cannot bring myself to leave you. Besides . . ." She held his gaze, watching emotion sweep across Neeheeowee's face, though it was just as quickly masked.

He didn't, however, say anything, and so Julia continued, "I have discovered within myself a desire, a love perhaps, for the prairie. I find I yearn to be out on it. But I have found amongst my talks with Yellow Woman tonight something more. I have discovered that I desire to see my friend, Kristina. I know she still lives with the Lakota, and I wonder how she fares. It is within my ability now to go and see her, if you will take me. But I must tell you. I will not sleep with you. I will not make love with you again until the day we are married. And I would ask you to help me keep this resolve. So if you agree to take me, you would have to agree, also, to keep away from me."

Neeheeowee swallowed. It was the only movement that exposed his emotion. At length, however, he said, "I will take you to her if that is your decision. I will also try to keep away from you, but I cannot give you my word on that because I am not sure I can do it. I will try. It is the best I can promise you. You will have to decide if that is good enough for you."

Julia glanced at him and had the oddest impression of time standing still.

She hesitated. At last, though, she nodded her head. "If that is the best you can do," she said, "I will accept it."

He inclined his head briefly before moving farther into the room. "We go at once, then," he said. "I will leave now to speak with my cousins and Little White Man. When I return, we will go."

And Julia, hoping she knew what she was doing, agreed.

Chapter 15

"We will need horses in order to cross the prairie to your friend, Kristina," Neeheeowee informed her as they set out from the fort on foot. "I gave the gentle mare to Little White Man, and it is just as well. The mare would only hinder us crossing the plains. She was too slow."

"We will ride there?" Julia asked, gazing out over the land where they traveled.

"*Haahe*," he said and nodded. "The distance there is great and would take us too long on foot. I am now in my own country and that of my brothers the Arapaho and Lakota. I do not need to be careful to cover my tracks and so there is little reason why we should walk. We will obtain some horses."

Julia looked at Neeheeowee, wondering how he intended to "get" horses. She had heard that Indians often obtained horses by stealing them from one another or from the white man. Is this what Neeheeowee intended?

She sighed, deciding she had to say something. "I must tell you, Neeheeowee, that I do not believe it right to steal horses," she said.

"Steal? A horse?" Neeheeowee gave her a puzzled glance. "I do not steal. I might capture a horse from

245

an enemy and this, like counting coup, is a great honor."

Julia held her ground. "I believe it is stealing."

Neeheeowee shrugged. "Sometime I will enlighten you as to the honors of counting coup and what it means to us and why. But not now, I think. And do not worry about this 'stealing.' You will like what we will be doing, I think."

"I cannot—"

"We will be journeying to Black Lake," he said. "You have heard of it?"

She shook her head no.

"It is a spot of much mystery and much beauty. The water there a man cannot drink, its taste is bitter, but the wild horse loves it there. The wild pony comes to this lake to drink of the bad-tasting water, even to roll around in it in delight. Julia," he said, "I take you to capture the wild pony."

Julia gasped, immediately contrite. "You do?"

He nodded his head. "You are in the land of the Cheyenne now. This land is full of wonders, but mostly it is full of buffalo and wild pony herds. Did you not know that it is from these pony herds that the Cheyenne have obtained so much of their wealth? The Cheyenne have little need to capture ponies from another, not when there are horses in these herds so easily taken."

"I didn't know that."

He looked back over his shoulder. "No two tribes are alike. We may be allies with some, but we are not the same. Sometime I will have to teach you the differences."

Julia smiled back an acknowledgment, saying only, "I would like that." But deep within herself, she felt brighter. What he said gave them a future. And to Julia, who remained unsure as to how to find a place

in this world for the two of them, it gave her cause
to hope.

For the moment it was enough.

Black Lake was truly a land of enchantment. Situated, along with other small lakes, near the upper
snag of the Sand Creek, the lake lived up to its description. Shallow and small in diameter, probably
not more than four to five hundred yards across, the
lake, which appeared black from a distance, sat in a
valley that looked more like a fairyland of trees and
deep, blue sky than wilderness. Horse trails from
every direction led up to its shores, their routes
deeply entrenched and heavily traveled. Off in the
distance the sharp peaks of the Rocky Mountains
loomed large.

Immediately Julia began to think of fairies and gob-
lins and stories of magic and adventure, and as she
looked out over the lake she said to Neeheeowee, "It's
beautiful."

"Yes, and here we will find many horses, when
they all come to drink."

Julia smiled, and said, "I'm parched. I think I'll take
a drink, too," she bent down to take a sip.

"Julia, don't!" But he was too late. She had already
put the water in her mouth. She gasped and spit it
out at once while Neeheeowee stood beside her—
laughing.

"It is not funny."

"Truly, you are right," he said, still laughing, and
Julia, after a moment, began to smile, too.

She sat down beside the lake. "I'd forgotten what
you said about its bitter taste. It doesn't seem as
though it should taste so awful. The lake looks like
some enchanted land from a fairy tale."

"What is this 'fairy tale'?" He said the words in
English, as she had.

"It is a story," she said, "about enchanted places and people. People who hold much mystery, who work in magical ways. And though we in my culture know these stories are not true, we nevertheless love to hear them over and over."

Neeheeowee nodded. "As do my people. We also like these stories. There is a myth about this place, too. Would you like to hear it?"

"Yes," Julia said, immediately turning toward him with interest.

Neeheeowee came down on his haunches beside her and, picking up a rock, he tossed it into the water. "At the bottom of this lake," he began, "lives a huge serpent. It is very big and very strange, for it creates this bitter water that we see here. It is the reason the water is so hard to drink. This is the environment that the serpent needs in order to live."

Julia smiled. "It is there, right now, as we speak?"

Neeheeowee nodded his head. "It is there."

"Can I see it?"

"Only if you are foolhardy enough to swim in its waters. For the serpent guards its home well. And though it allows all those horses, you see over there, to drink its water and roll around in it, if a man ventures into its depth, he is immediately captured by the serpent and taken below the water to his death. It is why no one bathes here, either. The serpent allows no one near it."

Julia grinned. "I see. Could I stick a toe in?"

Neeheeowee chuckled. "You can try it and see."

Turning from him, she did. When Neeheeowee roared like a beast beside her, Julia was startled into snatching back her foot. He grinned at her.

"If we cannot drink this water," she said, "where will we find water today to drink?"

"There are other lakes nearby. Do not worry. This is not like the land that we crossed at the beginning of our journey together. There is much water here to drink and to bathe in."

"That is good," she said, then after a while she asked, "How will you catch those ponies? I always thought you needed a good horse in order to ride down and capture a wild one."

Neeheeowee nodded. "It is always best to catch a horse that way, but when you don't have a pony to ride, there is another way. Do not worry. I will show you how to do it." He looked down at her. "Tell me, *Nemene'hehe*, do you wish to learn how to capture a wild pony?"

And to his question, Julia replied with a firm, "Yes, sir," translating its meaning when she saw him smile.

It was sometime later that Neeheeowee took Julia into a ravine on the other side of the lake. "A ridden horse," he was explaining, "cannot overtake a free animal except in the early part of spring, when the ponies are half-starved and have no endurance. So at this time of year, we sneak up on a herd of the wild mustangs, hauling ourselves over onto the sides of our horses so that the wild ponies cannot see us."

"What would they do if they saw you."

"They would run," he said. "The mustang has a keen eye and will run from you if he spots you from very far away. That is why we have to sneak up on them before we ride them down and tame them."

"But Neeheeowee," she said, "you do not have a pony to ride to catch them."

"Do not worry. There is one other method of taking the wild pony, but it should never be used unless you have to. It is said that this method has come to us from the white man. I do not know. I only know this way breaks the spirit of the pony forever. So it is never used unless you must. Do you have the hair rope and the hoop made out of willow?"

Julia nodded, holding up the rope and hoop for

Neeheeowee's inspection; the rope was woven from buffalo hair and the hoop formed from willow branches tied with strings to hold the ends together. He took them both from her, hauling the items onto his shoulders.

"Stay here and watch. This first animal I must take by this way called 'ceasing,' but all the others I will ride down and tame in the usual way so that the animals keep their spirit."

Julia heard the playful neighing of the ponies off in the distance and spotted the herd just up ahead of the ravine. There must have been fifty of them, all arrayed in coats of different colors, frolicking and playing out on the prairie like children. The wind blew their manes, which were thick and straggly, all over their necks and faces, while their tails, long and full, swept over the ground with their every move. There were so many colors of them, from milky white to midnight black, that Julia had trouble keeping track of them all. Here was a cream color, there, a gray, a sorrel, a pied. She lost track of them all.

Neeheeowee had sneaked up to the edge of the ravine, his position there facing the wind, while he readied his bow and arrow. He took aim. *Swish*... The arrow hit the gristle at the top of the neck of one of the ponies. The pony fell, stunned.

Neeheeowee grabbed the rope he'd slung across his shoulder, leaping out of the ravine at the same time, and within seconds he had the feet of the mustang hobbled. He then approached the head of the pony, a mare, slowly, placing his hand first over the animal's eyes, then gradually bending down to breathe into its nostrils.

To Julia's amazement, the pony became instantly docile, leaving Neeheeowee with nothing more to do than let the mare rise. He petted the animal, he crooned into her ear, he then removed her hobbles, transforming the hair-rope into a sort of bridle, and jumping onto her back, he rode her over to Julia.

Julia stood amazed while Neeheeowee grinned.

"Now," he said, "I will use this mare to capture three more ponies."

"You will ride that mare?"

"Yes," he said. "She will not fight me. She is docile and will remain so. She is conquered."

"But how can that be?" Julia asked. "It is not long enough for you to be certain she is docile."

Neeheeowee gave Julia a strange look. "How long it takes," he said, "has no bearing on whether she is tame or not. She will not fight me." Here he leaned down toward Julia, the look on his face at once wicked. "Be careful, woman," he said, "or I will use the same technique on you."

She snorted, though a smile pulled at the corners of her lips. She had climbed out of the ravine and had begun to approach the mare, slowly at first and then with more certainty. She reached out a hand toward the mustang, cooing softly to the animal at the same time. After a while, she asked, "Why do you breathe into the pony's nostrils? Is there a reason?"

"*Haahe*," he said. "When I breathe into her nose, I impart some of my spirit into her. It helps her to obey me later."

Julia smiled, petting the mare a little more. "Why do you need to take three more horses?" she asked after a while. "There are only two of us."

Neeheeowee looked away, pointing to the herd. "We will each one of us ride a pony," he said, "while the other two will carry our supplies. Besides"—he sent her a lopsided grin—"we do not want to come into the camp of my brother, Tahiska, as though we were poor relatives. Two of these mounts will be a gift for your friend and her husband."

"I see," Julia said, nodding. "That is very thoughtful of you."

Neeheeowee grunted in response to her compliment, and then handed her his lance. "Take this and keep it with you. I will be gone for a little while taking these ponies. Use it if you must."

Again, Julia nodded, looking on as Neeheeowee turned his wild pony, now docile, and lay down flat on her back as he approached the remaining animals in the herd, a few miles distant. Julia shielded her eyes from the sun as she watched the whole procedure of taking wild ponies, which seemed to be the same as what Neeheeowee had done before except that here each pony was taken by running him down, choking him, throwing him to the ground, and then hobbling his feet. The rest that followed was always the same, with Neeheeowee breathing into the mustang's nostrils as a last action.

Amazingly, the whole procedure took less than an hour for each pony thus obtained. And by sunset Neeheeowee led four new mustangs into their camp.

He hobbled them all, then petted each one, pampering them, talking to them soothingly, and there was not one part of ponies' bodies that did not feel his hands. Julia looked on, mesmerized by what she saw, especially when she considered how little time it took to accomplish it.

She said as much to him as she walked up to him where he still petted and groomed each animal.

"These are not the best of the herd," Neeheeowee said in explanation. "The fleetest and the best of the herd get out of the way the fastest, and there is no catching them at all, for they are always the leaders of the pack. The only way to capture them is the same way I captured this mare, but it is not worth it to be done, for it kills the character of the horse. Those horses I traded for you at the Kiowa camp—do you remember them?"

"Yes, I do."

"They were horses that were the best I could find out here on the prairie, leaders all. It took me some time to capture them for I would not take them by the 'ceasing' method you saw me use earlier. To capture ponies like that one needs a gentle mare to lure them and then to capture them and tame them. Once I had them I then trained them to be the best warhorses on the plains. They were a special trade."

"I see," Julia said, then hesitated. "Why did you spend so much time with them? You must have had some plan in mind."

Neeheeowee looked away from her, his attention still seeming to be on the mustangs. At last he said, "There are some things it is better not to mention, for in broaching these things, one can hurt another or possibly make them feel indebted. You have asked me about this so I will tell you if you truly wish to know, but I fear that it may not be to your liking. Do you still listen?"

"*Han*," she said. "Yes."

"I was going to trade those particular mustangs for the fine guns that the Kiowa possess. I wanted them so that I could track and kill all the Pawnee who were involved in the killing of my wife." He shrugged suddenly. "I traded for something else instead." He smiled. "Someone else. I do not regret it."

Julia couldn't speak for a moment. At last, though, she said, "How you must have resented me."

He paused. "I did at first," he agreed, "but it did not last long. One look at the way your fringe moved with each step you took gave me so many more problems that I forgot to be angry." He chuckled, but still he did not look at her, his entire attention centering upon the animals he had taken today, or so it seemed.

And then he added, "I am glad I have met you again. I do not regret giving those horses away."

By the time he said this he was on the farther side of first mare he had caught this day, his hands still rubbing up and down her. After a while, he glanced up and over the mare, his gaze catching Julia's, and the two lovers looked at one another for a very long time. Julia was uncertain what to say. At last she averted her gaze. "I did not know," was all that she said.

Neeheeowee patted the mare one more time, then coming around the animal, he stepped over toward Julia. He came up behind her and, placing one hand on her shoulder, he bent toward her, saying, "My regret over the fate of that trade lasted but a moment. If I could, I would give more for you now than all that I possessed at that time."

Julia spun around toward him. "Would you?"

Neeheeowee grinned, but he said nothing; instead, he pulled her into his embrace. He brought her head in so very close to his own and Julia, looking up at him, thought her world surely spun. She closed her eyes, bringing her head back to rest on his chest. And that's when she heard it, the whispered words that meant so much to her, "Do it again for you? Never doubt it," he said, and Julia hardly even dared to breathe.

Chapter 16

⌒◯◯⌒

Julia had prepared a stew for their evening meal and both she and Neeheeowee sat around the fire, satisfied, their hunger sated. Off to one side, the horses nickered to the accompaniment of one cricket after another while a thousand stars gleamed in a black sky overhead. Neither Neeheeowee nor Julia spoke. Neither one felt the need, their silent companionship enough.

At length, Julia said, "Tell me about the Lakota camp where Kristina lives. I know already that the Lakota are the same tribe as the Sioux, that the tribe calls itself the Lakota, that the name Sioux is a name given to them by the white man."

"*Haahe*, yes," Neeheeowee said, and then thought a moment. "There are seven bands of tribes within the Lakota," he began, "and your friend lives with her husband in the Minneconjou band. It is like any other Lakota camp, only the Minneconjou generally range a little north of the other bands. Their people are known for their excellence in hunting and in warfare as well as for their intelligence. They have many great orators, and their wisdom is always sought in council. Your friend does well for herself."

"I am so glad," Julia said. "Please, Neeheeowee, tell me about her life there."

He paused. "She and her husband, Tahiska, have three children now, I believe; a boy and two girls, and the children keep their mother and her many relatives busy."

Julia thought for a moment. "What do you mean *her* relatives? She left her mother and father behind her. How could she have relatives in a Lakota camp?"

"There are many rules of living amongst our people that may be different than yours," he said. "Let me explain. When Kristina came to live with the Lakota, she found herself amongst in-laws, and it is always hard for a new wife to settle in when she must always guard what she says. Around in-laws there are a great many taboos, and so Kristina was not able to find a place where she could relax. After a year, there was a man and his wife who saw that the young Kristina, though happy with her husband, could never be herself amongst the people. They took pity on her and because they had lost a daughter two seasons of the moon ago, they adopted Kristina into their own family, to replace the daughter they had lost. It is a pleasant situation for Kristina, for now there is always a place where she can go and never worry about doing or saying the wrong thing."

"That was a good thing they did for her."

"Yes," he said, "but now, too, they are happy grandparents, for her children are their own and are treated as though they are blood relatives. For our people, it is the same thing."

"I see," Julia said. "Tell me, Neeheeowee, do you like it amongst the Lakota?"

"Yes, particularly in certain bands of the tribe."

"With the Minneconjou?" she asked.

He nodded his head. "It is so."

Julia glanced at Neeheeowee. "What are their rules of living?"

"What do you mean?"

"Well," she said, "let us take a young couple—like us, for instance. Let us say that this young couple stole away to be married. Is there much trouble in the camp if they do this?"

Neeheeowee shrugged, giving her a knowing glance, but he said nothing. After a while he began, "It is always best for the girl if she is bought—that is if a suitor feels strongly enough about her to give horses or other gifts to the parents. A girl must guard her maidenhood well, for if she slips, and the boy throws her away after, the incident is never forgotten. She will never marry. But this rarely happens. Most elopements work out, and the parents and others in the kinship accept the girl's choice and everyone settles back down to the harmony of their lives. It is more often done in the Lakota camp than in the Cheyenne."

Julia paused while she mustered her courage, but she could not hold back for long, and finally she asked, "Would we be considered a married couple to the Lakota?"

Neeheeowee sent her a quick look. "*Hova'ahane,* no," he said.

"Why would we not?"

"Because," he said, "I do not consider us married. And there is the difference."

There was little Julia could say to that, and so, shifting away from Neeheeowee, she gazed out over the landscape.

"It is there, up ahead, only a few hours away."

"We have arrived so soon?" Julia asked Neeheeowee, who had just this moment dismounted. "I . . ." Julia looked down at herself, at the travel-weary dress she wore, at the moccasins, caked with dirt and grime. "I would like to freshen up, maybe wash my dress and bathe before we get to their camp."

Neeheeowee nodded, pointing to a stream that ran nearby. He smiled, then said, "It is so I thought. It is why we have stopped. We will both of us bathe and put on our best clothing before we reach the camp of my Minneconjou friends."

Julia smiled a relieved "thank-you" to Neeheeowee as she, too, dismounted, bringing her pony and her packhorse close to the stream for grazing, hobbling both.

"They know we are here."

Julia heard his deep voice and gasped. "They do? You mean the Minneconjou?"

"*Haahe*, yes," Neeheeowee said. "The scouts from the Minneconjou would have reported our party to their camp several days ago. I saw them watching us, and one of them I recognized. They will know it is I who approaches them. They may not know who you are, so I think that your friend, Kristina, will be surprised."

Julia sent Neeheeowee an acknowledgment with her smile and then glanced up toward him. "Where do you go to bathe?"

He smiled. "I will bathe here, too."

Julia's head came up in an instant. "That is not possible."

He lifted his shoulders. "There is nowhere else."

"There must be somewhere else. Neeheeowee, you know we cannot bathe in the same area. You know that if you watch me, or if I watch you . . . there . . ."

"I do not know anything of what you say. Do you think these last few days that I have not guarded you as you bathe? Do you think I haven't looked?"

"Yes, I knew you guarded me, but I didn't know

you were watching, too. Now I know. Now I would
. . . it would . . . I would . . . I could not do it, Neeheeowee."

He shrugged. "That is your choice."

It was the only thing he said before he proceeded
to untie his leggings and, finishing the job, threw
them off to the side.

Julia watched with something akin to amazement
and something else more akin to lust. "Neeheeowee,"
she said, "you cannot do this." Yet, for all her talk,
she did not take her gaze from him, not even after he
removed his moccasins and began to untie his breechcloth.

"I hear you," he replied to her. "But I do not think
you have it right. *You* seem to be the one who cannot
do this. *I* am going to bathe. Do you watch, then?"

"No, I . . ." Julia stood as though struck dumb. She
knew she should move away, or at least turn her head
away. She couldn't, however, do it.

She watched as he removed the breechcloth, drawing in her breath as she beheld the beauty of him, for
he stood before her now in nothing save the beaded
necklace that she had given him so long ago.

He looked over to her and, upon seeing her heated
gaze at him, he grew in size, Julia's eyes widening in
response to it.

"Do you forget your rules?" he asked, bringing Julia's attention straight up to his face.

She thought she saw him smile, but she couldn't be
certain. "No," she said, at last. "I do not. I will go up
the stream a little way and I will bathe there. I will
try not to disturb your bath."

He grinned. "I would like you to disturb my bath."

"Neeheeowee!"

"Julia!"

She sighed. "I cannot do it. I resolved to myself—"

He'd taken a step toward her.

"Neeheeowee, you said that you would help me to do this."

He took another step. "I said I would try."

"You are not trying."

"I am." He suddenly stopped and breathed out loudly. "I find I grow weary of this, and I find I want you, Julia. I want you in my arms, I want you to lie with me in my sleeping robes. I want to feel you next to me when I awaken each morning. I—"

"Neeheeowee!" She had stopped the flow of his words, but she couldn't stop the damage done to her strength. She yearned for him, and she found herself aching for him in ways that were entirely feminine. But she managed to say, "Marry me, then," before, with the sweep of her arm, she flung back her hair.

Neeheeowee became sober all at once. "You know I cannot marry you, Julia, but I will promise you that I will love you all of my life." He closed the gap between them with a quick step and, pulling her in toward him, so very, very gently, he kissed her. "Here," he said, stepping back from her. He pointed to her heart, resting his hand there. "Here I feel the beating of your heart telling me of your desire for me. So, too, does mine beat. So, too, do I love you. There is nothing more that I can give you but this. But this I give you freely."

Dark eyes stared down into her own as one slow moment after another passed. "Neeheeowee," she said at last, "you must know that I love you, too, but without marriage I cannot—"

"Shh," he said. "I know. I do not fault you for what you do, it is only that I want you. I—"

"Neeheeowee, I can't. I—"

She had no chance to say more. Neeheeowee had already taken her lips against his as though in coup. His tongue explored her mouth, then left it to trail

kisses over her cheeks, her eyes, her brows, back to
her lips, over to her ear, down her neck. She was
swept up in the excitement of his kiss, and Julia felt
herself weakening with the need for fulfillment.

"Julia," he said, his head coming up for a moment.
"Touch me."

"Neeheeowee, I can't—"

"I need to feel your hands on me."

Julia gulped, breathing in his intoxicating scent as
she did so. Never had she wanted to do something
more in her life. Never had she felt that she couldn't.
Still . . .

She reached out toward him, toward his engorged
shaft. She touched him, gently at first and then with
more and more vigor.

She heard his indrawn breath and felt her resolve
weakening, her own needs beginning to take prece-
dence over her conscience.

"Neeheeowee, please. I can't . . . I . . ."

He shuddered, and though he moaned, he drew her
hand away from him all the same. "Yes, I know," he
said, and pulling her in closely toward him, he rested
his chin upon the top of her head. "I know you cannot
do this. I know I have tested you too far. And though
I may regret it in the days yet to come, I will honor
your requests. But know this, Julia, married or not,
with me or not, I vow to you that I will love you the
rest of my life."

And with this said, Neeheeowee stepped away
from her, turned, and sprinted toward the water, div-
ing in and swimming away with all the vigor of love
unrequited.

And Julia, watching him, pondered, if only for a
short while, the wisdom of letting him go.

Chapter 17

"**J**ulia!" Kristina called out, and Julia turned her head to catch sight of her friend, waving. Julia laughed, then waved back, finding herself crying back, "Kristina," despite the fact that there were other people she did not know huddling around her.

"Julia!" Kristina hollered again, and Julia saw her friend hurrying through the crowd. Julia and Nee-heeowee had just arrived at the Minneconjou camp minutes ago, there to be met by a group of perhaps fifty to sixty people.

"Kristina!" Julia reached down to grab her friend's hand as Kristina rushed up to her. Julia bent down, giving her friend a hug. "Oh, how I have missed you."

Kristina grinned. "And how I have missed you," Kristina said, keeping step alongside the pony Julia rode, for the animal had never stopped moving. The two friends clasped hands. "I hope you have come to see me," Kristina said, "Although I'm sure you have news from home, I do hope you have come here with the desire of visiting and enjoying yourself."

Julia beamed down at her friend. "Yes," she said. "I have come here for all those reasons, plus one other."

"*Ma!*" Kristina uttered the Lakota expression. "It probably won't take me long to discover what that other reason is, especially if the reason is male and is under thirty years of age."

Julia grinned. "You still know me well, don't you? I guess some things never change."

Kristina chuckled. "Come, let me lead you to my lodge. We can let one of the boys in camp take care of your pony while you and I catch up on all the latest news and gossip."

"Yes," Julia said. "I would like that."

"I thought you would," Kristina said, and, taking hold of the pony's reins, Kristina set out toward her lodge.

Once there, Kristina called to a small boy and, handing him the pony's reins, she asked him to care for the animal in her stead. The young boy nodded eagerly and, in the midst of a rush of Lakota words, led the pony away.

"Come inside," Kristina beckoned Julia, holding up the rawhide covering to the entryway. "I have so many questions for you, I barely know where to start, but let me ask you this one first: However did you run into Neeheeowee again?"

Julia grinned and cast a quick look up toward the heavens. "That is a long story. If you have several days, I might be able to tell it all."

Kristina nodded. "It is one of those stories, is it? I'm fascinated. Come on in. I'll make us some coffee."

"You have coffee?"

Kristina nodded.

"Ah, I'd love some," Julia said, and bent down to enter the tepee. She looked up, noting at once the interesting array of Indian versus American trade articles strewn throughout the dwelling.

In one corner stood Tahiska's bow and backrest; in another lay Kristina's guitar. Hanging from the tepee lining were Tahiska's quiver and arrows as well as a flower arrangement from Kristina. Over to the right was an Indian cradle board and next to it an actual cradle. It went on and on. Here was Tahiska's medicine bag, there were Kristina's cups and saucers.

Julia smiled, her mood lightening to see that Kristina had been able to keep a part of her own culture with her.

"You seem to have made your mark here in Indian society. Tell me, Kristina." Julia paused. "Has it been difficult to blend the two cultures together?"

Kristina glanced at her friend from over her shoulder. "Not very," she said. "Tahiska indulges me."

"I see," Julia said. "And do you nag him just a little to buy some of these things for you?"

Kristina laughed. "Often," she said. "Often. But he never seems to mind. He just figures out a way to trade for these things and before I know it, I have them."

Julia grinned. "I envy you."

Kristina, two cups of coffee in her hand, came around to sit beside Julia. "Now, I wonder," she began, "why you would envy me?"

Julia shrugged.

And Kristina leaned forward. "It couldn't be because of the certain man who brought you here, could it? He didn't capture you, did he?"

"No!"

Kristina smiled. "That is good. That is one part of Indian culture that I cannot quite condone, although I suppose I can understand it a little. Listen, Julia, it has not been that difficult bridging these two cultures. Every society has something to recommend it, and so it is with Indian society. There are many things that I could teach you that I think you would enjoy. And the life here is very independent, very free. There is much about the Lakota to recommend them. Above

all, though, I couldn't think of being anywhere else
but with Tahiska." Kristina cast a shrewd glance at
her friend. "Which reminds me . . . what *are* you doing with Neeheeowee and why are you dressed in
Indian clothing?"

Julia rolled her eyes and grinned. "It is a very long
story."

"*Ma!*" Kristina said. "It is good that we have a very
long day stretching out before us then, because I will
want to hear every single little detail."

Julia laughed, and, reaching out to take hold of her
friend's hand, she proceeded to tell Kristina everything, right from the beginning.

"And so Kenneth is dead now?"

"Yes," Julia said. "It was not a good marriage, Kristina. Kenneth was too wound up in himself and his
own problems to be a good husband and he was often
cruel to me."

"Oh, I am so sorry."

Julia shrugged. "I have not mourned him much.
Not as much as I should."

Kristina laid her hand over Julia's. "I can understand. If I were in your same place, I would not
mourn him too much either."

Julia sighed. She and Kristina had been reclining
inside the tepee now for quite some time, talking, gos-
siping, catching up on the latest news. Julia began to
worry that she was keeping Kristina from fixing the
evening meal, but when she queried Kristina about it,
Kristina waved away her concern, saying that her
mother-in-law would see to their supper. "She knows
you and I will be talking away most of the day," Kristina had said. "Don't worry about it. Tahiska's mother
will enjoy helping us."

Julia had relaxed after that and had related to Kristina all the facts of her capture, Neeheeowee's rescue

of her, and, minus a few pertinent facts, had told how she had asked Neeheeowee to bring her here.

Kristina had listened, had smiled and then had said, "He's quite a handsome warrior, is he not?" to which Julia had not responded at all. But Kristina had gone on to say, "Someday when he has put his past behind him, he will make a fine husband. In the meantime he can be moody and distant, although . . ." Here Kristina had leaned in toward Julia, dropping her voice to a whisper. "Wouldn't you say both he and Tahiska fill out a breechcloth well?"

And to Julia's shocked giggle, Kristina grinned. "You can stay here with me," Kristina went on to say, "while Neeheeowee will sleep in the guest lodge, safely away from you. I would presume," she said, "that you presented quite a temptation to him."

And when Julia burst out with a spurt of laughter, she assumed Kristina had her answer.

The evening meal had come and gone, and while Tahiska and Neeheeowee sat outside the tepee, relating stories of their various coups, Julia and Kristina reclined inside catching up on more news, more gossip and, after introductions had been made, teasing the children. Julia had learned that Kristina and Tahiska had three children; *Wowaste*, or Goodness, the eldest; *Cikala Peta*, Little Fire, the younger girl; and *Keya*, Turtle, the youngest of the three and the only boy. The two girls sat with their mother and their newest "aunt," while *Keya*, who was no more than two years old, alternated between staying with the men outside and venturing back inside to his mother, as though to ensure she was still there for him.

Kristina and Julia each leaned back against a willow backrest, their legs stretched out before them and crossed at the ankle.

"So tell me," Julia had said after a while. "Are you happy in your new life here?"

"I am happy," Kristina answered, nodding at the same time. "Though at first it was very hard. There are many customs and taboos here and I knew none of them. I'm afraid I made more enemies than friends when I first arrived. And, of course, getting used to sleeping on the ground took some adjustment."

"Yes," Julia said. "I can see how that would be tough. Do you ever regret making the decision that you did?"

Kristina thought for just a moment, her gaze taking in the tepee, her children, skirting to the tepee entrance, where her husband sat outside. She sighed. "No, I don't regret it," she said. "Without Tahiska, I would be half-alive. I have discovered also that white society is not all that it's made out to be. And I miss very little of it, though I do wish from time to time that I could get news of how things are at home. My father has visited us twice, and I hear my mother went back East. But other than that I have no news of the fort, and I wonder how things are there. And," she said, gazing over to Julia, "I have wondered about you. I have worried. I did not think Kenneth would make you a very good husband. I didn't want to say anything to you at the time, but after the way he treated Tahiska, I never wanted to have anything to do with that man again."

Julia gave Kristina a smile that was half–self-conscious, half-apologetic. "You were right," Julia said. "He did not make a good husband."

"But Neeheeowee will," Kristina said. "Someday."

"Yes," Julia agreed. "But that day may not be until I am an old lady and much past the age of needing a husband. Though perhaps it is a good thing that Neeheeowee does not wish to marry me. I am not all that certain I *want* to remain in Indian society."

Kristina glanced up quickly, Julia noted, though all Kristina said was, "I see." A few moments passed before she added, "Have you always felt this way?"

Julia shook her head. "No," she said. "Not at the beginning. When Neeheeowee first asked me to stay with him, to come with him, I thought I might be able to make the change, but now ... Though I did not find much happiness in the white culture, Kristina, I am not convinced I would find it any more pleasant here. There is too much here that is foreign to me, too much I don't understand. No, I think perhaps it is for the best. If Neeheeowee truly wanted to marry me, I am afraid my feelings for him would force me to stay here and I'm not entirely certain, the more I think about it, that this is what I want."

"I see," Kristina said again. "Perhaps you had better tell me again how Neeheeowee rescued you. I'm afraid I didn't understand it all."

Julia sat forward, though her gaze centered downward. "He bargained for me. He had eight fine ponies he had brought to trade. He traded them for me."

"*Maaa*! Tell me it is not so."

Julia glanced up suddenly, sending a startled glance to her friend. "Is there something unusual with that?"

Kristina nodded. "It is a high price to pay for a woman, even though he was rescuing you. Just so you know, most men give one, maybe two horses to the parents of a young girl when they seek her hand in marriage, although not always do they give that much and sometimes nothing is given for the girl at all."

"But you ... Tahiska brought in plenty of horses for you."

"Yes," Kristina said, "but that was an unusual situation, for my father did not know of our marriage. Julia"—Kristina's voice was firm—"you may not realize it, Neeheeowee may not see it, but the man does truly love you if he did such a thing for you."

Julia stared at her friend. "He did it as a point of honor, he told me. I was a friend."

"Bah, he may have told himself that, he may even believe it. But I know that no man will give that many horses away for a woman unless he truly loves her. Now tell me again, what was it he did after he paid the price for you?"

"He took me home to Fort Leavenworth."

"Ah." Kristina nodded her head. "An honorable thing for him to do. What happened then?"

"Well, it was strange at first," Julia said. "All the way there, Neeheeowee barely paid me any attention. Nor did he speak to me, since we neither one remembered that we could communicate in Lakota, and you know I never did master that sign language. Kristina"—Julia gazed up to her friend in earnest—"I almost left him there, I almost rode back to Fort Leavenworth, but at the last moment Neeheeowee asked me to stay . . . in Lakota. It took me a while to translate it because I had forgotten the language. But when I did, when I realized he wanted me to stay, I . . . Kristina, I had fallen in love with Neeheeowee on that trip. I came riding back to him. I am not so sure now, however, that I did the right thing."

"No," Kristina said emphatically. "You did the right thing. It is good."

Julia frowned. "You think so?"

Kristina nodded. "Yes, I do. You loved him enough to leave your home, all that you knew, for him. This love that you two share . . ."

"Yes?"

"It is good, I think." Kristina paused. She chewed on her lip for a moment before she said, "But he will not marry you."

"Yes, he says he cannot." Julia lifted her shoulders, looking away. "He is haunted by his past, Kristina, and I don't know how to set him free of it. Nor am I certain I want to. These things he has told me, these customs and beliefs he holds are much too strange for me. He tells me he made vows to his dead wife and child not only to avenge their deaths, but to remain forever tied to them in marriage. He vowed he would never marry again, I believe. In his heart, he is not free and Kristina, though I long to be with him, I cannot understand him nor will I stay with him unless we are married. So you see, there is not much that can be done for us. A joining between the two of us? It may never happen."

"Hum . . ." Kristina sat for a moment, while her two little girls looked on, watching. At length, Kristina said, "I will need to think on this, my friend. This is truly a dilemma. It is odd. Neeheeowee has been like a shell of a man for these past five years, and all who know him realize that he has made it the purpose of his life to avenge the deaths of his wife and child. That is why it is good to see him so happy. I have not seen him this way in many years. But you are right. This man is not free. Still, do not give up hope. You know that he loves you and when you have love, anything is possible. I will have to see what can be done about your dilemma. In the meantime, please stay with us. You are my dearest and best friend; I will do whatever I can for you."

Julia smiled, taking Kristina's hand in her own. "Thank you," she said.

Kristina nodded, squeezing Julia's hand. "Take heart, my friend," Kristina said. "You are good for Neeheeowee, and he will someday be a good influence on you, too. I am sure of it. Come now," Kristina said, sitting forward, "I have a surprise for you," she said, holding up a white elkskin dress she had earlier set before them. She gestured toward the dress. "This dress? It is now yours. I wish to honor you in the tradition of the Lakota. It is odd. In the white man's world, when you have a special day, you receive presents. Here, on a special day, you give gifts away, or others in your family may honor you by giving gifts away in your name. The way the people think here is different from what you and I were used to. I am now giving you this dress to show you my sincerity. I wish to make you my sister, *hakataya*. From here on, throughout our camp, I would like you to be known as my sister, my kin."

"Your kin? You don't mean as in a real—"

"Sister?" Kristina queried. "Yes, I do. I wish to give you the highest honor a woman can bestow upon another. I remember seven years ago when no one in the fort would stand beside me. You did. You were always my friend without question. I have never forgotten that. And now that I have the chance to do something for you, I am happy to be able to do it. Sister."

"Kristina!" Julia cried and, sitting up, leaned over to hug her friend. "Always," Julia said, "we will be friends."

"*Hau, hau kola*, my friend, Tahiska," Neeheeowee said as the two of them sat outside Tahiska's lodge. They had been discussing many things, most of them trivial, but now Neeheeowee wished to ask his friend some serious questions. He leaned forward. "Tell me again," he said, "how you counted coup on the Crow. I have heard of the story all the way into the country of the southern Cheyenne. I have been waiting to see you to ask you about it myself."

Tahiska grinned. "Ah, yes. The Crow. I will tell it to you if you truly wish it, do you?"

Neeheeowee nodded. "I have been waiting to hear the story from you."

"Ah, I see," Tahiska said. He sat back, then began, "It was almost one full season ago. It was a cool and clear morning and I was out on the hunt. None of the scouts had seen the enemy and so none were on the alert for danger." Tahiska paused. "I saw the tracks in the snow and I knew, as you would, too, that the tracks were fresh and were not Lakota-made. They were Crow. I sneaked in upon the Crow, having been looking out for them, and when I found them, I saw that they were cold and were miserable, although determined to raid our camp for food. That's when I decided to have some fun."

Neeheeowee nodded his head. "What did you do?"

"Well, you know that I have always been able to run quickly. That morning my wife had given me a new robe. It was quite long and covered me from head to toe. I looked up and saw a tree branch about my height and so I walked into the Crow camp alone, greeting them. But then I threw my robe over my shoulder, covering my entire body from them while carefully hanging the robe on the branch. I ducked down and ran away as silently as I could and disappeared into the growth of trees while I watched them throw their spears and arrows at the robe. When they found out nothing was there, that their spears and arrows had hit nothing, they became quite alarmed, thinking me a ghost. They started to run home. I followed them, playing the same trick on them again and again. It was quite amusing."

"*Eaaa*. The story is better when you tell it. It is such a good tale. Your children will be proud to carry the story on down to their children."

Tahiska smiled. "I would hope so," he said.

Silence ensued between the two men. At length, Tahiska asked, "Do you still seek out the Pawnee who murdered your wife and child?"

Neeheeowee nodded his head.

Tahiska sat silently a moment more. "I would help you rout out this enemy and be done with it so that you can start your new life." It was all Tahiska would say on the subject of Neeheeowee's arriving in their camp with Julia. It was all a man would ever say to another man about so personal a matter. No questions asked, the best always assumed.

But Neeheeowee only shook his head. "I have always sought out these murderers myself. I will continue to look for them alone."

"I know this, but we have made the pledge of the *kola*," Tahiska said. "We have made the man's pledge, the pledge of brotherhood, to live and die for one another. Haven't I vowed to treat any concern you may have as my own? Is it not so that I should help you?"

Neeheeowee frowned. "What you say is true, my friend, but we have talked on this before, and nothing has happened since then to make me change my mind. You know that this is something I must do myself."

Tahiska nodded his head, saying, "Yes, I know the way that you feel about this. I will not press you. At least, not now. But come," he said, getting to his feet, "*Wanituka*, my friend. You are tired. I will show you to the guest lodge."

"The guest lodge?"

"Yes," Tahiska replied. "Julia stays with us and though I know, by custom, you would usually stay with us, too, I sense there is much more between you and the white woman than what ordinarily passes for friendship. I am afraid she would prove too great a temptation to you. Or am I wrong? Is there something you need to tell me? You haven't made her your wife, have you?"

"No," Neeheeowee said. "But we have been together now for so long, I had thought to keep her with me."

"Not in my lodge." Tahiska grinned. "My wife would never cease to talk about it if I did such a thing.

Have pity on me, my friend. I wish to love my wife, not listen to her scoldings."

Tahiska chuckled and Neeheeowee, shaking his head, smiled.

The afternoon stretched out warm and sunny before them. Both Kristina and Julia reclined beneath the shade of a cottonwood tree, the heat keeping the women from engaging in too strenuous a task. Kristina worked over a pair of moccasins, ornamenting them for her son, while Julia relaxed against the tree. A clear, effervescing stream rushed past them as though in a hurry to get somewhere, the constant gurgling and babbling of its waters a welcome background noise to the women's talk. Julia sat up, and, rising to her feet, walked a few steps down to the water. She dipped a hand into its cool depth and sighed.

"Did you know," Kristina said, looking up, "that the Indians believe that it is water that gives life? It is why each morning the young girls refill the water bags. Water that has sat all day is considered 'dead.'"

Julia smiled. "No, I didn't know that. I guess that explains why Neeheeowee refilled the water bags every morning as we journeyed. You have learned many of their beliefs, I see. What do you think of their convictions? Don't you consider them primitive?"

Kristina gazed away, seemingly lost in thought for a time. Finally, she said, "Some of their beliefs I consider primitive, yes, for they are based on fear and superstition. But I have found their religion to be much the same as ours; there is no idol worship and there is so much good that I see here in their everyday life, so much understanding of life that I wonder if our own civilization wouldn't be better if we understood the Indian a little more."

Julia said nothing, simply gazing back at her friend, and, after a while, Kristina put down the moccasins she had been working on and sat forward. "For instance," Kristina began, "have you noticed the way the Indians handle their children? It is incredible. I had never witnessed anything like it. Whipping is unheard of here, and a parent who would do it would be shunned and perhaps ostracized by the rest of the tribe. Children are taught by appealing to their sense of duty and to their desire to help and contribute to the family. They are rarely scolded, but as soon as they have their senses about them, they are talked to as though they were adult, they are told that such and such behavior will either benefit them in later life or not. The Indian appeals to the child's desire to take pride in himself, showing the youngsters examples of bravery and stellar behavior that are revered throughout the tribe. In such a way the child grows up deciding for himself what is a correct action or what is not."

"Truly," Julia said, "that is good. I have seen this, too, in Neeheeowee. I have found Neeheeowee to be wise beyond his years. Plus," she said, "he has never treated me with anything but kindness. It is odd"— Julia straightened away to look more directly at Kristina—"he is everything a man should be, honorable and honest beyond belief, brave and willing to risk his life, and yet, in all his dealings with me, he listens without scolding, often taking my advice. I have never known anyone like him."

Kristina grinned. "*Ma*! So spoken like a woman in love. I am glad to hear it."

Julia grimaced and shook her head.

At that moment, Keya, or Turtle, Kristina's youngest child, rushed up to his mother, his sister, Wowaste, in quick pursuit. Julia surveyed the young boy and his sister, deciding that both had the best, yet different features of their parents. Keya had the coloring of his father, while his sister's skin color looked just slightly darker than Kristina's. The young boy's hair boasted golden highlights in its dark depth, a legacy from his mother, while his sister's was a deep, rich black. Julia had noticed that both girls had inherited the coal black eyes from their father, while Keya's were a bright green. In all three children the combination of white and Indian blood had created startling beauty, and Julia felt certain that in years to come, all three offspring might become the breakers of hearts. Certainly, she thought, there would be no absence of suitors.

But for the time being, the boy needed the comfort of his mother's arms, whom he sought out often, while his sister, four years older, always accompanied him, it being her duty to watch over him. Wowaste came to sit by Julia, while her younger sister, Cikala Peta, who usually played with other girls her own age, decided to join her mother, too, taking her place quietly at her mother's feet. Perhaps it was curiosity about their newest aunt which kept them so close to their mother's side this day. The cause of it didn't matter to Julia. She enjoyed each moment she spent with the children.

Julia had observed that Kristina followed the many Indian traditions in the raising of her children, though there was one thing she did that was entirely different from anything else done within the tribe: she taught her children to read, an action that couldn't help but bring good things not only to her children, but to the rest of her tribe, also.

Her tribe? Julia scoffed at herself. Since when had she begun thinking of Kristina as Indian?

Kristina's son looked toward Julia now, and, startling Julia, he said, "*Waste Win*," pretty woman, pointing toward Julia.

And while Kristina crooned softly to the little boy on the ill manners of pointing, Julia grinned down at the lad. He looked at Julia, he stared, and then transferring his attention from his mother to Julia, he hopped off his mother's lap and came to sit on Julia's, where he proceeded to play with Julia's dark hair, the lad murmuring words of no meaning in her ear.

Kristina smiled, and in English she said, "He is so good-hearted, this one. But already, he loves the women, and often goes from woman to woman kissing them. I'm afraid he could cause trouble to a young girl's heart when he gets a little older."

Julia laughed. "I think you speak the truth on that."

Kristina smiled. At length, she sighed. "My life here is good," she said. "Tahiska thinks I work hard, but look at me. I sit out here, in the cool shade beneath a cottonwood tree, working over a pair of moccasins. The work is not difficult and is not great and no one puts tremendous demands on me, seemingly happy at whatever I manage to produce." Kristina paused, then looking up at Julia, said, "But I miss my family sometimes, my father. I think next year, if we have a good year hunting, I will take the children and go to see my father. What do you think?"

Julia frowned. "I wouldn't do it."

"Why not?"

Julia looked away, her gaze catching onto a piece of rawhide left hanging in the sun to dry. "It is hard to explain. But there is more and more animosity between the white people and the Indian. As Easterners flood our fort going west, they bring with them ever new and unusual prejudices. Often the white people I have encountered do not distinguish between one Indian tribe and another, thinking they can inflict damage on an innocent tribe for the wrongdoing of another. If you go back, Kristina, they might not let you come back here again. People will think you have lost your mind to want to stay with the Indians."

Julia paused, looking back toward her friend. "When we stopped at Bent's Fort on our way here," Julia continued, "there was ever the threat of someone discovering I was white and taking me away from Neeheeowee. It is why I dressed as an Indian. It is why I still am dressed like one."

"But I have family and friends back there, my father—"

"Let him come and see you. He is a good man. He would not take steps to hurt you. But there are others who would. Kristina, I have seen it. Some white men have strange ideas about the freedom of white women. Hatred grows within the white man's fort, and I fear that soon it will overwhelm any real attempts to make peace between our two races. If you love your husband and wish to stay with him, do not go back." Julia tried to ease the harshness of her words by smiling, though ultimately, she began again, saying, "Kristina, if you went back, I'm afraid we'd see Tahiska taking on the entire cavalry in war." Julia chuckled a little. "It would be something to see though, wouldn't it?"

Kristina smirked. "In thought, yes. But I think you are right. I do not wish to see such a thing take place in fact. We will see. Maybe I could have scouts go there and see what is there for themselves, or perhaps I could send word back to my father." She sat back. "I will think of something."

Julia smiled. "As I will, too, my friend. As I will, too," she said, pretending fear as Keya got down on his knees to threaten her with an invisible bow and arrow. The young boy laughed as did his two sisters, and before long the children were frolicking about again, ever seeking new adventures.

Chapter 18

Kristina and Julia sat beneath the same cotton-wood tree the next day. The temperature was simmering and, to distract them from the heat, Kristina had collected her guitar from her tepee. She, along with her three children and Julia, whiled away the afternoon beside the clear, running stream. Kristina strummed out the many songs she remembered while Julia hummed along, sometimes even singing.

They had just finished one particular melody when Julia said, "I don't recall you taking your guitar along when you left with Tahiska seven years ago."

"I didn't," Kristina said, scooting over a little when the sun hit her full in the face. "Tahiska traded many a buffalo robe for this at one of the trading posts. He knew how much I missed being able to play music, and so he bargained for this shortly after we were married. My only frustration is that I can hardly keep it in tune."

"Ah, yes, I can understand that," Julia said. She looked around her, hearing the ever-present drumming in the background. "You must feel strange here, with all this music that is so monotone and unmelodic—and the dancing—why, it would appear that only the men are allowed to dance, or so it seems to me."

Kristina grinned. "Actually," she said, "that isn't so."

"Isn't it?"

"No," Kristina said. "I have to admit, when I first came here, I thought their songs lacked melody and inspiration, too. But then I started listening, I started asking questions. And while it's true that their songs have little harmony as you and I know it, they do have a structure. Here, I'll show you. Listen carefully. Do you hear the drums in the distance?"

Julia nodded.

"Good, now, do you hear the men singing?"

"Yes."

"All right now, do you hear that one voice that started singing before the others?"

"Yes," Julia said, "I think so."

"Good. That is the lead singer. Now here comes the second voice and then the others. It isn't the drums that set the pace of the song. It is the lead singer."

Julia grinned. "Is that so?"

Kristina laughed, nudging Julia with her elbow. "Behave yourself. Now, here is something else you should know," Kristina said. "Did you hear those three heavy beats in the middle of the song? Those are what the people call honor beats. They are usually in the middle of the song. It has a pace, a sort of movement to it. You see?"

Julia grinned. "That's remarkable. Leave it to you, Kristina, to figure out the complexities of an Indian song. I will have to listen to the music more carefully and find these things in there myself. I have noticed that Neeheeowee often sings to himself. Sometimes I think he makes up the songs."

"That is probably true."

Julia sat back against the cottonwood tree and

closed her eyes. "Kristina," she said, after a moment, "how about dancing? Don't you miss dancing?"

Kristina smiled. "When you have a husband who looks like mine does in only breechcloth and moccasins, one does not think of dancing too often."

Julia giggled, Kristina joining in with her. And soon all three young children chimed in, too, just as though they had understood every word the women said, though the women spoke distinctly in English.

"Here," Kristina said after a while, and transferred Keya to the lap of her eldest daughter. "If you want to know about dancing, let me show you a dance I saw a young girl of the Omaha tribe do. I have heard that it is starting to be a dance women in some of the tribes are doing. I don't know about that, and no one seems to know where the dance originated, but it is quite pretty."

"But I thought that Indian women didn't dance."

"Nonsense," Kristina said. "Maybe the women don't do the wild contortions that the men do, and maybe the women aren't always allowed within the circle to dance, but we certainly dance," she said, and Julia smiled as she caught the "we dance" in Kristina's words.

"Now let me show you this particular step, but I need a robe, preferably a small one to do it. May I use yours?"

Julia nodded and handed Kristina her elkskin robe, which looked more like a shawl with fringe.

"Now watch." Kristina waited for the beat of the drum, then, coming up on her toes and stepping in time to the beat, she spread her arms, the shawl fanning out around her as though she had wings. Fringe from her dress, and from the shawl, swayed like prairie grass waving in the wind. And while Julia watched, Kristina swayed, turning in circles, her arms outspread, always in time to the drum.

She stopped, smiled, and said, "See?" before dipping her head in a quick "bow."

Julia grinned and clapped, singing out a "Hear, hear," while the children, in perfect imitation of Julia, added to the noise.

"That was a lovely dance," Julia said, after Kristina had returned to her seat beneath the tree. "What is it called?"

Kristina shook her head. "I honestly don't know. As I said, we first saw it when someone from the Omaha tribe danced it at the summer get-together last year."

"Will you teach it to me?"

"Of course," Kristina said. "Do you want to try now?"

Julia nodded.

"This is good," Kristina said, coming up onto her knees. "Now the first thing I must tell you about this is that in Indian dancing, a woman must always conduct herself in an honorable, yet proud fashion. Others will look to her to see that she feels pride for herself. To do this, the woman seldom moves from her waist up. Movement is done from her feet, her legs, her knees. It's an up-and-down movement. Here, watch."

Again, Kristina rose, indicating the correct way to dance. "Of course," Kristina said, "to be a really good dancer, a woman must dance from her heart, she must dance what she feels inside. It is not always easy to accomplish both of these things, but if a woman manages to do it, she is greatly admired."

"I see," Julia said, though, in truth, she wasn't sure that she did.

One must dance from the heart? A woman must dance what she feels? What did that mean? Had she ever, in all the parties she had attended, danced from the heart?

In truth, Julia couldn't be certain, and as she reminisced over the past, she began to wonder about this phrase. Dance from the heart?

Perhaps, she decided, she would have to know her heart before she could express whatever was in it. Was that the key?

Whatever it was, it left Julia pondering over it for many, many days to come.

As the days passed, Julia began to see less and less of Neeheeowee and more and more of the women. It was the way of the camp circle. Women spoke to women; men to men. And while they did not avoid one another in public, married couples tended to drift toward the more socially accepted circles—men with men and women with women.

Julia missed Neeheeowee. She missed his quiet talks with her, the baritone of his voice, his way of joking with her, the way he touched her, the feel of his skin against her. She even missed the aromatic scent of his skin, and she began to wonder at the wisdom of keeping him at a distance.

She kept him company only at their evening meal, when Neeheeowee joined Tahiska's family circle. With both Tahiska and Neeheeowee providing food for the family, Kristina and Julia found themselves with an abundance of meat and often the evening meal would include others in the camp, who were themselves unable to provide such quantities of meat. It seemed to Julia that it was during this time that Neeheeowee should have lavished her with great attention, but he didn't; often he sat alone, moody and sullen amidst the gaiety of feasting.

He often stared at her, and Julia caught his gaze upon her more often than not, but he never spoke to her, nor otherwise approached her. And Julia began to despair.

She said as much to Kristina.

But Kristina shrugged off Julia's comments, saying only, "He will soon change. He is only sulking. Sometimes a woman has to be strong and allow the man time to ponder what he is missing."

But Julia was far from comforted.

And then it happened after they had been in the Minneconjou camp a little over two weeks. Julia had begun to know a few of the other Indian women by sight if not by name. One of them, Kokomikeeis, a very pretty Indian woman, spoke to Julia often, and Julia had soon recognized the woman as the wife to Wahtapah, another of Tahiska's friends who had accompanied him into Fort Leavenworth seven and one-half years ago.

That same woman approached Julia now, and, smiling at her, Kokomikeeis took Julia's hand. "Come," she said. "The women are all gathering into *tiyospaye* parties, or groups of friends. It is time for us to gather the *hu-te* or the *pomme blanche*, as the French say, the root that grows out on the prairie. If we wait much longer, the roots will no longer be good. Come, your sister Kristina and I want you in our party."

Kokomikeeis hurried with Julia through the camp, toward the side of the circle that faced the valley, explaining that the women were going to dig roots this day. Julia was amazed to see that Kokomikeeis acted as though it was a great social event.

It turned out that it was.

Julia heard the voices of the other women before she came in sight of them; the incessant chatter, the unrestrained laughter and bantering of the women as they told jokes, some lustier than others. Julia smiled at one particularly funny story, and lifted her head to see a gathering of perhaps fifty to sixty women. She heard the sudden cries of joy as the women caught sight of her and soon she found herself surrounded by a party of young women and girls.

They were going root digging, a chore that seemed to Julia as if it should have been laborious and difficult. It didn't happen to be that way.

The women set off in groups, many of them carrying awnings to set up and use as shade. Once they came out onto the prairie, the women set down their water and any food they had brought with them in the shade and, leaving only a few young girls to watch over their things, the entire group of women scattered out onto the prairie, hunting for roots.

Julia followed Kristina, who had given her a "root-digger," a stick made for just such a purpose. Julia bent down, and, as she worked, she began to smile. The women truly made this a party. There were jokes bantered about that would have made even the most seasoned soldier blush, and Julia began to giggle at the ridiculousness of them. Feminine laughter resounded throughout the valley, with an occasional barking to a child who had drifted into danger, or a shriek as someone found a particularly great source of roots.

And before Julia knew it, it was noon, a time to quit the work and rest.

They came back to the awning and seated themselves into several high-spirited groups. They had just finished their meal, when up on a hilltop came a sight Julia thought most peculiar: There upon the hill stood several of the young men and teenage boys from the camp. The women, upon seeing them, instantly flew into furious chatters, each one quickly gathering up their roots and running out en masse onto the prairie.

"Come on." Kristina rose, pulling Julia up with her as she jostled Julia onward toward the group. "Now is the fun part."

"The fun part?"

"Yes," Kristina whispered excitedly. "It is a game. The young men and boys up there are going to come down here and try to steal our roots. They call it counting coup. We call it defending our home. You are allowed to throw as many roots at an attacker as you can and he will try to get to you and steal your roots. If he steals them, he gets to keep them."

And so it was that Julia found herself stretched out atop a small hill, throwing roots at various teenage and young men. But it wasn't until the game was almost over that she saw Neeheeowee running toward her.

Immediately, she grabbed any roots she had remaining and threw them, one at a time, at him. Neeheeowee dodged them all, coming closer and closer to her. She burst out with laughter as he came right up to her and, bending over, took all of her roots.

"You can't have them," Julia cried out to him and, tripping him, pulled him down to her just as he'd started to leave.

He stumbled over onto her, the weight of his fall causing the both of them to roll over and over, down, down the hill.

He laughed, the sound of his masculine voice a sweet harmony to her ears. They continued to roll, over and over, until they stopped, and Neeheeowee became the clear victor in the fight, coming up on top of her.

Grinning at her, he said, "I count coup on you, which makes you my own. And this"—he suddenly gazed down at her, his look potent—"is your punishment." And he kissed her. Right there on the prairie, before the multitude of maybe a hundred pairs of eyes, he kissed her.

It should have been a sweet peck. It wasn't.

He kissed her with all the fervor of one who has been away from his love much too long. His tongue swept into her mouth, his teeth nibbled at her lips and he rained kisses over her face, her eyes, her nose, her ears, her cheeks. It was as though he couldn't get enough of her.

And Julia, in a gesture of sweet rapture, surrendered to his potent power.

Still, it was some moments before Kristina came upon them and giggling, she said, "Come on you two, before you become the gossip of every lodge in the camp circle."

But when they didn't move, when they made no attempt to pull away from one another, Kristina simply ushered the others in their party away, leaving the lovers to reacquaint themselves with one another as best they could out there upon the prairie.

Julia and Neeheeowee sat in the honor place within Tahiska and Kristina's lodge. It was an area closer to the entrance which most Indians kept to show recognition to visitors and guests, it being easier from that vantage point either to enter or to leave the tepee. As is the way of things, it was the general custom that when in the lodge, the women sat with women and the men with men, but tonight the couples had gravitated toward one another and no one seemed to mind, least of all Julia.

Tahiska had passed around a pipe to Neeheeowee and the two men were smoking comfortably when there came a scratch at the entryway, and a male voice asking to come inside. Tahiska answered the call and bid the visitor to enter. Wahtapah pushed back the entrance flap and both he and his wife, Kokomikeeis, filed into the tepee.

Julia was supposed to move to accommodate them, but she didn't know this. It caused Neeheeowee to have to put his arm around her, pulling her around the circle to allow room for the newcomers. Kokomikeeis smiled, while Julia's body responded to Nee-heeowee's touch as though she were starving.

He didn't remove his arm from around her shoulders, and Julia breathed in deeply in an attempt to calm her heart.

She glanced up at Neeheeowee, finding his gaze riveted on her. She stared, he looked back. Little knowing that she did it, her face came closer to his, until, with a groan, he moved closer, his lips brushing down over hers.

The moment came alive with magic. Julia's stomach quivered, her head spun, and her world tilted out of control for a moment. All she knew was the feel of his lips over hers, the warmth of the night, the fragrant scent of skin, his clothing. And she moved toward him, wanting more.

"There are buffalo on the ford of the Teton River, I have heard," Wahtapah began, breaking the spell.

"Yes." It was Tahiska who spoke next. "I have heard this, too. There are several from our camp that think to go there to hunt."

Neeheeowee brought his head up, away from her, while he breathed in deeply, as though to regain control. And Julia did notice that his breechcloth had settled in a way that made her stomach do flip-flops.

"Do you go down to the Teton?" Wahtapah asked Tahiska.

Tahiska shrugged. "I do not think so. There is plenty of meat here, and it is only the beginning of summer. There will be time to hunt more buffalo. I am content for the moment to stay close to home and to my wife." He gazed over at Kristina and smiled, Kristina returning the gesture, catching his hand and squeezing it.

"Some say the Pawnee are there in our hunting grounds," Wahtapah related. "I have heard that because the white man is crowding them in their own country, the game in their old hunting grounds have fled. It appears that our brothers, the animals, fear these white men. Some say that the Pawnee are dispersing into our country, taking our game."

Tahiska merely shrugged, while Neeheeowee sat up, all at once interested. After a while the Cheyenne warrior asked into the silence, "Is anyone going down there to protect Lakota territory against these invaders?"

"There are a few parties," Wahtapah responded. "Though I would not choose to follow any of the leaders of these parties. Few have good war records. Let us hope that any fight they have with the Pawnee will bring them honor."

Tahiska nodded while Neeheeowee stiffened, sitting forward and pulling away from Julia, if not physically, then in spirit.

"Ho, are you in there?" A male voice called out from the entrance and Tahiska responded with, "We are here, please come in and be our guest."

An older man entered, holding up his hand in greeting to everyone as he came fully into the lodge, standing up and coming around to take a seat at the honor place, Kokomikeeis and Wahtapah scooting down to allow him room. And while in most Indian circles, the females might have tended to huddle together at this point, the males, too, none here made the move to do so. And for this, Julia was glad.

"We are pleased to see you," Tahiska said. "This is *Capa Tanka*, Big Beaver." He made the introductions to everyone present. "I have asked Capa Tanka to visit us, to bring us entertainment. He is the camp's memory, its historian. He remembers everything, even the small details of camp life. And he is a great storyteller of all these minor facts. It is a pleasure for you to visit us."

Capa Tanka nodded, taking the pipe from Wahtapah, and smoking it before anyone else did or said anything. Then, at the urging of Tahiska, Capa Tanka began in due time to talk of many things in the everyday occurrences of camp life. Julia's attention fell away from him and she began to think of other things, mostly her own problems, stifling a yawn at the same time.

". . . there was a murder in the Brule camp to the south of us several months ago when it was time to make meat," Julia heard Capa Tanka say.

"This is a very bad thing," Tahiska spoke up and everyone agreed. It was a serious thing when a Lakota took the life of another Lakota. It didn't happen often, and news of such a thing spread quickly. "What did they do to the murderer?" Tahiska went on to ask.

Capa Tanka hesitated, "That was an interesting thing," he said after a long hesitation. "It is something I have not heard of in many, many years."

All were quiet as the camp historian paused once more.

"What did they do?" Kokomikeeis asked, breaking the silence.

The old man looked up, hesitated, then began, "They invoked the kinship appeal as the way of handling the murderer."

Julia heard several gasps from around the lodge and she almost asked what the "kinship appeal" was until she realized that Capa Tanka had every intention of telling them.

"I have not heard of such a thing happening in many, many years," Tahiska spoke up. "There is probably nothing I know of to show higher respect to one's dead relative than that, though the price is high, for each person related to the deceased must battle with his own hatred and pride first and overcome both before the kinship appeal will work."

"I agree," Wahtapah spoke up from the side.

"There is nothing more noble, if one can manage it."

The women waited for the historian to continue, but Capa Tanka held back, as though awaiting something else... or perhaps someone else. He glanced over toward Neeheeowee once, though Neeheeowee remained studiously silent, the younger man's gaze centered downward.

At length, the camp historian continued, saying, "It is well to think on such things, for there is nothing better than the kinship appeal to put out the fire of hatred in oneself. It is also said that it releases the anger of those who were slain as well. But it is not easy to achieve."

Julia still waited expectantly for someone to tell her what this "kinship appeal" was.

But it never came. The old man began to speak of other things and then, with one last glance at Neeheeowee, Capa Tanka started to rise, but Julia held him back with her carefully chosen words, saying, "I know I should not speak out like this, but I am new to the Lakota camp circle and I do not know what the kinship appeal is. Would you be so kind as to explain it to me?"

The old man looked at Julia, his keen eyes appraising her before he said, "You have blended in so well with us that I forgot for a moment that you are new to us. I would be happy to tell you of the kinship appeal. But first I must tell you that it is a true story. It comes to us from our ancestors many hundreds of years ago. No one knows who first started it, and it is not used often, for it is so difficult to attain."

All sat quietly while the old man stretched out his legs. "Let me tell you what has happened in the Brule tribe to explain this appeal. It happened only two seasons of the moon ago down there upon the Rosebud River. There was a man, a Lakota man, *Shonka*, The Dog, who killed another from his own tribe, a man by the name of *Mato Waste*, Good Bear. This is always a bad thing when it happens within a band, for one murder leads to another and soon there is one family fighting another of close kin, and sometimes it never stops.

"Now the murderer in this case, Shonka, escaped and was roaming over the hills, avoiding the victim's relatives, for he knew these people would kill him if they could find him. It so happened that there was a man amongst these particular Brule relatives who was known to be a wise and very just old man. His name was *Ogle Sa*, Red Shirt.

"Now Ogle Sa listened to his relatives. He heard their arguments, their fighting, and when it became Ogle Sa's turn to talk, here is what he said, 'My brothers, this is a very bad thing that has happened to us. Our relative, whom we all loved, lies dead while his murderer roams free. Therefore, would it not seem that we should find this murderer, Shonka at once? Is it not our duty to kill this man for the evil he has done?'

"Well, you can well imagine the response of the relatives. It was what they were all wanting to do and they all agreed that they should go out at once and seek revenge upon this murderer. But old Ogle Sa was not done speaking yet, and here is what he said next. 'My brothers, I, too, want justice. I, too, lost my kindred. But hear me. There is another way to resolve this. It is a harder path to take, but it is a better path. Now, it is true that we have lost a brother. But a murder is not always best met with more murder, especially if it means killing one from our own band. Hear me, my kindred. Would it not be better to handle this matter with no further killing? There is a way. Go and bring from your lodges your very finest. Bring here things that you value above all else. Bring them here for we shall give all these things to Shonka, the killer, as a way of showing him that we are not deceitful in what we propose to do. My brothers,' old Ogle Sa said, 'we will take this murderer into our own Brule kindred. He will take the place of our dead relative. And he will serve us and be to us what our relative was. But you must, everyone of you, search within your hearts to see if you can do this, and if you are able, then, bring me here, the finest things you possess that we may show Shonka our single-minded purpose.'

"Well, you can imagine that every single member of that kindred had to struggle within himself to conquer the hate and anger he felt. For no Lakota man would agree to this without feeling it truly within his heart.

"And that's when the wise old Ogle Sa pointed out that hatred and revenge are but flighty things at best, but that to live with Shonka in benevolence day in and day out required the most supreme qualities of a human being that could ever be put forth. And wasn't that what all we Lakota men strive to do?

"Well, all of the kinsmen looked into their hearts and saw that what this wise old man said was a good thing, for it is easy to kill, it is easy to hate and seek revenge. It is not always the easy way to love despite all. And perhaps such is a true test of whether one is a great human being or not."

"And did they all do it?" It was Julia who spoke up. "Did they all decide to live this way? Even Shonka?"

"Yes," Capa Tanka said. "It is said that they found the murderer in the hills, for it is always easy to track a man, and they brought him back to the village. You can probably guess how Shonka felt to be placed among the family of the slain man, for he knew all wanted to kill him. But Shonka did not hesitate to step back into the camp. He seemed to accept his fate with a great calm.

"He was taken into the lodge of the elders, there to await his fate. And that was when wise old Ogle Sa came up to him. Here is what he said: "My friend, my fellow Lakota of our Brule band, I am going to ask you to look into your heart before I tell you what we do. Look around you. What do you see? Over there is the brother of the slain man. Over there, his cousin. In the corner over yonder is his father and another brother yet. To me, the man who is dead, my cousin. Now, my friend, do you see all these gifts here? All of us have looked into our hearts. All of us loved our brother well. We bring these gifts to you now to show you our earnest intentions. These gifts here, they are for you. From this day forward we ask of you that you take the place of our dead relative. I ask you to look into your heart and tell us if you are able to truly take the place of our beloved. For if you are, from this day forward you will be a part of our family."

Julia gasped.

"Ah," Capa Tanka continued, "now Shonka began to shake, so deep was his emotion, and when each member of this kindred began to give to him the gifts they had brought and to speak to him kindly, the murderer began to cry, the tears falling from his eyes to the ground for he could not control them. And it is said that from that time forward Shonka became the best kinsman of all, because, you see, he had to prove himself worthy of that kindred's trust, and so he strove at all times to be the best of kin.

"Now, this is a good story. It is a true story. I tell it now because it is the love that one feels for another within his heart that can conquer hate. It is never anything else. But, there is more." The old gentleman held up his hand when Kokomikeeis would have spo-

ken. "You may want to know what happened to the
dead relative. That is the best part of all, for this slain
man, seeing what terrible hardship his relatives went
through to do this, seeing that they conquered their
own hate, that they took the most strenuous course of
all, felt that he, too, must do the same. And so this
slain man departed for the afterworld, free himself
from all hatred. And that is the end of the story."

Julia sat, unable to say anything for a short while,
though at last she said, "I thank you very much for
telling me this story. Now you say that this is true?"

The old man nodded his head.

"And you say that this happened just recently?"

"Yes," the old man said, gazing intently at Neeheeowee. "In the Brule camp to the south of here. It
is a remarkable thing and one well to remember.
Now," he said, "I will take my leave from you. There
are others here in the circle who have requested that
I speak to them this night."

The old man rose, to the accompaniment of "*Hau,
hau, kola,*" and left.

No one spoke for a long time, though it was Neeheeowee who seemed to be the most lost in thought.

At length, it was Kokomikeeis who spoke, saying,
"That is a truly incredible story. For people to do that
requires the most strength of all. I do not know that
I could do it."

All agreed except one, Neeheeowee, who alone remained quiet for the rest of the evening.

Chapter 19

◠◠◯◯◠◠

The drums beat out an intoxicating rhythm. At least eight to ten men, young and old, sat around the two big drums. All beat to the rhythms, all sang. Boys and young men danced in the center of the circle, around a fire that was needed more for the light that it gave than for its warmth, since the heat of the day still hung in the air. The full moon outshone the stars up above, casting shadows over the ground and making the night sky so bright, one had to look past it a long way to find the stars.

Kristina, Julia, and Kokomikeeis sat together, watching their men and others dance around the center circle. Some of the men, Julia noticed, danced wildly as though in a hunt; others enacted scenes from a kill, or perhaps a fight. Some threw their bodies into hideous contortions. But Neeheeowee and his friends did none of the above, and Julia saw that they seemed content to dance a dignified, steady dance.

Some women chose to keep time to the beat of the drums, moving up and down, there on the outer rim of the circle. Their steps were simple, merely picking up the feet in time, and Julia observed that they all managed to maintain a proud, dignified pose.

"Come"—it was Kokomikeeis who spoke—"let us

stand on the edge of the circle there with the other women. There we can see our men better and also we can dance."

Kristina muttered an agreement and nudged her friend. "Come on, Julia. It's time. I've seen you practicing."

"But Kristina," Julia said, pulling back, "I've never done this before. And I feel like I don't belong."

"You do and it's easy," Kristina replied. "Just stand there and move up and down. The movement is nothing compared to what I've been watching you do. You'll be fine."

Julia rose with a bit less grace than she might have otherwise had at any other time and allowed herself to be moved through the crowd toward the outer ring of the circle. There they joined the other women, creating a line around the circle, all keeping time to the rhythm.

As Kristina had said, the dance was easy. One just moved up and down, the main ingredient being to stay in time to the beat of the drum, and Julia found herself relaxing.

The drums stopped but Julia kept on, Kristina taking hold of her arm. "I forgot to tell you, when the drum stops, the dancers stop. It's not always easy to tell when they'll stop, it's more a feeling that you have to get for it, but you'll get used to it after a while."

Julia nodded, asking, "When do the women get to dance, besides just swaying here at the edge of the circle?"

"There will be women's dances later," Kristina said as the drums started again. Both Kristina and Koko-mikeeis began to move in time with the beat, and Julia joined in, realizing that after a while the drums acted as a sort of balm for her, her troubles forgotten. What was it Kristina had said? To dance with your heart? What did that mean? Julia still didn't know.

She closed her eyes as she stood there on the sidelines, moving with the beat of the drum. Fresh smells
of grass permeated her consciousness, while the
scents of fire and smoke, of paint and body heat
added to it, all of it mixing with the sound of the deep
singing, with the ebb and flow of the drums. Julia
swayed to the rhythm, though her movement remained up and down, and all at once she wished she
could be out there dancing, putting into motion what
she felt.

She looked up at that moment to catch Neeheeowee's glance at her, his look at her intense, sensual. All
at once emotion swept through her, deep, fierce emotion . . . love. Her gaze met his as they both kept time
to the music, her movement up and down, his steady.

Dance with your heart. She heard Kristina's voice.
Dance with your heart. And then it happened. All at
once Julia knew what that meant, knew what she felt.
And she knew she had to express it, she had to tell
him.

She moved forward.

Neeheeowee paused.

Dance with your heart. She swept into the circle as
though she belonged there, her gaze sought out Neeheeowee's and never left him. She lifted her arms, her
shawl and all its fringe falling around her like a second skin, making her look more butterfly than human. She never lost time to the beat as she came up
onto her toes.

She began to swirl and sway to the rhythm, to the
music of the voices. She twirled, the fringe of her regalia falling out around her as though it were a part
of the rhythm itself. And with each swirl, she looked
toward Neeheeowee.

I love you, she said with each sway of her body. *You,
with your kindness and gentle ways. You, who have never
left me, despite your vows. Whatever scars I might have*

had from the past are gone. I am free again to love you, to love these people. You have healed my heart. I am whole again because of you.

She came up on her toes to express what she felt. The swirl of her dress conveyed her pent-up emotions; the flap of the fringe, the swaying motion of her body became a significant incantation; the series of steps she took, the way she danced on her toes pronounced the affection she felt more effectively than words could have. Neeheeowee knew it, he felt it along with her, and he began to dance with her, around her, making his movements connect with hers, become a part of hers.

It looked more choreographed than the finest ballet, the love between these two more evident with each step, each sway and swirl.

For a moment all other dancing, all other dancers stopped, though if the onlookers were entranced or critical remained hard to discern.

And so enraptured was Julia for Neeheeowee, Neeheeowee for Julia, neither of them heard the raised voices, neither of them saw that Kristina watched the faces of those around her, that Kristina, grabbing her husband and leading him out into the circle, began the dance of the shawl.

The drums kept beating, the voices kept singing, and Kokomikeeis came forward, too, her arms spread wide as she, too, danced and twirled. Voices that had been raised were stilled as all around the circle watched the couples in the center. Other young girls began to join in, other boys and men as well, and soon old and young alike, male and female, entered into the circle, dancing.

Old people from the sidelines began to clap at so wonderful a sight, while they, too moved in time to the rhythm. Other voices began to sing, and still Julia and Neeheeowee danced within the circle, around the fire, unaware of anything, save themselves.

I love you, she said with the sway of her head, the shawl coming around her as she twirled.

I honor you, Julia, my love, his steady dance said as he followed her around the circle, his steps intersecting and becoming a part of hers. He took her in his arms and kissed her.

The drumbeat all at once stopped, the singing ceased, and Julia and Neeheeowee, a part of the music, a part of the rhythm left off all movement, Neeheeowee still holding her tightly to him.

"Taku kin oyas'in isanbya canteciciye," he whispered in Lakota. "I love you more than anything else. Julia," he murmured into her ear alone, "I want to marry you."

And Julia, there under the softening light of a full moon and a million stars overhead, agreed.

The drums started again, the singing, the voices, but Julia and Neeheeowee walked away from it, out of the circle, unaware that all within the circle observed them go.

But nothing lasts forever, and as the drums kept on, the people began to look back, away from the two lovers, and all began to move again in time to the rhythm. A new precedent had been set this night and no one said a word when the women stayed inside the circle with the men, dancing.

They could barely wait until they reached the guest tepee, both scooting inside with a fluidity of movement that denied their haste. Julia's dress fell to the floor without pause, Neeheeowee's breechcloth followed close behind. Moccasins flew into the air, one after the other, neither of them caring where they landed.

He took her in his arms. "I love you more than anything else, more than my vows, more than my hatred. I think I have loved you this way from the moment I first saw you, I was just too stubborn to admit it."

"And I love you," she said.

"Julia," he fell to his knees, taking her with him. He kissed her cheeks, her eyes, her nose, her lips. "I know I cannot give you much. There are so many men who could offer you more. Are you sure you wish to stay with me? Are you sure you want to marry me?"

Julia half smiled. "I'm sure," she said, then fell silent. Memories came back to her; Neeheeowee fixing her moccasins, though he'd been more than a little upset with her at the time; Neeheeowee rubbing ointment onto her feet; Neeheeowee listening to her point of view, nodding and taking her advice more times than not; Neeheeowee protecting her against harm as they crossed the prairie together. He had provided her with food, clothing, protection, and now he gave her the warmth of love and companionship.

Stay with him? Yes, she thought so.

"Julia? *Nemene'hehe*?" he asked, his tongue glazing over her neck. "You seem to think about it for a long time. Do you have doubts?"

"No, my love," she said. "I did at one time, but tonight at the dance, I saw things clearly. I love you; I wish to stay with you. You, with your kind and gentle ways, have healed my heart, taken away my doubts. I wish to spend the rest of my life with you."

Julia saw him close his eyes as he inhaled sharply. But all he said was "Julia," before he rubbed his hands up and down her spine, his touch ranging lower and lower, until, grabbing ahold of her buttocks, he pulled her up close, letting her feel the state of his arousal.

"Tonight," he said, "I honor you. I have been too much like a young boy in the past, but tonight I pay tribute to you."

He took her weight into his arms and set her onto their sleeping robes. "You have been married before," he said, one arm resting around her, the other over her body, his hands playing havoc with her breasts. "Did your husband ever initiate you into the more subtle forms of lovemaking?"

Julia arched her back, giving him more access to her body. She could hardly speak, but at last she said, "I am unsure what you mean."

"Did he ever kiss you here?" He touched her feminine mound.

Julia gasped. "Neeheeowee!"

"*Eaaa*," he said, "I was right. He did not take the time to show you the more pleasurable forms of love." Neeheeowee suddenly smiled. "I am glad," he whispered, then began to inch his way down her belly, kissing every bit of skin he came in contact with.

"Neeheeowee, you can't!" she said, trying to pull him back up toward her.

"Julia, I want to do this," he said, looking up. "There is not much I can give you. Let me give you what no other man can. This is my gift to you."

He had come up onto his elbows over her, and, as Julia gazed up at him, she was struck by the sincerity of his gaze. Still . . .

"But Neeheeowee, you would embarrass me."

"Embarrass you? How could I do this?"

"Because," she said, "you . . . I . . . what I mean to say is . . ." She gazed at him, at the love she saw there in his eyes and right then in her heart, she capitulated. She sighed, "All right," she said, running her fingers through his long, dark hair. "But you must promise me that if I let you do this, you will let me return the favor to you."

Neeheeowee smiled at her, and, lifting her head slightly toward him, he kissed her. "*Eaaa*," he whispered, "my Julia. How I do love you, but this is my gift to you. It is given freely. There is nothing expected in return—"

"But I—"

"Sh-h-h-h," he murmured into her ear. "Later, much later, if you are comfortable with me. For now, if you so much as touched me, I would explode. I hold myself back by the thinnest of strings. I would give this gift to you. I would know you as I want you to know me. But I warn you that if I do this, it will draw us closer and closer together."

"It will?"

A smile was all he gave her as answer. And Julia, the beginnings of a grin on her lips, said, "I would like that very much."

"*Eaaa*! My Julia, My *Nemene'hehe*."

He touched her there, his fingers like smooth velvet against her. He spread her legs with a gentle hand, grinning a bit as he said, "You resist me as though we have never made love. This is just another way for me to love you. You will like it, I think." And then he kissed her there, and Julia thought she had never been so scandalized.

She thought she would simply endure it and thank him very much for his gift, but his lips seemed to work magic, and Julia found herself responding to the overpowering sensuality of his touch.

She moaned, arching her back a little in silent invitation to do more. And he did, his kiss going on and on, his tongue exploring hidden areas. She began to move with the power of it, she began to respond to the magic of it. She began to feel. She . . . she spread her legs a little farther.

And still it went on and on.

"Neeheeowee, Neeheeowee, I—" Pleasure built and built within her until she was completely certain she couldn't take more of it. And then, and then, a thousand explosions went off inside her. She reached for Neeheeowee, and he was there for her, never withdrawing his touch until the very end.

"Julia," he said, reaching for her when her heartbeat had settled back down. "Julia, I am afraid I cannot hold back, I try. I—"

Julia didn't even think twice. She arched her hips up toward him, feeling his joining with her as though it were a sort of release.

"Julia," he said again, looking down on her as he thrust deeply within her. "I have never loved anyone as I love you."

"Nor have I," Julia murmured back, her movements meeting his, becoming a part of his.

Julia looked up to him as he strained over her, and, seeing him gazing back at her, she felt herself let go. Gone were the prejudices, gone were her doubts. Somewhere along the way, she had become a part of this man, and as he met his release, she felt herself merging with him, and yet spinning apart from him. Something had just happened between them. She had looked at him, she had touched him; she knew him now with a certainty of just who and what he was, and, as she smoothed back his hair as he settled over her, she knew she would love him always.

Yes, she had looked at him and she had found him beautiful. Was there any person on earth as lucky as she?

Somehow she didn't think so.

Chapter 20

⌒⌒⌒○○⌒⌒⌒

It came early in the morning. Neeheeowee and Julia had barely fallen asleep, after awakening to love one another yet again. It came with no warning, without any preparation for it. It came without asking: the dream.

He saw the face of his former wife before him and in her arms she held their child.

"How could you forget your promise?" her eyes exclaimed. *"The Pawnee who murdered me still roam free. And I am forever trapped here until the moment of full justice."*

Neeheeowee tried to wake himself, but he couldn't. She held out the body of their baby.

"Do not forget your baby," she said. *"You must seek out these murderers. Only then will I and your son be free."*

Neeheeowee awoke with a start, cold sweat already beading and pooling on his body. His breathing was shallow, his pulse raced, and as he lay there, he reached out to touch Julia.

Julia. Somehow she had become the only thing real

305

in his life. He didn't want to think of his past life anymore; he didn't want to remember his thirst for revenge. Hadn't it already claimed five years of his life?

And then he remembered his vow. He sighed.

The ghost of his former wife must surely have a heart filled with hatred, for she could not even allow him a moment's happiness.

Neeheeowee shut his eyes. What did she want with him?

He moaned. He knew what she wanted from him. Revenge, sweet and simple. And at one time, he would have done anything to give it to her.

But he didn't want it anymore. He wanted Julia. He wanted a life with her. He wanted to laugh with her; he wanted to see her full with his children. He wanted to grow old with her. He wanted her for his wife.

He stared up into the flaps of the tepee, noticing that a dim light had begun to fill the sky. He had awakened later than usual, too late to go out upon his early morning hunt. He grimaced, upset with himself. He would have to do better in the future.

Dogs barked outside, making Neeheeowee instantly alert. More dogs joined in barking furiously and Neeheeowee flew to his feet, grabbing his breechcloth and weapons as he had been taught to do from childhood. He rushed out of their tepee toward where the commotion took place. And there he paused.

A war party returned. A beaten war party; the same party that had gone out to teach the Pawnee a lesson about Lakota borders.

Neeheeowee groaned. How many were dead?

He watched the men filter into the camp, noting that no packhorse carried a body. Were there no casualties, or had the warriors been unable to recover bodies?

If this latter were the case, it was indeed a grim day for the Minneconjou camp.

By this time, Julia had awakened and had come out to see what was the matter. She stood behind Nee-heeowee, and, for a moment, just one delicate instant in time, his head spun. Perhaps it was her scent, perhaps it was simply her presence, or maybe it was a premonition of things to come; whatever it was, Nee-heeowee found himself wanting to reach around him and take her into his arms, never to let her go.

Something had happened between them last night. He had told Julia that if he made love to her in the way that he did, that it would draw the two of them closer together.

He had been right.

He had touched the essence of exactly who and what she was last night, and he had found himself loving her more now than he could ever remember loving anything or anybody. He didn't want to leave her now, he didn't want to lose her.

And yet, here were the warriors that had set out against the Pawnee. Beaten, defeated.

Could he allow the Pawnee to triumph? Could he allow the Pawnee into his own country, letting them commit murder again? Could he allow them anywhere close to Julia?

He knew the answers to his own questions before he even asked them, just as he knew what he had to do.

He had to go find the Pawnee. But this time, in tracking his enemy, he had to be successful. He had to bring an end to this once and for all.

Turning around, he stalked away from Julia without so much as a glance at her. He knew his action hurt her; he knew he should at least smile at her and give her tender greeting, but he couldn't.

If he turned to talk to her now, he would most

likely break down in front of her, in front of the whole tribe. He didn't want to go to war. He didn't want to do what he had to do.

He must.

There was a difference.

"What's wrong?" Julia wanted to know.

She had seen Neeheeowee return to their tepee, she had noted the grim expression on his face, and she didn't understand. He had merely watched the war party return to the camp. What could have happened to him so quickly? True, the war party had not done well, but neither had they done too badly. No one had been killed during the skirmish; and for that all the people were happy. So why did Neeheeowee look so dispirited?

She came into his tepee. He didn't turn around to acknowledge her, nor did he even look up.

"Are you going to answer my question?" she asked, then repeated, "What is wrong?"

He drew a deep, steady breath, though he still did not look at her. "I go now to find the Pawnee. I have been too long off of this purpose. It has brought us harm."

"I disagree," she said evenly. "The Pawnee have been routed home. Didn't you hear the stories of the warriors? The Pawnee are on the run."

Neeheeowee merely shrugged his shoulders, not even turning around. "It makes little difference to me. The one or ones I look for are still here. I must seek them out; it has been my duty these past years. It is time now for me to bring this to an end."

"And what about me?"

"What about you?"

"Are you going to leave me now after you asked me to marry you last night?"

Neeheeowee stopped all movement. And though

his back was still toward her, she saw him gaze upward while his hands came down to his sides. Finally,
he bent his head. "I should not have said that to you,"
he said. "I am not free to take you as wife. I do not
know what happened to me last night."

"Do you shame me before the whole camp then?
All in the camp circle know I spent the night here
with you."

He breathed out heavily. "I do not throw you away.
I would never do that. You may stay here while I am
gone, you may tell everyone here that I married you
last night. I would see that you can hold up your head
with pride. I would not take that from you."

"Do not go," she pleaded.

"I must."

It was all that he said, but it was enough. Julia knew
without doubt that nothing she could do or say would
keep him here.

"I will follow you."

"You will not."

"I will," she said. "There will be no one here to stop
me."

"No, Julia, you will not come with me," he said.
"You would only get in my way, and you would get
yourself killed, and probably me, too. You do not
know the prairie well enough to survive on it."

"True enough," she said. "Nevertheless, I intend to
follow you if you insist on going alone."

"I will not allow it."

"And why not?"

Neeheeowee turned back toward her, but still he
didn't look at her, and Julia knew he pretended interest in the parfleches in his hand, if only to hide the
emotion she thought she had seen there within his
composure. At length, he said to her, "That is how
my first wife perished. I allowed her to talk me into
letting her go with me on a hunting trip. I did what

she wanted and she died. I will not allow that fate to happen to you."

"Neeheeowee," Julia said, scooting forward toward him. "It is not the same thing. I am not the same person as your former wife. You are not planning to be gone on a hunting trip. This is not five years ago. This is now, and I promise you, if you leave, I will follow. Besides," she said, "I am not so certain you are following the correct path in your life."

He looked down his nose at her. "Say what you mean."

"You talk about your purpose in life, you tell me about your lack of a vision and you tell me that you arrived at your purpose now because of the death of your wife and child. I believe that you chase a ghost. I do not think that you follow the right path."

He shrugged. "It makes little difference now. I am set upon this course, I have long put this into action and I must now complete it. The Pawnee must die."

"Neeheeowee," she reached out to touch his hand. "I ask you to think about this. Will killing the Pawnee make you a better person? Will your life be better because of it?"

He shrugged, throwing back his head. "Perhaps not. But it makes little difference anymore. I do this thing now not because I want to but because I have to. I could never live with myself if the threat from the Pawnee walked into our own camp, putting you in danger. Who could I turn to then? Could I say that I had decided that protecting my loved ones was not my chosen path? What man who would claim this has any pride? No, Julia, I do what I have to do. I tried to make you see that. I'm sorry that the day for me to leave has come so soon."

Julia bit her lip. "Neeheeowee . . ."

Neeheeowee shook his head. "I do not have time to argue with you. I must leave today and quickly before the tracks of these Pawnee are forever gone. If I could change this part of my life for you, I would. I cannot."

"All right," she said. "If you have to go then take Tahiska or Wahtapah or both. Don't go alone."

Neeheeowee shook his head. "What I do is mine alone to do. It is not something I can charge another with, nor share. If I had done this a few years sooner, the Pawnee would not now be here threatening and scaring our villages."

"Fine," she said, "then take others."

Neeheeowee sighed. "Julia," he said at last, "I cannot change the way things are, nor can I change the vow that I made to put this to an end."

"I see," she said. "Then I will come with you."

"You will not."

"I will."

He drew himself up to his full height. "We will see," he said, and stepping past her, he flung open the tepee entrance.

And as Julia watched him walk away, she began to make her plans.

"Keep her safe, my brother," Neeheeowee told his *kola*, Tahiska, the two of them standing outside Tahiska's lodge a few hours later. "And do not let her follow me."

Tahiska grinned. "My friend, if you cannot keep your own wife here with wise counsel, how do you expect me to?"

Neeheeowee grunted, the sound deep in his throat. Shaking his head, he turned, jumping onto the mustang whose reins he held in his hand, while he clicked his other pony forward. He threw a quick look over the supplies he had stashed on the pack pony, satisfied that he had enough to get him into the country of the Pawnee.

He glanced down briefly at Tahiska, saying, "Do what you can to keep her here. I am afraid she would perish out there and I have no time to teach her the means of survival on the prairie, nor to watch over her."

Tahiska nodded. "I understand your concern."

Again Neeheeowee grunted, and with a quick jerk of his head, he scanned the crowd for a glimpse of Julia. He could see her nowhere. Was she purposely staying away? He hoped not, for he had wished to see her one more time before he left camp.

But he could not find her, and he would not demean himself by going to look for her in their lodge. If she had decided to send him off with no farewell, so be it. Her pouting would do her no good. He would still go.

A crowd had milled around him, but he ignored the people, himself not seeking the glory and admiration they gave. He had turned his horse around, he had started to click his mount forward when—

"Neeheeowee!" Julia ran up toward him. "Do not leave yet! I have something for you."

Neeheeowee watched her run toward him, observed her as she tied a blanket onto his pack pony. "I just decorated that blanket this morning," she said, albeit a little nervously. "I did not want you leaving without it."

Neeheeowee nodded and Julia came around toward him. And though she knew it went against Indian etiquette to show affection in public, she reached up to take Neeheeowee's hand in her own. And looking up to him, she said, "May you put this thing to rest once and for all."

Neeheeowee acknowledged her with a quick nod and, bending down to touch his forehead lightly to the top of her head, he said, "Wait for me," to which Julia simply smiled.

Chapter 21

❦❦

"I worry about her."

Tahiska sent his wife a look of agreement. "She does not know the prairie well enough to do this. Did you see her sneaking away to follow him?"

"Yes," he said. "I saw it."

"Will you follow her?"

He nodded his head. "Of course. I will watch over her for a little while, at least until she reaches my Cheyenne brother."

Kristina frowned. "I wish I could be certain she would find him right away."

Tahiska grinned. "My wife," he said, "I will have to teach you better in observation. Did you not see that blanket she put on the pony? It is one of those white man's gifts we received recently."

"Yes? And?"

"It is a very cheap blanket and I have often thought it was not worth what I traded for it. It unravels too much . . . all the time . . . in fact, it will catch on everything it comes in contact with, leaving Julia with an easy trail to follow. I gave it to her to put on the pack pony."

Kristina smiled. "Why, my dear husband," she said, "I believe you have devised an excellent plan.

Let us only hope that what I did will slow him down long enough to allow Julia to catch up to him."

"What did you do?" Kokomikeeis asked, as she and her husband, Wahtapah, came to stand with Kristina and Tahiska. All watched as Julia made plans to sneak away.

"I did not do much," Kristina said, "just enough to make him slow down. I put a cut into his reins. After an hour or two, the reins will break."

"Ah," said Tahiska. "That will work well with what I did, for I slipped a few sand burrs beneath the blanket where he rides his pony. Within a short time, his pony will buck and refuse to move. That, too, will slow him down."

"My friends," Wahtapah said, shaking his head. "Perhaps we should have talked to one another first before we let him leave the camp."

"Did you do something, too?" All three people stared at Wahtapah.

He shrugged. "I simply put a small hole in his water bag. He has others. I ensured that. But this first one will leak and he will have to stop for a while to refill it."

"Oh, dear," Kokomikeeis said. "I think someone should follow our friend to be certain he comes to no harm since he may find himself defenseless soon."

"My friend," Kristina said, looking closely at her. "You did not do something, too, did you?"

Kokomikeeis looked away. "I thought I did it for the best. I did not want him to go without Julia when she was so determined." She gulped. "I untied his supplies. They will fall off soon."

The other three people stared at one another for a short while before laughing, Kokomikeeis the last one to join in. And so involved were they in their own conversation that no one noticed the camp historian, joining them until the man came right into their midst.

"I have come to ask you and your friend to follow that young man. He will need some protection on this, his first day on his trek," the old man said.

Tahiska was the first to respond. "What do you mean, grandfather?" he asked, addressing his elder with the customary term.

"Our friend, the Cheyenne; he will not get far," the old man said. "I am afraid I have done something that will require you to follow your friend. I began to get distraught over our friend having to leave when he seemed so happy. I have known that young man as long as you have and I do not remember ever seeing our friend so contented. And when I saw his wife making plans to leave to follow him, I decided she should have the opportunity to catch up with him."

"Grandfather"—it was Tahiska who spoke—"what did you do?"

"It seemed a harmless thing at the time. Now I am not so certain," he said. "I gave him a draft with a small amount of a sleeping aid in it to make him tired. I did not mean harm, I only thought to allow the young white woman to find him."

All four friends stared at their grandfather, then at one another.

"It is all right, grandfather." It was Wahtapah who spoke. "We, too, did something to slow our friend down, and my cousin and I were about ready to mount up and follow our Cheyenne brother anyway." He glanced toward Tahiska. "We had better get our mounts and take our friend some new rope and water bags and watch over him when he falls asleep. I believe he may need our help soon."

Tahiska nodded his agreement, but before the two men left to collect their mounts, all five people looked toward one another, and together they all laughed.

Sometime later, Julia began to despair. She had been riding most of the day, following the path of the raveling blanket, but now she could find no trace of it. Either the blanket no longer existed, or it had developed a knot in it. Whatever the case, she could find neither it nor Neeheeowee.

She glanced around her. None of this landscape looked familiar, and the sun had begun its descent from the sky, Julia estimating the time at around eight o'clock in the evening.

That would account for her hunger, she thought, and, dismounting, she quickly hobbled her pony while she reached into one of her bags for some *wasna*, the same concoction that Neeheeowee called *ame*. She left her mare to graze while she strolled a short distance away to sit down on a nearby stone, preparing to enjoy her lonely meal as best she could. That's when she heard it: the neighing of a horse, then the deep, human sound of a moan.

She sat up straight, her head tilted as though that angle might help her to hear better. There it was again, the sound of . . . an injured man?

Julia gazed around her, seeing that she was quite alone. She listened again. There. It came from the other side of that slight rise in the land, just over there to her right.

She stood up and moved toward the sound, slowly, quietly at first. Would it be friend or foe? Should she prepare herself to fight, draw her knife, perhaps? Should she run back to the camp to get help from the others? She gazed in one direction and then in the next. Which way *was* the camp?

Suddenly she realized she was quite lost, and she found herself awash with a terrible feeling of helplessness. Still, she edged farther toward the sound, the action conquering her fear to some degree, and getting to her hands and knees, she inched her way for-

ward. Before she reached the top, she drew her knife;
for safety, then with more curiosity than courage, she
popped her head over the rise. Up, then down.

She hadn't seen a thing. She tried again. Horses,
two horses, that's all she'd seen. She looked back at
her own mare, still safely hobbled a short distance
away. She sighed, knowing she would have to take a
better look. She didn't want to, and she debated a
short time with herself, finally deciding she had no
choice but to look more closely.

She raised her head again, espied the horses, and
was about to fall back down the rise, when her gaze
caught upon a sight that looked more ridiculous than
she would have cared to admit. Her blanket, or at
least what remained of it, lay stretched out on the
ground before her, its yarn bunched up into neat clus-
ters, looking more like a cat plaything than a blanket.
She gulped and looked again.

Was Neeheeowee down there? He must be.

She inched her way farther and farther up the rise.

Then she saw him; down there, off to the right of
the ponies. Neeheeowee. He lay stretched out on the
prairie, one of his parfleches full of clothing acting as
his pillow. Why, it looked as though he had suddenly
taken the urge to nap.

Strange.

Beside him, the packhorse had thrown off all her
bags into a mess stretching out across the prairie, and
though hobbled, his favorite mount had chewed her
way through her reins, the buckskin noose lying flatly
upon the ground. Neeheeowee's water bag lay empty
beside him.

Odd.

Neeheeowee would never have been so careless
with his supplies, nor would he have taken the time
to rest during the day. She gasped. He couldn't be . . .
he wasn't . . . ?

She picked herself up in a hurry, throwing herself over the rise, falling down in her rush and sliding all the way to the bottom, her descent stopping no more than an inch from Neeheeowee's head. He didn't awaken. Oh, dear, he had to be sleeping . . .

She reached down to him. She put her fingers next to the pulsebeat at the base of his neck. He seemed to be all right. Perhaps he just slept. He had reason to be tired, she realized, recalling the night they had just spent together—last night—neither one of them getting more than a few hours of rest. Had he needed to sleep this desperately? Somehow it didn't seem plausible, and yet, the evidence that he required rest seemed to be stretched out before her.

She threw a quick look at the mess surrounding her, at the disorder of robes and blankets, of parfleche bags and clothes, of weapons and broken rawhide rope. Perhaps, she decided, it would be best if she were to clean up the clutter. She could make camp right here, attend to his needs, and then, when Neeheeowee awakened, he might find reason to let her stay with him.

She rose, starting about her tasks, and, as she did them, she began to wonder, thinking back on it, what the noise had been that had led her to Neeheeowee. She could have sworn it sounded like a human's moan. But it couldn't be. Neeheeowee slept too soundly to have made the noise and yet . . .

She gazed down at Neeheeowee, then looked around her, even glancing up into the sky. She could see no evidence of anyone or anything else. She raised her shoulders in mock defeat, and, unable to make sense of it, she went back to her camp chores and to the task of preparing dinner from Neeheeowee's ruined supplies. So busy was she, in fact, that she missed seeing the shadows of two men, Indians, who slid down into the camp, leaving behind them rope and bags, the same men who would watch, who would guard the two travelers all night long.

Neeheeowee was not pleased to see her.

He hadn't awakened until the next morning and when he did, Julia was already up, simmering some of her own food over the fire. The day before them had dawned clear, yet hot and humid for all that, and when he awoke, the sun had already brought its heated touch not only to the land, but to all its occupants as well.

Neeheeowee managed to roll over onto his elbows first, although one hand came up to hold his head. And the first thing he asked was "What happened?"

Julia gave him a curious glance. "It is odd," she said, her voice barely over a whisper. "I was going to ask you that same question."

He grimaced, still holding his head. "Would you mind speaking more softly?" he asked, and Julia almost laughed.

"I will try," she said in a quiet, though distinct voice, and Neeheeowee winced. "Neeheeowee," she said, as softly as she could, "you did not imbibe in drinking whiskey before you left camp, did you?"

"Wiss-kee?" he asked, flinching when she replied with an, "Oh, yes."

"What is this, wiss-kee?" he said the word in English and then, "*Eaaa*, it is the white man's fire water. I remember. No," he said, shaking his head and then cringing.

"I see," she said. "It's odd, you know. You are acting in much the same way as a man does after he has had some whiskey the night before. You haven't . . ." she trailed off with whatever she was about to say as Neeheeowee suddenly rose and rushed from their camp as though he ran from a demon.

He came back, looking a little white and a little sick,

his glance barely resting on her. "I need water," he said after a little while. "I need to lie in it, to soak my head in it. I must find some rushing water to heal whatever has come over me."

It was quite a usual thing for him to request, Julia thought, remembering that it was a common belief in American Indian culture that water, especially rushing water, healed. He looked around him slowly, turning his head only the minutest degree. At length, he said, "I know this place. There is water to the south and west of here. It is only a short distance away. I will go there now."

Julia nodded and, peering up at him, asked, "Do you need any help?"

He looked taken aback, and, had he been feeling a little better, he might have flinched. As it was he had to settle for a scowl in her direction. "I am no woman that I need your assistance." And with this said, he jumped up toward his pony, not quite making the mount and having to squirm his way into a seating. Once there, Julia observed that he had to lean forward, resting his head against the pony's neck before giving his signal to the animal to move.

Julia watched their slow departure from the camp with a set expression on her face. She wouldn't follow him—she knew he wouldn't want her to—which left her to do what? Looking around her, at the mess stretched out there across the prairie, she knew just what her chores would be for the next several hours, and, with a sigh of exasperation, she made a move to start.

The cleanup of Neeheeowee's supplies was not an easy task, Julia decided later, for most of Neeheeowee's rawhide had been eaten through, leaving a minimal amount of rope for her to use. She had long ago dumped all their belongings onto the ground, in her search to find some decent buffalo hide rope, finally finding some in the very last bag where she looked. He packed in an odd manner, she decided, finding an extra pair of moccasins hidden below ointments and paint in one bag, extra food tied up in clothing as though stuffed away, to be forgotten. But perhaps he had his reasons for packing this way, and she made a note to put his things back together the way she had found them.

She struggled now to determine just how to arrange all their things onto the pack pony, since she had very little rope to use. But finding no easy solution, she set her attention onto stuffing all his belongings back into his bags, making sure to "hide" the moccasins and food as she had found them.

She ignored her hair, which had fallen into her face, pushing it back occasionally only when it became a nuisance to her work. She held too many objects in her hands at the moment and she blew up at the few strands of hair that had fallen over her eyes, Neeheeowee choosing that same time to walk his pony back into their camp.

He gazed at her for a while before saying, "That rawhide that you have there—it is cut through." He scattered some long willow branches on the ground as he spoke. "We can use these willow branches here to tie on our supplies and restock our rope once we get back to camp."

"This is good," Julia said, "but I do not need it. I found some fresh rope here in camp."

Neeheeowee gave her a puzzled look, but Julia, after glancing up at him and pushing her hair back from her face, didn't give it any further thought. "Tell me," she said after a while, "why are you going back to camp?"

Neeheeowee came to sit down beside her, having just hobbled his pony off to the side. His hair was still wet, she noticed, and he smelled clean, refreshing, his fragrance reminding her of the fresh, rushing streams of water which were scattered throughout this land.

He put his hand over hers, his skin still feeling cool next to her own. He cocked his head to the side, looking at her before he said, "We take you back to the camp."

Neeheeowee scooted around behind her as he spoke, and, squatting down, he placed his legs about her while he took her hair into his hands, brushing it with his fingers and styling it into two neat braids, one on each side of her head. "I did not realize," he said, "that having your hair loose became such a nuisance."

Julia stared away, not answering at first. At last, she said, "It won't work, you know."

"What?" he asked. "Brushing your hair?"

"No," she said. "It will not matter if you take me back to camp. I will follow you again."

He frowned, a groan forming deep in his throat. "You cannot. Where I go, I go alone. What I do is mine alone to do. This is not your fight. You must go home."

"I know," she said, closing her eyes against the sensation of having him work over her hair. "But Neeheeowee, we have been all through this before, and it makes no difference to me. If it concerns you, it concerns me."

"I disagree," he said. "The warpath is no place for a woman. Is it your intent to follow me into every fight?"

"No," Julia said, shrugging just a little. "Only this one."

He raised an eyebrow. "Why?" he asked.

Julia shook her head. "I do not know," she said. "I only know that I must follow you this time. I feel that if I do not do this, my life will never be the same. I cannot explain it."

Neeheeowee took a deep breath and sighed while Julia, sitting in front of him, yet so close to him, knew that he struggled to contain his anger; she could feel it. At last, he finished with her hair and came up onto his feet, saying only, "I must think," before he strode from their camp, as quickly as all that, each step that he took reminding her that his temper was barely restrained.

And though a part of her wanted to rush to him and explain why it was so necessary that she go with him, deep within, she knew he would fare better if left alone to decide for himself what was best. She could only hope that he would honor her decision, because in truth, he had little choice. She would accompany him. She didn't know why it was so necessary, nor did she know how she would do it, if he chose to leave her behind. But somehow, some way, she would accompany him.

She vowed it.

Neeheeowee had never felt more torn. He debated his predicament as he strolled out over the prairie, the setting sun before him. On the one hand, he could not let Julia accompany him; he knew what disastrous consequences it could have. Yet, on the other hand, he remembered how *he* had been as a boy, stealing along with the men as they went to war, hoping that no one would send him home. He knew the burning ache that she felt, that need to be a part of something, and he knew he should honor her courage, for what she did was heroic—stupid perhaps, but heroic.

Yes, he should honor her. Wasn't it what the grandfathers would do? Wasn't it what his fathers had done for him?

And yet he found himself reluctant to allow her to

go with him. He wanted to protect her, to cherish her, to keep her from any and all dangers. How could he let her accompany him when that very thing that could free him from his nightmares might also be the agent that would kill him and perhaps her, too?

He hung his head as he strode along the prairie, not far from camp, never far from camp, contemplating his problem. If he sent her back to the village, would that action squelch the valor he admired in her?

A weakness within him cried out, urging him to do just that; to ignore her own power of choice, to do what he knew was best for her; wisdom, however, implored him to nurture her strength as though it were a wild thing needing care.

Which path did he follow? The path of fear? The path that said this could be exactly like the time before? The path that told him he could cause her death as he had caused another death before her?

Or did he bow down to the wisdom of his fathers? Should he cherish this show of strength in her, sowing her fortitude as though it were a seed, letting it grow into a thing of beauty and wisdom?

Did he truly have a choice? He grimaced.

Perhaps the true question was: Did he have the strength to allow her to have her own life?

Neeheeowee frowned and looked skyward as if for guidance. But at last, knowing what he must do, what his grandfathers before him beseeched him to do, he set his pace back toward their camp. And though he trembled at what he had to do, he knew he would not waiver from his decision.

"We will leave before dawn tomorrow," Neeheeowee said some time later as both he and Julia reclined before the fire. "I want you to be ready to go because I cannot afford to be long on this trail."

"I understand," Julia said. She paused, then, "You have decided to take me back?"

Neeheeowee looked sullen, but all he said was, "No, I have decided to let you come with me."

Julia looked up at him, her gaze startled. "Y . . . you have decided . . . that—"

"There are conditions and there are rules," he said. "But if you agree to them, then I will let you accompany me."

Julia nodded her head. "I would agree with—"

"We will discuss the rules first and then, if you agree, we will set out together."

"I see," she said. "What are these rules?"

"The first rule is that you will engage in no fighting unless you have to once we reach the enemy. When we get to his country, and if I fight him, I want you to stay well back and attend to the horses. This would be a big help to me."

"I would agree—"

"There is more."

Julia nodded and fell silent.

"You will attend to most of the camp chores," Neeheeowee said, looking at her sternly. "You will bring water for both me and the horses in the evening and you will fetch it without complaint no matter what I do or say."

She nodded.

"And," he said, pausing only sightly, "there will be no lovemaking."

He caught her startled glance, and, though he didn't have to, he went on to explain, "It is considered a very bad thing for a man to engage in sex if he is on the warpath, and if he does this, it is said that he will be wounded in battle. We will not test these teachings. While we travel, and until I meet the enemy, there will be no kissing, you will refrain from touching me, and we will not sleep with one another at night. If you agree to these things, you may come with me. If not, I will take you back now."

Julia glanced at him, certain that he held back his anger, yet he said nothing more, merely awaited her reply and at last, when she said, "I agree to these conditions," she saw a spark of emotion flicker there within his gaze.

He said nothing as he stood up and then moved off to where his buffalo robe lay in a heap upon the prairie. He picked it up and brought it over toward her, dropping it and stretching it out next to the fire. Before he lay down upon it and surrendered himself to sleep, he turned to her and said, "So be it."

And Julia nodded back, whispering to him in the dark, saying in English, "It is done, my love. I agree."

Chapter 22

How could he keep his attention on the matter at hand when Julia's well-shaped buttocks loomed before him?

Neeheeowee let out a groan of despair as they sat around the fire in their evening camp. They had only been on the trail for seven days and already he yearned to feel her, to touch her, to make love to her. He turned his back on her as though this would help him regain control. It didn't work. The action did him no good whatsoever. Her womanly scent reached out to him, begging him to kiss her; anything, if it meant feeling her body against his. She began to sing as she worked, her voice soft and pretty, and he wondered if he would go slightly out of his mind before this journey ended.

He'd spoken the truth when he'd said that a warrior refrained from sexual intercourse when on the warpath. Those that did it, those who shunned the teachings of their elders for the pleasures of the moment, had been known to die or to sustain a life-threatening wound in battle soon thereafter. Neeheeowee literally knew of no Cheyenne or Lakota warrior who had sex before, during, or after a fight.

327

Which meant that he couldn't touch Julia, though he knew she would welcome it.

It left him—what? Frustrated, eager for her company, and ... He stared down at his body, not really needing to see the physical proof of his desire for her.

Well, he could not become a victim to his flesh. There were some things a man never did. There were some restraints that a man must place upon himself and this, he knew, was one of them.

Stifling a groan, he rose from his position within their evening camp and strode as calmly as possible toward the river, where he hoped the cooling freshness of the water would ease his passion. It was all he could hope for at the moment.

Julia bent down to hand Neeheeowee his bowl of stew where he reclined on the ground, just having returned from a lengthy bath. She saw his gaze move toward the cut of her dress, where a firm outline of her breasts could be seen. She drew in her breath in anticipation, but just as quickly let it out. Neeheeowee had meant what he'd said; he didn't touch her, he didn't kiss her, he didn't even acknowledge her except with his glance, which strangely enough, Julia found focused upon her more and more rather than less and less.

They had been traveling about a week and the country into which they were entering now had become more arid, the prairie more inclined toward the shorter grasses, with long stretches to be found without a single tree in sight. She saw buttes and mesas in the distance, and she knew that soon they would leave the friendly country of the Lakota and Cheyenne for the more hostile hunting grounds of the Pawnee.

She hadn't realized they would be traveling into the land claimed by the Pawnee. She had assumed the

Pawnee still trespassed on Lakota ground, and she shivered at the thought of moving closer and closer to the territory of their enemy.

But she couldn't complain. Though Neeheeowee ignored her for the most part, despite what he said, she awakened each morning to the feel of his arms wrapped around her, holding her tightly to him, and she gloried in the sensation. If this was all he could give her for now, she would be content with it.

She wasn't certain why she'd become so intent on accompanying Neeheeowee on his journey. Just what she could do to help him settle this score, she couldn't even fathom. She had no skill with a gun and less than that with a bow and arrow. And while it was true that she might be more burden than helpful mate, she was determined to change that. She knew she was needed here.

Neeheeowee had faced his nightmares alone for much too long. Now he had her. If he were to perish in this venture, then they would perish together. But if not, if he were to confront these ghosts, then he would have her beside him. And despite the careful teachings from her early life, Julia believed Neeheeowee: her man, her love, was haunted, if not by real people, at least by the past. And Julia knew it was time to do something about it.

She glanced at him now where he sat only a short distance from her.

"Are we close to the Pawnee now?" she asked.

Neeheeowee placed his right hand before him, the back out. He swung it to the right, palm out and thumb out, and then back. Julia frowned, having learned that this was the sign for "no."

"Will we be there soon?"

He lifted his shoulders and said, "Within five or six days."

"How will you locate the specific men that you want?"

He held back speaking for a while as though giving his answer much thought. After a short time, he said, "I have spent these last five years determining just who it was that attacked our camp that day. I have made inquiries into many camp circles, some who are friendly with the Pawnee. I know now the men that I seek. I also learned that these men usually hunt or war together. So it should be easy to set a trap and snare them all. It is what I intend to do."

"I see," Julia said. "But, you are only one person; how many of *them* are there?"

"Three," he said. "It will be a fair fight."

"Ah," she said. "I know it will be a fair fight, for you are a warrior to contend with, but do you not think you should teach me some skill with a weapon in case I am needed?"

"You will not go near the fight. You will stay way back, guarding the ponies as we agreed."

"Neeheeowee," she said, "I still think you should teach me to be of some use."

He cast her a sulky glance, then he frowned. "Do you know nothing about fighting?"

"No," she said. "Nothing at all."

"*Eaaa.* I see. You are right," he said. "You must know something about fighting, for by following me, you may need some skill. I will teach you a little each night and you must practice. But realize that by carrying a weapon, if you do not use it well, that weapon can be turned against you. It is the first thing you must know."

Julia smiled. "I will remember. I will look forward to our lessons. Is there any other way I can help you to overcome this enemy?"

He smiled. "Yes," he said, looking meaningfully at her breasts. "Do not tempt me with your body."

"I do no such thing!"

He chuckled. "You do not have to do a thing, just your being here is enough." He looked down at himself, his breechcloth already straining against his need. "Do you see?"

Julia caught her lip between her teeth. "There is very little I can do about that."

Neeheeowee laughed outright. "No, my love," he said. "There is a great deal you *could* do about it, it is only that we cannot allow such things to happen between us right now."

"Neeheeowee," she began, "could we go to sleep tonight with you holding me? No lovemaking, just holding? Is that not allowed?"

He shook his head. "It could be done, I would say, if you looked like a bear and smelled like a rotting buffalo. As it is, though, I would never sleep."

She chuckled, not missing the backhanded compliment. "But Neeheeowee," she said, "I wake up each morning with you holding me. I am only asking to go to sleep that way, as well."

He moaned. "I am afraid it would be painful for me: to have you in my arms, to want you and not be able to take you...I do not know if I am man enough."

Julia didn't know what to say to that and Neeheeowee, after putting out the fire, chuckled, lying down to sleep, and, despite what he said, he invited Julia into his arms and into his bed, putting his arms around her and holding her the whole night through.

Evidently, she thought, he was man enough.

She awoke to the sound of Neeheeowee flipping through the parfleches. And though it was dark outside, she could see that once again, a mess lay strewn out all over their camp.

She came up onto one elbow. "What is it you are looking for?"

He glanced over to her, then back toward the bags. "I thought that I had packed more food than this. I do not wish to spend the time this morning hunting for our morning meal. I had hoped to snack on some *wasna* and be on the trail before the sun rises. But if I cannot find this food, it will mean I have to hunt."

Julia sat up, letting her sleeping robe fall to her waist. "I know where it is."

He gulped, his attention suddenly diverted to her chest and the parfleche bag he'd been holding fell to the ground.

Julia came up onto her feet, shoving her dress over her head at the same time, and paced over toward Neeheeowee, who, now that she was dressed, seemed to have recovered himself . . . somewhat.

"I know where the food is," she said, again. "I'm surprised you do not remember it for it was in a special spot—it looked to me as though you'd hidden it. When I had to repack our things several days ago, I found the food wrapped up within your clothing. I put it back the same way I found it, thinking you had reason to pack it that way. Ah," she said, "here it is now." She pulled the food out from underneath clothing.

Neeheeowee stared at it blankly. "I did not pack it this way," he said.

Julia merely shrugged her shoulders, but Neeheeowee thrust out his chin. "It is most strange," he said. "That first day I left camp odd things happened to me. First all my supplies fell off my pack pony and then I became tired, so tired that I took down a blanket from my horse and threw it out on the ground. That is all I remember, except awakening the next morning to find you there and me with a severe headache."

Julia tilted her head to the side. "Perhaps your water was laced with whiskey?"

"Maybe," he said. He narrowed his brow and looked at her. "No, I think someone put a medicine into my water or perhaps gave it to me in a drink I had before I left the camp. I think someone cut my rope and someone pierced a hole in my water bag. Julia," he said, "I believe I have been tricked. Someone went to much trouble to slow me down." All at once he chuckled. "And whoever it was, did a good job of it."

Julia gazed over to him. "Why do you laugh if you think this?"

"Because," he said, "it was done so well and because it means that whoever did it protected you. Someone wanted you to find me. It means someone in the Minneconjou camp cares for you. I am pleased with it. Did you find anything else like this?"

"Yes," she said, "I found your moccasins hidden beneath your paint. I thought at the time that it was odd, but I didn't want to question the way that you arrange your things."

Again, Neeheeowee grinned. "Show me," he said, and when she did, she had the pleasure of hearing the deep, resonant beauty of his voice, for Neeheeowee laughed, and Julia after a while, joined in his with a chuckle of her own, their joy in one another's company extending well into the night.

And when they fell asleep that night, he held her in his arms, Julia deciding there was nothing quite so wonderful as the feeling of his embrace around her. Contented now, she fell asleep.

It came without warning. Just when Neeheeowee thought he couldn't be happier, it came to him: the dream. He saw his wife and baby again, alive, then dead. He heard their screams, he heard their pleas for pity, he listened to their voices now, demanding retribution.

He moaned in his sleep, he tossed, and cold sweat began to cover his body. He tried to call out to the ghost, he tried to explain about Julia, about the change in his life, but he couldn't. He couldn't talk, and she wouldn't listen.

"Avenge my death," she said. *"Avenge the death of my child."*

It was all she said. It was all she would say. And she would not listen to his thoughts, or to his pleas, silent though they were. She wanted revenge; he was her instrument. She would not let him rest until it happened.

He tried to cry out his frustration, but nothing would come, and, at last, he had no choice, he awoke.

Julia awakened to the feel of Neeheeowee stirring beside her. He groaned in his sleep, his body twisting out of his sleeping robe. She sat up and leaned over, taking him in her arms, but he shrugged her off, reminding Julia that in an Indian culture, a man wanted no sympathy when he showed any sign of weakness. To do such was considered the ultimate of insults.

So she lay back down, listening to the sound of his breathing as it became more and more normal. At last he took a deep breath and shuddered.

"The enemy is close," he murmured to her after a while. "We will have to be on guard at all times from now on during the day, most of our movements being done at night when there is a moon to guide us."

"I see," she said. "How do you know this?"

"I know," was all he replied.

"Ma," Julia let go the Lakota expression. "How far away do you think the enemy is?"

"I am not certain of that. I will scout ahead tomorrow while you stay here well hidden. I will find out where the enemy is so that we can make plans to overtake him."

Julia nodded her head in agreement, yet listening to him, envisioning what was to come, she felt her stomach wrench, fear sweeping over her. And when she lay back down to rest, she was not at all surprised to find that the sleep which she needed eluded her.

Chapter 23

Neeheeowee returned to camp the next day when the sun was at its highest peak. He looked weary, even a little downtrodden.

"They are less than a day's ride from here," he said in answer to her unspoken question. "We can intersect with them tomorrow."

"Tomorrow?" she repeated. "So soon?"

"*Haahe*, yes," he said. "We will make our plans tonight, for we must take them by surprise. Because they are in their own country, they have become lax and I can use that to my advantage. They will not expect an attack so close to home. And Julia," he said, looking at her closely, "I will show them no mercy. Expect none."

Julia looked at him, understanding in her eyes, yet within her heart, she wished it could be different.

As it turned out, there were five of them, not three, and Julia grimaced, shutting her eyes when she discovered it. They were big men, all well armed with lances and bows and arrows, but all right now were asleep. The sun had not yet made its appearance in the sky, and Julia realized she was witnessing the darkness before dawn.

336

The enemy had pitched their camp high upon a flat-topped mesa, and Neeheeowee and Julia had last night climbed to a spot above where the enemy slept. Both Julia and Neeheeowee lay flat on their stomachs, overlooking the Pawnee camp. Neeheeowee had painted himself for war, the black paint stretching across his face, the look of him fierce enough to cause Julia to cringe.

He motioned her back down to a ledge on the mesa. Using hand signals he told her to wait there, unless he ran into trouble down there, at which time she was to mount the swiftest of the ponies and flee. She nodded, although she had already told him that if he died, she would ride right into the camp and perish, too. She had no wish to live her life without Neeheeowee.

They had argued about this point more than any other of their plans, and Julia kept her intentions silent for the moment, not wishing to cause further argument with the enemy so close at hand. Her glance, however, told Neeheeowee she had not budged on her decision at all.

He scowled at her before sending a helpless look toward the heavens, but he said nothing, only communicating by sign what he expected her to do. And Julia nodded, agreeing to all of it, with the exception of the one.

He nodded and, again, scooting to the top of the ledge, peered down into the enemy camp, Julia following him up onto the ledge. And then, all at once, it started. Neeheeowee shrieked out his war cry and dropped down into the camp, cutting the throat of one of the villains at once.

The Pawnee responded as they had been taught all their lives, up and starting battle even before they rubbed the sleep from their eyes. One attacked Neeheeowee with a knife, Neeheeowee pulling him down toward him and stabbing the attacker with that knife.

Two down, Julia counted.

Two of the Pawnee, seeing the strength and cunning of their enemy, fled the scene, disappearing down the mesa and into the night. It left Neeheeowee with one left to fight. Julia gulped and barely dared to look.

"You," she heard Neeheeowee say in Lakota, himself cornering his prey. "You are the one who killed my wife and my baby. You are the one I have sought all these long years. *You* do not deserve to live, *you* do not deserve to walk this earth, *you* will not walk the path to the spirit world, either. I will ensure it."

The two men circled one another, Julia noticing with an odd sense of detachment that the sun had just begun to rise on the eastern horizon. A breeze blew straight into her face and then quit. She shook her head.

Had it spoken to her?

It couldn't be. She must be going mad.

Again, wind rushed into her face. "Stop the fight." She caught her breath.

She had heard of what the Indians called the spirit wind, she had been out west long enough to know of these beliefs. But she had never thought it to be true.

"He follows the wrong path. Do not let him do it." The wind again rushed into her face, ruffling her hair this time and seeming to speak to her yet again. "It will sour his heart forever."

She gazed back down at Neeheeowee and the Pawnee. Perhaps the whining of the wind, the desolation of the plains had, at last, made her crazy. Or perhaps the men had spoken. But as the two men circled one another, grunting, screeching, screaming, she knew with certainty that neither of them had spoken.

The Pawnee howled, and Neeheeowee, not even flinching, pulled the Pawnee down, pushing his knife

to the other man's throat so fast, the Pawnee barely
seemed to know it before it was done.

"I will kill you now as you killed my wife," Neeheeowee said, Julia listening. "I will make you suffer
as she did, and never fear, you will never see the spirit
world."

Wind rushed up behind her, seeming to push her
down into the camp.

Neeheeowee raised his knife and in that moment,
there in the breeze, Julia saw the future before her, a
future with a sullen Neeheeowee, a Neeheeowee
without heart, without passion, and she understood
all at once why she was here: this murder would take
Neeheeowee's heart just as surely as his wife had
taken his spirit.

She looked around her for help, but knew that if
anyone were going to do something about this, it
would have to be her.

He screamed, and Julia jumped to her feet.

"*Hiya*! No!" Julia yelled it out as loud as she could,
running forward and stumbling over the rocky landscape to twist her way down into the camp.

At the interruption, the Pawnee howled, snapping
about to try to regain control, but Neeheeowee held
him fast, not letting him move even a little bit.

"*Hiya*! No!" Julia shrieked again. "You must not do
this."

"*Eaaa*!" Neeheeowee roared. "You are not to inter-
fere in this!"

Julia looked at the Pawnee, who, she noted, looked
more ferocious than anyone she had ever seen. "You
must not do this," she yelled again to Neeheeowee,
then more calmly, "You must spare his life." She advanced right up to them, falling onto her knees beside
them both. "You have lost a wife and a child, my love.
I know this is difficult, I know your wife haunts you,
but if you do this thing, if you see it through, it will

change you forever. Do you not see? It will harden your heart, even against me." She took a deep breath and plunged. "I know a harder way, but it is a better path," she said, her words rushing together almost in a slur. "You lost a child, a boy child I think you said. I say you should invoke the kinship appeal right here, right now. You had a son you lost, make this man your son. Do this deed as no one else has ever done it before you. Show mercy to your enemy. Right here, right now."

Neeheeowee, who held the other man's head in his hand, howled at her. "He is not Cheyenne!"

"He doesn't have to be!"

Neeheeowee screamed. "I cannot do it!"

"Yes, you can!"

Neeheeowee howled again, the sound a screech against the morning air. Then, pushing the man's head down hard on the ground, Neeheeowee jumped to his feet. And though he let the Pawnee come up onto his knees, Neeheeowee glared at the man. Proud Wolf's glance clearly let the man know that one move—any move—and the Pawnee would yet die.

"Your life might be spared," Neeheeowee spit out, clutching a knife in one hand while he signed out the meaning of his speech with his other. "My wife desires this revenge to end. My wife seems to think you are honorable enough to keep your word. My wife would have you take the place of the kin which you took from me five years ago. My wife would have me take you into my home as . . . my son." Neeheeowee's voice faltered, although his stare remained fixed. "You, my friend, have a choice. One given to you by the wisdom and compassion of my wife. You can either die the same death—here now—that you had delivered to my kin five years ago, or you can accept the gift that I will give to you now to show you my sincerity; the gift of my finest warhorse. For I will honor my wife's wisdom and the feelings from her heart. What say you now?

"But I would caution you. If you accept what my wife and I offer you, you must pledge to me—your solemn oath—that from this day forward, you will take the place of my lost kin, ever to be obligated to fulfill that role, that you will never falter from that duty. Know you now that it is hatred for you that has brought me to this camp on this day. Know you, too, that I will not leave it until I have obtained either your death or your vow of kinship. The choice is yours."

Julia had arisen while Neeheeowee had been speaking, moving off to the side to get Neeheeowee's war pony. She brought it down to them now; standing behind Neeheeowee, the three of them, the pony, Julia and Neeheeowee, awaited the Pawnee's decision.

The Pawnee warrior looked up toward the gift, looked up to Julia and then back toward Neeheeowee. He trembled, looking at the Cheyenne's knife, still clutched firmly in hand and poised to wield a death blow. The Pawnee then glanced up toward the sky, then down at himself and at last, not being able to withhold himself, he screamed, but as he cried out, tears streamed down his face.

Without further pause, he gestured back in the language of sign, "From this day forward you," he motioned toward Neeheeowee, "I am a part of your family, taking on the duties that beholds that station, no matter that you are Cheyenne and I am Pawnee. From this day forward, I am a part of your family. From this day forward my home is yours, my family is yours. There will be peace between us. I swear to it."

The Pawnee sank farther to his knees with his words, his head down, and with one last scream of frustration, Neeheeowee threw away his knife.

"It is done, then," Neeheeowee said, and in that

moment, the wind rushed in upon them all, the image of a woman and a small boy upon it.

All three saw the image, all three stood staring at it, Neeheeowee the first to recover and, crying out his war cry, he moved about the camp, picking up his own weapons plus those of the Pawnee. He marched then from the Pawnee camp as though a demon pursued him. He didn't look behind him, not even to check upon her safety, and it was this action, more than any other, which told Julia that her Cheyenne warrior was not yet free.

The Pawnee, still on his knees beside her, told her something in gestures, and at his urging, she hurried from the camp, following after her Cheyenne husband.

It was odd, she was to think later. The Pawnee had given his word and as easily as that, he became friend instead of foe, Julia realizing the kinship pledge, although forged in a moment of force, would be kept by the two of them, the Cheyenne and the Pawnee, forever.

It was no less than a miracle.

Neeheeowee knew he had to leave her, at least for the moment. He could not stay around Julia and think, not being as angry as he was.

He came back to it again and again: How could she have interfered in his life as she did? Hadn't he held the knife ready, just awaiting the moment of complete justice? Hadn't the moment been truly his? Hadn't he been ready to make the man an example? And Julia had made him stop. Julia.

He thought back to it now. Why had he stopped? He hadn't needed to. He had told Julia he would show the Pawnee no mercy. So why had he?

Because of Julia? Was that it, or was it because of something else?

He couldn't help thinking that five years of searching, five years of his life were wasted. When the time had come for him to commit revenge, he had made the man a brother instead.

Was he unable to kill the man? Was that it? Was he so weak that he could not do what needed to be done?

Neeheeowee shook his head. No, he would have gladly turned the knife. That was not it. It was something more—someone more. Julia had influenced him. Julia had suddenly brought a shred of light into his hatred. Julia had remained even stronger than the mightiest of warriors, for Julia's was the gift of understanding, and of love.

He lifted his face to the heavens and the wind blew right up to him and away. Ah, he thought, the spirit wind. This was no ordinary wind. This was the wind of knowledge, the wind that went everywhere, saw everything. This wind talked, the words plain if one only listened.

"What do you want of me?" Neeheeowee asked aloud.

It blew right up to him, whispering in his ear, "You are free."

"No," he yelled out, not daring to believe it. "How can this be? I failed my wife and child yet again."

"No," the wind seemed to say, "You are free." And as if to show him, an image of his wife and child materialized before him, both of them smiling, both of them waving, both of them, at last, letting him go.

And it happened right then. Before his eyes, right there in the wind, he saw his future, the things he must accomplish for himself, for his love, for his people. Neeheeowee began to tremble. He had not sought a vision this time, he had done none of the ceremonial rites, and yet, here before him lay the vision he lacked. And Neeheeowee realized what had been missing from his life in all the years past: love. It had taken love to show him his true path; it had taken the love of a strong-willed woman: Julia.

And there, on that ledge overlooking the land of his enemy, Neeheeowee cried.

That was how Julia found him.

She came right up to him, kneeling at his side and taking his hand into her own. "The Pawnee," she said as softly as she could, "your new kin is taking care of his dead. He awaits you, for he will follow you home. I was able to understand at least that much from his gestures to me. Neeheeowee"—she ran her hands through his hair—"it is over."

Neeheeowee didn't acknowledge her except with a brief shake of his head. He didn't look up; he didn't stand up. He couldn't. Tears streamed down his face.

Julia put her arms around him and knelt with him for a very long time, feeling the raw emotion within him as though it were her own. It was no show of weakness on his part, and both knew it. Rather, it was a strengthening. Together, they were more than the forces that had sought to overwhelm them.

Gradually, Neeheeowee looked up, placing his arms around her as he did so. Finally, he got to his feet, bringing Julia with him, and, as he did so, as he stood, the wind whipped around a corner, blowing its strength upon them.

Their hair rippled back against the breeze, their faces softened under its caress, their clothes and fringe ruffled back because of it, but before it went on its way, before the spirit wind left them forever, it whispered to them, "Together you are strong. Together you will bring wisdom to your people. Use the power well."

Neeheeowee stared down at Julia. She looked back up at him, and she knew then that love had conquered all. Both of them were whole again. Both of

them had set the other free. She began to smile. The
wind whipped around them again and Julia laughed,
Neeheeowee joining in until the happy sounds they
made mixed with all of nature, and had anyone been
there to observe them, it would have been a difficult
task to distinguish which was the most beautiful: the
joy of the human laugh or the sweet sighings of the
wind.

Truly, both sounded one and the same.

Epilogue

Neeheeowee had given Tahiska and Kristina the best horses that he could, since they now were the kin of his betrothed. He smiled at the gesture he had made while relief swept over him. At last he was free to follow his heart.

He sat within his lodge now, awaiting his bride. And though he knew the Lakota were not familiar with the Cheyenne wedding custom, it was the one ceremony he insisted upon despite anyone else's rituals. Besides, his own relatives, Mahoohe and Aamehee, Voesee and her son, had recently arrived in the camp to witness it. They received word of his formal marriage and his invitation to them to join him from, of all people, his new Pawnee kin.

Neeheeowee shook his head at the thought. The Pawnee man, who only a few weeks ago had been his worst enemy, was fast becoming the best kin Neeheeowee had ever known. The man remained aware of all the kinship taboos and acted accordingly. The Pawnee had even brought his own family here, to raise his own children in this Lakota camp.

Neeheeowee heard noise outside and knew that out there, Kristina led Julia toward his lodge on one of the best horses which she and Tahiska possessed. He could even hear his own male relatives beside his lodge, Mahoohe and Tahiska, Wahtapah and others, all waiting anxiously outside, a fine blanket spread out upon the ground.

Neeheeowee could barely stand the anticipation, and he rushed to the tepee entrance to peep outside.

He caught sight of her and for a moment all conscious thought fled. Never had he seen anyone more beautiful than she. Never had he witnessed anyone so fair.

She dressed in white elkskin, her costume beaded across the top in shades of blue with an occasional yellow or red bead giving the creation designs. Long fringe fell from the arms of the gown and also from the bottom, hanging straight to the ground. Her hair had been braided with ribbons and ornaments, her face painted in the fashion of the plains Indian, with vermillion slashed down the part in her hair. His stomach fell at the grand sight of her, his loins jerked in pure reaction, and, at last, Neeheeoee smiled. It was good, their love, their marriage.

Kristina led the pony Julia rode right up to his door, where some other women lifted Julia off her mount and set her upon the blanket which had been lying there on the ground all this time. As soon as she was settled, Neeheeooee's male relatives picked the blanket up by the corners and, lifting it entirely, prepared to carry Julia into Neeheeowee's lodge.

Neeheeowee let the tepee flap fall as though he hadn't watched the whole thing and when his male relatives opened the entranceway, to bring Julia in, Neeheeowee felt himself trembling as though he were a young boy again.

Several jokes were exchanged between the men before they left, but at last they were gone, and Neeheeowee stood within his own lodge, looking down upon his wife. At last, with these ceremonial rites, Julia became his wife, in fact, in deed, and no one could dispute it.

Julia suddenly smiled at him, Neeheeowee returning the gesture, and, as she fell into his arms, they laughed, the sound of their happiness seeming to rebound throughout the entire village.

All the people heard it. All the people smiled, shaking their heads and walking away from the newlyweds' lodge as quietly as they could.

Soon the feasting would begin, the partying most likely to go on well into the night. And although no one really expected the young couple to join in the festivities that night, it wouldn't keep the others from enjoying the feast given in the young married couple's name.

Truly, this night, all had cause for great happiness; the love between these two people, a part of their life and blood now, would serve as an example of strength in years to come.

The drumbeat sounded louder that night than ever before, the beat, which symbolized the heartbeat of the people, drowning out the vows exchanged between the two people who stood alone in the tepee on the edge of the camp circle. And there, had anyone looked, he would have seen two silhouettes illuminated on the tepee's lining, Neeheeoee's hand over her heart, Julia's over his, vowing their love to one another forever.

But at that moment in time, no one gazed back toward the tepee. Perhaps it was for the best, for, as it is said by the wisest of men, love, forged and once pledged, needs no warranty from another to last forever.

Afterword

The wagon master to Colonel Sumner, Percival Lowe, delivered this address to the Kansas Historical Society on January 14, 1890:

The Cheyenne and Arapaho were the habitual occupants of these plains from the Platte to the Arkansas, and from the forks of the Solomon to the mountains. I then thought, and still believe, that the Cheyenne were the handsomest, noblest and bravest Indians I ever saw in a wild state. I met them often, knew them well and their way of living. They fought their enemies with an unrelenting vigor — that was their religious duty from their standpoint. They were as virtuous as any people on earth; whatever civilized man may say of their table manners, their family government was perfect — perfect obedience to parents, and child whipping unknown; veneration and respect for old age was universal. In their relations to each other crime was practically unknown. They worshipped God, in whom they had implicit confidence. They hated a liar as the devil hates holy water, and that is why, when they came to know him, they hated

349

the white man so intensely. For fortitude, patience and endurance, the sun never shown on better examples.

Percival G. Lowe

Avon Romances—
the best in exceptional authors and unforgettable novels!

THE MACKENZIES: LUKE   **Ana Leigh**
                              78098-4/ $5.50 US/ $7.50 Can

FOREVER BELOVED   **Joan Van Nuys**
                              78118-2/ $5.50 US/ $7.50 Can

INSIDE PARADISE   **Elizabeth Turner**
                              77372-4/ $5.50 US/ $7.50 Can

CAPTIVATED   **Colleen Corbet**
                              78027-5/ $5.50 US/ $7.50 Can

THE OUTLAW   **Nicole Jordan**
                              77832-7/ $5.50 US/ $7.50 Can

HIGHLAND FLAME   **Lois Greiman**
                              78190-5/ $5.50 US/ $7.50 Can

TOO TOUGH TO TAME   **Deborah Camp**
                              78251-0/ $5.50 US/ $7.50 Can

TAKEN BY YOU   **Connie Mason**
                              77998-6/ $5.50 US/ $7.50 Can

FRANNIE AND THE CHARMER   **Ann Carberry**
                              77881-5/ $4.99 US/ $6.99 Can

REMEMBER ME   **Danice Allen**
                              78150-6/ $4.99 US/ $6.99 Can

Avon Romantic Treasures

Unforgettable, enthralling love stories,
sparkling with passion and adventure
from Romance's bestselling authors

LADY OF SUMMER *by Emma Merritt*
77984-6/$5.50 US/$7.50 Can

HEARTS RUN WILD *by Shelly Thacker*
78119-0/$5.99 US/$7.99 Can

JUST ONE KISS *by Samantha James*
77549-2/$5.99 US/$7.99 Can

SUNDANCER'S WOMAN *by Judith E. French*
77706-1/$5.99 US/$7.99 Can

RED SKY WARRIOR *by Genell Dellin*
77526-3/ $5.50 US/ $7.50 Can

KISSED *by Tanya Anne Crosby*
77681-2/$5.50 US/$7.50 Can

MY RUNAWAY HEART *by Miriam Minger*
78301-0/ $5.50 US/ $7.50 Can

RUNAWAY TIME *by Deborah Gordon*
77759-2/ $5.50 US/ $7.50 Can

Discover Contemporary Romances
at Their Sizzling Hot Best
from Avon Books

**THE LOVES OF
RUBY DEE**   *by Curtiss Ann Matlock*
78106-9/$5.99 US/$7.99 Can

JONATHAN'S WIFE   *by Dee Holmes*
78368-1/$5.99 US/$7.99 Can

DANIEL'S GIFT   *by Barbara Freethy*
78189-1/$5.99 US/$7.99 Can

FAIRYTALE   *by Maggie Shayne*
78300-2/$5.99 US/$7.99 Can

Coming Soon

WISHES COME TRUE   *by Patti Berg*
78338-X/$5.99 US/$7.99 Can